Embers of the Nephilim:
Ghost Girl
and the
Ghost Giant

By
Andrew
R. H.
Quinn

Periodic Table of Contents

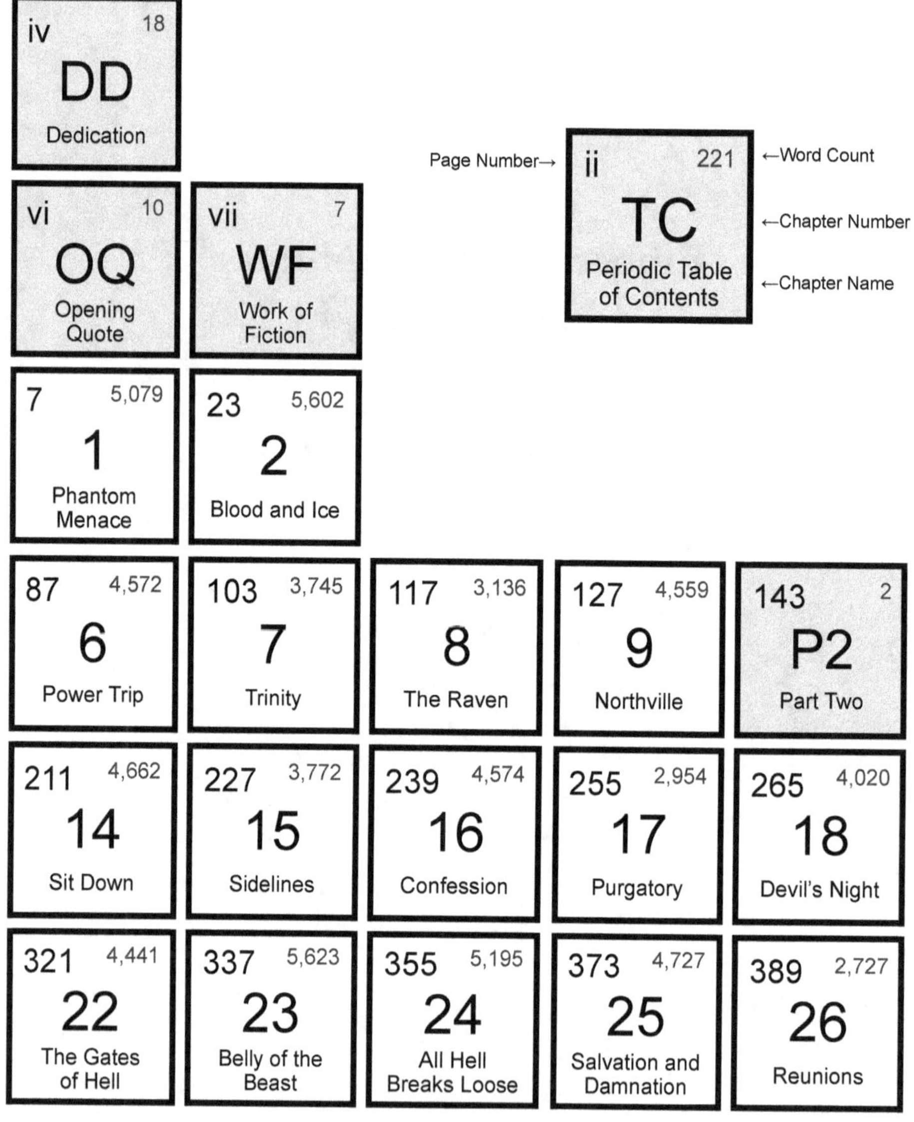

This book is dedicated to everyone who has ever had a dream that
seemed impossibly out of reach.

Acknowledgments

This book would not have been possible without the help and support of so many wonderful people. In the interest of brevity (and making sure that no one is left out) you can find a complete, up-to-date list on the website at https://fauxsaur.us.

In particular, I'd like to thank all my beta readers (especially those who were able to come together at the last minute to make this book a reality) and everyone who provided guidance in fields outside my expertise. Specifically, I'd like to give a special thanks to my editor, Erik Maloney, who helped bring out the best in this book (note: any errors are the sole fault of the author and any improvements that of the editor).

"The harder the battle, the sweeter the victory."
—Les Brown

The following is a work of fiction.

Michigan
696
5
275
24
102
5
Hawthorn Center
Northville Psychiatric
96
24
Plymouth
Spiritus Sanctus
Salem High
153
153
275
12
24
12

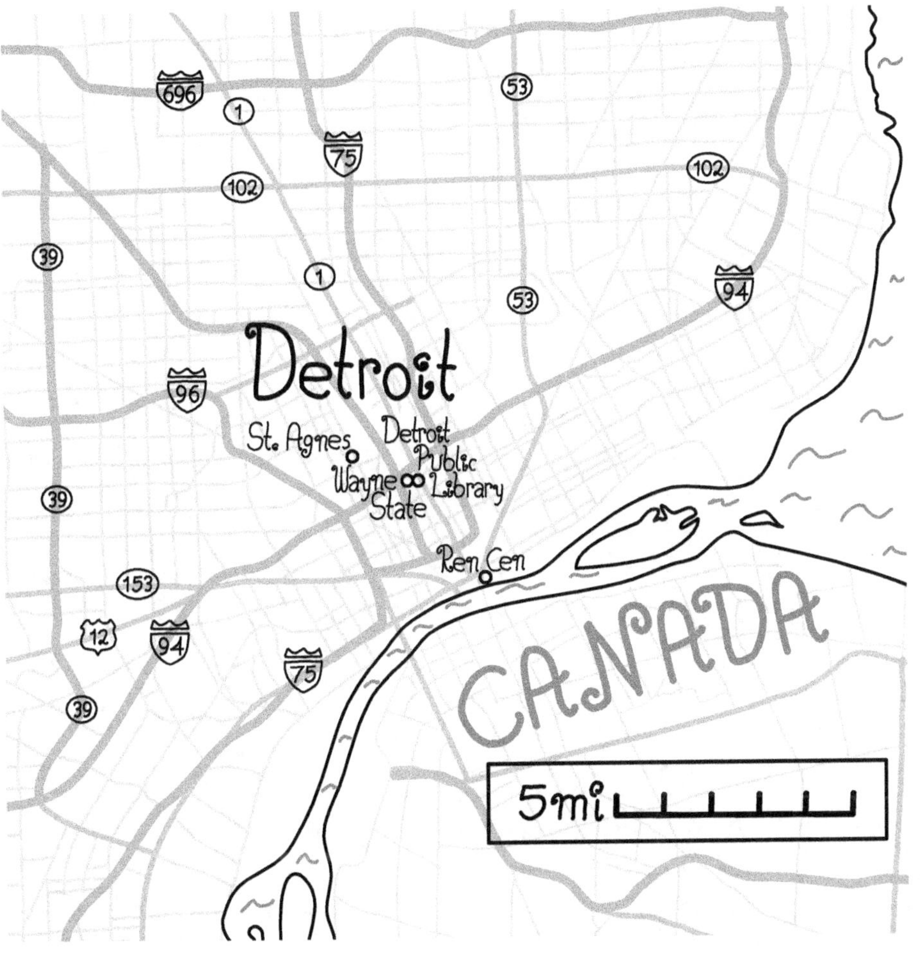

696
1
53
75
102
102
39
1
53
94
96
Detroit
St. Agnes
Detroit
Public
Wayne
Library
State
39
Ren Cen
153
CANADA
12
94
39
75
5mi

PROLOGUE

Sunday, May 31st, 2009 (Pentecost)

Olivia drew smiley faces by all the questions she got right on her science study guide. Naturally, that was all of them. "Yes!" she cried, moving on to her religion homework, wishing she could have finished it on Friday instead of moving to the new house. If she hurried, though, she could still get a few sketches in before bed. A twinge of guilt cut through her when she heard her mom approach from downstairs.

"Olivia! We're going to the store to pick up some light bulbs!"

"Thank you!" she called back, eyeing the lantern on the corner of her desk. She didn't need it yet, since there was still plenty of light coming in from the window, but it'd be awesome to have *actual* lights tonight.

"Don't burn the house down while we're out!" her dad called.

Olivia chuckled. She didn't hate their new place *that* much. "Don't worry! I'll wait till you get back!"

"That's my girl," he said, laughter echoing up to the attic room.

"You're terrible," her mom chuckled on the way out.

The door creaked shut below, and Olivia looked out the window, holding her breath until her mom made it to the car with the aid of her white cane. She waved to her dad and gasped when her mom returned the gesture. She was looking right at her. How had she adjusted to their new house so quickly? And would she disapprove just as rapidly if she knew her daughter wanted to be an artist?

Her parents left, leaving her with a vague sense of worry as she worked on her assignments. She only got halfway through by the time Cisco started barking. He *never* barked—except that one time.

Something heavy crashed downstairs, and Olivia winced. It sounded like glass broke.

"Cisco!" she called, hurrying down the creaky ladder.

The ancient retriever stood at the end of the downstairs hall, growling at fallen boxes all marked *fragile*.

Olivia inhaled sharply. "Cisco! What did you do?" she cried.

He whimpered, looking around before bolting away like a younger dog. She hurried after him, darting through the endless maze of stacked boxes until she knocked one over. Health insurance denials flooded the hall, multiplying, threatening to sweep her away, while Cisco yelped around the corner.

"Cisco!" Olivia cried, holding onto the door frame for dear life in a flurry of layoff notices. She pulled herself through the current of paper cuts with mounting dread. Cisco lay there on a chunk of ice in the sea of swirling prescription drug prices. She swam after him while he sank into the papery vortex.

"NO!" she screamed, diving after him only to hit the floor. The papers subsided, fluttering to the ground, and the lights flickered overhead. Bank statements devolved into unhinged scribbles, all depicting the same thing: an ever-shifting mass of black and white with angry red eyes. The papers went transparent.

Olivia backed away from the glowing eyes looming in the dark. "No, no, no."

She ran down the never-ending hall, panting, her frigid breath hanging before her, turning into mist. She panicked in the fog, trying to hide behind towers of boxes and stop her teeth from chattering. Sweat trickled down her face and froze, biting at her skin. Olivia screamed when the crimson searchlights fell on her.

She gasped, waking in a cold sweat. It was just a dream. A nightmare. Still, she felt her arms and legs just to be sure. No icy crystals—just dull bruises from her last encounter with the Ghost Giant.

In the moonlight, her eyes darted across the slanted, tentlike ceiling of her attic room. She was *home*, trapped in the new reality of their haunted house. If only her parents realized it was haunted. If only they believed her. Believed that the Ghost Giant tormented her when they were away. She'd had to *beg* them to call Father Tom after its last visit. The psych eval for the exorcism was supposed to be soon....

Rummaging through her research notes, Olivia checked her homemade calendar she had drawn on the back of an old envelope. Two days left. She just had to survive until then, and Father Tom would drive the monster out. She grabbed the Bible off her desk and hugged it under the covers, trying not to cry herself to sleep.

"If I should die before I wake, I pray the Lord my soul to take. If I should die before I wake, I pray the Lord my soul to take."

ᚦᛖ ᚹᛁᚾᚨᛚ ᚹᚨᚱ

PART ONE

Chapter 1: Phantom Menace

Thursday, October 29th, 2009 (Feast Day of Saint Narcissus)

The bus hit a pothole, jerking Olivia's pencil to the side and ruining her sketch of Lady Constance fighting the Ghost Giant. Olivia tried to salvage her drawing, and the last envelope, by erasing the taillike line. Ghosts didn't have tails. At least, this one didn't. It walked on two legs and stood nearly seven feet tall. She touched up the determination in Constance's eyes, wishing that heroes were real and that she shared their bravery—that she could slay the Ghost Giant.

Tears struck the paper, and hissing brakes brought her back to reality. Her dreams died a bit more when a group of girls in shabby green and white tops, torn to be more revealing, snickered at her. Like most things, fitting in cost far too much. She shuddered at the thought of herself in similar attire and wiped frost from the window, wishing that she was heading home with her parents like the little kids laughing in the back seat of a car passing by.

"Look at the little traitor," a freshman with a flip phone said. "See how the wannabe senior's all dressed in white?"

Her seatmate laughed. "Except for her hair."

They giggled until a senior chimed in, "There's nothing wrong with white."

Olivia sank into her seat and lowered her hood to better hide her ruined hair and puffy eyes. She'd gone to school today excited, dressed in her favorite outfit, only to be attacked by students armed with colored hair spray. Apparently, that was a Class Color Day *tradition*. Naturally, she'd changed into her gym clothes to protect her outfit, but then her classmates had turned on her for wearing the wrong color.

Olivia ignored the senior defending her. Sure, the upperclassmen had chanted "save her hair" when they'd sprayed her, but they'd just lightened the existing colors instead of removing them. All anyone had done was reduce her locks to a blotchy mess of irregular polka dots. Spirit Week *sucked*.

The bus engine whined, signaling that evasive maneuvers were about to begin. Everyone held on to the seats ahead while the bus zigzagged to avoid potholes, but Olivia did her best to put her art supplies away before her stop. She bounced in her seat, bumping a bruise on her leg. She winced, knowing that it was fading. Knowing that the Ghost Giant would return soon. Compared to it, bullies were just annoying. But they'd ruined her one sanctuary from home: school.

The bus began to slow as it passed two white pumpkins stacked into a jack-o'-lantern snowman. The brakes hissed, and Olivia stood as the bus lurched forward, trying to slip past the boys before they noticed her. She stumbled down the aisle, grabbing successive pairs of seats for support while momentum rocked the bus backward. For every action, there was an equal and opposite reaction.

"Nice hair, Wade," Devin said, sticking out his leg to trip her.

Everyone laughed, but Olivia landed on her hands and knees inches from the floor. She took a breath to calm herself, but the stench of cigarette smoke clinging to his clothes and the minty gum glued beneath the seats ruined the effect. So gross.

Devin wolf whistled at her backside to even more acclaim, and Olivia went red. She rose and adjusted her hood. It was damp, and her fingers came away green. Stupid hair spray. Everyone was laughing at her. For once her secondhand hoodie seemed more than warm enough. She tucked a stray hair behind her ear and wiped colored sweat from her brow, focusing on her dusty white Converse so no one could trip her again.

"Leave her alone, shrimp," said Jasmine, Plymouth's basketball star, standing tall in her jersey and *accidentally* stepping on Devin's toes.

"Ow!" he cried.

Everyone went silent in the senior's wake.

"Thanks," Olivia mumbled. The Machine was even taller up close.

Jasmine gave her a reassuring smile. "Don't mention it."

As Olivia descended the stairs and hopped over a flooded pothole, a little kid said, "I want to be a mummy this year."

Couldn't the driver have parked *anywhere* else?

"Well, I want to be a goblin or an ogre," another kid said.

Jasmine ducked to avoid catching her curls on the doorframe before stepping over the crater.

The door closed with a squeak and a hiss before the *Doldrum* bus —lucky thirteen—departed. Exhaust lingered, and someone threw a half-empty pop can out a window. It hit the pothole, splattering Olivia and Jasmine with muck.

"Scoooore!" someone yelled.

"Beat that, Jasmine!" Devin called over distant laughter as the bus sped away.

Olivia stared at her ruined sweatpants and Jasmine's muddy knee-highs. Their shoes hadn't fared any better. Bubbling ripples distorted their murky reflections alongside the floating pop can. Such a waste.

Jasmine shook her head, sending her Afro into frenzied motion. "I hate that kid."

"Yeah," Olivia said. The only way her day could get any worse was if the Ghost Giant showed up. She headed home, surprised to see that Jasmine was slowing down to walk beside her. Their footsteps crunched on a sidewalk that was practically gravel. Such was life in a place colloquially known as the Cracks, an apt name given the broken terrain and its denizens who had fallen through.

Olivia and Jasmine advanced in silence, flanked by overgrown lawns spilling out of the gaps in old, white picket fences. Even the grass wanted to leave. Olivia turned her nose up at a dying tree infested with spiderwebs and bagworm nests overhead and caught Jasmine staring at her hair. She waited for the inevitable question: who got you? But it never came.

"Hey, let me know if that doesn't wash out," Jasmine said, ducking under a branch. "I work at a hair salon on the weekends. Zedd's. Manager gave me a key to open up. So I can slip you in—even though we're closed for repairs—if you want help cleaning that mess out or covering it up before homecoming."

Olivia's shoe caught on a thorny weed. "I'm not going." Only creeps like Devin had asked her to the dance.

Jasmine frowned. "Trust me, you're not missing anything. Dances *suck*. Still, let me know if you need help."

Olivia nodded, spotting goosebumps between Jasmine's socks and short shorts. Her eyes widened. Any other day, Jasmine would have made it home by now, but despite the cold, she'd slowed down for her. And her offer? How could anyone be so kind? Olivia looked away. She couldn't afford a trip to Detroit and didn't want to ask for a ride. So she let the conversation die and zipped up her arctic camo hoodie to ward off the wind.

Maple leaves rustled against the faded *For Sale* sign next door, and her defaced gate blew open, knocking about in the breeze.

"This is my stop," she said, pausing by the mailbox.

"Yeah, hang in there, kiddo," the tall girl said, stooping down to hug her. She shook her head at the graffiti before taking a few steps backward and departing with a wave.

Olivia returned the gesture, wishing that she could be like Jasmine, head held high in the face of everything. Unbroken. Defiant. Kind. Her fingers twitched, yearning to draw her standing tall against the backdrop of faded fences and the pale sky beyond. Thunder rumbled in the distance.

A sketch for another time.

The horrendous burning bear head with an eyepatch on the gate glared up at her, eliciting a scowl. Olivia was just a beginner, but even she could draw better than whoever'd graffitied it there. If only jerks, supernatural or otherwise, would stop messing with their stuff. Why not tear up one of the abandoned homes further down the block? There were plenty to choose from.

The mailbox creaked open, raining down bits of rust. Silver and iron were said to be good at warding off ghosts, though, in Olivia's experience, they didn't work. But perhaps she just didn't have enough of them. She leafed through the mail, concluding the only things they had in abundance were bills and ads.

A chill passed through her as the wind picked up. She shivered and jolted at the sound of frost crunching underfoot. It wasn't cold enough for frost. Olivia stared back at the sea of grass and weeds, dotted with stepping-stone islands, that passed for their yard.

She must have crossed in a daze, lost in thought. She hadn't lost time. She just hadn't been paying attention. She didn't need to go back to the hospital. To those harsh lights, sterile floors, and blank walls.

Olivia slowed her breathing. Her stay would have been worth it if the subsequent exorcism had succeeded, but it hadn't. And despite the doctors concluding that she didn't have schizophrenia, Father Tom refused to try again. But no matter what he said, the Ghost Giant was real. Olivia didn't need meds, and she certainly didn't need to be locked away. *Again.*

Loosening her grip on the mail, she focused on the angel statue on the porch. Raphael, the archangel with whom she and her parents shared a saint name,[1] stood on guard at his usual post by the door with his staff and fish in hand, just as he had at their old house.

But the similarities ended there. Jagged scars ran across the aged facade like cracked ice, telltale signs of the former ivy infestation. And unlike their old house, no picturesque shrubs broke up the monotony of the glazed old windows that seemed to distort reality itself.

But despite the dreary exterior, Olivia far preferred it to what lay inside—that was another matter entirely. Despite the danger, she fumbled with the keys until the stupid lock deemed her worthy to enter the haunted house they'd been forced to take refuge in.

Floorboards squeaked as Olivia took off her muddy shoes. A single beam of light peeked through the curtains and reflected off a tall mirror in the corner, illuminating a painting over the hallway. She stared up at the image of Bartimaeus receiving his sight, hoping that her mom would get her sight back in a similar, albeit less miraculous, fashion. Ironically, they could afford the surgery, but not the daily immunosuppressants and steroids her mom would need to *keep* her vision and prevent tissue rejection. Stupid health insurance companies. Her mom would be more *productive* if she could *see.*

---

[1] A name chosen by Catholics during the sacrament of confirmation. Note: female confirmands can select the names of male saints when they are confirmed, as can nuns when taking a new name upon entering monastic life.

Locking the door merely protected them from lazy thieves. So to guard against the ghost—or rather give herself advance warning—Olivia slipped in a fraying earbud and turned on her portable radio, knowing it would crackle if the spirit showed up.

"Fjord Motors announced another round of layoffs today, and scientists say that increased solar activity...Breaking news!" the radio announced. "The vigilante many are calling the Exterminator has just been arrested after a failed sting on local rapper I.M.A.B.'s house."

Olivia hadn't thought the cops would ever catch that guy. Still, it gave her hope that she could accomplish her own impossible task. That said, she was in no hurry to see whether her next set of experiments would work. So she hurried down the hall to find her mom, knowing the Ghost Giant would only show up if she was alone.

After she switched to a less distracting station, quiet classical music filled her ear. Her stomach rumbled at the scent of yesterday's Granny Smith applesauce. Her mom wasn't in the kitchen, but, clearly, Olivia had fasted long enough to see if that helped her face the ghost, as Saint Mark described in some versions of his Gospel.

Yet Sister Paula had said that priests didn't fast before exorcisms. Nor did they burn fish hearts, as described in the Book of Tobit—only prayer, holy water, and relics. Olivia had tried two of these, but they'd never worked. Holy water just froze and shattered like her hopes, and her prayers must have failed because she hadn't had enough faith. It had to be that. She wouldn't question Church doctrine.

Across the hall, she pressed her ear to her parents' bedroom door, not wanting to disturb her mom if she was working. Nope. Farther down, the bathroom wasn't locked, and she doubted her mom was downstairs. She was probably in the back room. Olivia squeezed between the basement door and the pull-down ladder that led up to her attic room. Finally, she opened the creaky door at the end of the hall.

Vanilla candles lit the small room as the sky darkened outside. Working at the tiny table draped in an old-timey red and white tablecloth, her mom ran her fingers over her braille display. She smiled when Olivia joined her. "Be with you in a minute."

"Mm-hmm," Olivia said, looking away from the faint burn scars peeking out of her mom's vintage dress and the untarnished locks her own should have been identical to.

Olivia cut through an envelope with an intricate letter opener engraved with a lion, witch, and wardrobe—the coolest thing she'd found in the house. It tore open a utility bill with ease and preserved the envelope for future drawings.

Their tactic of keeping the heat down was paying off. Soon, they'd have enough to weatherproof. She frowned at the next mailer, an ad for jewelry. They wouldn't have *that* much money. Olivia set the thick, colored paper aside, wishing that it had come in something she could doodle on and that they could afford sketch paper and gemstones.

Not because jewels were pretty, but because one of Lady Constance's stories was supposedly based on a historical case in which precious stones stored mystical energies. Thus, they could trap the Ghost Giant, since it lacked a physical form. And if it lacked matter, it *had* to be made of energy. Unfortunately, that route was out of reach, just like the electronics in the next sheet of ads.

But those wouldn't help against the creature, since its presence generated interference. If it disrupted the electromagnetic spectrum, though, the reverse might also be true. A stun gun might have enough juice to harm the thing, but she didn't see an offer for one of those. Or printer paper, for her to draw on. Just an analog camera that was too expensive for her to test whether it could capture the ghost's existence on film. Why was everything that could help always out of reach?

Olivia froze at a note from the hospital. A request for a follow-up appointment. She watched her mom's braille display pins rise and fall with a series of clicks and slowly set the letter in the discard pile. She hated hiding things from her mom, but she didn't want to risk going back. And though she lamented wasting the blank side, she refused to chance anyone else finding out where she'd been.

After all, she had already transferred because Father Tom couldn't keep his mouth shut about his theory of a teenage girl *acting out*. Olivia made a fist. She wasn't *acting out*. She didn't give herself bruises, and she didn't ransack the house. And his insistence that nothing supernatural was at play—ugh!

Despite her clean bill of health, some of the psychiatrists at Hawthorn disagreed with Dr. Park's conclusion that she didn't have schizophrenia. Like everyone else, they thought their profession could explain everything. Of *course* they thought something was wrong with her. They just told her she'd *imagined* things. That her brain was misfiring, giving her hallucinations. That therapy and medication would solve *everything*.

Her mouth twitched at a dog food coupon. Nothing would bring Cisco back—not therapy and not the replacement dog her family had lined up. She hadn't *imagined* him dead on the floor, maw encased in ice, fur frozen in crystalline spikes. She wiped away a tear. One moment, he'd charged around the corner to save her, and the next, he was still. But worst of all, his death had been in vain. All the ice that might have convinced her parents of the ghost's existence had melted before they'd come home. And the vet said he'd died of a heart attack, which had been plausible at his age.

Olivia understood her parents' doubt. No one wanted to talk about things that couldn't be explained or to think that their daughter was being tormented by a demon—or at least an evil spirit rising from below. It was too hell-bent on destruction to be a different type of ghost. Sad, wispy souls lingering out of sorrow didn't hurt kids, and bright, happy ones returning with a message of hope or a warning didn't kill dogs. No, this was a malevolent entity that preyed upon her when she was alone. Olivia glanced at her mom, who continued pounding away at the keys. At least she was keeping Olivia safe, even if she didn't realize it.

Olivia lingered on the final letter. It was from school. She held her breath and read. Despite the semester being half over, they would let her switch her study hall for art class, like they would a transfer student —*if* a parent would sign off on it.

Her shoulders sagged. What would her mom think? That her daughter was a disappointment, chasing foolish dreams that would lead to poverty, wasting her potential? That they had let her skip a grade for nothing? Or would she be pained that she couldn't see what her daughter drew. Olivia couldn't bear to imagine the hurt on her mom's face.

Her mom grinned, hitting the keys one last time before taking a sip of water. "How was school?"

All the pain came rushing back. Kids in sunglasses and bandanas ran around, spraying everyone with different class *and* school colors. But that made no sense. Sure, the educational park was made up of three schools—but everyone attended classes in each building. Still, the school colors made more sense than the *unionists' made-up ones.* They'd sprayed everyone on the basis of *equality*, since *class* was an *arbitrary social construct.*

Her mom sniffed the air. "Is that *hair spray*? Oh, Liv, you didn't try a retro hairstyle? Did you?"

Olivia groaned. "No, Mom. Decade Day was yesterday." It wasn't like her to forget.

"That's what I thought, but still..."

Olivia sniffled, playing with her watch strap. Her mom scooched closer and took her hand, no doubt feeling the tension in her fingers.

"Liv, love, are you all right? What's wrong?"

Olivia broke away from her mom's scarred fingers to grip loose folds of her sweatpants before smoothing them like she would a skirt. She didn't want to talk about her hair. Her mom wouldn't understand.

"Liv, what happened?"

Olivia took a deep breath and slipped the art class form into her backpack alongside the envelopes. "It was Class Color Day," she said, fingering a stain on her favorite hoodie. Her *only* hoodie. "They tagged me. Over and over again..." She sobbed into her mom's shoulder.

"Oh, honey, I don't understand." Her mom rubbed her back, not encountering the usual resistance of the hood. "Why is your hood up?"

Olivia pulled away and pulled her hood down, crying at how ridiculous she looked, knowing her mom wouldn't understand. That she couldn't see out of those light blue eyes.

But *Olivia* knew how stupid she looked. All her life, she'd been told how lucky she was. How cool her white hair was. How it would take any color. But she had never wanted to dye it, because it was already so awesome.

After all, what color could be better than her natural shade? *None*. That's what color was better. And all of them together was way worse. She tried not to think about her long hair being marred with every color her fellow students had in their pockets and more. For, in their enthusiasm, colors had mixed.

"Liv," her mom said, running her fingers through Olivia's hair and finding stiff, dry spots. "Oh, *Liv*, what did they do to you?"

Olivia launched into an explanation between sobs, but she froze when static crackled in her ear. Shivers ran down her spine, and her breath caught, hanging in the air before her. The Ghost Giant was coming! But why? Her mom was here! Olivia's breathing quickened. The frigid air stung her nose and dried out her mouth. Her shoulders stiffened, and her mom recoiled, bumping the now-frozen glass on the table. Twinkling frost crept up the candles, snuffing the flames out with a hiss, plunging them into darkness.

Her mom looked around—as if she could see anything. "Olivia?"

No, no, no! Everything was wrong! The air quivered like a mirage by her mom. But it was far too cold for that. Olivia gulped and patted her pocket, doubting the bag of ordinary objects doubling as mystical materials would work. But she'd already exhausted scripture and outside help.

The haze quivered into a blur as she drew her rosary and squeezed the crucifix. Glowing red eyes in a swirling mass of white and black loomed over her while she held the prayer beads out. Olivia prayed they would help this time, even though they weren't a relic. "In the name of Christ, get out!"

The ghost jerked and shook, writhing with pain. But something was wrong.

"Olivia?" Her mom shuddered, frozen sweat glistening on her brow.

Olivia's eyes widened. The ghost wasn't in pain—it was stifling laughter! The monstrosity lashed out, filling her vision with lights. She flew across the room and hit the ground. Lightning flashed.

"Olivia!" her mom cried over the thunder.

The ghost swept the chair and table out from under her, and her legs snapped with a crack as wood and bone gave way.

Her mom screamed, and Olivia shrieked.

The heavy oak tabletop crashed to the ground with a thud, but the ghost threw it as if it were nothing. Olivia dove away. Wood, plastic, and glass, all brittle with ice, shattered against the wall, raining down frost, shards, splinters, and circuit boards. The letter opener skidded to a halt, inches from her fingers. She grabbed it, but the ghost rounded on her mom.

"Get away from her!" Olivia screamed.

Thunder shook the house. The phantom froze, turning its red-eyed gaze on her. She rose to her feet, blade in one hand and the contents of her pocket in the other. The creature's indistinct outline fuzzed in and out of existence while misty features shifted like paints swirling together.

It stepped forward, coating the carpet in frost, and she gulped, gripping the cold blade tighter. She lunged, and a spectral hand closed around her throat, coating it with frost. Pain radiated from the cold and pressure. The abomination raised her into the air. Despite its spectral form, it felt so real, so cold, like a cloud of ice.

Sensations flooded her mind like paints splattering on a dark canvas. A distant, crimson glow beneath a dim, golden sphere. Rows of twisted, half-formed bodies embedded in cylinders. A long roar shook everything. Then a burst of jagged light, followed by a boom and a relentless pounding from above, echoed in her head.

The visions alternated with reality, mixing in like afterimages from a strobe-light. One moment, she was at home, and the next, that *place*. She was disoriented, and her stomach churned. Worlds blurred together, and a long roar shook the ground. The scent of decay overwhelmed her.

Olivia kicked her dangling feet, gasping for air, struggling to see past the things bellowing in her brain, the things threatening to drown out reality. But between glimpses of flashing lights and bodies, she flung her monster-hunting materials and slashed at the beast.

As she expected, the letter opener passed through the creature's arm without resistance and frosted over. Its red eyes burned with laughter, but something bounced off its chest and rattled to the floor, while everything else passed through. Darkness crept in from the edges of Olivia's blurry vision. She struggled for air but grinned when the beast went rigid. The apparition let out an unearthly cry and threw her. She hit the wall hard.

"Olivia!" her mom screamed.

Rain struck the roof in a torrent. Free from the visions, Olivia groaned. Her arm throbbed harder than the storm pounding at the windows. But her stomach and heart lurched at the sight of her mom's shattered legs. Blood froze over broken bones while Olivia began to weep. "Mom," she groaned.

The Ghost Giant stepped between them, floorboards creaking far too lightly for such a massive figure.

"Olivia..." her mom croaked. "Run!"

Olivia stared into the Ghost Giant's malevolent eyes and staggered to her feet. With one last glance at her mom, she ran, and the ghost gave chase. Bittersweet tears rolled down her cheeks. It wouldn't get her mom. It was going to get her.

She slipped past the attic ladder, but the ghost just passed through and knocked her down. Light flashed in her eyes as it slammed into her, blinding her before she hit the floor. Blinking to readjust to the darkened hall, Olivia couldn't see anything but icy rungs glistening in the lightning.

Frost coated her leg, and Olivia screamed as a spectral hand pulled her through the floor and into the basement. The ghost roared and threw her through the ceiling. She sailed into the front room with a chill while rot hung in her nostrils. She hit the mirror standing in the corner with a crack as glass shattered.

Olivia hoped that luck wasn't real and prayed that she'd survive as she always had. The Ghost Giant rose up from below and lumbered down the hall, frosting over the painting as it entered the room, once more covering poor Bartimaeus's eyes.

With effort, Olivia forced herself to her feet and took hold of the mirror. "Get...out," she cried, shifting it to catch a flash of lightning. A million rays struck the ghost, only to pass through as though it were a prism, casting scattered beams of white, black, and sickly red on the wall.

The ghost lunged and struck her in the face. Her head bounced off the wall. The mirror shattered, and she hit the floor. Fear rose in her heart, but blackness swallowed her vision.

⠐⠣ ⠌⠂⠕⠦⠮⠃ ⠦ ⠈⠇⠲⠱⠃⠞⠌⠰⠷⠄ ⠌⠄ ⠘⠺⠑ ⠄⠄ ⠇⠈⠂⠌⠌⠰⠷⠄⠄
⠄⠘⠺⠑ ⠄⠇⠈⠂ ⠄⠎⠂⠌⠱⠇⠮ ⠗⠪⠄ ⠄⠌ ⠇⠔ ⠌⠄ ⠻⠰⠰⠮⠄ ⠏⠪ ⠄⠌
⠙⠄ ⠝⠪⠮⠻ ⠏⠣ ⠂ ⠌⠂ ⠌⠰⠷⠄

Distant Memories: Mother's Day

Little Olivia sat across from her mom at the kitchen table, doodling in the margins of her spelling worksheet and swinging her legs beneath the chair.

"*Height*," her mom said, typing.

Olivia crossed her arms. "I *hate* that word."

"*Olivia Linda*, why do you *dislike* that word?"

"'Cause I'm short. I'm so small!" She threw down her pencil. "I hate it!"

"*Because*." Her mom sighed. "Why don't we take a break from spelling? Come sit on my lap, okay?"

Olivia hopped down, around, and up, tapping her fingers on the table before frowning at the monitor. "Mommy, why doesn't Daddy use the computer?"

"Because the screen hurts his eyes. Now, can you double-click the fox?"

She did so. "Why's it on fire?"

"Because it's an homage to Samson when he set foxtails on fire to hurt the bad guys."

"Those poor foxes! I don't see why the boys like him! That's messed up."

"Hmm....The world can be a messed up place sometimes. But it can also be wonderful," she said, running a scarred hand through Olivia's hair. "Now, can you double-click the big white bar at the top?"

"The address bar?"

"That's right!"

"Done."

"Now, watch what I type."

```
javascript: document.body.innerHTML =

'<textarea></textarea><iframe>'
```

Olivia frowned. "You're just mashing words together! Text! Area!"

Her mom laughed. "Maybe I am, but if I was, could they do *this*?"

She hit Enter, and Olivia gasped. "The screen! It changed! It changed!"

"Good. Then it's still working. Now watch this." She typed so fast!

```
javascript: document.head.innerHTML +=

'<style>html,body{height: 99%;} body

> * {border: 0; height: 100%; width:

49%;}</style>'
```

Olivia squinted. "That doesn't look like what we learned in school."

"That's because this isn't *English*," her mom said with a smile.

Olivia frowned at the words between those strange symbols. "Then what is it?"

"It's *three* languages all working together!"

"*Three!*"

"Yes!" her mom said, tickling Olivia.

She giggled, fending off her mom's hand. "What are they? What do they do?"

"Well, HTML is like *you*. It's what the webpage *is*. CSS is like your clothes. It changes how things *look*. And JavaScript is like your brain. It lets the program *think*. Got it?"

"I think so," Olivia said, poking her tummy, shirt, and forehead. "Ugh, there's that word again, *height*!"

Her mom laughed. "It's doing something important here." She pressed Enter. "See!"

"Whoa, the boxes got bigger! I wish I could do that."

"You'll grow soon enough, kiddo. Now for the last step."

```
javascript: document.querySelector('body
> textarea').addEventListener('keyup',
function(event)
{event.target.nextSibling.contentDocument
.body.innerHTML = event.target.value})
```

"That's—that's a lot of big words."

"It is," her mom said, hitting Enter.

"They didn't do anything!"

"*Really*? Why don't you type your name in the left box?"

Olivia frowned at the keyboard and poked the buttons. "O-L-I-V-I-A. Whoa! Mommy, it's showing up in both boxes!"

Her mom nodded. "That's because whatever you put in the left box will show up in the right box—without reloading. Now watch this." She typed something in the left box.

```
<h1 style="color: olive;">Olivia</h1>
```

"Whoa, it's big. And *green*!"

Her mom laughed. "Just like your eyes. It's why your dad and I named you *Olivia*."

Olivia got quiet, staring at her mom's sightless reflection on the glassy screen. "Mommy?"

"Yes, dear?"

Olivia shifted in her mom's lap. "Daddy said you want my eyes to be the first thing you see when you get your sight back."

"It's true, kiddo," she said in a sad voice.

Olivia frowned. Her mom got sad a lot. And right now, she looked like she did when people told her that Olivia looked just like her. She was about to cry! Olivia had to cheer her up. The bracelet! She slipped it on her mom's arm. "Happy Mother's Day, Mommy!"

Her mom cried happy tears upon feeling the braille glue dots, and Olivia hugged her.

"Thanks, kiddo," her mom whispered.

ᚦᛖ ᚲᛟᛗᛁᛜ ᚹᚨᚱ

Chapter 2: Blood and Ice

Olivia groaned in the dark, wincing at a bump on her head. Did she have a concussion? Probably—lightning flashed, and the light stung.

She blinked, but that merely showed afterimages intertwined with faded vines beset by sickly fruit. What on earth? No, they weren't fruits. They were water spots. It was wallpaper. She was in the front room, not some garden.

Olivia shielded her eyes as light danced about the mirror shards at her fingertips. Beyond the sea of broken glass, frosty footprints melted into the hall. Something dripped from above.

I WARNED YOU was carved in the icy painting's glass frame, permanently blinding poor Bartimaeus. But worst of all, *Two Days* was smeared below. In *blood*. Olivia watched the lettering drip until it sank in.

"MOM!" she cried, dashing around the glass, pushing past the pain of throbbing bruises. Olivia was too dizzy to run, and she hit the wall in a daze. She tried the lights, but the power was out. It didn't matter —she clung to the wall and pushed on. Her fingernails clicked over the grooves between the wood panels with every step on the threadbare carpet.

"Mom!" she cried, passing the kitchen. Olivia held out a hand, seeking the incoming ladder. Her mom wouldn't have needed such a crutch. She'd have known how many paces away the ladder was.

Icemelt from the Ghost Giant's chilly footsteps seeped into her socks, making them squish against her feet while she stumbled into the ladder, now slick with ice and water.

"Mom?" Why wasn't she answering? Olivia slipped past the basement door into the back room.

"Mom..." she whimpered at the sight of a frosty blood trail glistening in the lightning.

"Oh, God," she whispered, looking around in panic but not finding her mom anywhere.

Tears flooded her vision, but she forced herself not to look away. Like brushstrokes on a canvas, the frozen blood and melting bootprints came in layers. Thus, they told a story, if she could decipher it.

A long smear lined with handprints had been trampled by icy footsteps, which meant the Ghost Giant had followed her mom when she crawled away. But both trails went cold two feet short of the door. There, they reversed amid elongated handprints.

Her mom had tried to cling to the floor when she'd been grabbed, but the blood splatters centered around the pile of icemelt showed that it had been for naught—because these meant that blood had dripped, not oozed, onto the floor. That *thing* had dragged her back and lifted her high, but, given the lack of blood or frost by the door, neither of them had gone through. And there was no sign of frost on the ceiling or the walls. They'd just *vanished*.

"No, no, no!" Olivia sobbed, falling to her knees with her head in her hands. Her mom was gone, and they were going to blame her. But she didn't do it! She couldn't have done it. She could *never* hurt her mom. But the fact that she couldn't remember crossing the yard gnawed at the back of her mind.

"I'm not insane," she whispered. "I'm not insane." There had to be *proof*. Olivia glanced around frantically, unable to think of anything until she wiped her tears. Her *hands*. She held them out until lightning flashed.

"Oh, thank God!" she said. There was no blood on her hands or her clothes. She *couldn't* have done this, and she certainly couldn't have reached that painting in the front room. The Ghost Giant had taken her mom, but *where*?

She gasped, recalling those glimpses of the strange place she saw whenever the creature touched her. Had it pulled her mom into that grotesque and chilly place? That other world?

Sitting against the door, Olivia racked her aching head but couldn't come up with anything else. She didn't understand why the ghost had attacked when her mom was there, but it didn't matter. She just had to get her back. But how?

Thunder jostled her to her core, making the floor dig into her bony backside until she stood. Reality struck her harder than the new wave of rain that was pelting the roof. So she brushed aside a salty tear, knowing what she had to do. Hunting down the ghost was a stupid girl's dream, but her dad had been in the Army. He'd get Mom back. She just had to call him.

Feeling her way to the kitchen, past the mess she'd have to clean up, Olivia grabbed the phone off the charger. The buttons and display lit up too brightly, so she squinted, realizing that the dimly glowing hands of her watch had stopped moving. Stupid ghost. It had broken her watch, and, given the way her pocket felt, it had probably destroyed her radio too. But thankfully, given the difference in time, she'd been unconscious for less than six minutes.

She sighed in relief and thanked God for not having lost much time or many brain cells. Olivia dialed the only useful number she had memorized with her eyes closed. Then she waited.

"Line disconnected," the phone complained.

"Idiot!" Of course, it wouldn't work while the power was out! She'd have to use the wired one in her parents' room. But first, she grabbed a sticky note off the fridge by the cell service maps and ran her thumb across the raised surface. Yes, this was the one with her dad's numbers, not the shopping list.

Using the phone like a flashlight—one she had to turn back on every fifteen seconds—she crossed the hall and clambered onto her parents' creaky bed. Their family photo at the lake glinted back at her from her dad's nightstand. Even without his beard, he stood out among them with his dark hair and rare dark green eyes. Moving to her mom's nightstand, Olivia grabbed the corded phone and tried the first number on the list.

It rang.

"Yes!"

"No one is available to take your call," the phone began in an automated tone. "If you'd like to leave a voicemail—"

"Dang it!" Olivia ran a thumb over the sticky note and tried her dad's newest number.

"No one is available to—"

She prayed that the final number would go through and that he'd have reception.

"Ada?" a garbled voice asked.

Tears welled up in Olivia's eyes. It had been weeks since she'd last seen him. "It's me, Dad."

"Olivia?" he asked as his truck hit a rumble strip in the background.

She sniffled.

"What's wrong, sweetie?"

Olivia put a blanket between her spine and the headboard before leaning back. "Dad," she said in an uneven tone. "The Ghost Giant...it took Mom."

"The ghost....It *took* her? She's *gone*?"

"Yeah," Olivia sobbed, taking Cisco's bone-shaped dog tag off the nightstand and holding it close. She prayed her dad would believe her like Cisco had.

Thunder roared.

"Dad?" Olivia said, nestling into the ugly blanket for warmth. "I'm scared."

"I...I am, too."

"You believe me, don't you?" she asked, holding her breath.

His breathing filled the other end of the line.

Olivia tried to control her tears. He thought she was crazy. He'd send her back! She didn't want to go back to the hospital. Back to the white lights and sterile halls—all too representative of the blank canvas doctors and orderlies wanted patients to revert to. In that place, she'd only had one true friend. A friend she'd abandoned when her parents took her home.

"*Please* don't send me back," she pleaded. "I didn't do this. I wouldn't hurt her."

"I know, and you're not going back. I..." He sighed. "I believe you."

Olivia nearly dropped the dog tag. "You do?" He wouldn't lie to her, but it didn't make sense.

"Yes....I—I don't understand, but Dr. Park said you weren't seeing things or having blackouts—"

Olivia gulped, unable to bring herself to mention the lost time.

"And Father Tom....Well, he didn't even try. As unlikely as it seems, a ghost might actually be the most logical suspect."

Olivia blinked and let out a sigh of relief. Maybe he had doubts, but he wasn't blaming her, and that was good enough for now.

He sighed. "Even now, I don't understand how this is possible, but there's plenty we've yet to understand. Any sufficiently advanced technology would appear like magic to us. Whether we want to admit it or not, science can't explain everything yet."

Olivia pushed back her hair and dried her colored tears before setting Cisco's tag aside. She recognized that tone. He'd used it when explaining the scientific method to her when she was little. He was at least *open* to a supernatural possibility, so she'd take what she could get.

"Before we continue," he began. "There's something you should know."

"Yeah?"

"When we considered pulling you out of the hospital, they offered to pay us."

"Why?"

"To study you."

Olivia gasped. Park. It had to be Park. He tried so hard, but there was nothing he could do to help, because the ghost was real. But paying to study someone....She didn't need to have watched horror films to know that was a red flag. He might have meant well, but she was *infinitely* thankful she'd left the center in time.

"You still there?"

"Yeah, just *processing*," she said, pulling the blankets tighter.

"Anyway, you're not going back. That's why I took up trucking again. So we can afford to keep refusing their offer."

Tears streamed down Olivia's face. They'd spent the whole day together after he brought her home, and then he'd said he had to leave. She'd felt so betrayed because it had hurt so much to spend weeks away from him and her mom, and then, just when she got them back, he had to go. She sobbed. "If we're that desperate, why aren't we using the savings for Mom's vision?"

Silence.

"Dad?"

He sighed. "That was in stocks that we didn't sell in time..."

Olivia hung her head. So *that's* why they were in the Cracks. They weren't just trying to get her mom's sight back more quickly. They were trying to rebuild from scratch.

"Anyway, those were for getting your mom's...sight back..."

"Dad?"

"No one's taking you," he whispered before the line went quiet. Muted.

"Dad?" she cried, shifting in the bedding. Given his silence, the fact that her mom was gone must have fully sunk in.

"Tell me *everything*," he said.

And so she did, from the beginning. Describing her mom's injuries was hard on them both. But when she got to the visions, he wanted to hear about them over and over again. Couldn't he just let her move on to everything else instead of forcing her to relive the worst moments of her life?

"These things you saw, they can't be random. Do you think it's another dimension?"

"I don't know. It's all blurry." It couldn't be Hell. It didn't look like Hell. Her mom wasn't in Hell.

"There has to be an explanation....*A burst of jagged light*—that's what you said, right?"

"Yeah." Olivia ran her fingers over a domino, engraved with braille, from her mom's nightstand. *Marry Me?*, it read. She sniffled, hoping she'd get the chance to ask her about that someday.

Her dad gasped. "Do you think it's lightning?"

Olivia's eyes widened, and she replayed the visions in her head. A burst of jagged light. Lightning. The boom could've been thunder. Incoming rain pounding on a roof.

"I think you're right!" she said. "It was a storm! And that sphere— it had to be the sun! That place is *real*!"

"Okay. Okay. If we continue this line of thought, what about the rest? What would that crimson stuff be? Flowers?"

Olivia shook her head, setting the domino aside. "Flowers don't glow."

"What then? Paint? A sign?"

Olivia gasped. "YES! A sign! A *neon* sign!"

"But you said it was low to the ground."

Olivia nodded. "It was raining! I saw its reflection! There's a building with a red sign!"

"Okay! Then that sound. The one that shook everything. Was that thunder?"

"No, it was too drawn out. But it sounded *familiar.*"

A car horn blared on the other end, and her dad took a deep breath.

"It's a train whistle!" Olivia cried. "That's why everything shook *before* the thunder. A train passed by!"

Her stomach churned. Those bodies. Her stomach heaved, but nothing came up. Instead, hunger and weakness dragged her down into the covers.

"Olivia! Olivia, are you all right?"

"I'm okay. It's just those *bodies.* I could see them in the cylinders. I don't know how they got there."

"Right....Did it look like a lab? Were they floating in tubes of liquid?"

"No, they're *embedded* in them, sticking out somehow with bones and flesh..." She didn't understand, and she didn't want to think about what those people must have suffered.

"Um...okay, that must be where the stench came from. Let's...let's move on. Where was the sun?"

"It..." she said, trying to remember, before pointing in the direction she'd seen it. "It was on the right. Just past the crimson lights."

"Okay. If it was on the right...then, given the time, it might have been in the southwest."

Olivia nodded. "If we assume the place I saw was in the Northern Hemisphere."

"Quite right," he said, pride evident in his voice.

"Which we could, since there was a storm both here and there."

"Hmm....Not so fast. How was the sun positioned on the horizon?"

Olivia inhaled sharply. There were probably other storms around the world. "Um...it was cloudy today, but I think it looked similar to when I got off the bus yesterday." The way it had illuminated overgrown houses had been particularly memorable.

"Okay, hold on..."

Olivia frowned and pressed the phone more tightly against her ear. That sound—it sounded like paper. He must be unfolding a map.

"Let's see...if there was a neon sign, that place is probably in a big city."

"Right."

"And given the sun's positioning, it's probably near Plymouth's longitude."

Olivia sat up. "You think it's in Detroit?"

"Hmm..." he said, probably tracing a finger over the map like he did when he planned a route. "83rd parallel. Cuts through Detroit, Columbus..."

"The storm wasn't going to hit Ohio."

"Right....Okay, no other big cities in the US, Canada, Cuba, or Costa Rica....And it misses South America entirely."

"So if we can confirm the storm didn't reach Columbus, we can bank on Detroit."

"*Hopefully*," he said. "We've got no other leads. That train, though...it's gotta be near the tracks. You said the ghost threw the table. Is the computer still in one piece?"

Olivia winced. "No. And the braille display's broken."

Her dad inhaled sharply. "That's too bad. Your mom loved that thing. We'll have to get a new one."

"Yeah..." Those were *expensive*. "I hope she doesn't have to go back to the screen reader."

"Radar," the phone crackled in a gruff voice. "Exit's closed, and there's a few bears making camp ahead. Over."

"Dad?"

"Sorry. Hold on." A button clicked on the other end. "10–4, Vinland. Thanks for the heads-up."

"Roger that. Vinland out."

Ah, he was using his trucker radio. "Dad?"

"Yeah..." he said, clearly lost in thought. Judging from the crinkling sound, he was trying to find a new route.

"The storm's worse up there, isn't it?" Olivia asked, leaning back.

He sighed. "Yeah. Full-blown blizzard. And this rig's doing me no favors."

Olivia winced. "I'm guessing you're not going to find a computer anytime soon."

"No..."

She frowned. "I can go to the library and check the maps online."

"Mmm....I don't think any of us are going anywhere with this storm. I'll call you in sick tomorrow."

Olivia stared up at the ceiling. *Tomorrow*? She hated waiting. There had to be something she could do *tonight*.

"Hey, look at apartment reviews if you need to figure out how far that train whistle carries."

"Good idea," she said, glancing at her busted watch. "And I can check the historical radar to see where it started raining around that time."

"Okay, that should be enough to narrow down the area—*assuming* it's in Detroit. Listen: with this storm, all flights are grounded, and I'm about thirty hours out if I don't stop. I don't know when I'll get back tomorrow night, and we can't go to the cops, since they'd treat you like a suspect, given the state of the house."

Olivia nodded, knowing what he was getting at. "I can ask Sister Paula for help. She'll probably be volunteering at the library."

"That's an excellent idea. Promise me you'll sleep with the ladder up, and call me once you've narrowed things down at the library, so I can check it out when I get—shoot!"

"What?"

"Phone's about to die."

"Wait, Dad! There's—"

The line went dead.

Olivia stared at the phone. They hadn't gotten past the visions or talked about the message on the painting!

She called back, only to find that the number didn't have a voice mailbox set up yet. Another number had a full inbox, and the last couldn't be completed as dialed. She tried several variants, with and without the area and country codes, before giving up.

She set the phone back on the receiver and fixed the spiral cord with a frown. It was snagged on something. "Ugh!" She followed the cord and pulled a photo album out from under the bed. It contained pictures of all the things her mom wished she had seen.

Olivia teared up at photos: her crawling beside Cisco when he was a puppy, her kindergarten graduation, her First Communion. Her mom was there in every photo. Always there, but never able to see.

What truly broke Olivia's heart was the bookmark. A paper bracelet she'd made for her *years* ago. *Happy other's Day*, it said, now that a few glue dots had fallen off. Once again, Olivia broke down in tears. Why had she kept it all this time?

She couldn't stop sobbing until she set the keepsakes down. The painting said they had two days. If that's when the Ghost Giant was coming back, that would be more than enough time. "I'll get you back, Mom. I promise."

Thunder boomed, and Olivia scowled. Stupid storm. There had to be something she could do *now*. They needed an *edge*. She froze. There was one object that hadn't passed through the ghost. Yes! That was *exactly* what they needed!

Phone in hand, Olivia raced to the back room, losing her balance when the rapid movement sent her head spinning. Her sudden stop nearly sent her to the floor. Still, she stumbled onward, falling to her knees. Her stomach gnawed at her like a beast trying to claw its way out of her body as she crawled forward, past the blood scattered across the floor that stank of blood and iron instead of spilled paints.

At last, bits of rust and salt pressed into her palms. Rowan wood shavings, garlic powder, and scraps of aluminum foil danced to the thunder alongside her silver friendship bracelet. Olivia scooped it up and, in a puddle where the ghost had choked her, saw her prize: a lead fishing weight.

Lead! It couldn't pass through *lead*! That's why it chased her down the hallway instead of passing through the walls! It was just like the teleporting baker in Lady Constance's first case! A wicked smile spread across Olivia's face.

Everything else had failed, but lead would save her mom. After all, if the ghost couldn't pass through lead walls, then it wouldn't be able to go through lead *knives* either. All she had to do was make them.

Unfortunately, pencils were made of graphite, not lead. She'd need another source. Olivia grinned. There was plenty of lead paint under the coat they'd added for safety when they moved in. And her dad even had a lead-rated respirator! Everything she needed was in the basement.

She cracked the door open until it hit the ladder, and she sucked in her stomach to slip past the knob. Old stairs creaked beneath her feet as she rounded the corner, lamenting that she had to keep turning the phone light back on.

Rooting through her dad's automotive supplies from his time as a mechanic turned up a crowbar, and the respirator wedged between a tire iron and a jack. Olivia smiled now that she could gather the paint safely, and she breathed a sigh of relief at the lead oxide label. Thank goodness her dad was always overprepared—she'd be protected from the fumes when she melted her harvest down.

But was there a high enough concentration of lead in the original paint to counter the Ghost Giant? She frowned. Her chemistry teacher said some old houses in the area had up to 50 percent in their paint, but was hers one of them?

No, it didn't matter. The paint must have had enough lead to prevent the ghost from going through the walls. So she'd still have enough if she melted it down, but she'd need a way to refine it. The stove would do, but, without power, she'd have to light it manually. She needed a lighter. To the camping supplies!

Olivia skirted a puddle glinting in the light, rippling from the thunder. She looked up at the dripping ceiling. That must have been where the ghost had grabbed her. The next time it did that, it would lose a hand.

She stubbed a toe on an overturned shelf. "Ow!" The camping supplies and handyman's equipment were mixed in with the unsold inventory from her dad's days as a traveling salesman at a now-defunct survivalist company, Indestructible, LLC. Olivia scowled. The ghost must have done this. Maybe it'd lose *two* hands next time.

She sifted through the mess and found an Indestructible lighter with a side compartment packed with magnesium powder. Better yet, she found a spotlight-grade flashlight! Olivia beamed, clicked it on, and winced at the brightness. At least she wouldn't have to keep turning the phone on every few seconds.

Awesome as all this was, she wondered if they had any other cool stuff that might help her and her dad with the Ghost Giant. Digging deeper turned up a military-grade Indestructible pack, somewhere between a purse and a satchel. Her dad's demo had shown that a five-inch blade couldn't cut through the material.

Olivia set the pack aside and dusted off a folding telescope, fondly recalling her part in his sales pitch—in the skit, she had used it like a baseball bat. He'd sold a lot more units whenever he'd brought her along. But even with her help, his commission never approached what he'd been paid before getting laid off. Stupid Wall Street bankers and automotive bigwigs.

Rummaging more unearthed a combination compass and signaling mirror. Currently, she used one as a compact, but in the past, she'd thrown them like mini-Frisbees to show how sturdy they were. They'd managed to sell quite a few before one ended up embedded in a rotting tree.

After that, word spread, and people started asking silly questions, like why neither of them tried to catch it. *A finger hazard*, her dad would say, before trying to spin it as a shuriken or a replacement for clay pigeons. Few bought that line or the product itself.

Olivia fiddled with the compass, weighing its utility. The needle would go crazy if the ghost were around, but there'd be plenty of other signs pointing in its direction. She tossed the compass back and raised an eyebrow at a tin caked in dust. Prying it open revealed a pair of night-vision goggles.

She gasped. Ghost hunters used these, but why did her dad have a set? Whatever the reason, it wasn't printed on the warning label. *Sensitive components: do not expose to bright light.* Regardless, they could come in handy, so they went into the pack.

Further searching yielded more Indestructible gear: a multifunction watch that she put on right away, a pair of rugged radios, and a water bottle with a bullet embedded in it (a demo she'd not been there for, though her dad had sold out of all but one, since the customer liked setting them up in pyramids to shoot down en masse).

Heading back upstairs with her haul, Olivia slipped through the door and stopped at the kitchen to appease her stomach. Unfortunately, the fridge light didn't come on. She groaned, hoping the power would return before things went bad. But, just in case, she made her favorite type of sandwich: turkey, lettuce, and pickle with mayo. After she finished praying and dug in, a side of cold peas and applesauce rounded out the meal.

That done, she brought a saucepan to the bathroom and donned the painter's mask, tightening the straps to make it fit. Time to get some paint chips. Hopefully, her dad would thank her for the help on the eventual remodel. She chipped away, trying not to damage the underlying walls while filling the pan.

But the lenses kept fogging up. Olivia was thankful for her better-than-perfect vision[2] and could only imagine the annoyance of glasses fogging up daily. Still, her mask did not constrain her vision well enough to hide her reflection. If only that hair spray would come off as easily as the paint on the wall or, better yet, the peeling fence posts.

With the pan half full, Olivia tried to add water but found that the sink wasn't working. Stupid power outage. She shrugged and added the next best thing: her mom's disgusting skim milk. It was practically water, after all.

---

[2] So-called *perfect vision* (i.e., $20/20$ vision) is a misnomer, because it's entirely possible to have better than *perfect vision* (e.g., people with $20/15$ vision can see as much detail from twenty feet away as the average person can see from fifteen).

She placed the pan on a burner,[3] and the stove lit easily with the lighter. While she was happy in this case that they didn't have an electric stove, she hoped the gas company was doing its job of properly filtering out all the toxic fumes. But she doubted it, because no one checked that sort of thing.

Periodically stirring the mixture, Olivia wondered if the sleep-inducing chemicals in warm milk could go airborne or slip through the mask's filters. She could live with drowsiness, but not acute lead poisoning; nevertheless, she threw a lid on to contain the fumes and speed up the process by trapping the heat.

To make the most of her time, she sharpened worthless butter knives with a whetstone, just like her dad had taught her. Well, maybe not *just* like that, since she'd soaked the stone in *milk* instead of water.

Soon, the skim came to a boil, and the lid rattled. Interestingly, the mixture didn't separate into layers. And naturally, no cream rose to the top, since skim wasn't real milk. Olivia prodded the chunky texture, breaking it up with a little more stirring before submerging the knives and turning off the heat.

She jumped with joy at her foray into metallurgy. She was practically a chemist! But the motion made her head spin. She bet chemists didn't get dizzy when they moved.

When her head calmed, she removed her creations with a pair of tongs and propped them up to cool. Interestingly, the blades were white, like cartoon swords. She grinned at the surprise she had in store for the Ghost Giant.

[3] WARNING: lead is not a substance to be messed with. The author and all veritable health care professionals urge against melting it, unsupervised or otherwise, in the *strongest* possible terms.

Detective Kurstin Wagner stared at the bloody evidence bags alongside her partner, Saul, waiting for the lab tech's report.

"Whaddaya think spooked him?" he asked, cocking his head towards the interrogation room.

"I don't know," she said, remembering how the tattered poncho before her had once hung over the gaunt man's shoulders like a cape. He'd looked bigger then, in all that body armor. He had been despondent since she found him, and she prayed that his state hadn't been caused by the *real* Exterminator—that the man she'd seen fleeing the scene hadn't been the real deal.

Saul grunted. "Chief says you *literally* caught him red-handed."

Kurstin nodded, remembering the blood dripping from the gloves while the vigilante stood over his victims, both beaten beyond recognition. And all the bodies she'd passed to get there....The crime scene photos didn't do it justice.

"The question is," she began, "did he really do all *that*? Or is he just a fall guy?"

Saul scratched his bushy brown beard, staring at the prisoner beyond the glass. "Either way, I'd like to know how a twig like *that* managed to carry all *this*," he said, gesturing to the bagged evidence: guns, ammo, and tear gas canisters beside the pump-action shotgun.

"Let alone beat the house guests half to death in the middle of a gunfight," Kurstin mumbled, holding up the skull-emblazoned gas mask. It had chilled her to the bone when she arrived on the scene, and all the survivors had mentioned cowering in terror at the muffled breathing.

The moment he'd taken it off was seared into her mind. He'd blinked under dim lights, revealing facial scars in the shape of a lopsided *X* marring the area around his left eye socket. And given that they'd cut through the bone, it was a miracle his eye was still intact.

Saul's pager chimed, and he cursed. "Tox screen's clean."

Kurstin sighed. "So much for our theory."

He nodded. "Was a good theory."

"Yeah..." she replied. If the man she'd arrested had taken a hit of the stuff the Exterminator had swiped off that German...well, it could've lent credence to the idea of them being one in the same and potentially even explained this guy's seeming ability to shrug off physical exertion.

"That footage of him going up against those addicts..." Saul said. "*Visceral.*"

Kurstin nodded. With another perp at large, they needed to get the one in custody to snap out of his despondency and to figure out what had sent him into shock. Per her tradition, Kurstin put her hair up in a ponytail; she would keep it like that until she was certain they had the right man. But his blank stare was *not* encouraging. "Gonna be a *long* night."

"Well, I'll leave you to it," Saul grunted.

Kurstin glared at him. "Are you seriously just going to leave me with *him*?"

"*Yep*," he said, walking backward toward the door. "Your prisoner, your problem. Besides, as much as I'd love to burn the midnight oil, I'd prefer to catch some Z's."

Kurstin rolled her eyes. "I swear, if I hear you were playing cards—"

"You won't," he said with a smirk.

Kurstin groaned and checked her phone when it buzzed, skimming the report. No sign of elevated adrenaline levels, and a CT scan hadn't revealed an enlarged pancreas or adrenal glands. Strangely enough, his bones were as dense as an athlete's. But the doctors hadn't found any sign of rapid weight loss or muscular atrophy. Had the lab screwed up the blood work?

Somehow, that seemed preferable to detaining a guy who might be able to tap into hysterical strength like moms who lifted vehicles to save their kids in urban legends. Verifiable or not, there was historical precedent for it—if the tales of ancient berserkers powering through fire and arrows were to be believed.

The secret of whatever drugs they'd taken had long since been lost to time. But of all the gangs whose operations the vigilante had busted, the Berserkers would be the most livid if they found out that a Black man had his hands on their namesake's legacy. Imagining Rice fuming all the more if word of this latest development got out brought a smile to Kurstin's face.

But the new text on her cell dampened her spirits.

35% OFF MATERNITY WEAR!

She rolled her eyes at her mother's lack of subtlety and typed in a fury on the tiny QWERTY keyboard.

Funny, but u already have a grandkid. And I told u, this #'s 4 work/emergencies ONLY!

"Detective," a mechanical voice said.

Kurstin spun. "Dr. Park." She'd been briefed on his synthetic speech and did her best not to stare at the nasty scar under his throat mic. Despite the glasses, turtleneck, and lab coat, his broad shoulders, perfect posture, and firm handshake made him seem more like a soldier than a child psychiatrist. Perhaps he was the right man for the job after all.

Kurstin cleared her throat. "Thank you for filling in for our shrink on such short notice. Heck of a day to be out sick."

"No worries, Detective. Happy to help," he said without moving his mouth.

That was a bit eerie, but it wasn't anything she hadn't seen before. Though this was the first time she'd seen it outside of a horror game.

"Have there been any developments?" he asked.

Kurstin shook her head, feeling her ponytail swing behind her as she led him to the observation window.

"No," she began. "He's still in shock and hasn't spoken since we took him in. And we still haven't been able to ID him."

The doctor nodded. "I'll see what I can do."

ᚨᛚᚹᚨᛁᛊ ᛊᛈᛟᚲᛖ ᛟᚠ

Chapter 3: Pilgrim

Friday, October 30th, 2009 (Angels' Night Morn)

Olivia laced up her hiking boots at the door before the sun rose. Favorite outfit: check. Thank God her army tank top didn't get ruined yesterday. Speaking of which, beret to hide that tie-dyed mess: check. Maybe it would've washed out, but she'd showered quickly when the power had returned, in case the Ghost Giant showed up while she was deprived of dignity and defenses.

To ward off the cold and child services, she adjusted her scarf to hide her bruises before slipping on a pair of aviators. Between those and the military pack, she looked more like an army brat instead of a ditzy model. But her smile faded as she slipped on her backpack. Winter coat...Olivia snapped her fingers. It was at school! In the chaos of yesterday, she knew she'd forgotten something!

Slowly, she turned to the coat tree, put her mom's on, and raised the faux fur hood. The puffy coat was far too long on her and in desperate need of sewing, but it was warm. And it still smelled like that fragrance they'd tried at the store, Verdant Lime. Olivia's eyes grew misty as she pulled it tighter.

Time to find out where that stupid spirit had taken her mom. She just had to get to the library and avoid cops looking for unattended minors skipping school. But first, she had to get out of the Cracks. Olivia stepped into darkness so cold that it bit into her teeth. Part of her waited for her mom's familiar shout of 'learn something new', but a metallic clang startled her instead.

Her mouth went dry as a can of green hair spray rolled into the angel statue. On the canister's side, someone had scrawled *Redemption*. Olivia made a fist. *Devin*. But compared to her mom's peril, his antics were *nothing*. Besides, she could use his gift. Improvised mace would be better for self-defense than resorting to a knife. She pocketed the hairspray, praying she wouldn't need it, before locking up and heading out.

Her watch said she was on time to catch the bus, so things were looking up. But the graffiti on the gate dampened her mood, as did the rancid chunks of milk and trickles of sour wine leaking from her neighbor's trash bag. Olivia gagged, unsure of which smelled worse, the place from her visions or the garbage. The working streetlight flickered overhead.

Save for the Cracks, Plymouth was a prosperous town largely unaffected by Detroit's current plight. But Olivia couldn't understand how it had a subdivision this bad. Maybe every carton had a rotten egg. Still, she wished the road didn't look like it had been bombed.

Unlike some of the other houses on the block, Jasmine's was well maintained and even had a pumpkin-emblazoned basketball on the porch. Olivia smiled. No one had stolen it! Perhaps there was hope for humanity yet. Unfortunately, she had to revise her estimation at the sight of a TP'd[4] tree so laden with the stuff that it looked like a weeping willow.

The houses on the next street over weren't decorated, but they didn't need any help to be scary. Poison ivy and sumac choked overgrown buildings, and the wind made creepy sounds whenever it passed through broken windows or creaky doors. A raven perched atop a chimney added to the effect.

A multitude of black cats meowed when she reached the crazy cat lady's home, sending her neighbor's Norwegian Elkhound into a frenzy. The little guy ran up and down the fence, barking.

"Hey, Sigurd," Olivia said, tossing him a bit of her lunch.

The little guy devoured the turkey, wagged his curled tail, and smiled before looking around and whining.

"Sorry, Cisco's still not here," Olivia said, trying to move on.

Naturally, Sigurd trotted beside her until the corner.

"Gotta go."

He whimpered behind the fence, uncoiling his tail.

"Oh, don't be like that," she said, patting his head through a gap in the fence. "I'll be by...when there's light outside. And my dad's home."

---

[4] TP'ing is an activity where idiots throw toilet paper over their victim's property, particularly their houses and trees.

She lowered her head. "Mom too..."

The little guy turned and growled.

Olivia paled. There was a hooded guy ambling right for her! "Thanks for the warning," she whispered, crossing the street.

She checked her compact and discovered that she was being followed. Crud! There were only two blocks between them. Olivia picked up her pace. Blood pounded in her aching legs, but her pursuer was still closing in despite his strange gait. He was going to get her!

Olivia shook the can of hair spray like spray paint, only to inhale sharply. What was she *thinking*? He'd grab her if he got that close! She checked her compact. One and a half blocks.

Her mind raced, and she fumbled in her pack. Knives—deadly, and too close for comfort. Throwing? Nope. Telescope bat—risky. Flashlight? Heavy enough to hurt him and bright enough to blind him *if* he was within arm's reach....One more block.

Compact? Sharp enough to cut. Light enough to throw. But what about her aim? Half a block.

Olivia's shaky fingers closed on the lighter. Hair spray was *flammable*. A flamethrower. Yes! Unexpected enough to shock him, drive him off, or burn him if necessary. But could she really set someone on fire? She gulped, hoping it wouldn't come to that.

Footsteps pounded on the gravel, and Olivia whirled. "Back off!"

Flames erupted, burning scorch marks on the sidewalk, and the glow highlighted the terror on her pursuer's pasty face.

He cursed, stumbled back, and fell, raising skinned-up hands before running off. Unfortunately, he tripped over his sagging pants and had to pull them up with every step.

Olivia shook her head. "Idiot." What did he think *belts* were for?

Plymouth proper soon greeted her, and she smiled with glee at the lampposts. Not only were they all working, but they'd also been decorated for the city's Halloween contest. Frankenstein dummies, stuffed scarecrows, and wicked witches, mixed in with a few zombies, adorned every block.

Ahead, bleary-eyed college students with equally lifeless expressions crowded the bus stop. Olivia kept her head down and pulled up her scarf, hoping they wouldn't question her age or lack of Wayne State attire. Thankfully, they were too preoccupied with books and naps. The bus soon appeared, and everyone boarded, though Olivia doubted anyone else had used their birthday money for their ticket.

She frowned, settling in. There were no profanities scrawled anywhere, and it was *quiet.* Too quiet. She peered over the seat. No one was gossiping. In fact, they were all studying. If this was what college students were like, then college must be *awesome*!

The bus departed, and Olivia passed the time by sketching a world-hopping princess from Constance's series. She grinned, thrilled that it almost looked like the character on the cover. The sword even looked right! By the time the bus reached campus, all that was left was the shading.

Olivia hopped off with the students, thankful that, next to them, people assumed she was just short. Not a child. But with everyone's eyes glued to their phones, no one even noticed her or her struggle to avoid getting trampled.

Finally, the oblivious crowd thinned, and she found herself trailing behind two guys, doing her best not to gag. They smelled like they'd been sprayed by skunks. If college was full of people like them, then perhaps it wasn't quite the paradise she'd imagined. Olivia held her breath until they wandered right past the library.

High windows loomed overhead while she entered. Intricate vaulted ceilings, polished marble floors, fine paintings, and stained glass windows stretched as far as the eye could see. Even without crucifixes, it reminded her of a cathedral. And today, there were nuns out and about in their white habits and black veils.

At the front desk, Sister Paula looked up from her book, and Olivia lit up. Part of her wanted to run and hug her godmother like she had when she was a little girl, but those days were gone. And the suspicion on her former teacher's face only deterred Olivia further.

"*Olivia Linda*, what are you doing skipping school?"

She wilted, and the nun's expression softened.

"Is everything all right?" Sister Paula asked.

Olivia bowed her head. "No. Can we talk...later?" She needed to find that place from her visions first, to prove she wasn't going mad.

Her godmother put a scarred hand on hers. "Of course, dear. My break's in a few hours. Would you like to join me for brunch then?"

Olivia nodded. "That'd be perfect."

"You'll be near the computers?"

"Yes. I need to look something up."

"Marvelous," Sister Paula said, handing her the sign-in sheet. "I'll see you there."

"Thank you."

"By the way," the nun said, returning to her book, "Sister Martha ventured out today."

Olivia scowled. *Martha* was a disgrace to the order and unworthy of the title of Sister!

Her godmother chuckled. "Keep your wits about you, dear. Now, hop to it before she finds you on her *rounds*."

"Thanks," Olivia said, hurrying off. "Speak of the devil," she muttered, finding Martha patrolling the area with her stuck-up look. Ducking behind some bookshelves, Olivia worked her way to a computer in the back. Hopefully, there'd be no interruptions while she gathered intel.

First off, Columbus. That was easy enough. Yesterday's weather reports showed that the storm hadn't touched Ohio. Excellent. Next up, Detroit. To see where it started raining when the Ghost Giant attacked, Olivia used what little code her mom had taught her to overwrite the page's contents and inject a Minutecast from when her watch had broken.

Overlaying a map of the rail lines, she tweaked the transparency to find two tracks intersecting the storm front. But, according to the schedule, only one had a train running at the time! Zooming in on Good'ole Maps revealed a single red, lighted blob in that area: a nightclub called Helvete.

Olivia twirled her pencil. Now, where had she seen that sign's reflection? The club was on the northwestern corner of the block, leaving only the surrounding structures as candidates. Additionally, the lighted signs were only on the western side. So that eliminated the sprawling scrapyard to the east. And with the museum's shadow, she wouldn't have been able to see the sun from that pho place. Scratch that. The angle of the sign's reflection was wrong for both the restaurant and the museum—which left only the club itself! And the parking garage next door....But which one was it?

She frowned, scooting back in her chair to stretch. Her mom had to be in one of those buildings. But if she wasn't, they'd waste valuable time if her dad searched the wrong place. Somehow, she needed to double-check her work in case this was all just a big coincidence. Who knew how accurate those visions really were—or *what* they were, for that matter?

Her gaze settled on the art museum across the street. It was *tall*. Tall enough that she should be able to see into the other buildings with her telescope.

"Gotcha," she said, a bit too intensely, judging by the look a guy in a gaudy button-down gave her. Olivia blushed but kept jotting down the address before stuffing it in one of the many pockets on her surplus fatigues, hoping that standard women's pants would one day have pockets large enough to be for anything other than show.

After logging out, she headed to the front desk. She needed to let Sister Paula know that she'd be back in time for brunch, but her godmother was nowhere to be found. So Olivia left her a note on the sign-in sheet and went to hail a cab. But the drivers and passengers kept giving her odd looks.

Raising her scarf to obscure her face further, she wandered away from the curb, not wanting to risk anyone reporting a lone kid. But walking to the museum was a frightening prospect. It was in a sketchy area, and going alone would be unwise, teen or otherwise.

The flamethrower had worked before, but she didn't want to tempt fate. She turned back and froze. A cop was heading her way. If he hauled her off to school, she'd miss her chance to investigate her visions before her dad got back.

Unable to retreat, Olivia advanced, sticking to the main street. There had to be a way to get to the museum safely. The wind shifted, bringing a guy's singing to her ears:

> Father stands upright and generous. Stooping only to
> break the law by burying the dead. Looking up only to
> be blinded from above. Sinking into poverty, head
> downcast while the bride-to-be raises her voice—
> weeping over seven dead.

She frowned at the guitar solo. Were those lyrics telling the tale of Tobit? She strained her ears.

> And so the son set out to save his family, walking in the
> company of one from above now below. Boy's bringing
> in a fish while taking in advice being handed out. And
> soon he's drivin' out a demon beside his bride!

Olivia gasped. It *was* Tobit! But would the singer live up to the moral of the story and help a stranger in need? Only one way to find out.

> Finally, son, bride, and guide returned, restoring dignity,
> wealth, and sight. Then, at long last, after the story's
> past, the father's eyes closed, and the son's opened in
> time for his family to flee before the Prophecy of Jonah
> came to pass!

Olivia stopped by a guy in his twenties with a wavy ponytail. He played the final chords with his eyes closed and she stood there, mesmerized.

He smiled, teeth unnaturally white against tan skin, and opened his eyes to look directly at her.

She flinched. How'd he know she was there?

"Yo, do not be afraid, chica," he said with the faintest hint of an accent as he continued strumming. "My friends call me Rafe. What do they call you?"

"Liv," she replied. At least, that's what her classmates had called her before she transferred.

Rafe nodded. "And what brings you here on this fine morning, Miss Liv?"

Olivia stared at her hiking boots. All her life, she'd tried not to burden others by asking for help. But now she had no choice. "I...got a little lost...." Well, she knew the way, but getting there...

"Physically or spiritually?"

She raised an eyebrow, eyeing Rafe's necklace, a cross composed of melded music notes.

"Oh, I jest!" He laughed. "Pray tell, where are you headed?"

"The art museum."

Rafe nodded. "I know the place. Come, let us go!" He put his guitar in a case plastered with stickers from cities around the Lakes and hefted it over his shoulder.

Olivia froze, unable to believe her luck. She wanted to trust his kindness, but part of her was wary. After all, that princess she'd drawn had been saved right before getting attacked by her rescuer. But the medical textbooks he hefted from the bench made him seem more trustworthy—as did the Bethesda Hospital logo on his coat and scrubs. She hoped those were more than just a Halloween costume.

"Ready?" he asked.

Olivia gulped, nodding. She prayed Rafe could be trusted and followed a few feet behind, only to blush at his books. She could almost hear Sister Paula scolding her about manners.

"Thank you. Do you need help with those?"

Rafe turned to her, walking backward. "I'll manage. 'Tis good exercise," he said, rolling up a sleeve, revealing a toned arm adorned with wrist weights and intricate tattoos.

Olivia stared at the school of fish swimming around a green whale with a hole in its belly. A tiny man knelt at the center.

"Whoa," she said, noting the detailed scales on each fish. "Nice lines." Tattoos really weren't her thing, but—her eyes widened. She'd gotten too close.

"That Pinocchio?" she asked, stepping back and hoping Rafe wouldn't notice her discomfort.

"You wound me, Liv!" he laughed. "'Tis the prophet Jonah! Not some puppet! Only an unbeliever would confuse the two! Why, Jonah himself proves that they aren't the same! Incidentally, all would do well to learn from him and remember that disregarding wisdom leads not to freedom but to *suffering*."

"I..." Olivia didn't know what she'd expected today, but it wasn't a theological lecture. Then again, she only expected those on Sundays and at midweek Mass.

Rafe winked. "Oh, I am messing with you, Liv. But nice catch on the parallel! And remember that patience in the belly of the beast only becomes necessary after one cuts one's lifelines, ensnaring oneself in the nets and depths of tribulation."

Olivia chuckled. "Lotta sea metaphors in there."

"¡*Sí*, Señorita!"

As terrible as that pun was, Olivia laughed so hard she almost missed a step. But Rafe caught her, still managing to keep ahold of his many books, until she regained her balance. They continued on, side by side.

"So, Tobit?"

Rafe lit up. "You know it!"

Olivia nodded. "Write that song yourself?"

"Sí."

"So you're a musician?"

"'Tis a hobby. You have any?"

Olivia looked away. "I draw sometimes."

"Reaaally? Have anything with you?"

Olivia blushed. She'd never shared her work with anyone, let alone a stranger.

Rafe clicked his tongue. "Oh, Liv, one's world expands in proportion to one's bravery. And it's *easy* to be brave with strangers. For even if they judge us, we'll *never* see them again."

Olivia frowned. That...actually made sense.

"Case in point: occasionally, I *dance*." Rafe flashed her a smile and launched into a series of breakneck, spinny dance moves. Miraculously, he made it down the sidewalk without losing his balance, footing on the slippery pavement, or stack of books.

Her jaw dropped at the skill and absurdity of it all, unable to stop herself from laughing and applauding.

Rafe bowed near an indifferent stranger passing by. "Ah, nothing fends off the cold like movement. So, how about those drawings?"

Olivia hesitated. Rafe seemed so genuine and somehow *familiar*, even. Like a long-lost friend, one she didn't want to let down. But what if he thought her sketches sucked? No, he was right. This might be good for her. Before she could chicken out, she handed over some drawings. And despite his words, she held her breath, anxious to see what this stranger would say.

Rafe leafed through her sketches atop his books. "Liv, these are fantastic! You should be an artist!"

She blushed, waiting at the crosswalk. "You think so?"

"Absolutely," he said, handing them back.

Olivia's spirits rose, only to fall at the impossibility of it all. Such a compliment was easy to give but hard to live up to. "I don't know..."

"That's okay," Rafe said, tapping two fingers on his forehead. "I do. See, it's clear you enjoy art—"

"But I'm not good at it," she said, shuffling through her papers, embarrassed by figures with asymmetrical eyes and no necks. "Look, this guy's legs are way too short!"

"Don't sell yourself *short*, chica."

Despite not usually liking height jokes, she laughed anyway.

"Liv, could you put those in chronological order?"

When she did so, her eyes widened. The mistakes vanished over time. She'd gotten better *without* help. But how much faster would she improve with a teacher or just another set of eyes?

Her heart went out to that art class form and faltered at her selfishness. Her mom was in danger, and here she was talking about *art*!

"So," Rafe said, turning a corner. "You enjoy art and are improving—"

"But it's just art...." Olivia hung her head and ran a thumb through the edges of her beloved pieces, feeling ashamed at how much of her self-esteem was wrapped up in something so worthless. So wasteful. Those pencils and paper could have been put to use on homework.

"Just art?" Rafe said. "Blah! You see, Señorita, people seek out art and entertainment in their downtime. Thus, recreation shapes their thoughts and, in turn, their actions. Why, the works of Lucas inspired many to become archeologists and scientists! But there's a *dark side*. See, people *crave* originality. Art must be novel, more exaggerated than real life—"

A bus passed by, shifting into higher gear. Olivia's mind likewise raced to keep up with Rafe's ever-accelerating speech.

"—and so it is. *Until* it is imitated. Then, the line is *moved*. Entertainment shapes culture and vice versa. One need look no further than the race to the bottom that is advertising!" he said, gesturing at a racy billboard.

Olivia blushed and looked away.

"And tragically," Rafe continued, "those who complain about the state of the entertainment industry are the very ones who've abandoned it to what it's become! Why, if they just *participated* in it, things might improve! Hence my *guitar*," he said, rhythmically tapping the case.

Olivia's eyes widened. "Wow. You make it seem so important."

"Because it is! ¿Comprendes?"

She nodded as they crossed the street.

"Excelente. So, since art's important, you enjoy it, and you can be good at it, the only thing holding you back from your *ikigai*,[5] your *raison d'être*,[6] is sustainability."

"That's why I can't," she sighed, putting her sketches away. "I need to find something less *risky*." Maybe if her family had been richer...But they weren't. And she couldn't bring herself to tell her

---

[5] Japanese: a reason for being. Western understanding paints it as the intersection of what one's good at, what one can be paid for, what one enjoys, and what's important for the world.

[6] French: reason for being.

mom. To make her constantly worry that her daughter would end up a starving artist like Van Gogh or Vermeer.

"Oh, chica....*Everything* is risky. Success is *never* certain." Rafe gestured to a shuttered factory and a soup kitchen across the street, bowing his head. "Many took *safe* jobs only to be laid off this past year. Where luck is involved, one must rely on *Him* to provide. For if it is *His* will, how then will He let you fail?"

Olivia sniffled. The idea of God providing for her as He had for Isaac seemed too good to be true. The idea of the Almighty wanting her to do what she wanted to do felt *delusional*. But what if he made her that way? Surely, He couldn't be so cruel as to put a desire in her only to place it out of reach....Surely, she'd get her mom back. But what if that wasn't His plan? What if she tried and failed?

"Liv?"

"What if I'm scared," she whispered, holding back tears.

"Of failure?" he asked, concern clear in his eyes.

Olivia nodded, staring at the sidewalk. Like rescuing her mom, a career in art would likely fail if the first attempt didn't pan out. And if she worked on backup plans for either endeavor, her focus would be split, potentially dooming all her efforts.

Rafe cleared his throat. "As your philosopher-king, Alexander, once said: through every generation of the human race, there has been a constant war. A war with *fear*. Those who have the courage to *conquer* it are made free, and those who are conquered by it are made to *suffer* until they have the courage to defeat it, or death takes them."

Tears fell from Olivia's eyes. She'd been living in fear ever since they moved. Worried that the Ghost Giant would show up, that she'd be locked away, out of her mind on pills—afraid of what she'd find if she went to visit her friend, afraid that her new classmates would find out she'd been institutionalized.

No, she'd been terrified long before. Scared her parents would be disappointed in her pursuits. That others would mock her work. Scared of what her mom would say—that she wouldn't understand. But now, faced with the possibility of never getting the chance to ask....That hurt even more.

"You see, Liv, if your soul yearns for this, then it is your calling. Sadly, not all heed the call." He looked on with sorrow at a group of homeless people gathered around a burn barrel. "But ignoring it will destine you to a life of hollowness. Many turn to chemicals and recklessness to fill the void. Perhaps one day, they'll find their way back, back to what they were born to do."

Olivia wiped away her tears. She *would* get her mom back. Why was art.…Why was that scarier than facing the Ghost Giant? But she knew.

"But what if," Olivia whispered, "not everyone understands?"

"Oh, chica, not everyone understands the mysteries of the cosmos above or the marvels of engineering beneath their feet," he said, tapping the asphalt. "And yet their lives are all the better for those who do. Those who make the most of their gifts."

Olivia shook her head. He didn't understand. "But what if they can't understand? What if my mom can't *see*?"

Rafe put a hand on her shoulder. "Oh, Señorita, perhaps your mother cannot see. Cannot enjoy the things you do. The things you create. But parents *yearn* to experience joy through their children in things they cannot. And it is a parent's *eternal* hope that their children will live better than they."

Olivia sniffled. Maybe her mom would be supportive. Maybe she'd been worrying about nothing this whole time.

"Food for thought," Rafe said, patting her on the shoulder and gesturing to the museum. "Till next we meet, Miss Liv," he said, carrying on.

"Goodbye, Rafe," Olivia said, watching him go before turning to face the buildings across the street. "Thanks for everything."

Kurstin yawned, trying to cover up the circles under her dark green eyes with concealer. Saul joined her in the car as she dialed her best friend.

"Hey, Kay!" Jay said with her usual enthusiasm, eliciting a groan from Saul.

Kurstin shot him a glare. "Hey, Jay. Listen, I know you're between assignments, but I need a favor."

"Dangerous words, Kay." She giggled. "I'm not *Saul*."

"I heard that," he growled.

"Oh, *goodie*, you're here too," the phone crackled.

"*Jay*, play nice," Kurstin said, glaring at Saul.

He threw up his hands, and Kurstin rolled her eyes. "We've got an unidentified witness in the wind and a lunatic in lockup."

"How crazy are we talking?" Jay asked.

"*Search not for the man in the moon*," Saul began, "*but above all, flee the mad one and the hanged man*. Those were my favorite lines."

"Uh-huh, yeah, I'm sure," Jay said.

"He's not joking," Kurstin said, holding up a hand to ward off Saul's retort. "But I'm more concerned with the fact that our perp didn't talk until he saw the psychiatrist we've got on loan."

"You're thinking witness intimidation?" Jay asked.

"I can't rule it out," Kurstin replied.

"You should go to Standards," Jay said.

Kurstin sighed. "I don't trust them to handle this....Look, Saul's covering that angle, but I need you to work your magic on some surveillance footage."

"Okay, I'll bite," Jay said.

Saul grunted. "Partygoers were all too high or hammered to remember anyone matching the description of the guy Kurstin saw fleeing the scene."

"In their defense, most of them were blinded by tear gas," she added.

"Lemme guess," Jay said. "All the other guests were accounted for, so Cole and Holland didn't look into it too thoroughly."

"Yes," Kurstin replied. "And all the footage we managed to subpoena or get the neighbors to hand over goes staticky a few minutes before and after I arrived."

"Interesting..." Jay said. "Consider me intrigued. Out of curiosity, do you have audio of the interview?"

"Yeah," Kurstin said. "But his voice is *creepy*. And more disturbingly, he refers to his victims as animals."

Saul snorted. "Can't say I disagree."

"Saul—" Kurstin said, turning on him.

"The way they behave," he continued. "Without honor or humanity....And *victims*? I mean, come on, anyone he's ever killed turned out to be guilty as sin. Worthy of the death penalty ten times over."

"*Saul!*" Kurstin said, closing her eyes and massaging the bridge of her nose. They'd been over this twice already.

He just held up his hands. "I know you did the right thing bringing him in, but if it were me—"

"*See*," Kurstin said, shaking her head. "It's crap like *this* that's forcing me to look into this unofficially."

"Uh, Kay," Jay said, "even if the department *wanted* to keep the vigilante on the streets, I don't think we're well funded enough for a cover-up."

Saul grunted. "Well, we're still well funded enough for them to throw up red tape to prevent us from looking into this or anything else worthwhile."

"Uh-huh," Jay replied. "And just how are we supposed to know that *you're* not in on it?"

"I would *never* let an innocent man take the fall," he growled.

"Okay, fair enough," Jay said. "Look, I get why you think this is some big conspiracy—"

"Pot calling the kettle black—" Saul muttered.

"But, Kay, why are you even *considering* that?"

Saul chuckled, and Kurstin sighed. "Just tune into the press conference, and you'll see," she said, glancing at her watch. She had to get going.

"Well," Saul said, opening the door and letting in the cold. "I'm off to see what's so scary about our child psychiatrist. Wish me luck."

Kurstin groaned, starting up her car.

After a moment, Jay asked, "Is he gone?"

"Yeah." Kurstin yawned, heading out.

"Kay, promise me you're not going off the deep end like him."

"I'm *not*," she said.

"Okay, okay. I just don't want this to turn out like your brother's—"

"This is *nothing* like that!" Kurstin snapped. "Look, I *just* want to make sure that we've got the right guy. I mean, the stuff the perp was saying—the things Dr. Park just went along with. Well, they were *out there*."

"Isn't that what psychiatrists are supposed to do? Get people to talk?"

Kurstin sighed, putting on her turn signal. "That's what *Saul* said. Said it's their *job* to talk to sick people. Indulge their fantasies. Get them to open up. Said Anania did it *all* the time."

"Ugh! Forget I said anything. Look, I'll help, but I need something in return."

"All right," Kurstin said, not liking that tone.

"So, because we're besties, you'd tell me if you were pregnant, right?"

Kurstin narrowed her eyes and took a deep breath. "Are you kidding me?"

"So you didn't hear it from me," Jay said. "But you know that interview you just pulled an all-nighter to conduct?"

"*Yeah*," Kurstin said, resigned to where this was going.

"Well, *someone*—"

Meaning Saul.

"—shared the juiciest bits around the office..."

Kurstin groaned, hitting her head on the seat. "What *exactly* did he share?"

"Well, it starts out with this bit about *auras*. Quote: *the eyes are the windows into the soul. I see what I see. And yet so often, I do not*

understand. Sometimes, I think it madness. Other times, folly. End
quote. The shrink then asks what he saw when he looked into yours."

Kurstin squeezed the steering wheel, wishing it were Saul's neck.

"To which the perp replies," Jada continued, "*I saw a woman
giving birth to the land, air, and sea. It is a sin to harm a pregnant
woman. So I stayed my hand and surrendered.* You then responded, *For
the love of God...I'm not pregnant.*"

"We've also got this bit about him reciting Revelation: the fourth
seal, seeing a pale horse whose rider's name was Death when he looked
into the shrink's eyes. As well as his claims that Dr. Park got his throat
slashed in North Korea, but those weren't the predictions the boys
started betting on."

"I'm gonna kill him."

"So, Kay, did you forget to tell your bestie that you're—"

"I'm not *pregnant!*"

"You're the *best!*"

Kurstin slid her cell shut and pulled into the station. At least
someone was profiting off her misfortune. *Again.* Ugh! Why was she
surprised? Saul had done the exact same thing the *day* she'd gotten
back from her honeymoon.

"I'm gonna kill him." She yawned. But first, the press conference.
Then sleep. Then murder.

ÞM ‹ΩMIϙ ΡFR ÞM‹›

Chapter 4: Kindred

Olivia stared down the buildings across the street, hoping that her mom both was and *wasn't* being held captive in there. Because if she was, well, it broke her heart to think about what she was going through. But if she wasn't, then Olivia had no idea where else to look.

She hated that she was too young to enter the club and looked away from the *Condemned* sign chained across the parking garage. Waiting was hard, but they'd have better odds of getting her mom back if her dad went in. She just had to make sure he searched the right place when he got back. But to do that, she needed to do recon from the art museum.

According to the prices listed on the window, she had enough to get in, but she doubted they'd take money from an unaccompanied minor. They'd just have the police haul her back to school. The fire escape around the corner looked promising, but the ladder wasn't down. Assuming that there was a back door, that would be her best bet, because there was no way she was getting in through the front.

As if on cue, buses flooded the street. Sycamore Junior High School kids surged out, and Olivia smiled. Unlike the kids at her old school, they weren't in uniforms. And there were *far* too many students for them to all know each other. But best of all, they looked like they were in the eighth grade, the grade she would have been in if her parents hadn't let her skip a year.

Blending right in, she joined the tide, thankful the staff weren't checking bags or tickets when everyone spilled into the lobby. She didn't want to think about what would happen if they found the lead knives in her pack.

"Stick with your group," a staffer told a boy venturing off on his own.

Olivia frowned. She'd need to find a group to tag along with, lest she get kicked out. But even if the students didn't speak up, the teachers would. There had to be a way. Slipping through the crowd, she searched for opportunities.

"You seen Frances?" someone asked.

"*No*, Keemia!" a moody girl in a scorpion tee replied.

Not helpful.

A boy sighed. "But Carmilla's in the other group."

Nope.

"Relax, Adrian," a goth guy replied. "Miss Norma's filling in. She'll never notice."

Huh, he was kinda cute. Wait, they had a sub!

"Seriously, Otto?" Adrian said, adjusting his glasses. "She's counted us off *five* times."

The other boy shrugged. "Yeah, who does that?"

Adrian shook his head. "She'll know *immediately*."

Olivia grinned. *This* was her chance. "I'll switch with you."

They turned, and Otto looked her up and down. Olivia wished her coat was more presentable. No! She was here to scout for buildings, not boys!

Otto elbowed his friend. "Could work. Adrian's a girl's name too."

Adrian rolled his eyes. "Lemme guess. You think Allison won't notice."

Olivia followed his gaze to a teacher flirting with a tour guide. "How'd you know?" Drat, she should've gone with them.

Otto smiled, and Olivia blushed. Maybe it was okay if she went with this group.

"Thanks," Adrian said, heading over to the moody girl, miraculously lifting her spirits.

She chatted with him for a moment before mouthing *thank you* to Olivia.

"Guess everyone's happy," Otto said with a grin. "Name's Otto."

"Uh...Sabrina Kaspar," Olivia replied, not wanting to give her real name in case she got caught.

"What kind of a name is Cass-par?"

"It's derived from the name of one of the Magi." Thank goodness she paid attention in class. Oh, how she missed the academy. The Park wasn't bad—especially Mr. Bialy's chemistry classes—but she missed the teachers at Spiritus Sanctus.

"So, you're like a wise man—er, *woman*?"

"Something like that."

"Otto," a woman called from the front.

"Here!"

"Adrian."

"Here!" Olivia said.

Some of the boys turned around, but no one said anything.

"Well, *Sabrina*," Otto said, "it's a pleasure to meet you. I knew this'd work."

"Yeah." Now she just had to figure out how to slip away. When the time was right, of course.

"*Hello*," a woman said in a Russian accent. "My name is Anastasia, and I'll be your tour guide this morning. If you'll follow me, please."

"Come along," the teacher said, prodding them forward.

Olivia sighed, glancing back at the sub. Sneaking away was going to be hard.

"Today's exhibition," Anastasia began, "will showcase contemporary pieces by local students alongside more traditional works."

Olivia groaned with some of the other kids, knowing how torturous this would be since she couldn't take her time to enjoy everything.

"This piece, entitled *Leaves of Grass*, is a literal interpretation of Walt Whitman's work of the same name."

Olivia perked up. Whitman was one of her mom's favorites.

"Notice the surreal feel of the leaves budding up from the ground."

Olivia studied the bunnies taking refuge in the grass and weeds sprouting from the branches. Doves nested below. It was all so detailed and yet so simple. If only her mom were here....She bowed her head, wishing her mom could *see* this.

"*Lame*," Otto said.

Olivia glared at him.

"I mean, neat. If you're into that sort of thing."

Olivia rolled her eyes. "I *like* art."

"I'm more of a *science* guy," he said with a smirk.

"I happen to like *both*."

Otto chuckled. "You do? Then explain that tree. No way it can support itself with the surface area of those—"

Olivia lit up. He was talking about gas exchange rates!

"Shhhh!" the teacher said, standing between them.

"No, it is fine!" Anastasia said. "Art is supposed to be a conversation!"

The sub glared at the tour guide. "Then it's one they can continue *later*."

Olivia scowled. That wouldn't be possible. Why'd what's-her-name have to ruin a perfectly academic discussion?

Anastasia shook her head but continued on with the next painting. "This Lovecraftian work was inspired by the artist's love of literature and kaiju films."

"Now *that's* a painting," Otto whispered, nodding at the dragon octopus thing perching atop a lighthouse, beset by hydroplanes amidst a stormy sea.

"Why?" Olivia asked, playfully snickering at his kraken tee.

Otto grinned, but the sub—Miss Norma—cleared her throat.

"*Killjoy*," he coughed.

Olivia stifled a laugh, prompting Miss Norma to move her beside a girl in a sweater-vest. Olivia sighed. At least sneaking away would be easier now that the sub was preoccupied with Otto.

"Sorry my mom's a buzzkill," sweater-vest girl said.

Olivia blinked. If she looked past the girl's beaded hair and Miss Norma's glasses, the two looked quite similar. "Sorry you have to *live* with her."

"Yeah, she can be a total pain!" the girl moaned. "I'm Harriet, by the way."

"Sabrina," Olivia replied. It felt wrong how easily deception was coming to her, but she had to maintain her cover.

The tour guide led them to an odd sculpture composed of an avocado, a chalkboard, an old-timey terminal, some cash, and a picture of a turtle at the center of a two by two grid.

"This self-contained composition quite literally illustrates what it takes to construct itself."

Olivia stared at the plaque below. Apparently, the bills equaled the total cost. She turned her attention to the code on the terminal, unable to decipher it.

"Oh my gosh!" Harriet whispered.

"What?"

"The chalkboard outlines the list of materials, and that code applies a mask to the avocado to generate the turtle!"

Olivia blinked, having no idea what that second part meant. "Huh, that's pretty neat."

Harriet laughed. "The sculpture, or how I knew?"

"Both." Olivia chuckled. "How'd you learn to code?"

Harriet's gaze lingered on the terminal while they moved on. "Mom made me. Says programming's a high-paying job. But I just wanna draw stuff with it. She doesn't like that, though."

"I'm sorry," Olivia said, knowing how that felt. But did she *really*? Her mom never ridiculed art. And now that she thought about it, that seemed unlikely, given her love of poetry.

"Don't be," Harriet said. "Not like it's your fault or anything."

"Yeah..." Olivia said, hoping her mom was all right and feeling guilty for almost enjoying herself here.

Otto, standing near a painting of a pale dragon in a forest, rolled his eyes at Miss Norma, causing Harriet to giggle.

"So, Sabrina, are you and he...?"

"What? No, no, no," Olivia said, shaking her hands. "Nothing like that!" She didn't even go to this school!

"*Really*?" Harriet asked. "I bet you could totally get his number. He seems pretty cute and *really* into you."

Olivia blushed. "What?" Was it just her, or was it getting hot in here?

"I mean, come on, he was practically ignoring the paintings before my mom moved you."

Harriet might have been right, but that was irrelevant in light of her mom's plight. But even if she was safe and sound at home, it wouldn't matter.

"I don't have a cell," she said, staring at her boots. She wouldn't be able to text him.

"Oh..." Harriet said, following the others. "I don't either."

"You don't?"

Harriet shook her head, knocking beaded braids together. "Everyone else does, and, till now, I thought I was the only one who didn't. And no one likes calling..."

"Yeah." Olivia *did* know how that felt.

Anastasia cleared her throat. "Come closer. Gather round."

Everyone bunched up around a chalk sequence of two boys growing up. They started out crawling as toddlers' scribbles and grew into detailed teens walking side by side. But why did the first lean on the younger one after teaching him to walk? Things only got worse from there as he devolved into a series of wispy lines before fading away and leaving the other in anguish.

Anastasia gestured to the composition. "This piece is called *Brothers*. The green figures represent the artist, and the white his brother. Each segment is a re-creation of their art styles at that approximate age. Any guesses why the artist's work becomes more advanced faster than his older brother's?"

Harriet's hand went up.

"Yes," Anastasia said, pointing to her.

"His brother helped him learn."

Olivia nodded slowly. It made sense.

Anastasia smiled. "Very good. And does anyone know what happened to the older brother?"

No one raised a hand. Olivia squinted at the drawing. The older brother's art style regressed, but the wispy lines started in his head. She gasped, and the tour guide nodded.

"Brain cancer?" Olivia asked, unable to come up with a better explanation.

"Yes," Anastasia said somberly.

Olivia stared at the piece. It must have been terrible to get worse at something that had once brought him so much joy. If she could make anything half—no, even a quarter—as good as this piece just once in her life, she'd be happy. Strangely, relative to the other works on display, this one was much cruder, and yet it was the one that got to everyone. Even Otto looked a bit moved.

"There's something about these paintings," Harriet said. "Something...*simpler*."

Olivia nodded. "They're slightly less than perfect."

"Exactly! They're less like stuff I've seen on other field trips and more like something I could make. They're more—"

"*Feasible*," they said together, grinning.

Harriet looked around. "I mean, they're all still above my level, but it's easier to imagine making this sort of stuff than the things at the fine art exhibitions my mom drags me to."

"Yes! Why, this one even shows how to get from where I am to there," Olivia said, pointing to the final drawing of the now-photorealistic brother in anguish.

"All right, kids," Anastasia began in her Russian accent, "we'll head upstairs in ten minutes. In the meantime, here are your sketch pads and pencils. Feel free to check out other exhibits or stop by the restrooms."

Olivia's shoulders slumped. This was her chance to slip away. But they were getting sketch pads...premium hardcover ones with fancy lettering. Her eyes watered. With one of those, she wouldn't have to keep drawing on the back of used envelopes.

But Miss Norma shook her head when the tour guide tried to hand them out. "No, everyone, stay together! Come along," she said, ushering them to a staircase.

Olivia and Harriet groaned, but Anastasia put her hands on her hips. "The whole point of art is self-exploration."

"They can do that on their own time."

"And just how many will get that chance?"

One by one, the students slipped away while the adults argued.

Harriet elbowed Olivia. "Let's get out of here."

"Yeah," she said, feeling strangely guilty for leaving. She'd never ditched a school tour before. Still, following Harriet's lead, she tore her gaze away from the stack of sketch pads. One day.

Unlike the others, Harriet walked straight past the restrooms and toward the gallery. Olivia stuck with her, since the security guards only paid attention to lone students. Plus, Harriet was pretty cool.

They stopped by a vase seemingly woven from ceramic snakes, but Olivia paid more attention to the window, confirming that there was nothing on the first floor she couldn't see from the sidewalk. They had to go higher. "Hey, wanna check out the stuff upstairs before your mom gets us kicked out?"

Harriet grinned. "Heck, yeah!"

They dodged groups of visitors on their way to a staircase free of bickering adults.

"And just where are you two going?" Otto asked.

Olivia froze, and Harriet blushed.

"We were...." Harriet began, turning to Olivia with a grimace.

"Going upstairs," Olivia blurted out, not wanting to hide things from him. "Wanna join us?" she asked, hoping that would prevent him from tattling.

He shrugged. "All right."

Harriet gave her a wry smile and hurried upstairs.

Walking beside Otto, Olivia hid a smile of her own. This still felt wrong, but she was getting closer to her goal alongside her new friends.

Marble statues, jade figurines, and bone carvings filled the first exhibit. But there were no windows in the room. And Olivia wasn't really into sculptures. All the same, she had a hard time keeping her eyes off a guy sketching an Inuit artifact. His drawing was so detailed that it looked like a black-and-white photograph! But acne-ridden bullies bumped him, causing him to drop his things.

"Whoops!" They laughed, stomping his stuff underfoot.

Olivia made a fist when the boy's pencil snapped, but Harriet held her back.

"Take it easy, Sabrina. There's nothing we can do."

The artist's fingers contorted before he picked up his ruined sketch.

Olivia gasped. He'd cursed at them in sign language!

"Come on," Otto whispered, peeking around a corner. "A security guard's coming!"

Olivia hurried after them, but looked back one last time. She blushed, making eye contact with the Indigenous guy. Her heart melted at his black eye, and the bruises on her neck ached. There was nothing she could do, but she had to try. *I like your drawing,* she signed.

He froze and looked down at his ruined sketch with a bittersweet smile. *Thank you.*

Unlike voice, sign language didn't convey tone through pitch but through body language. Thus, Olivia could have wept at how gentle his movements were. Her comment had meant the world to him.

"What was that all about?" Harriet asked.

Olivia turned to her. "What was what about?"

"Those gestures," Otto said.

"Sign language," Olivia replied.

Otto frowned. "What? Like what Deaf people use?"

She nodded, and Harriet tilted her head to check behind Olivia's ears. "But you're not....How'd you learn it?"

"My best friend," she said, staring at her boots. Fearing that it was already too late to see her again. But she didn't want to think about that. *Couldn't* think about that. She shook her head and looked around for a better view of the street before blushing at revealing sculptures and paintings of pale people.

Harriet and Olivia hurried Otto along, but he kept gawking at everything, forcing them to follow suit and do their best to *admire* things whenever a security guard passed by. Nervousness would imply they didn't belong, while staying calm was less likely to get them questioned.

Olivia shifted on her toes, checking her watch. Why hadn't Harriet's mom noticed they were missing yet? She hoped their names wouldn't be called over the PA system, putting all the guards on high alert for wandering students.

"Hey, Sabrina," Harriet called. "These look more...interesting."

Olivia nodded, following her into a room full of lush landscapes and plenty of windows. Perfect vantage points. If she could just confirm which building she'd seen yesterday—yes, maybe then she could relax a bit here before going back to chat with Sister Paula.

Otto groaned, leaving the scantily, or less, clad works behind. They took in paintings of vibrant forests, rolling fields, and striking gardens, reaching the windows just as storm clouds rolled in.

Olivia sighed. If only she'd been quicker! Her night-vision goggles might do the trick, but she couldn't whip those out in public. Were there any bathrooms on this level? No, the signs all pointed downstairs. She'd have to go higher still and hope for a secluded area.

"Wow," Harriet said, coming to a stop beside a colossal painting. "This one's really something."

Olivia glanced at the placard. *The Edge of Light and Shadow* depicted the boundary between two forests, one of which was shrouded in darkness. At the center stood a curved wooden blade driven into a stump. Otherworldly flowers bloomed from its hilt.

Otto scoffed. "There's no way those branches could be woven into bridges. And the scale between the sword and the trees—they'd have to be *hundreds* of feet tall!"

Olivia frowned. While the bridges did look odd, the lighting looked right. This Samuel Immanuel Rhys must've been a true master to bring such an imaginative piece to life.

Harriet chuckled. "It's totally possible. Redwoods and Baubotanik could explain it all."

Olivia and Otto raised their eyebrows.

"What?" Harriet asked, messing with her bulky beads. "I know a few things."

Olivia shook her head. "I know redwoods are big, but what's Baub—Baubo—"

"*Baubotanik* is an architectural form that makes living structures from interconnected plants."

Olivia's mouth fell open, and Otto grinned. "*Interesting*," he said.

Olivia nodded, spotting a distant staircase. "Look, another floor!"

"Well, what are we waiting for?" Otto asked.

"But we haven't even finished with this one!" Harriet called, stopping alongside them upon seeing the *Closed* sign.

Olivia's shoulders sagged, but Otto turned to her with a mischievous smile. "Who's up for more sneaking?"

Harriet tilted her head. "I dunno. Maybe we should head back..."

Olivia nodded before gasping at the fine print. "Oh my gosh, it's a *Constance* exhibit!"

They stared at her.

She blushed. "I mean...if we go back now, we'll just be looking at the same stuff again, right?" That was plausible. Besides, she *really* didn't want to break the rules alone.

Otto shrugged. "She's got a point. I say we go."

Harriet crossed her arms. "You're just saying that because *she* said it."

"No!" Otto protested, scratching his curly hair. "Look...if we get caught, your mom'll get fired."

Harriet grinned. "Let's do it," she said, ducking the velvet rope.

"Wait!" Olivia called.

"Come on," Harriet said. "It's a *Constance* exhibit."

"But—"

"Hurry up, slowpoke," Otto called. "Last one up's a rotten egg!"

Olivia groaned. She had to go up there anyway, but sneaking into the museum and away from a tour group didn't hold a candle to *trespassing*. Checking for security guards and tour guides, she hurried upstairs.

"Harriet? Otto?" she called, scanning the massive darkened space. No one answered, and there was no sign of movement. Her shoulders slumped. She'd known they'd have to part eventually. She just hadn't expected to get ditched.

"Farewell," she whispered, heading for a distant window. Thankfully, the entire floor was closed, and there were no workers in sight, so they were probably on a break.

What little light came through the dusty panes silhouetted mannequins dressed in sophisticated lab coats, elegant nightgowns, and lavish dresses. All of them bore Constance's face. Olivia stared up at the larger-than-life figures, hoping she would succeed like her hero.

Pushing away the desire to stop and read everything, she pressed
on. Wandering through a tangle of mannequins, scaffolding, and plastic
sheets, she passed the Winter Wraith Trio, the Friendly Phantom, and
even the little Ghost Goblin in his swamp.

Ducking under the Pugilist from *The Poltergeist Heist*, Olivia
climbed into the Acrobatic Apparition's exhibit and opened the frigid
window with a squeak.

Slipping on her night-vision goggles merely showed that it was too
far to see anything clearly in the parking garage's dark recesses.
Looking through her telescope—with and without the goggles—didn't
yield any better results.

But the club....Even with the clouds, the interior was bright enough
for her to see inside with the telescope. She gasped. There were no
pillars! By process of elimination, the bodies from her visions *had* to be
in the parking garage.

Olivia jumped at the sound of heavy footfalls on the stairs.

"Uh, where are they?" an anxious guard asked, swinging his
flashlight back and forth.

Crud!

"The lovebirds are in the hedge maze," two radios crackled in
unison. "And the other one's by the window."

Olivia's face burned, and betrayal cut through her. They'd ditched
her to—

"I'll let you grab the third wheel," a confident-sounding man
snickered, patting his heavyset colleague on the shoulder.

"Oh, uh, okay," the other replied, passing under the Hunchbacked
Reaper's scythe and sack of souls. "Um, which exhibit is the
window by?"

Crud! Thinking quickly, Olivia pulled out a radio from her pack,
hit the scan button to match their frequency, and tapped transmit while
quietly blowing into the mic.

The heavyset guard paused, his radio emitting staticky sounds.
"Come again?" he asked.

Olivia turned off her volume and kept blowing, continuing to jam
his comms as she crept through in the shadows, past his sweeping cone

of light.

From her hiding spot behind the Silk Merchant Spectre, her way to the rooftop exit was clear, but she felt a pang of guilt as the more athletic guard passed the troupe of Spirit Brides to enter the maze.

She hesitated for only a moment before calling out, "Run!"

The heavyset guard's light fell on her, and Olivia broke into a sprint.

The athletic one's curses echoed out from the maze, along with rapid footfalls.

Olivia dug frantically in her pack and dashed between a Ghost Queen mannequin and the lanky plumber it was lunging for. She whirled, momentarily clicking on her spotlight-grade flashlight.

Blinded, her pursuer crashed into the display, barely maintaining his balance. When the mannequin snapped, he cried, "Oh, no!"

"Sabrina, look out!" Harriet screamed.

Olivia spun, deftly avoiding a bit of scaffolding. "Thanks!"

"*Hey*!" Harriet shrieked when Otto pushed her down to slow their pursuer.

"*Jerk*!" Olivia spat, clicking her light on before racing up the stairs.

Otto struck a wall headfirst, but Olivia hit the door running. "That's what you get!" she hissed, stumbling into the cold. Gravel crunched beneath their boots, but her pursuer was thankfully out of breath *and* shape.

"Wait!" he called, panting.

But Olivia ran down the fire escape and kicked the rusty ladder free.

"Stop!" the guard wheezed above, while the ladder slid free with a metallic screech.

She hurried down the ladder and out of the alley, looking both ways before dashing across the street. Those bikes by the parking garage were at the wrong angle for her to hide behind. Wait—the parking garage! Olivia raced underneath the *Condemned* sign and hid around the corner, gasping for air.

Someone burst out of the museum. "Which way'd she go?" a long-haired woman demanded.

Olivia peered past an antique army bike as her pursuer hurried out of the alley. "Syd, I—I...dunno..." he groaned, hanging his head and hunching forward with his hands on his knees.

Thunder boomed, and it began to pour. The woman shook her head and hurried inside with her colleague. Heart racing, Olivia leaned against the concrete wall and slid down to catch her breath.

She'd *escaped*! And, more importantly, she had ID'd the place from her visions. This very building....She stared at the cracked ceiling. Was her mom still up there? All alone? So *close*?

If her dad didn't get back in time...if something happened to her mom...Olivia wouldn't be able to live with herself, especially if she'd had a chance to save her. She eyed the dark interior, trembling as she pulled out a lead knife. There was no turning back.

Distant Memories: Cellie

Olivia stepped into her new room and shielded her eyes. The walls, bedsheets, and tiles were all so white they were nearly as bright as the lights above and the thin curtains in the back. So this was to be her prison.

"And there's your roommate," Dr. Park said in his mechanical voice.

A girl a little older than her sat at the foot of a bed among papers filled with equations made up of strange symbols. Her waist-length hair spilled onto the blankets and disappeared amid the sheets.

Craning her neck to see past the girl's glasses, Olivia frowned. Pale blue eyes. Despite Olivia's freckles and light green irises, she'd often been asked if she had albinism. But compared to her cellmate, no one would ever make such a mistake.

But was this some sort of sick joke? The odds of two white-haired girls being checked into this facility, let alone being roommates, were nearly impossible. Was this a trick to get her to doubt her sanity? Fine, she'd play along. "Hi, I'm Olivia."

The girl ignored her. She just kept staring at the wall and tapping her pencil to her paper. But her lips were moving. Olivia yawned to pop her ears and enhance her hearing. But her roommate was simply mumbling to herself, strange sounds that were not words.

"Felly mae naw teyrnas gyda'r Nefoedd uwchben, y Ddaear yn y canol, ac Uffern isod..."

Olivia sucked in air through her nose to pop her ears closed and turned to Park. "What's up with the tapping?"

In contrast to her roommate, Dr. Park spoke without moving his mouth yet still made sense. "She thought you might ask about that, so she told me to tell you that she communicates with the voices she hears using Morse code. Right now...she's telling them they'll talk about it later."

Olivia folded her arms. Unlike her roommate, she didn't belong here. She narrowed her eyes at the girl's medical bracelet. *Nonverbal Epileptic* and *Schizophrenia** were marked down. She'd seen plenty of bands along her tour, but she and her roommate were the only ones with asterisks. Whatever those were supposed to mean. They probably meant as much as the hospital's hypothesis on her condition: absolutely nothing. The Ghost Giant was real, and she didn't belong here.

"What's with her tracking anklet?" Olivia asked. If this place was so bad even the despondent tried to flee, then Olivia hoped they'd decide she was sane as soon as possible.

Dr. Park shook his head. "Miss Sigfried has epilepsy. That monitor warns us when she has an episode," he added, kneeling at the girl's bedside.

"Victoria, this is Olivia. She's going to stay with you for a while. Take good care of her."

Olivia rolled her eyes. If anyone was going to be taking care of anyone else, it'd be the other way around. And this was a *complete* waste of—Victoria was smiling at her. Olivia couldn't help but smile back.

Her roommate made an odd gesture with her hand.

Dr. Park laughed, which his mechanical voice box amplified into an unsettling sound. "She says she likes your hair."

Olivia chuckled. So, despite the babbling, Victoria could communicate—with sign language. "Thanks."

Victoria smiled and nodded.

Huh, so she did understand English. She just didn't *speak* it.

Dr. Park turned to Olivia. "If you'd like to talk to her in ASL, you can say *thank you* like this," he said, putting his hand to his chin and moving it down and away towards her. "Just use your dominant hand and move your arm in her direction."

Olivia copied the gesture. She wished she could capture Victoria's return smile on paper. Whatever this place was, she wouldn't let them hurt her new friend.

ᚨᚾᛞ ᛟᚠ ᚹᚨᚱ

CHAPTER 5: SPIRITS

Olivia peered into the darkness of the condemned building, safe from the downpour but not from the Ghost Giant. Why'd that monster drag her mom here? And, of all places, why was it haunting a *parking garage*?

Her hand trembled on the lead knife as she braced it under her flashlight, just like she'd seen in the movies. But her thumb twitched over the switch. The light would give her away. So she slipped on her night-vision goggles.

Unlike the flashlight, they had no switch—because they were analog—and she soon became wrapped up in the green landscape. Jumping at the sight of distant people, Olivia shook her head when she realized they were part of an old mural.

Elegant as their happy faces might have once been, cracks and demolition markings now marred their features, like those of the classic cars bustling around elm-lined streets. A bygone era washed away nearly as cleanly as the runoff scrubbing the painted shoes and tires away, leaving nothing but grime.

Olivia followed the stream to the lower level, to make sure that no one sneaked up on her, but found only trash floating in a sea of green. Given the lack of ice covering the painted machinery, it seemed unlikely that the Ghost Giant was lurking in the depths.

Thankful that she wouldn't need to keep looking over her shoulder, Olivia headed back up. Balancing atop a parking block, she peered outside. As expected, the club's crimson sign was reflected in the puddles, but it was at the wrong angle.

Following rusty signs pointing to the upper floors, Olivia kept a white-knuckled grip on her gear, ready to blind or stab at a moment's notice. Mesh safety fences slowed her progress, forcing her to cut through them with her knife like an explorer in the jungle. It was much less effective than a machete but did surprisingly well for what it was.

Underneath the sounds of rain and of distant cars splashing through puddles, there was something else, masked by running and dripping water. A rhythmic tapping that grew louder with every step she took.

Advancing on tiptoe and trying to maintain her nerve, she crept forward until her foot snagged on something. A grating sound echoed throughout the level. She froze, eyes darting from side to side.

Crud! She'd been too busy keeping an eye out for the ghost to watch where she was going! She tensed, ready for something to leap out of the darkness, not daring to move until her heart rate settled.

Glancing at her boots, Olivia carefully stepped out of a torn safety vest lying on the ground, trying not to disrupt the clipboard tangled in it. Interesting. According to the sign-in sheet, no one had been here since last year. But, more ominously, no one had signed out. Had the Ghost Giant scared them off?

Finding the source of the tapping did nothing to disprove that theory. Water dripped from a crack in the ceiling, splattering on the fragments of a shattered hard hat that littered the ground like broken glass. What on earth had enough force to do *that*?

Her night vision goggles picked up something shiny, flowing down the ramp ahead. Olivia pinned it underfoot when it passed by. A candy wrapper with a gargoyle.

She gasped at the sweepstakes deadline. *October 24th, 2009.* Someone had been here *recently*. But, given the caramel flavor, it wasn't something her mom would have eaten. Hopefully, the litterbug had long since moved on, but she wasn't about to count on that.

Olivia sloshed up the ramp as quietly as she could, thankful she'd worn boots and waterproof fatigues. But when the odor hit her, she recoiled viscerally, wishing she'd brought the gas mask. The second level stank like a latrine. Which, while bad, wasn't the odor she remembered from her visions.

She tiptoed farther, her heart rate increasing at each new sign of human habitation. Broken cots lay at the feet of the vintage mural of the Statue of Liberty, now caked in dirt, and busted camping chairs blocked out the waters beneath the Golden Gate Bridge. But it was the partly torn-down wall of the broken St. Louis Arch that chilled her to the bone. For in its wreckage, needles practically glowed in her goggles. She gasped at the people passed out in soggy sleeping bags. *Addicts.*

Thunder shook the building, but they didn't stir. Hopefully, they'd be out for a while. Not wishing to linger or to leave and potentially abandon her mom in this squalor, Olivia crept forward. Pulling her scarf up dampened the stench of unwashed bodies and human waste, but she still wanted to gag. Focusing on what little perfume still clung to her mom's coat, she tiptoed toward the edge. But the neon reflection still wasn't at the right angle.

She stared at the water running down in sheets from the fissures above and crept through the maze, trying to remain dry—ever thankful that the waterfalls masked her steps.

In place of the next ramp, Olivia was instead greeted by a massive pile of rubble. She thought she could climb the rocks, but the stones were slick with all the water spilling from the gaping hole overhead. And each time thunder boomed, more and more of them tumbled down.

Olivia took a deep breath in preparation for her task but paused at an even fouler smell. Further sniffs only revealed what she'd dreaded most. It was getting stronger, its source closer. She spun.

"You mustn't go up there, pretty flower!" a twitchy woman in a dirty shawl said.

Crud! Olivia backed away, trading her knife for hair spray. "Why not?" she asked, trying not to look afraid.

"Because the *Giant* lives up there," the crone said with an odd tone of reverence.

"*Giant*?" Olivia's eyes widened. Did she mean the *Ghost Giant*? Did this woman actually know something?

"But of course! He lives up in the sky!"

Olivia frowned. Maybe not....Thunder rumbled before she could speak, and something heavy crashed down upstairs. With a yelp, she jumped to avoid dust and moisture falling from an ever-growing crack above.

"SHHHH!" the woman said, holding a gnarled finger to her lips. "He'll hear you. Doesn't like guests!"

"Then why are you yelling?" Olivia snapped, hoping the others wouldn't wake. "By the way, have you seen a blind woman?"

"Hush! Enough of your nonsense! Now gooooooo!" the woman cried with a shooing motion.

Someone sighed behind Olivia, and she whirled, primed to mace them with hair spray. A middle-aged guy in a tattered coat that stank of old booze held up his hands, limping back.

"Ignore her, Miss," he said, ambling around scattered rubble. *Not right in the head*, he mouthed.

His words cut through Olivia like ice. Glimpses of Hawthorn Center flashed in her mind. No one had believed her there, just as no one believed this woman here. It was a twisted version of the future she feared. Babbling in the streets instead of being locked in a cell. Destructive freedom versus oppressive care.

"Know what I saw!" the woman said.

Olivia tried to catch her breath, but her heart kept racing. She was hyperventilating!

"We've been over this..." the man said, fingering the creases on his brow. "There's no giant."

"There is! Saw him, I did! Got red eyes and claws, he does—"

Olivia gasped. It *was* the Ghost Giant. This *was* the place.

"—and his footsteps..." the woman said, lowering her voice and leaning in to whisper to Olivia none too quietly. "Even shakes the earth when he walks!"

The man sighed. "The train, Milda....The *train* shakes the building."

"But the screams!" Milda said, turning to Olivia. "No explaining those, 'cept he eats his victims!" she said, *whispering* as usual.

Shaken, Olivia tried to get ahold of herself. "*Okay*," she said in a sarcastic tone, hoping it came out slow and even. It must have worked, because both nodded like they believed her—Milda, her words, and the man, her tone.

"See!" Milda said. "She believes me! Got good sense in her!"

"*Right*," the man said, sending Milda on her way.

Olivia's heart went out to the old woman, but she blushed under the man's gaze, knowing how strange she must look in her green beret, night-vision goggles, and oversized coat, clutching a flashlight and a can of hair spray. No doubt he thought she was a crazed runaway.

"Best of luck with *whatever* it is you're doing," he said, pulling out a flask and departing.

Olivia glared at him, simultaneously hating him for leaving a teen who *clearly needed help* and being ever so grateful that he wasn't getting in her way. But on the off chance he changed his mind, she started climbing as soon as he settled down in a corner.

Lightning flashed halfway up, and her night-vision goggles went bright white, blinding her. Covering the lenses in a panic, she hoped the delicate components weren't fried. Blessedly, when her vision returned, it was obvious the equipment was okay. Still, she stashed the fragile goggles in her pack to preserve both the gear and her sight.

Until her eyes adjusted to the dark, she had to clutch at slippery handholds whenever lightning flashed. *Red* lightning. As ominous as the color was, it only meant there was rain in the clouds. Still, it made the moss and water look like clumps of blood. But the liquid running over rocks was light like water, not thick like paint. Until it wasn't.

Olivia froze, feeling a stream of warm liquid running over her hand. She yanked it back, and it was stained red. *Blood. Actual blood.* She recoiled with a shriek, and her voice echoed through the chamber. Rocks shifted beneath her, and she clambered up in a panic, kicking off a rock slide. Lunging for the ceiling, she clung to the upper level while the pile collapsed like a pyramid of apples at a grocery store.

Running water soaked her to the bone and weighed down her coat, yet she managed to haul herself over the slippery edge, against the current.

A stone's throw away lay a cluster of twitching rats crushed beneath a concrete slab. Olivia eyed a missing chunk in the ceiling. That must've been what had fallen earlier. But was this place really that unstable? Or did the Ghost Giant do this?

She readied her knife while lightning flashed through shattered skylights, reflecting onto the ceiling from shifting puddles below. Glass twinkled in the shallow depths alongside countless eyes above. The endless squeaking made it obvious what they belonged to. *Rats*. But why were there so many of them?

Thunder rumbled, raining down concrete pebbles from the ceiling. Vermin scurried away from splashing debris, and Olivia covered her head while sloshing through puddles that dotted the unstable structure. If the Ghost Giant wasn't here, she'd rather not stick around until it—or the train—arrived.

She hurried past murals of flying cars on their way to the North Pole, whizzing by fjords and glaciers. Past a ramp crumbling away to nowhere. Over a submerged chunk of rubble depicting a family in retro space suits flying over Mars.

Four paces later, she stopped, not needing to peer over the edge, for the crimson glow from below matched yesterday's vision exactly.

She shuddered. This was the place. But where were the bodies? As if in answer, the wind passed through with an eerie whistle, bringing a familiar stench to her nostrils.

Her stomach churned while she looked around. Bones slick with rain jutted out of broken pillars, the floor, and even the ceiling—all hidden from the street. Each form contorted in a twisted pose with a look of anguish as if yearning to break free.

Sweat formed on Olivia's brow, and she gripped her knife tighter. There was no way they could get stuck in there like that. No way the concrete could dry like that, riddling ribs and limbs with rock, rusty rods, and PVC pipes. No way rubble and wire could be so entwined within the bones.

"Get away!" she cried, kicking a rat off her boot. It hissed at her but fled with its kin when she took a step toward it. Wait...the rats....Olivia neared a skeleton and gasped, eyeing chewed-up bones. Was her mom—no, she couldn't be!

Splashing around, she dodged glass and rodents, running from skeleton to skeleton. But they were all too old, covered in algae, mold, and moss. She searched the room twice and wept. Twelve bodies, none fresh enough to be her mom's. She might still be alive.

Olivia bowed her head, hating herself for feeling relieved that others had died. There, surrounded by the dead, she said a prayer for the departed. These people had had lives too. Friends and family. But now they were gone, trapped in this foul place.

A train whistle sounded. CRUD! Olivia dashed for a skylight, bones cracking underfoot, and dove through a sheet of water when the building shook even harder than before. She crashed into a pillar skeleton, but the train drowned out her shriek.

Losing her footing, she fell among rain and rubble. Rock pelted the standing water all around her, widening the skylight. But, in the chaos, she noticed the skeleton's tapping finger *and* what was carved below. *Northville H266*. But that was—

"No! Please!" a man screamed over the noise. Water splashed, and he howled.

Olivia winced and stuck her head through the waterfall, catching the silhouetted man and his intermittent shadows cast upon the wall.

"MERCY!" he cried, arching his back. Bloody glass twinkled in the lightning before the darkness enveloped him.

"Oh, God!" Olivia whispered, clamping a hand to her mouth. Her eyes widened, and her breath hung before her. "No, no, no, not again!" she whimpered.

Red light bathed the chamber ahead. *Consistent* light. Water froze, and the sound of cracking ice bore into Olivia's soul with every unseen step. At last, a massive, red-eyed figure emerged. The Ghost Giant.

It stomped on the man's chest, grinding its foot and the man farther and farther into the glass beneath the rapidly freezing water. Olivia wept at the man's cries and gripped her knife so hard it hurt. She had to do something! But her legs merely shook.

"Mer—cy," the man croaked.

While the beast was distracted, Olivia forced herself through the waterfall and around the pillars. She had to save him!

The Ghost Giant tore its victim from the water. Its red eyes flared, and its form writhed, blurring together with the man's like paints mixing. Distorted screams echoed through the noisy chamber. Then it slammed him into a pillar and let go.

Olivia froze. No!

In the illumination of the red light, the man's hands twitched, and his arched back gave him a horrific silhouette with his hips and shoulders vanishing into concrete. Rats surged forward as the man coughed up bloody bits of rock.

Olivia looked away, sobbing through his short-lived screams. Tears and rainwater flowed down her cheeks. She'd been too slow! She shook with rage, and tears froze on her face when she lunged. "MONSTER!"

The Ghost Giant spun, and the red beams of its eyes hit Olivia like headlights. Still, she plunged her knife into its shoulder. The red light went out, and the creature howled, throwing her across the room.

She splashed down, skidding across submerged debris. Olivia winced and rubbed her eyes, catching the silhouette of the giant tearing the blade out. Metal clattered on ice and frosted over.

The ghost's eyes ignited, and Olivia forced herself to her feet. She could have sworn the beast had felt more solid after she stabbed it. Oh, well. She drew another knife, knowing it would work. She stared the creature down while its breath and hers hung in the air. Incorporeal blood dripped from its arm, pelting the ground like hail.

"Where's my *mom*?" Olivia hissed, tightening her grip. Her hair stood on end, and red light came from *behind* her. A light that *lingered*. Her mouth went dry, and she looked over her shoulder.

The *second* Ghost Giant growled.

Olivia took a deep breath and braced herself. "God, help me."

The beasts charged, freezing and crushing water in their wake. Olivia slashed about, trying to see past her lingering breath. Mist swirled, and the ghosts lunged in and out of range. Olivia attacked, only for them to vanish before her blows could land. They were *toying* with her. "Face me, you cowards!"

They punched through columns, exploding rock and bone. Dust and debris struck her from every angle. She clicked on her flickering flashlight and swept it around until it went out. There! She slashed at a hand emerging from the dust. The ghosts roared in unison, and the entire structure shook.

A pillar crumbled, and Olivia leaped away, gasping at the water spewing from the new hole torn in the ceiling. Time to go! She clicked the light off and ran.

The twin ghosts lunged at her from behind and through pillars. Olivia dodged incorporeal claws, feeling the temperature plummeting behind her. She jumped, narrowly avoiding a ghostly hand. But the second spirit materialized in front of her, grabbing her by the throat midflight.

Olivia's vision doubled, and her head felt like it was going to split. Frozen metal burned her fingers, and frost pricked her skin, forcing her to drop her gear.

She went for another blade only to gasp. Despite her double vision, there was only one pack. Two of her four hands merged whenever she touched her backup blades, splitting back apart each time one of the weapons slipped through her numb fingers. Her vision blurred, and her sight faded entirely by the time her hand closed around the final knife.

"DIE!" she screamed, stabbing the monster in the arm. The ghost roared and went solid. Olivia fell, leaving the blade embedded in the beast, and hit the ice. She fumbled blindly for the fallen knives, but her fingers only closed around her flashlight. Sight returned as she clicked it on to blind the ghost. But the light only flickered. "Crud."

Red light blinded her in turn, and the ghost struck like a freight train, slamming her through a column and deeper into the flooded floor's depths. Olivia's ears rang, and the rats screeched.

She tried to rise, but frigid fingers forced her under the rapidly freezing water. She tried to keep her head above the bobbing ice before it trapped her under. But her tears only mixed with the grime.

"I don't want to die..." she sputtered. Ice closed in around her chin. Olivia shook, sending shivers up and down her spine. More water froze, and the ground writhed. The Ghost Giant's eyes widened, and Olivia fell through the floor. The *solid* floor.

Dr. Park Sung-Min fired a silenced warning shot from a distant rooftop before Subject A could follow the girl through the floor. His quarry broke for cover when the bullet struck near its feet. It had been a calculated risk, but now that the girl had manifested *abilities*, she'd be better able to defend herself. There was no way he'd let her come to further harm.

"Do it," Sung-Min hissed in the voice he'd used all these years, scanning for movement. If Subject A came up here, this op would end, and he could go home. Unfortunately, that didn't seem to be happening.

Extracting his prey from the parking garage would have been a nightmare, so Sung-Min raced down the fire escape to disappear, confident that the Subject wouldn't pursue the girl until it had ascertained that the coast was clear.

He stashed his gun behind the dumpster and adjusted his lab coat before strolling into the bustling pho shop.

"Ugh, *now* you come back!" Miss Tran groaned in a nasal tone, removing the washrag from his table and hurrying to clear another booth. "Your noodles went cold."

He nodded to her and slipped back into his seat, watching the parking garage out the window for any sign of the girl or of hostiles as he procured metal chopsticks from his coat.

"Don't mind my sister," a younger waitress said in a warm tone, procuring an iced coffee from a fridge. "Did your call go well?" she asked, setting his drink down and putting his bowl on a portable stove.

"Very," he said, seeing the girl emerge in a daze. She'd figured out Subject A's weakness to lead all on her own. And now that she had abilities....Well, Subject G was *brimming* with potential.

ᚠᚭᛉ ᛁᚼᛏᚱᛁᚷᚢᛗᛍ

CHAPTER 6: POWER TRIP

Olivia screamed, passing through the dark. Vibrations filled her ears and dug into her bones until she fell into the dim light and struck the concrete. But she didn't hit the ground. She just *stopped*. There was no pain or blood, but her stomach churned at the lack of deceleration. Vertigo struck her when she stood.

Frigid water dripped onto her forehead from the frost above. Olivia braced herself, barely able to see, but the ice didn't spread. Neither Ghost Giant emerged. Her vision cleared, and she squinted. The frost looked like an outline of *her*. But how? Why didn't she get stuck in there like all the others?

Milda's jaw dropped. "She fell from the sky!"

Her voice rang through Olivia's head like an alarm, nearly sending her to the ground.

"Blessed child of heaven!" Milda cried, surging forward with outstretched arms.

Olivia fled the horrid noise, pushing through the pain as her echoing footsteps drove daggers into her skull. Milda's voice, rattling in her head, was excruciating. She had to keep running. Get away from the sounds. Away from this place. Before the ghosts gave chase.

Clouds cleared, and Olivia's frosty coat sparkled in the resurgent light.

"It's her!" Milda screamed. "She's an angel!"

From halfway across the chamber, the woman's voice was more bearable, but Olivia kept running for her life, past a stirring junkie.

"Shut your mouth, fool woman!" he called.

His deep voice reverberated through Olivia's bones, nearly making her stumble.

"Know what I saw!" Milda shouted, her echoing words striking Olivia when she reached the ramp.

"Whoa, slow down there, Angel," a drowsy addict called.

But Olivia only ran faster. His voice cut into her like a palette knife, driving her out. Her footsteps pounded in her very being like a hammer alongside the gentle murmur of flowing water headed to the lower level. But she wouldn't let the water's soothing sound lull her into a false sense of security. She kept looking over her shoulder while she ran, waiting for the ceiling to frost over. For a Ghost Giant to grab her.

Racing into the street, Olivia stumbled under the overwhelming bass of a distant car. Snow fell from white clouds, chasing off their dark counterparts, and the nightclub flared to life. A loud beat pulsed through its walls, echoing off the bikes outside and making her head want to split.

Olivia screamed, clamping her hands over her ears to no avail. She fled downtown in a daze, away from the music, the buzzing power lines, and the hum of the museum's indoor lighting.

Block after block, she ran in heavy, waterlogged clothes that were rapidly freezing. At last, she reached an empty area full of rundown vacant buildings, abandoned lots sprouting wilting weeds, and a bus stop. Shelter!

She ran against the howling wind into the enclosure and scraped the icy buildup off her mom's filthy coat. But the sound grated on her ears. What was *happening*?

Blue lightning flashed. Hail! But it was the thunder that shook her to her core. Olivia fell onto the bench, holding her throbbing head. She could feel *everything*: the cool air rolling in, the tremors reverberating beneath her feet from distant cars, and the hail pelting the bus stop's roof. She even felt the bench moving, vibrating ever so slightly.

What was *happening*? What had happened to her? Had she snapped? Why did she survive? The pulse of everything bore down on her, and she shook uncontrollably in the cold. Frost raced up the bus stop's walls.

"No, no, no!" It was here! Olivia reached out to wipe the frost away, teeth chattering, but it kept growing back. She turned away, hands pressed to her head. No, she'd just *imagined* the frost. The Ghost Giants hadn't come for her. She wasn't dead meat.

Olivia fell to her knees, waiting for the end. She tried to steady herself on the wall—to face her final moments with dignity—but it didn't catch her. She jerked back and blinked. She tried again, but her hand passed through the wall with a tingling sensation.

No, everything was okay! Her hands were just going numb. She was hallucinating. She'd hit her head. *Again.* That was bad. She'd ruined her vision. Lost her depth perception. But she wouldn't go blind like her mom! She just had to touch the wall. Prove everything was okay. She had to be able to see. Had to get her mom back. She had to be alive. But her fingers slipped through the glass with the same sensation as before.

"No, no, *no!*" she screamed, recoiling as the shrill sound tore through her and echoed all around her. Still, she tried to tap the glass. Her fingers were *transparent.* She trembled, pulling them closer, and saw through them like glass. Olivia cried, trying and failing to slam her fist against the wall.

"I'm not insane. I'm not insane," she chanted, hugging herself. See, her hands still worked! They weren't going through *her.* Everything was fine! No! She could see the sidewalk through her legs! Her heart rate skyrocketed. She was hyperventilating. Another panic attack. She had to stop!

Closing her eyes, Olivia took a deep breath, holding it as long as she could before gasping for air. She continued until her breathing slowed. When she finally had the courage to peek, her hands were opaque.

"Perfectly sane," she said, clamping her eyes shut, not daring to look. Her fingertips touched the frigid glass and didn't slip through. But when she opened her eyes triumphantly, she could feel the vibrations.

Dancing molecules pulsed as if the wall were alive. Focusing on that feeling, she likened it to the throb of music. But it was unlike any music she'd ever heard. So quiet. So distant. Distant until she pressed her hand closer, becoming one with the beat. Olivia stepped through the wall.

Wind and hail assaulted her. Grains of ice pelted her numb face and frozen clothes with sharp clinks, but she could feel each and every chunk vibrating when it struck her. They were all unique, each melting or shattering at its own rate, but so too were they alike—like voices harmonizing in a choir.

She focused on their frequency, joining in the harmony until she vibrated in sync with them. They passed right through her, and she walked down the empty street with weightless steps.

Hail floated all around her, and even the tiny crystals from her frosty footsteps rose in her wake. All sparkled in the lightning like a kaleidoscope of prisms. A wave of awe washed over her. Her transparent reflection stared back from a store window before the glass frosted over.

Placing a palm on the window, she felt its vibrations. Its fragility. One wrong note and the whole thing would *shatter*. Olivia turned her attention to the hail. She shattered bits on impact as she hummed their breaking tune. Their *Shatter Song*. Such power...

She stared at her ghostly hands. Was this the power the Ghost Giants felt when they destroyed concrete with their fists? And if so, why did she have their abilities? Was it proximity or the blood that flowed from their wounds? And if these were indeed their powers, had she taken them for good? Was one gone? Would the other come after her for vengeance?

Her eyes widened. *This* was why she hadn't gotten stuck in the floor. Thank the Lord she'd been able to bring her clothes with her! Olivia went red, thinking about what could have happened to her in that place and in the cold. She felt the comforting rhythm of each and every scrap of fabric on her. Each layer and item in her pack called out to her, like a separate instrument in a collective song.

Mind still numb from everything that had happened, she grabbed a stone from the ground. It quavered in her ghostly hand until she took it into her song, making it a part of her, like her clothes. Hail passed through it, just as it passed through her.

With another shake, the ice that lined its surface shattered until it was just another stone, completely itself amid the storm. With a grin, Olivia did the same to her attire, expelling ice and grime from the fabric and her skin. A pleasant warmth washed over her whenever her body shook. Her new powers seemed so entwined with that shaking sensation.

Olivia smiled, returning her attention to the rock. She tossed it up and watched it become solid before catching it and bringing it back into her song, making it incorporeal like her. Feeling the lightness in her limbs, she chucked the stone high and *jumped*, rising through the air, story after story, to snag the stone at the height of its arc.

But Olivia kept going. Buildings shrank beneath her feet as well as a sidewalk mural of snow geese taking flight. A trail of hail followed her like a comet's tail.

She grinned, looking skyward. The clouds were getting close, and the air was getting thin! Lightning flashed, momentarily turning her solid. She gasped. Her powers had been disrupted like a radio interrupted by static in a storm. She'd been right! Enough electricity could—

Thunder struck like a tidal wave. Its song drowned out her own, overpowered her, and sent her plummeting to the earth, entirely solid. At first, she screamed, shaking in terror, and became a ghost. But then she went solid, squealing with glee, hands outstretched. Was this what roller coasters felt like? The wind running through her hair was exhilarating! Then her beret blew away.

"Crud!" Olivia twisted in the air and shook to become intangible. Gravity no longer held sway over her like it did over her hat, which quickly caught up with her and passed right through! She went solid, dove, and fell faster, reaching for it. The bus stop and sidewalk art grew larger, closer. The ground's song cried out in alarm, growing louder.

Still, Olivia raced toward the earth, not allowing herself to be caught up in its tune as she shifted back into the physical world, landing with none of the speed she'd accumulated. She laughed. She had broken the law of inertia!

For her next trick, she embraced the sound of the earth and slipped through the sidewalk before realizing that she couldn't breathe! Olivia touched the dirt with her ghostly fingertips, like she had the solid rock, and swam back to the surface.

Gasping and giggling with glee, she hopped up and down the street with weightless bounds, laughing at the specks of frost floating alongside her, following her. She modulated her song to become partially solid at the top so gravity could pull her back down, then bounded up again like an astronaut on the moon. Around the block she went, lap after lap, until she wavered like a top.

Olivia ran for the bus stop and through her panicked reflection. The songs abandoned her, leaving her in the cold's embrace. She collapsed onto the bench with a racing heart and a smile, trying to take it all in. She could soar! Slip through things and break them with a thought! At least, she could a moment ago.

Staring at a frosty wall, Olivia felt its song as a nearly imperceptible sensation. But it was there. Wiping frozen sweat from her brow, she rested a hand on the chilled glass, unable to slip through. But with every passing moment, the song's volume grew with her returning stamina.

Were these powers like a muscle that could be strengthened? Or a pigment capped in how much light it could absorb? Not knowing, she waited for her breathing to return to normal, watching the hail. Finally, Olivia embraced its song and kicked off to fly through the winter wonderland of twinkling, crystalline hailstones. She needed to call her dad. She had *so* much to tell him.

Street after street passed by below. Her mind raced. She'd survived the Ghost Giants and gained their powers but hadn't found her mom. But she did have a lead. *Northville*.

Olivia shivered, shutting down that line of thought, and landed with no acceleration in a phone booth. A few coins and button presses later, she stood by, hoping the call would go through.

"No one is available to—"

Slamming the receiver down, she reached for her pack to retrieve the sticky note with his numbers, but her hand hovered over the zipper. She could *feel* the braille dots from within her pack! And so she grinned, prayed, and tried again, dialing accordingly.

"Olivia?" her dad asked, crackling through a mass of static.

She jumped with joy and went halfway to the ceiling before the tether of the metallic phone cord went taut, holding her in place like a balloon.

"Dad," she said, descending.

"Are you all right? Why'd you wait so long to call?"

She closed her eyes and took a deep breath, hoping he wouldn't get mad. "I...just wanted to make sure I had the right place."

He sighed. "Okay. I'm just happy to hear your voice. So where was it? And how'd you confirm it was the right spot?"

Olivia stared at the sticker-covered ceiling, trying to find a more positive way of explaining her decisions to follow a stranger into a shady part of town, sneak into a museum's off-limits section, and explore a condemned building. Naturally, she couldn't come up with anything.

"*Olivia*, don't tell me you went there..."

She pursed her lips. "Okay, I won't."

"*Olivia. Tell* me you didn't go there."

"No can do..."

"And why in heaven's name not?"

"Because...that'd be a lie," she said in a small voice.

"*Olivia Linda*....You *went* there?"

"Yeaaaah," she said, going red. He wasn't happy. "Promise you won't be mad."

"I'm not promising *anything* until you tell me what happened."

She sighed. What had she expected? "I found the place and sorta ended up there..."

"YOU DID WHAT? How do you *sorta* end up there?"

Olivia held the phone away while he shouted. She'd never seen— or rather heard—him this angry. There had to be a way to calm him down. Maybe she could try a tactic she hadn't used in years. She just had to wait until he finally ran out of breath.

"Daddy—"

"Don't you *dare* try that little girl routine with me, young lady!"

She winced. That had backfired spectacularly. Even with all the powers in the world, there was no way to abate his anger.

"Explain yourself. *Now*."

"I'm sorry! I didn't mean to go there! But once I was there, I had to look for Mom!"

"What if you—"

"What if you got back too late!"

The line was quiet for a long while.

"Dad?"

He sighed. "*Please*, don't do anything like that again. And what do you mean, you didn't *mean* to go there? How did you just *end up* there?"

Olivia frowned, trying out of habit to twirl the metallic cord around her fingers, but failing, before shaking her head. "I went to a museum to scout out the building. It was a con—"

She shuddered, realizing her mistake. It would be better if he didn't know the structure was condemned.

"You're breaking up. What'd you say?"

Right....Shaking triggered her powers, which, by extension, disrupted electronics the way the Ghost Giants did.

"I said it was a parking garage. I—" Was chased by a security guard? Nope! "—ended up in there to shelter from the storm. But I got worried you wouldn't get back in time. So I looked around..."

The phone crackled. "Okay. I understand. I'm not happy, but I *understand*. But why on *earth* did you look around? What if the ghost had gotten you?"

Olivia tilted her head to the side, pinning the phone between her cheek and shoulder, wondering how best to explain. "I discovered that it couldn't go through lead."

"And?"

"I, uh, had some lead-coated knives for self-defense."

"*Olivia.*"

"Yeah, Dad."

"*Where* did these lead knives come from?"

"That's a good—"

"*Olivia Linda*, just answer the question."

Her shoulders slumped. She'd heard her middle name more today than she had in the past few years. "I melted lead paint from the bathroom and coated sharpened butter knives with it."

"*Olivia...*"

"Don't worry. I used the respirator. And I feel fine! No symptoms of lead poisoning!"

He sighed. "Olivia, if you *ever* get the idea to *melt lead* or venture out unsupervised, *call* me. I can't lose you both..."

"I understand," she said. "But what choice did I have? If that *thing* came back, I would've been defenseless without them!"

"Point taken....Anyway, I'm guessing they worked?"

Olivia grinned, until she remembered that guy choking on concrete. She shouldn't mention that. Not over the phone, at least.

"Yeah. But, Dad, those bodies from the visions—"

"Weren't Halloween decorations."

Her stomach rebelled with an unsettling sound. "Yeah. The ghosts could put people in concrete."

"Ghosts...ghosts, *plural*?"

Olivia pursed her lips. "Yeah. There were two of them."

"How'd you get *away*?"

She turned, trying to pace around the tiny enclosure without getting tangled in the cord.

"I fell through the floor." Naturally, that didn't explain anything.

"What do you mean? Did it collapse, or was there a—"

"I think I have their powers," she said, watching her hand fuzz transparent. Static filled the line until she stopped.

He gasped. "You're serious?"

"Yeah," she said. She held her breath.

"Okay, well, lead with *that* next time....What—what can you do?"

Olivia shook with excitement, ready to share, but had to get ahold of herself before the phone could pick up anything. This shaking thing *sucked*.

"I can feel vibrations! They sound like songs! If I match their frequency, I can pass through them or bring them with me. And shatter them. Dad, I can fly—uh, float!"

"Whoa, whoa—slow down. You can feel vibrations and shift, or—phase, through solid matter?"

Phase, that was a good way to describe it! "Yep."

"Huh, just like Guillermo," he mumbled.

"What?" She frowned, looking up at the ceiling. Wasn't that some old sci-fi character?

"Nothing," he said. "You must be doing some form of quantum tunneling or higher-dimensional slippage to go through things....Overwhelming resonant frequencies to break stuff..."

Olivia frowned. He seemed lost in thought. "Dad?"

"Sorry. You said you could *fly*?"

"Yes—or at least, I can become weightless and float along using my previous momentum."

"Interesting....Can the ghosts fly?"

She paled. "I hope not! I've never seen them fly. But if they could, why haven't they?"

"Hmm, good deduction. But we're deep in uncharted territory, so I don't think it's safe to rule out that possibility quite yet."

She sighed. "Agreed. But we still need to get Mom back."

"So...she wasn't...one of the bodies?"

"No," Olivia said, staring at her boots. "I searched the whole floor. *Twice*."

"Okay. Then she's prob—she's still out there. But we need to go to the cops about the others. Especially since we don't have any more leads to—"

"Dad, they'd be defenseless! And they wouldn't believe—"

"You said the ghosts can't go through lead."

"Yeah, so?"

"Bullets are made of lead."

"They are?" Olivia blushed. She thought they'd make them out of something less toxic nowadays.

He chuckled. "Yes. They're made of lead. The police will do just fine."

Olivia sighed. The power to go through solid stuff was *awesome*. But if she couldn't go through lead in an era of *firearms*...well, that was a pretty big weakness.

"Olivia?"

"Sorry, lost in thought."

"Okay. I'm going to call the police when we hang up."

"Wait! Mom wasn't there, and I'm the only one who knows about that place! What if the ghosts decide to hurt her when the cops bust in?"

He clicked his tongue. "Aside from waiting for me to get home, do you have a better idea?"

Olivia's shoulders slumped, then she tightened her grip on the phone. "Actually, *yes*. We have another lead."

"How so?"

The phone beeped. "One minute remaining."

She groaned, withdrawing a clump of frozen change, and shattered the ice holding the coins with her powers together before putting them in.

"You still there?"

"Sorry, had to feed the machine. Anyway, I found a message carved into the rock by a skeleton. It was a...it was a Northville room number," she said, forcing the words out.

"A *skeleton*? *Northville*? The old psychiatric hospital?"

"Yes, the one across the woods from..." Olivia couldn't bring herself to say it aloud. She didn't want to go back.

"From Hawthorn Center?"

"Yes," she whispered, feeling guilty for leaving Victoria there without saying goodbye.

"Olivia, why would you think—"

"Dad, why do people leave messages behind before they die?"

"To identify the killer. But they left a *room number*, not a name."

"Right, so there's probably evidence there. Why else would they spend their final moments carving that in *stone*?"

"Unless they wanted a way to identify themselves—no, then they'd have left *their* name. But if they left something behind in that room, it might've been *their* room."

Olivia inhaled sharply, knowing where he was going.

"How much stock can we realistically put in a mentally ill patient?" he asked.

"I know, but what if they were sent there because they tried to *warn* people about the ghosts and no one *believed* them?"

He was quiet for a long moment. "I know what you're saying. But, after the psych eval, we had to send you there for observation."

"I know," she said. "I understand. I'm still not happy, but I *understand*."

He gave her a half-hearted chuckle. "Using my own words against me?"

"*Yes*," she snapped, instantly regretting how forcefully she'd said it, knowing how much it must've hurt to send her away. How much she'd missed him when she was in that place. And how much she missed him each time he left for weeks at a time.

"Dad, I—" Olivia began, eyes watering.

"I suppose I deserve that." He sighed. "Regardless, if the ghost went after a patient, it could've been trying to silence them. So, logically, there might be, or may have been, something in that room."

"Right," she sniffled, trying to move on like he had.

"Okay, this is a lot to take in, but it's worth looking into until I get back..."

"Which'll be when?" she asked, wiping frost from the glass, staring out at the indistinct horizon, only now noticing the clink of hail striking overhead.

"Dunno," he yawned. "Tonight—if I can stay awake. And if the roads stay cleared. I've made good time so far, but I hear there's another storm on the way. Just promise me you won't go to Northville alone."

"Yeah, I'll take Sister Paula." Her eyes widened, and she glanced at her watch. Phew. She had *plenty* of time. Wait, electronics! Olivia went transparent, and the watch stopped. Crud! How much was it off by? She hit the sync button and winced.

"I was supposed to meet her for brunch!" she stammered.

"One minute remaining."

"Come on! I just fed you!" She patted her pockets for coins but, as expected, found none. All these abilities and she was *still* powerless against poverty!

"Olivia, what's going on?"

"Just the phone. We're almost out of time. And I need to meet Sister Paula. I hate time limits." She gasped. "Dad, there's something we didn't get to last night!"

"What?"

"Last night, I hit my head and saw two messa—"

The line went dead, humming and begging for more change.

"Oh, come on! That wasn't a *minute*!" Olivia slammed the phone down and bowed her head. Tears dripped onto the ground. She hated this. Being at the mercy of things she couldn't control. Being so *powerless*.

No. She wasn't powerless. Not anymore. She made a transparent fist, feeling her powers bore through every fiber of her being. Feeling the echoes and songs of everything around her.

Olivia straightened up and stared into the hailstorm. She couldn't do anything about the stupid phone, but she had plenty of time to *end* the Ghost Giants and get her mom back.

To Northville. She shuddered and clenched her fist tighter. She'd go to Northville for her mom. But she wouldn't go alone.

Saul chased a drug dealer down an alley, berating himself for letting the shrink give him the slip near the Berserker's den. According to that interview transcript, Park losing a tail shouldn't be surprising, given the perp's claims about the doc being a former spy. But Saul refused to believe a crazed vigilante who insisted his name was *Vigil*, of all things. With all the uncertainties, he decided to focus on what he did know: how to chase perps *and* get them to talk.

Turning the corner, he tackled the runner. "Where are they?" he growled.

The biker grinned. "Don't know what—"

Saul slammed the dealer into the dumpster headfirst.

"I'm not going to ask again," he growled. "Now, where'd you toss 'em?"

The dazed Berserker sneered. A blow to the head sent him face-first into the pavement. Still, the man gave Saul a bloody smile.

"Guess you'll have to book me for questioning," he wheezed. "*And* go through the garbage."

Saul stared at him. Surely no one was *that* stupid.

"Too bad you won't be able to prove it's mine." He laughed. "And then I'll walk. We'll file a countersuit for police brut—"

Saul sent the idiot and many of his teeth flying with a single kick. He knelt, waiting until the biker stirred. "First of all, you won't *walk*," he said, breaking the dealer's leg.

The Berserker screamed, but Saul drove the air from his lungs with a punch and leaned closer.

"*Second*, your boss and I have a little understanding."

The man spat on the ground, so Saul hauled him up by the beard, dangling him over the pavement.

"See, it's a waste of my time and city resources to bring you in only for him to get you out. And your *boss* doesn't want you guys getting sloppy. So we have a common interest in keeping trash like you off the streets."

Terror descended on the biker faster than a gambler on unattended winnings, and Saul gave him a fake smile.

"That's the spirit. Now, hold still," he said, wailing on him. Given that he wasn't a full-patch member, there was no reason to hold back. One way or another, he'd scare the man straight. Still, part of him wished this guy had put up more of a fight, like the twins had.

The phone rang, and Saul cursed. "Gotta take this," he said, dropping the man onto the concrete.

"MY LEG!"

A sharp blow to the throat quieted him.

"You'll keep your mouth shut if you know what's good for you," he said, sliding open his cell. "Hey, Kateri—uh, Paula." It'd been awhile since he'd slipped up and used her old name.

"Sorry to bother you but there was a young lady I was supposed to have brunch with, and—wait, it looks like she signed back in while I was looking for her. Sorry about that."

"No problem." Saul slid his cell shut and stared down at the wheezing biker. "Right, then. Where were we?"

ᚳᛆᛏᛂᚳᛁᚱᚠᛂᛁᛗᛂ ᛂᚳᚺᛗᛆᛗᛂ

Chapter 7: Trinity

Olivia pushed off icy lampposts and buildings, going faster and faster, until she rocketed into the library. Her shoes squeaked on the frosty marble, but she did her best to look for Sister Paula quietly. She checked the front desk and searched among the bookworms waiting out the storm.

Curiously, her powers let her *feel* things she couldn't see. Every volume on the bookshelves called out to her, their shapes and materials becoming infinitely clearer whenever sound waves bounced off of them. In this way, echolocation told her which aisles were worth checking.

But no matter how many figures she investigated in the maze of shelving, none *felt* like a nun. Olivia froze, feeling a distant habit, but the hands were wrong. No scars. *Martha.* She hurried through the botany section and stopped her search.

Even with her powers, she couldn't feel everything in the multistory chamber. Besides, she and her godmother were probably going in circles, looking for one another. So she headed for the computers to stay in one place and took off her mom's coat.

To make the most of her time, Olivia searched for a map of Northville Psychiatric to find room H266. Stories of abuse and of Northville's infamous overcrowding had worried her that Hawthorn would be the same, but she hadn't seen either of those things during her stay. And, thankfully, Northville had been closed for years, so there'd never been a chance she'd end up there.

An old map of the sprawling campus left little wonder why there'd been multiple *successful* escape attempts per day. But was it really escaping when patients were just *walking out*? The Center seemed to have learned from its neighbor's plight by keeping most of its patients in a single centralized structure.

In contrast, Northville had so many buildings they'd started naming them after letters. Logically, H266 would be on the second floor of Building H. Curiously, the building looked more like an *X*. Olivia searched for a map of the interior but couldn't find anything.

Broadening her search, she learned that they'd stopped using the building in the '80s and that it had caught fire shortly after. *Lovely*—another abandoned place rendered unstable by years of neglect. At least this time she had her powers to help her navigate.

Still, Olivia recoiled upon finding pictures of hallways covered in satanic graffiti. But that didn't hold a candle to the rare unvandalized sections. Those were far scarier, due to the peeling paint. Given the building's age, it had to be *lead* paint.

And the crumbling walls themselves had to be stuffed with asbestos, which had probably long since gone airborne. They'd need masks to walk out with anything other than a heightened risk of cancer.

"Well, look what the cat dragged in," a woman said.

Olivia's skin crawled as she turned in her chair. *Martha.*

"What's the matter? Didn't *feel* like going to school today? Or are you just too good for that now?"

Olivia held her tongue, trying to keep her nerves—and powers—in check. But this was the woman who'd made her life a living hell. The one who'd spread Father Tom's *theories* among her friends. The one who'd made her ashamed to show her face.

"What's that? You have no excuse for your actions? Well, do you at least have a defense for what's on your screen?"

Olivia went red, knowing that Martha would tell the others she was a devil worshiper no matter what she said.

"You're coming with me this *instant*," the vile nun snapped, grabbing her wrist and yanking her out of the chair.

"You can't do that!" Olivia cried in a hushed tone, going red upon literally feeling all eyes on them.

But the woman ignored her protests, dragging her away. "I'm reporting this to your truancy officer, and it's going on your record."

"I don't *have* a truancy officer," Olivia hissed, unable to break the evil nun's iron grip. Taking a risk, she made her arm *slightly* incorporeal and yanked it free. Still, the crone's claws tore at her skin.

"What just—"

Olivia held up her arm. Nail marks stung and quickly reddened on her pale skin. Blood soon followed. "You just assaulted a minor!"

Distant spectators gasped, but Martha sneered. "You did that, you little bi—"

"*Martha*," Sister Paula hissed, whirling between them. "We do not raise our voice in a library. And we certainly don't put our hands on *children*," she said, jabbing an accusatory finger.

"Practically a priest," Olivia muttered.

She flinched as Martha tried to backhand her, but her godmother caught the woman's wrist.

"This is *not* a school. And you're *not* in charge of discipline. Now take a walk, *Sister*."

"Hmph! Mother will hear of this. And what'll she think of you and your godforsaken goddaughter then?"

Olivia glared up at her, but Martha just departed with a smirk.

"Pft," Sister Paula scoffed. "I never understood why they put women who didn't want children in charge of them."

Olivia gasped. Her former teacher's logic was impeccable, but still, she'd said it *out loud*.

"Oh, come now, child, don't pretend as though the thought never entered your mind," she said, putting her hands on her hips. "And that priest comment was over the line."

Olivia bowed her head. "Yes, Sister." She wished she hadn't said that...in front of her godmother, at least.

"Come now," the nun said, giving her a handkerchief for her wrist. "Be careful not to get blood on your sleeve," she added, ushering her to an open table by the computers.

"I saved you some dessert, but you didn't show. What happened?"

"You remember what we talked about before I...went away?"

Her former teacher nodded. "We spoke of spirits and such."

"Yeah, well, I kept trying prayers and fasting after the exorcism, but they didn't work for me..." Olivia said, hoping she didn't sound like a heretic. "It took my mom," she whispered.

"Heavens, child," her godmother said, scooting over to hug her. "If Tom had just...never mind. What happened?"

Olivia fought off tears, worries for her mom, and fears that her observations were proof of false doctrine. She squeezed the handkerchief, unable to meet her godmother's gaze. "It broke Mom's legs..."

Horrific images flashed in her mind.

"It chased me..."

She squeezed the fabric tighter.

"And when I came to, she was *gone*," she said, loosening her grip. "Poor Ada..."

Olivia kept staring at her wrist, feeling the throbbing in her veins. But her powers picked up on the nun's soft expression, hardening into problem-solving mode.

"You said *when you came to*. Did you black out?"

Olivia nodded, wiping the blood away. She didn't want to talk about that. She hoped most of her brain cells were still intact. That her mom hadn't passed out too. That she was okay.

"Are you all right? Have you seen a doctor?"

"I'm fine," Olivia said, realizing it was true. She was tired and sore, but with her powers, she hoped she'd find her mom within two days. Still, she'd been unconscious for a few minutes. "But I can't go to the hospital."

"And why on earth not?"

"They'd call my parents."

"Ah, yes, William's out of town....A pity godmothers don't count for guardians." Her former teacher narrowed her eyes. "You told him, didn't you? About your mother?"

"Of course."

"There's something else, isn't there?"

"Well, even if he were here, I couldn't go," she said, looking away again.

Sister Paula put a scarred hand on Olivia's, but she didn't look up.

"Why's that?" her godmother asked.

"Because," Olivia whispered, loosening her scarf. "They'd find bruises." She was so tired of trying to hide them. Pretending to be clumsy, always late getting dressed for gym. Everyone thought she lacked self-confidence and made fun of her all the more for the fact that she hadn't grown.

"What exactly am I looking for, dear?"

"What?" Olivia checked her compact and gasped. Sure enough, there were no bruises. When did that happen?

"They were there this morning!" Surely she hadn't imagined those. All *this*. She couldn't be losing her mind.

Sister Paula tilted her head. "Well, they're gone now. Count your blessings."

"But how?" And why didn't she have new ones? Could the ice from the ghost's cold fingers have soothed the wounded tissue? No, that hadn't helped yesterday. Was she too light? Its grip too weak? Nope. Nope. Both were the same as yesterday.

But why weren't the bruises *worse* after being amplified by the ones from this morning? Even if the ones from yesterday had faded, new ones should have at least started showing by now. Did her new powers include healing?

Sister Paula cleared her throat. "I presume you're here to ask for my help to find Ada."

Olivia nodded.

The nun sighed. "I took the liberty of checking your browser history when you didn't show for brunch. You were headed to a very dangerous area, young lady."

"I know," she said, nodding and not looking up until she felt a smile spread across her former teacher's face.

"Well, you shan't be doing anything so foolish as that again, since I'll be with you."

Olivia chuckled, hugging her godmother. "Thanks."

The nun patted her on the back. "So, did your ill-conceived expedition yield any results?"

"Sort of."

"Do tell."

"Well, I saw things when the ghost grabbed me last night. Dad thought it might be another place on Earth. So we put our heads together and concluded it might've been in Detroit. And this morning, I found a parking garage that matched all the clues online. And, yeah, it was the place."

Her former teacher crossed her arms. "So rather than forwarding this to the police, naturally, you decided to go it *alone. Olivia Linda,* have you no sense?"

Olivia sat up straighter, like she had whenever the nuns reprimanded her in a similar tone for slouching, and blushed when she realized what she'd done.

"But it's a *ghost.* I didn't think they were equipped to deal with that!"

Sister Paula raised an eyebrow. "And you *were?*"

Olivia fidgeted in her seat. She was now. Ugh, it was like she was in school all over again! Sister Paula had never needed any mystical ability to see right through her.

"So tell me, what if the ghost had hurt you? Or worse? Why not give the police an anonymous tip?"

Olivia lowered her head. "I thought I could handle it."

"And what on earth made you think that?"

She looked away. "They're weak to lead."

"Lead? *They?*"

Olivia nodded. "Turns out there are two of them."

Sister Paula frowned. "And they're weak to *lead?*"

"Yeah."

The nun snorted. "That's not in scripture. More and more, I think these things are neither ghosts nor demons but *men.*"

Olivia pursed her lips. "What do you mean?"

"See, if your exorcism failed, you either didn't believe—which I very much doubt—*or* it's not a ghost but rather a person, who possesses free will."

Olivia's eyes went wide. She had its powers, so obviously, it could be a man! That's why it *toyed* with her when she prayed. It was a cruel *man.* She gasped. "It's just like the T. rex and the allosaur!"

"That's right," Sister Paula said, clearly remembering the lesson well. "They may have looked similar on the outside, but we well know that the bones are completely different! Take heart, child. If this thing didn't back down after your exorcism, then it is a man. And men are *fallible.*"

Olivia smiled, relieved to know that she wasn't up against some ancient being or one of the damned returning from beyond the grave. "I have something to show you," she whispered.

"Okay."

"Do you remember how you said that sometimes, we're the answer to our own prayers?"

The nun nodded. "Sometimes, when we are ready, God gives us the strength and ability to see things through."

"Well," Olivia said, looking and feeling around with her powers to make sure no one was watching. "I think He's leveled the playing field." She made her hand immaterial and put it through the table.

Her godmother put a hand to her mouth, and, after a moment, she grinned. "Interesting sense of humor He has, giving you your adversaries' abilities."

Olivia wiped frost from the table, gave her former teacher a smirk, and went white at the sight of Jasmine staring at her from behind Sister Paula. "Jasmine! What are you doing here?"

"College day," the senior muttered, shambling forward with a blank expression. She looked as if she'd seen a ghost. "Storm cut my tour short. Thought I'd work on homework while stranded....Olivia, please tell me I'm not going crazy. Please tell me that I saw what I think I saw."

The nun stared up at the senior. "You look faint, dear. Have a seat," she said, pulling out a chair. "I'm Sister Paula, by the way."

"Jasmine Jackson," she replied, sitting down unsteadily.

Olivia gulped. "Jasmine...what is it you think you just saw?"

"I—I was at the computer," she said, jerking her thumb back, "listening to music, and my headphones crackled. The screen flickered. And I—I saw you in the reflection. It—it looked like your hand went *through* the table."

Olivia winced and turned to her godmother.

But Sister Paula just smiled. "Remember, setbacks might be blessings in disguise."

Olivia sighed. Jasmine was so cool and kind. Hopefully, she could be trusted. Because Olivia wasn't about to make her think she'd cracked. She wouldn't do that. It was cruel. She wouldn't be like the Ghost Giants.

This time, though, Olivia looked and felt around more thoroughly, searching for anything reflective before making her hand transparent. Sure enough, the closest computers flickered.

Jasmine gasped. "You're like the specter!"

Olivia's eyes widened. "What *specter?*"

"The one that attacked me. I thought I was having a nightmare!"

"Hmm....So you *both* have haunted houses?" Sister Paula asked.

"Looks like it," Jasmine said.

"On the same block, no less," Olivia added.

"Curious," the nun said, touching her chin. "I wonder just how many other *ghosts* are in your neighborhood."

Jasmine shook her head. "I dunno, but I didn't tell a soul. Doubt anyone else did, either. People'd think we were *crazy*."

"*Yeah,*" Olivia said, knowing all too well how that felt. "Long story short, there are at least two of them. They took my mom, and I somehow have their powers now."

"And they're probably just men, not spirits," Sister Paula added.

"That's...a *lot* to take in..." Jasmine said. "And did you say they got your *mom?*"

Olivia nodded. "I don't know where they took her, but we have a lead," she said, waving them over to the computer. Even with her back turned, she felt the senior's eyes bulge.

"Well," her godmother began. "I see how you got Sister Martha riled up."

Olivia sighed, clicking through images. It wasn't like *she* was the one who'd written on those walls like a child. A very immature, profane child.

"Anyway," she said, "it's not much, but I found a room number in the creatures' lair, Northville H266. I think there might be a clue inside."

"Cheery place," Jasmine said dryly. "Almost makes me yearn for the Cracks."

"Hmm," Sister Paula said, looking over her shoulder. "We'll need respirators."

Olivia nodded. "Yeah. But I've only got one at home..."

Jasmine shrugged. "No biggie. We can borrow some from my employer."

"Really?" Olivia asked, craning her neck to look up at the senior. Why was she so tall?

"Really," Jasmine replied.

Olivia frowned. "I thought you worked at a hairdresser."

"Yeah," she said, looking away. "But we're closed for repairs, and we have extras sitting around."

"Excellent. Then let's be off," Sister Paula said, rising.

"Wait," Jasmine said, pointing. "Those look like no trespassing signs. Does this place have guards?"

"Not anymore," Olivia said, logging off and falling into line behind her godmother. "They pulled them a couple of years ago due to budget cuts."

Jasmine just shook her head. "Everything comes down to money."

"Speaking of which," Sister Paula said. "Does either of you have cab fare?"

Olivia nodded, hoping her Christmas money would be enough to cover the trip.

"Yeah," Jasmine said, "but we can take my folks' car."

Olivia lit up. "Really?"

"Heck, yeah," Jasmine chuckled. "'Less you wanna take the bus."

"Then lead the way," Sister Paula said, falling back to Olivia.

The senior took point, and the nun lowered her voice. "Word to the wise, young lady—when someone offers you something, don't question them unless you think they can't deliver. Instead, say thank you."

Olivia blushed. "Oh...by the way, Jasmine, thanks for...you know, everything."

Jasmine snorted. "'Course. What kinda person would I be if I didn't lend a hand? 'Sides, I wanna get those specters too."

Olivia froze, and her boots squeaked on the marble floor.

"What's wrong?" Sister Paula asked as Jasmine turned.

In addition to their footsteps echoing in the hall, Olivia's powers picked up on more subtle vibrations around the corner.

"That's right, Officer," Martha said. "One way or another, they all end up on corners, and the only difference is what they're selling."

Olivia's face burned. "Martha's on the phone. I think she's calling someone a—"

"Yeah," the evil nun said, "so I've got a girl skipping class."

Olivia balled up her fists and shook with rage. That vile woman was calling *her* a whore!

The lights flickered, and the line crackled.

"Hello? Hello?" Martha called over the disconnect tone.

"*Olivia?*" Jasmine muttered, staring at her half-opaque form and the flickering lights.

She blushed and became solid again, wiping frost from the marble floor with a squeak.

"Hello?" Martha called, hammering away to redial. No one needed powers to hear that.

Sister Paula narrowed her eyes. "I take it she was reporting your absence?"

"Yes."

"Wait here." The nun stalked forward, rounding the corner, and Jasmine turned to Olivia.

"You cause that blackout?"

Olivia blushed, staring down at her boots. "Happens whenever I use my powers. The frost, too."

"So you killed the phone?"

Olivia shrugged. "Not intentionally. But I'd do it again in a heartbeat."

The tall girl laughed. "Atta girl. Hey, what else can you do?"

"I can float. And *feel* sounds and stuff from a distance."

"Cool," Jasmine said. "So you can...*feel* what they're saying now?"

Olivia nodded. "*Martha,* I suggest you reflect on how you've treated her and do penance before Mother makes it *mandatory.*" She winced at the sensation of enamel grating away.

"What?" Jasmine asked.

"The evil nun ground her teeth."

Jasmine frowned. "Evil nun? Did I miss something?"

Olivia raised an eyebrow, before noting the headphones around Jasmine's neck. Right, the senior hadn't seen or heard the nun-fight. Thank goodness for that.

"Long story," she said, shivering at the idea of Jasmine having witnessed that.

"Hey, ice maker, 'less you want the whole world to know what you can do, ya need to keep that under control."

"I know," Olivia groaned. "It's just...shaking activates my powers."

Jasmine blinked. "That sucks. That *really* sucks."

Olivia kicked the frost half-heartedly. "I know, right? Happy, sad, angry, cold. They all trigger it!"

Jasmine just gave her a smile. "Yep."

Sister Paula returned triumphantly. "Right, then. Now, where were we?"

Olivia's Notes: Spirits in Scripture

Of all the "supernatural" abilities associated with the saints/scripture, here are all the ghost-related ones I was able to find in the Bible:

> Evil spirits have proceeded from their bodies; because they are born from men, and from the holy Watchers is their beginning and primal origin; they shall be evil spirits on earth, and evil spirits shall they be called....And the spirits of the giants afflict, oppress,

destroy, attack, do battle, and work destruction on the
earth, and cause trouble: they take no food, but
nevertheless hunger and thirst, and cause offences. And
these spirits shall rise up against the children of men
and against the women, because they have proceeded
from them.
(Enoch 15:9–11, translated by R. H. Charles)

Okay, so it's not canonical, but it does raise the possibility of a
fourth type of ghost, descended from demons. But if the Ghost Giant's
as ancient as this passage is purported to be, I don't think I can stop it...

When the donkey saw the angel of the LORD on the
road ahead with a sword in hand, it went off the road,
and Balaam struck it to get it back on the path.
(Numbers 22:23)

Cisco was certainly able to see the monster, but if a "mystic" like
Balaam couldn't, I don't know why I could....I miss Cisco so much :(

1 Samuel 28 (The Witch of Endor) and
Matthew 17:1–13 (The Transfiguration)

Whether the ghost summoned in the Old Testament was Samuel or
a demon masquerading as him, the idea that souls can return from
beyond the grave is confirmed by the appearance of Moses and Elijah
in the New Testament, but if the Ghost Giant's not a demon, it certainly
didn't come from heaven.

The angel replied, "With regards to the fish's heart and
liver, you may burn them in the presence of one afflicted
by a demon to permanently drive it away."
(Tobit 6:8)

I don't understand. Sister Paula says the Church doesn't use this method, and, regardless, fish hearts won't keep in a readily burnable state for me to try it.

> And when the disciples saw him walking on the sea, they
> were troubled, saying, It is a spirit; and they cried out
> for fear.
> (Matthew 14:26, KJV)

Obviously, he's not a ghost, but this does show that they believed ghosts didn't follow the laws of nature. There's got to be a way to contain this menace, though...

> And the man in whom the evil spirit was leaped on them,
> and overcame them, and prevailed against them, so that
> they fled out of that house naked and wounded.
> (Acts 19:16, KJV)

I can't be possessed, since I've been baptized, but I don't know how I'm supposed to beat the Ghost Giant if it's harboring super-strength on top of everything else! I wish that Father Tom believed me. That *someone* believed me. I wish this never happened to me. I wish—I wish I....*No*, I wish that stupid ghost would go away! God, pleeease send it away!

ᚦᛖᛁᚱ ᚳᛁᚢᛏᛋ ᚠᚫᛗ

Chapter 8: The Raven

Jada Johansen clattered away on her laptop in the van while her automated pentesting suite brute-forced more rich dudes' networks.

"Let me get this straight," a reporter growled over the radio. "The *vigilante's name* is *Vigil Lee?*"

"That's what he said," Kay replied, defeat clear in her voice, "and given his current state of mind, we don't believe he's fit to stand trial."

A reporter cursed, and Jada winced. The media were tearing into Kay like a kid ripping open candy wrappers on Halloween. All because she was the first one to arrive on the scene yesterday. Well, that and the *crazy* backstory the perp—or someone else—had cooked up.

"And you said he's a *gypsy?*" another reporter asked.

"Supposedly," Kay replied. "And as I said before, he prefers the term *Romani.*"

"So you're telling us," a man began, "that a *Black Gypsy fortune teller* busted up a bunch of white-power gang operations?"

"Among others—yes, that appears to be the case," Kay began. "But—"

Jada couldn't help but snort. The bikers were *totally* flipping out right now.

"But there's barely any meat on his bones!" someone shouted.

"Which is why we believe that he may not have acted alone," Kay said for the umpteenth time. "So if anyone—"

"This is outrageous!"

"If *anyone* has *any* information—"

"This is a sham!"

"Any information on the other—"

"We'll be right back after a word from our sponsors!" the radio chimed. "Do you suffer from—"

"Unbelievable," Jada said, muting the radio and leaning back in her seat. They couldn't even broadcast the conference in full. And no wonder Kay wanted her to look into this! The idea of a scrawny guy going out at night and in broad daylight to wage a one-man war on crime in full body armor was *laughable.*

That said, the idea of the Exterminator being a nomad seemed plausible. As crazy as that premise was, she was rather impressed with Dr. Park's line of reasoning when presented with a perp with no prints, ID, or missing persons reports. She doubted she'd have come to the same conclusion, despite the fact that few groups were as resistant to documentation or as adept at staying off the grid as some of the more militant Roma. Fabricated story or not, Dr. Park seemed criminally underutilized as a child psychiatrist.

The laptop beeped, and Jada winced. "*Password123*? Seriously, *Bentlee4Life*? Are you even *trying*?" she asked, watching the ping sweep and port scan results come in.

"Come on, come on," she said, watching devices pop up. "Laptop, laptop...game console, game console, *another* game console....Cameras! And, given the manufacturer, the default password is...correct! *Wow*, you suck at security," she said, flipping off the packet analyzer before she could see what shady sites he visited.

"Let's see," Jada said, flipping through surveillance feeds. It was funny how those devices were supposed to bolster physical security, yet they'd been left so digitally insecure that they actually made the owners *more* vulnerable.

"Okay, if the van's *there*, then you're...house number 7734. Which means that I want the cameras on the north side...for yesterday..." she mumbled, scrubbing through footage.

"And just like everyone else, your feed goes blank," she grumbled, scratching off yet another address. At least she was getting a clearer idea of which direction Kay's mystery suspect had fled.

Rolling around to the next block, Jada hoped Kay appreciated how much gas money she was throwing away for her. Her laptop attacked new networks when they came into range, and she checked the houses with lawyers or unreachable residents for cameras, crossing off the cameraless ones as she went.

Whoever she was chasing had somehow managed to simultaneously hack multiple devices on the fly without leaving any trace in the logs. In other words, he was a man after her own heart. But their elusiveness was seriously *ruining* her day, because she couldn't let a slob like *Saul* be the first one to find a lead.

"Oh, what do we have here?" she asked, spotting outdated cameras and coming to a stop. Those probably weren't on any network. So neither she nor their mystery human could hack them! Perfect!

Jada left her laptop to do its thing and hopped out with a clipboard to knock on the door, full of confidence and charm. But there was no response. And the house was so low-tech it didn't even have a doorbell. She pressed her ear to the door and, hearing footsteps, shied back, repocketing her bump keys.

"Can I help you?" an old White lady asked, opening the door with frail movements.

"Yes, ma'am," Jada said, smiling and clicking her pen. "Your HOA's[7] got us checking for water damage." She pointed to the magnets she'd plastered onto her vehicle. *Duckie's Water Damage and Restoration: Sink or swim, we've got you covered.*

Jada beamed with pride as the homeowner stared at her jacket, which bore a matching logo, with its adorable little umbrella and floaties.

"Would you like me to take a look around now or schedule a visit later?" she asked, pen hovering over an empty spot on a schedule she'd hastily scribbled gibberish on.

"Oh...well, since you're already here," the little old lady said, opening the door wider.

"Thank you, ma'am," Jada said, stepping inside. "You won't even notice I'm here."

"Oh, all right," her host said. "I made cookies, so be sure to grab some on your way out."

"Aw, thanks," Jada said, feeling a twinge of guilt. Maybe she could find a light bulb to change or something.

Going door to door and room to room, Jada searched each floor of the sprawling house for any sign of electronics or cohabitants but came

---

[7] Homeowners Association: a group that collects monthly fees to maintain a given neighborhood and/or set overly restrictive rules for residents.

up empty until she found what she was looking for in the corner of the unfinished basement.

"There you are," she said, settling into a worn-out rolly chair in front of a bunch of ancient video equipment covered in dust. Having found no trace of anyone else in the house, she flipped between inputs on the bulky TV, rewinding when she found the right angle.

"Come on, come on..." she said, watching sped-up trees and flags rustle and billow in the wind while cars and people raced by in reverse. Static.

"Are you *kidding* me?" she cried. "How in the world?"

The image cleared up, revealing a *motorcycle* parked under a tree by the park. As the footage continued, static engulfed the screen again, and, when it cleared, the bike was nowhere to be seen.

Jada grinned. "So *that's* how you escaped..." Given that the biker gangs had been gunning for the vigilante, it would be an awfully big coincidence if there *wasn't* a connection between them and this mystery man.

In her professional opinion, they weren't dealing with an accomplice or someone who'd set up an impostor. No, they were dealing with a would-be *assassin*.

But why had he fled if he'd gotten so close to killing his mark? Had Kay scared him off when she came charging in? Or had the prospect of injuring a cop made him decide that risking a brutal citywide manhunt wasn't worth it?

Whatever the reason, Jada didn't like how things stood. Due to the angle at which the hitman had parked, only the cameraless homes had a clear view of the license plate—assuming there'd been one to begin with.

Regardless, the guy had to be a pro. But pros had records from their rookie days. Finding a match among the biker gangs' known associates would be a breeze if she could find a witness.

Jada returned the old machines to how they'd been, thankful that she wasn't chasing an—or *the*—Exterminator. But she was still a bit conflicted about him being behind bars—implausible though it seemed that the skinny man was him. Legally or not, he'd been effective out on the streets, uprooting gangs and shutting down drug dealers. Meanwhile, the department had been busy pulling back and shuffling districts to cut costs when the public needed them the most.

But she wasn't shrewd enough to argue, like her mother, that the vigilante's actions were a necessary evil, not with all the bystanders the gangsters had gunned down in the shoot-outs and the inevitable turf wars that erupted in his wake. Nor was she soft enough to argue that crooks could have been rehabilitated like they were in her father's birth country. The prison system just wasn't set up for that.

But those were bigger problems for another day. Jada took comfort in her small victory and hurried upstairs, eager to bring in the mystery man and ask how he pulled off the camera trick.

"Did you find any damage?" the little ole lady asked, emerging from the kitchen with a tray of cookies.

"Nope, all clear!" Jada declared, maintaining the act despite her mounting guilt.

"Oh, wonderful!" her host said with a warm smile. "I'm so relieved! After all the rain we got last night and this morning."

"Happy to be of service, ma'am," Jada said, tipping the brim of her hat in a show of respect and hoping that she'd actually cleared up worry instead of introducing it.

"Please, take one for the road," the woman said, holding the tray out so that the chocolaty mint scent could work its mouthwatering magic.

Jada resisted temptation only out of sheer guilt. "I'm actually trying to watch my fig—"

"I insist," the lady said. "I'll be offended if you don't."

"Well, when you put it like that," Jada said, scooping one up and taking a bite. "Mmm, they're so *good*."

"Thank you," her host said. "Grab another before you go."

"Don't mind if I do! And thanks for the treats!" Jada said, waving farewell with a cookie in hand and heading out with chocolaty mint goodness in her mouth.

The little ole lady nodded in return before Jada trotted over to the tree the suspect had parked under. But as she feared, the rain had long since removed any trace of tire tracks or shoe prints. And a quick flash of her black light turned up no sign of bodily fluids.

"Darn," she said, scanning the park for visitors and spotting an old dude in a flat cap heading her way. Hopefully, he was a regular—if he'd been here yesterday, he might be able to fill her in.

A raven landed on a nearby branch amid the wet leaves and cawed, watching her with its beady black eyes.

"Hello yourself," she said with a smile.

In response to her kindness, it betrayed her trust by flapping its wings to spray her with water droplets.

"Stop that!" she snapped, frantically wiping her face and hands with sanitizer. Birds were cool, but their feathers were *filthy*, riddled with mites and diseases. Hopefully, she hadn't gotten anything in her mouth!

"How would you like it if I tried to shoo you?" she asked, waving her aloe-scented hands at it. "Go on, shoo! Shoo!"

"Shoo," it replied, in the creepiest, deepest voice ever—completely devoid of emotion or a soul.

Jada shrieked and jumped back, never once taking her eyes off the demonic creature as she instinctively reached for her gun.

"I was told they do that," an old geezer chuckled.

"Do what?" Jada asked, turning to the man in the flat cap she'd seen earlier, hoping he hadn't seen her go for her piece. The boys in the office'd never let her live that down if they got wind of this.

"Talk," the old man said, admiring the bird.

"*What?*"

He chuckled. "Didn't you ever read 'The Raven?'"

"Yeah, in school, but we all thought that guy had lost it."

The old dude just shook his head. "The education system these days. See now, when we read that poem, our teacher, Mr. Dambrauskas, told us that ravens were like parrots. They can mimic sounds. Though the wild ones usually don't talk much."

"Thank goodness for that. They sound *possessed*," Jada replied, looking at the menace with disgust.

"Begone, *fowl* spirit..." she muttered, failing to cheer herself up.

"Well, I very much doubt that they are, but we don't need to linger. Where are you headed?"

"To talk with you, actually," she said, showing him her badge. "I'm Officer Johansen, but you can call me Jada."

"Well, Miss Jada," he laughed. "You can call me Ervin, but why on God's green earth would you want to talk to me?" he asked, holding out a hand toward the path.

Jada nodded and walked beside him, jerking her thumb back at the tree. "A person of interest parked a motorcycle there yesterday afternoon, but I have no idea what he looks like."

"Ah, that fellow. You're looking for a tall, thin young man with a beard and long dark hair."

"Thank the Lord," Jada mumbled to the sky, grateful that Ervin had actually seen something *and* was willing to talk. "Notice anything else?"

"Well, I only got a brief glimpse of him in passing. But from what I could tell, he had the darkest irises I've ever seen on a White boy. Black as night. Same color as his hoodie."

"Interesting..." Jada said, writing everything down on her clipboard, not knowing any bikers or known associates matching that description. But he could have been wearing colored contacts. Or maybe a bounty had opened up and the Ninevites had sent one of their own.

"Any chance you could identify him if you saw him again?" she asked.

"Hmm....As I said, I didn't get a good look at him, but yeah, maybe. Yeah, I think I could do it."

"Great! Would you mind coming down to the station with me?" Jada asked, hoping he was a sucker for a pretty face.

Ervin laughed. "So long as I make it back in time to walk my grandkids home, we can go wherever you'd like, Miss Jada."

"Great!" she replied, turning on her heel to reverse course right back to that *infernal bird.*

"That teacher I told you about," Ervin said, eying the vile thing. "Mr. Dambrauskas."

"Yeah, what about him?" she asked, looking over her shoulder to make sure the menace didn't divebomb her.

"Well, he went off on tangents all the time. And I remember the day we covered Poe. He threw in a—and I quote—a *traditional Lithuanian fairy tale*. 'The Twelve Ravens.' And do you know how we could tell it was legit?"

"Because it got its own movie?" Jada asked, unlocking the van.

"Naw," Ervin said, taking shotgun. "You see, we knew he wasn't just making stuff up because there was a princess and an evil stepmother."

"Ha!" Jada laughed, starting the vehicle as the raven took flight. "How cliché!"

⠈⠄⠇⠄⠁⠄⠒⠼⠀⠙⠿⠉⠉⠀⠦⠇⠰⠹⠃⠄⠧⠰⠃⠀⠄⠂⠒⠀⠇⠆⠄⠣⠀⠍⠒⠰⠂⠀⠨⠉
⠂⠄⠃⠃⠆⠄⠂⠆⠀⠂⠙⠂⠀⠹⠆⠉⠀⠃⠆⠀⠹⠒⠉⠌⠎⠒⠂⠀⠷⠒⠒⠂⠼⠀⠂⠊⠀⠇⠶
⠠⠄⠀⠱⠂⠈⠀⠱⠦⠀⠋⠙⠒

"Yes, that looks just like him, Officer. Consider me impressed!" the witness said in a deep voice through the Blackberry's speakers as Sung-Min parked a few blocks back from the girl and her friends.

It was good to discover that those bugs he'd planted at the station were already bearing fruit.

"Thank you so much for your help!" Detective Johansen replied in her peppy tone. "For looking through all those photos and sitting down with Woodson here."

"Pleasure's all mine, Miss Jada. I hope you find your guy," the witness said.

Sung-Min did too. Anyone or any*thing* capable of spooking Subject B was an entity worth noting. And a potential quarry to add to his list. A third target, to offset the one that had been brought in without his intervention. One down, two to go. One left to identify.

"Thanks," Detective Johansen said, "Well, I'm off to drop Erv off. Take care, Woodson."

"You too," the sketch artist drawled.

Sung-Min frowned when the audio went quiet. His work had once been simple. *Go behind enemy lines and take out the leadership. Make it back if you can.* He'd done all that, but then he'd learned that there was more to the world than most knew.

He'd stepped up to protect humanity from the paranormal, the extraterrestrial, and the supernatural—or whatever else people wanted to call it. Because regardless of whether they believed it or not, they still needed protection.

But ever since government funding had dried up, they'd had to become more *resourceful* to get things done.

He rewound the audio on his phone and hit the Calibrate button on his throat mic before pressing Play.

"Yes, that looks just like him," the phone said.

"Yes, that looks just like him," Sung-Min repeated in the witness's deep voice, moving his mouth to get the throat mic to re-create a more natural sound. Good—despite the source, the tone didn't sound artificial. Satisfied with the new voice in his collection, he pulled a burner from his lab coat and dialed the department.

"If this is an emergency, please hang up and dial 911," an automated message said.

"Detroit PD, how may I direct your call?" a woman asked in an idle tone.

"Yes," Sung-Min said, using the witness's voice instead of that of the general whose throat he'd slit. "Can I have the extension for Officer Woodson?"

"One moment, please..." the operator said, typing away on a mechanical keyboard. "That'd be 9376. Would you like me to transfer your call?"

"No need, I'll call when I get back from lunch," Sung-Min replied.

"All right. Bye now," the woman said.

Sung-Min hung up, used the Blackberry to change his voice, and redialed.

"Hello?" the sketch artist said.

"Yes," Sung-Min began in Detective Johansen's voice with a fake smile plastered on his face to replicate the intended tone, "Before I forget, could you forward a pic of that sketch to this number?”

“Uh, no. You took the only copy, remember?”

“Oh, right!” Sung-Min said without missing a beat. “I’m such a ditz! Too much going on!”

“Somehow, I don’t find that surprising,” the man groaned.

“All right, bye!” Sung-Min said, returning to his usual straight face before removing the burner’s battery. It was a pity the detective was covering her tracks this well, but it didn’t matter. He’d get hold of that sketch one way or another.

His Blackberry chimed.

Status?

G has manifested abilities, and C remains stable, he replied. The discovery of the latter had led them to identify Subject A and a handful of others. Thankfully, she was hanging in there.

That complicates things....Do you need backup?

No.

They were stretched thin, and there was no need to pull Famine or Conquest off their current missions. He could manage Subject A and the new players for the time being.

Acknowledged. War out.

Chapter 9: Northville

"What's taking so long?" Olivia muttered, twirling her pencil and glancing out at Zedd's boarded-up exterior. The sooner they got to Northville, the sooner they could leave that place behind forever.

"Patience," Sister Paula said, leaning back in the passenger seat. "Perhaps Miss Jackson's still looking for the masks."

"No, I felt her pick those up shortly after she—"

Jasmine hurried out and locked up before hopping in. Despite being counterbalanced by both Olivia and her godmother, the car leaned heavily to the senior's side. Between Jasmine's height and athletic build, it was clear that she'd packed on a lot of muscle.

"*Okay*—to Northville," Jasmine said, tossing them masks.

As they took off, Olivia caught hers and a glimpse of skeletal clown graffiti through gaps in the boarded-up windows. "Ugh."

"You all right back there?" Jasmine asked, switching lanes.

"Yeah," Olivia said, tossing her mask back and forth between her hands. Catching seemed *way* easier now that she could feel trajectories in her bones. "I just don't like vandals."

"You and me both," Jasmine mumbled.

Olivia felt the smile spread across Sister Paula's face, but the nun said nothing. She was probably still processing everything they'd gone over on the way. And Jasmine must've been doing the same, because they continued on in silence. At least, that's what it must've felt like to the other two.

Sure, the hum of the engine and the tires on the pavement provided subtle background noise, but the molecules in the leather seats, the floorboards, and the metal frame all called out to Olivia. Her powers made the old saying *actions speak louder than words* true in the most literal sense.

Jasmine, for example, was tense. She kept squeezing the wheel and relaxing her grip whenever she noticed. Meanwhile, Sister Paula remained still and calm. Her breathing never fluctuated. Clearly, she was more at peace with what they were about to do.

To attempt to calm her nerves and pass the time, Olivia worked on the sketch of Lady Constance's team she'd drawn while waiting at Zedd's. She'd almost finished the dog by the time they neared the end of the Seven Mile leg of their journey.

Rather than heading directly to the hospital grounds, they turned off onto Haggerty. That way, they could avoid the prying eyes of all the cops driving to and from the crime lab.

Olivia looked away when they passed Hawthorn Center. How many times had she stared out those windows, yearning to be free? And now, even facing her fear and finding out whether Victoria had passed away seemed preferable to going to Northville.

Jasmine pulled into a shopping center by the woods, and the three of them emerged without a word. The tall girl stretched while Olivia took inventory of her pack with her powers.

"Pleasant day for a stroll," Sister Paula said, taking in the chill autumn air.

"Yeah," Jasmine laughed, hefting her purse. "We might not've gotten to enjoy it if the entrances weren't swarming with cops."

Olivia shook her head. "Even if they weren't, they're blocked off by gates, and what little pavement's left is more bumpy and overgrown than the Cracks."

"Besides," her godmother said, taking the lead. "We don't want anyone reporting a suspicious vehicle."

"Fair enough," Jasmine said, following through the sea of cars. "A walk in the woods it is..."

"Come, children. A little nature never hurt anyone," Sister Paula said, nearing the forest and taking in the vibrant autumn colors on full display.

"Yeah," Olivia replied with a nervous laugh. "I'm sure it's just called the *Evil Woods* for no reason."

"Seriously?" Jasmine asked.

"Well, technically, it's the Hundred Acre Wood," Olivia began. "But locals are weird."

"I like the second name better," the tall girl replied. "Sounds more inviting."

"Yeah," Olivia said, crushing leaves underfoot. Perhaps the locals *didn't* call it that. Maybe it was just Hawthorn patients. But was it because they were *crazy*, out of their minds on pills, or just bored?

Sure, they did strange things now and then, but, given their conditions, that was understandable. No, what was truly unexpected was when *regular* people acted weird. What excuse did they have? Maybe everyone was just a little *odd* inside.

"Anyone nearby?" Jasmine whispered.

Olivia stiffened, feeling every sound wave radiate out from the rustling leaves. Those sounds would betray them even if they didn't talk!

She felt out with her powers and breathed a sigh of relief. "Just an underground passage."

Jasmine blinked. "Seriously?"

Olivia nodded, and Sister Paula smiled. "Probably maintenance tunnels."

Normally, Olivia would've loved to follow up on that theory, but she felt no desire to slip under the soil to see what sort of hellscape lay beneath. The sooner they left, the better. As such, it was hard for her to enjoy the hike, knowing their destination and lamenting that she was sneaking into yet *another* forbidden place.

She didn't like the trajectory of her day. Hopefully, things wouldn't get much worse, because she was already uncomfortable with the possibility of getting picked up by the police for trespassing. And she didn't want to see anyone else die. She lowered her head, falling behind, hating herself for failing to save that guy. If only she'd been faster...

Despite the distance, her powers brought Jasmine's question to her ears.

"So do we, uh, need to worry about her blowing our cover? Because she's *not* that stealthy....Too fidgety..."

Olivia went redder than the leaves she'd been sliding through and carefully stepped between gaps in the fallen foliage.

"She's always been a little noisy when she moves." her godmother chuckled. "Helps her mother keep track of her."

"*Aw*, that's so sweet," the senior said, much to Olivia's horror.

She'd never realized she'd done that. She felt so embarrassed that she wanted to sink into the leaves and hide.

"But I assure you," her former teacher continued. "She's quite adept at being sneaky when she wants to be *mischievous*."

"Cute," the tall girl laughed.

Olivia winced, desperately wishing that Jasmine would have thought she was *cool* instead of *cute*.

"Regardless of whether or not you find that trait endearing," the nun said, "I think we're getting ahead of ourselves."

"Oh, right," the tall girl whispered, glancing back.

Olivia forced herself to pick up the pace and pretend she hadn't heard anything. She felt out more carefully with her powers and lightened her strides, bouncing up and down so high that she couldn't help reaching out to touch a branch.

Jasmine stared up in wonder, but Sister Paula merely looked back at the frosty leaves twinkling in the sunlight.

"Hand *and* footprints?" she asked.

Olivia blushed and kicked off the ground one last time to float alongside them.

"Better?" she asked, hoping she looked cooler than a little kid bouncing up and down.

"Indeed," her godmother chuckled.

"Bit chilly," Jasmine said, adjusting her coat. "You're giving me a *literal* cold shoulder."

Olivia shook her head at the tall girl. Suddenly, her *I'm a Standup Gal* tee made more sense.

"Olivia," Sister Paula said, narrowing her eyes. "What did you do to your hair?"

"Nothing," she said, adjusting her beret to no avail. Now that she was floating along at eye level, there was no way she could hide every strand of ruined hair.

Bullies, Jasmine mouthed behind her back. Presumably, Olivia wasn't supposed to know that, but she could feel it, which only made it hurt worse.

"Hmm," Her godmother said with a somber look. She raised her head. "We're here."

She and Jasmine paused to take in the view, but Olivia kept floating.

"Whoops..." She dropped down and fell back to join them.

A red brick building overrun with trees stood nearby, with similar facilities off in the distance. Building H was the closest to the woods and, thankfully, the farthest from the road and its police patrols. But it was also the most overgrown—so much so that tiny trees had sprouted on the roof. Blessedly, no one was nearby.

"All right," Sister Paula said, slipping on her mask. "Let's hop to it."

Olivia and Jasmine followed suit.

"Should've done this a long time ago," Jasmine said. "Keeps my nose warm."

Olivia couldn't help but agree. She stepped into the warm sunlight, strolling past a keep out sign. Like it or not, they had no choice in coming here. And, given her newfound abilities, sending anyone else in would be irresponsible.

"Forgive us our trespasses," her godmother said, stopping by another sign at the entrance.

No Trespassing: Violators Will Be Prosecuted.
DANGER: Do Not Enter. Risk of Collapse.

"Creepy," Jasmine said, peering into a broken window lined with scorch marks.

"Yeah..." Olivia nodded, imagining all the people this place had housed. Those who'd slept in the halls when it had gone beyond capacity. Everyone who'd missed out on the arts and rehabilitation programs. Who'd been forced onto pills and into solitary when budget cuts set in. The ones who'd been *assaulted.*

"Well," Jasmine began, eyeing the dusty window sill, "I don't fancy climbing through."

"Me neither," Sister Paula said, examining the beefy chain padlocked around the door. "Can you get us in?"

Olivia frowned, feeling around with her powers. The walls had lead paint, but the door didn't.

"I think so," she said, grabbing Jasmine's wrist and trying to take her into her song. The tall girl was a lot bigger than the rock she'd experimented with at the bus stop, but their harmonies melded nonetheless. They passed through with ease.

Jasmine shivered and shook frost from her Afro. "That was *cold*."

"Really?" Olivia asked with a smirk. "I thought it was pretty easy."

The tall girl laughed, and Olivia reached outside to bring Sister Paula in.

The nun wiped her shoes off, staring at their icy outlines on the door. "Good to see you're putting the gifts He gave you to good use."

"Yeah. *B and E*," Jasmine said, crossing her arms. "We're off to a great start."

"C'mon," Olivia grumbled beneath her mask, motioning for them to follow.

In contrast to Hawthorn Center's white blankness, a riot of infernal color lined Northville's graffitied halls, and rubble blanketed the floor, rendering the tiles too dirty to reflect the crumbling ceiling above. But sparse portions of ungraffitied walls were smooth and shiny enough to gleam in the dusty air.

Those big, cream-colored bricks looked innocent enough, but no amount of spray paint could cover up the dead feeling she got, or rather *didn't* get, from the original coat of paint. Lead felt so wrong.

The tall girl ducked under a rectangular lighting fixture hanging by a thread. "Epic," she muttered beneath her mask.

Sister Paula stopped to stare at something, and Olivia turned. *Evidence-Based Practice and Innovation Center*, the badly defaced sign had originally said. But now it featured a creepy, weeping beast composed of twisted veins. Under all those layers of graffiti were the remnants of a sprayed-on skeletal clown.

Olivia gasped. "That looks like the one at Zedd's!"

The nun nodded.

"*Jesters*," Jasmine hissed.

"Jesters?" Olivia asked.

"They think vandalism and violence is funny, so they go around terrorizing people."

Sister Paula shook her head and looked around. "Always a shame when youths give in to their worst impulses."

"Yeah," Jasmine said, glancing at a room whose door hadn't been rusted shut. "And they're not the only gang that's been through here."

Light shone through a poorly painted window like sinister stained glass, made all the more disturbing by its subject matter.

"Those cards are the mark of the Tarot Cult," Jasmine said.

Olivia stared up at the tall girl with a raised eyebrow.

"Voodoo exiles from New Orleans," she said.

The nun frowned. "Have you run into them before?"

The corner of Jasmine's lip twitched. "Gangsters killed my mom's roommate the day I was born, so I got a different middle name instead of a godmother..."

Olivia lowered her head. "That's horrible." She couldn't imagine life without Sister Paula.

"Yeah," the tall girl mumbled. "And before that, another group ended my pop's ball career before it even began....Let's just say he's got an obsessive streak. Pored over all this stuff..."

Sister Paula nodded. "Know thine enemy."

"Exactly," Jasmine said. "Dove back into it when we moved. Wouldn't stop going on about it."

"Hmm," Olivia mumbled, hoping they wouldn't run into any creepy clowns, cops, or cultists. "We should keep going."

The other two nodded and followed, keeping up with ease.

"Not fair," Olivia muttered beneath her mask, glaring at the tall girl's long legs.

"Says the chick that can walk through walls," Jasmine snorted.

"Unless they've got lead paint," the nun added.

"Which is *all* of them around here," Olivia grumbled.

"Fair point," Jasmine replied. "Say, these colored doors—"

"Lead."

The tall girl nodded, sticking her hands in her hoodie. "Well, at least most of 'em have been forced open."

Hearing and feeling Sister Paula's footsteps go silent, they looked at one another and turned.

"What's up?" the senior asked.

"These motifs," the nun replied.

Jasmine shrugged, and Olivia followed her over, deftly avoiding broken glass by the guard enclosure. They studied a creepy mural of a beast riddled with red veins and weeping *blood*. It was just like the figure down the hall.

"Miss Jackson, does this mean anything to you?"

"No....I don't think it's a gang thing..." she said, looking around nervously.

Olivia shifted uneasily in the rubble, spotting more and more of the Blood Beast impressions. "They're all in different art styles. *Lots* of people drew this."

Sister Paula frowned. "All of these markings, most of them satanic clichés, profanities, gang signs, or one-offs..."

"But this one repeats," Jasmine began, "layer after layer..."

"There has to be a reason," Olivia whispered, giving voice to what they all feared.

Sister Paula shook her head, adjusting her habit. "I suggest we tread lightly and pray we don't run into anyone or any*thing*."

Olivia and Jasmine nodded, creeping forward. They searched for stairs with their heads on a swivel. But the courtyard outside held no dangers. Just dying trees and a multitude of milk jugs hiding under fallen leaves.

Taking out her telescope, Olivia peered into the adjacent wing, spying rusty refrigerators packed in tighter than the art supplied she'd crammed into her pack. Jasmine stopped beside her, and Olivia passed her the telescope.

"Must be where those jugs came from," the tall girl whispered, handing it back.

"Yeah," Olivia said, hurrying to catch up with her godmother. They turned the corner and found a pair of stairs at either end of the new hall.

"Hope the room's on this side," Jasmine muttered, peering down the central corridor and the collapsed ceiling blocking off the other half.

Olivia nodded, hoping the same.

"There's probably a sign with room numbers," Sister Paula said, trying to find and decipher directions hidden beneath vandalism.

They searched high and low but only found obscenities and helpful messages like *you won't make it out alive* and *don't come in here I will kill you*. Naturally, many of these had depictions of the Blood Beast nearby.

"Found it," Jasmine called.

It turned out that H266 was in the seclusion wing. The worst of the worst.

Olivia gulped, following the half-buried red line on the floor to the other stairs. She floated up to scout ahead but saw nothing in the darkened hall. Her night-vision goggles only confirmed what her powers felt: it was empty, save for a distant barricade. With all the doors closed, it was eerie just how dark the place could get. She motioned for them to follow, and she kept watch without her goggles as they climbed.

The stairs creaked under Sister Paula's footsteps, so she turned back to Jasmine. "Catch me if I fall."

The tall girl nodded, but it didn't come to that. However, when it was her turn, the stairs groaned under her weight.

"You hear that?" she asked.

"Yeah," Olivia said. "They sound like they're about to give."

Jasmine scowled. "No, not *that*. The tapping. Hear it? Tap tap. Tap tap."

Sister Paula shook her head, but Olivia felt out for the source and homed in on it. Something was hitting the window in the central corridor. She crept forward and peered around the corner.

Frosted privacy glass blurred out branches swaying in the breeze, bringing them in and out of focus when they hit the window like charred, skeletal hands in a perpetual fog.

"Just the wind," she whispered.

"Lovely," Jasmine said, stepping onto more solid ground.

Leading them down the hall with her flashlight, Olivia felt claustrophobic because of how close the doors were to one another. The rooms had to be *tiny*. She prayed she'd never be trapped in such a space.

"Need to let some light in," Jasmine said, tugging at the handles. But they were all locked.

Ahead, the barricade gleamed in their cone of light. They inched around rusty wheelchairs, bed frames, and a dusty gurney with leather restraints.

"Getting close," Olivia whispered, illuminating 252. At last, her light shined on 266.

The tall girl pulled on the door to no avail. "Lemme guess. Lead paint."

"Yep," Olivia said, trying to force her transparent hand through. But that only made their light source flicker.

She sighed, tapping the cold metal and feeling nothing but emptiness. No vibrations—just another void among all the dead space.

Jasmine scratched her head. "Any ideas?"

Olivia frowned, feeling out her options. "Guess we go through the floor. Or the ceiling."

"Right. Flight," Jasmine said. "Thank goodness you can fly."

"*Float.*"

"Close *enough*," Sister Paula whispered.

"If you say so," Olivia muttered, shining her light upward.

Drooping ceiling tiles were coming apart in layers, like two-dimensional stalactites, but, with the lighting, they looked more like teeth bearing down on them in the shadows.

She shook her head. "Floor's probably less likely to collapse if it gets weighed down by ice."

Jasmine nodded. "And if it holds, we won't have to deal with icicles dripping on us."

"You'll just need to watch your step." Sister Paula snorted. "And hope the floor doesn't give out..."

"Right..." the tall girl said, glancing at Olivia. "Can you take us both at once?"

"I'm not sure," she said, putting a hand on both of their shoulders and trying. But it was beyond her.

"I think it's a one-at-a-time thing."

"That's all right," Sister Paula said. "You two go on ahead, and pop back when you find whatever's in there."

"But—"

"Doubt we'd all fit," Jasmine said, putting a hand on Olivia's shoulder. "I mean, calling these things *rooms*'d be generous, given the lack of space—I mean room. Get it, *room*?"

Olivia groaned, and the tall girl chuckled.

"On a serious note," she said, "maybe we can get the door open from the other side. Add a bit of illumination."

Olivia frowned. "That'd be pretty bad design if the patients could get out that way."

"Fair enough," Jasmine said with a shrug.

Olivia turned to her godmother. "Here's the ligh—"

"Pft. I fear neither the dark nor what lurks within it. Now go. I await your return."

Giving in, Olivia took the tall girl into her song and through the floor. They kicked off an old piano with an ominous chord and bounded into the sealed room.

Rusty window bars, all too emblematic of the cage this cell truly was, obscured their view of a tall, brick building looming over the complex at the center of the campus.

"Cheery sight," Jasmine said, shaking frost from her fro.

"That's one way to put it," Olivia said, looking around and gasping.

"What the..." the tall girl said, eyes wide. She stretched her arms out, nearly touching both sides of the room. "Wait, is that..."

"*Blood*," Olivia said, realizing what the creepy Blood Beast depictions were drawn in. Suddenly, the etchings of helmed figures with pointy horns and axes on the bricks seemed tame by comparison.

The senior shied back from the mad scrawlings and bumped into a rusty bed frame that took up half the room. A metallic screech grated on Olivia's very being when it creaked.

"This must be what we came for," she said through gritted teeth, prying a bulging filing folder free from the rusty contraption with her powers. Frost and bits of rust rained down as she brushed it off.

Jasmine nodded slowly. "Hopefully, whoever put that together was more lucid when they—"

"Shh!" Olivia said, pressing an ear to the frigid door.

Jasmine followed suit.

"In the name of Christ, I command you to leave this place," Sister Paula said.

Olivia paled, grabbing the tall girl as they turned to one another. No, no, no! They bounced back downstairs, off the eerie piano, and into the hall. The temperature plummeted, she shook with terror, and the flashlight flickered.

Red light bathed the chamber, emanating from two weeping eyes emerging from down low, giving way to a transparent body composed of glowing veins. They pulsed with every beat of the creature's visible heart. Blood and spittle oozed from its maw, dripping onto the floor and evaporating as it ambled forward on all fours, despite Sister Paula's prayers.

Olivia's breathing accelerated, echoing off her mask and into her bones.

Jasmine stiffened at the Blood Beast's sharp teeth. "Maybe that guy wasn't so crazy after all."

Olivia gulped. She couldn't take both of them with her! She needed to defeat the creature here and now. Unable to calm her nerves or keep her form steady, she traded her flashlight for the telescope and held it like a bat.

But Sister Paula shook her head. "Olivia," she said, ceasing her chanting, "no creature under heaven or earth resembles this *thing*. And yet, it does not back down. It is no abomination from Hell, but a *man* masquerading as one. You can only take one of us—"

"No!"

"*Olivia*, take Miss Jackson and go. *Now!*"

"I can't..." Olivia wept, but Jasmine pushed her aside.

"I have a better idea." She pulled a revolver from her purse and fired. Loud shots echoed through the hall and Olivia's bones as the beast howled. But the bullets vanished on contact. And its veins glowed brighter and brighter with every hit.

Gunsmoke lingered along with everyone's misty breath, and the creature scratched at the ground with faster movements than before, tearing up tiles like a bull about to charge.

Jasmine's hands shook as she lowered the smoking gun. "I—I...I'm so sorry..."

"*Olivia*," Sister Paula said.

"I won't leave you!"

The beast snarled and charged.

Olivia screamed and ran through her godmother in an ethereal dash. She swung at a dense cluster of veins on the monster's paw and knocked it aside. It roared in retaliation, sprang off the wall, and took her through the ceiling with a crash.

She groaned, rolling into a rooftop sapling, evading its claws until she tripped. It leaped for her, but she phased into the hall. The roof gave way, and Olivia dove away from the falling debris, inadvertently letting the thing land between her and the others. It snarled, and she gasped, realizing her mistake.

"Run!" Olivia screamed, trying to close the distance, trying to distract the beast, *trying* to get it to change targets.

Her world slowed as Sister Paula turned. The abomination slashed through the nun's back, tearing through fabric, flesh, and bone. Blood froze before it could spurt.

"NO!" Olivia shrieked. She swatted at the monster, but it leaped, landing with a crouch, ready to pounce.

Sister Paula collapsed with a look of anguish.

"Oh my God!" Jasmine cried.

The creature lunged for her, but Olivia kicked off the wall and pushed the tall girl away before it could land.

"Forgive them," Sister Paula croaked, locking eyes with Olivia, "for they know not what they do."

Olivia sobbed, slipped through the floor, and bounced off a lead wall, landing with Jasmine in a rubble heap.

The tall girl groaned, forced herself to her feet, and tossed Olivia through a broken window.

The Blood Beast crashed through the ceiling and crushed the piano in a cacophony of dust and sour notes.

"Jasmine!" Olivia shrieked beneath her mask.

The monster pounced, but the tall girl was quicker. She leaped through the window, leaving the creature to crash into the frame, unable to squeeze through. It clawed at the structure, widening the gap.

"Go, go, go!" Jasmine yelled.

Olivia grabbed her, kicked off, and soared through the woods with the weightless senior in tow. The monster burst through the chained door and roared, freezing at the tree line.

Olivia wept, passing through the trees in a blur. "I'll kill you. Do you hear me? I'll kill you!"

The beast spewed mist from its nostrils in contempt and disappeared into the dark.

"Olivia," Jasmine hissed.

She felt cars ahead and went solid, landing unsteadily in the brush. Jasmine put a shaky hand on her shoulder.

"She's gone," Olivia sobbed, hugging the bulky folder. "And it's all my *fault.*"

⠈⠎ ⠯ ⠳⠇⠮⠄ ⠟⠦⠮⠄ ⠐ ⠯ ⠣⠇⠺⠄⠾ ⠟⠍ ⠾ ⠷ ⠮⠗⠌ ⠳⠄⠅⠄ ⠄⠳⠄⠍⠄⠾ ⠟⠗⠄⠅⠌⠄ ⠐ ⠶ ⠉⠇⠄⠾⠌⠃⠄⠾⠳⠄⠍⠄⠾ ⠟⠍⠄⠑⠍⠅⠾⠅⠄ ⠡⠻⠄⠾

"Deliver us from evil....Amen..." Paula sputtered, her vision slipping in and out of focus.

"Oh, Lord...help those girls..." she said, lamenting her lack of Last Rites, hoping she wouldn't linger in Purgatory for centuries. But what really mattered was the girls. She'd eventually reach salvation. But they needed to live.

"Save them...their souls....Saul's, Martha's...my killer's...my precious Ada's..." She wept. "Restore her as you did, Tobias...so long ago....Sight and status..." She coughed.

Her vision narrowed like it had when she'd endured her father's beatings. But the pain was worth it, both then and now. He'd never gotten her sister. Until he had. Paula wept, reliving the worst day of her life with her dying breaths. The time she hadn't forced herself to her feet. The time he'd hit her with a bottle.

She'd crawled on broken glass. Found her little sister dead at his hand. She'd wept, screamed. Fled the reservation in a haze. She couldn't save her. She hadn't even avenged her. She hated herself.

A foreign fisherman had picked her up. Bound up her wounds. Dropped her off at the orphanage. She'd met Saul there. Come to forgive the Church. And taken a new name to join the sisterhood. Tried to speed change from within. Tried to heal old wounds. Hers. And those between her tribes and the Church. She'd taught children. Ada. Olivia. Paula wept, remembering Ada's wedding. Olivia's baptism. Save for the priest and William, she'd been the only other soul present.

The fisherman's final words to her echoed in her mind, just as they had so many decades ago. *Rest now. You'll save another. Maybe even two. Till next we meet, Miss Kateri.* Paula smiled with tears in her eyes. Yes, they'd be safe. She could rest now. She went still, remembering the tune she'd heard so long ago.

Someone held her, humming it. Clouds flew by. Brilliant light shone above, stretching out to eternity, radiating from a man shining brighter than the sun—brighter than infinity. Light poured from his eyes and the holes in his hands along with the rest of his skin. And at his side stood a little girl welcoming her with open arms.

ᚦᛖᛋ ᛖᛏᛁᛚᛚ ᛖᚳᛟᚴᛗ

PART TWO

Interlude: Vivian's Journal

I knelt beside Bryce, helping him hold the bugle his wife gave him until he took his last breath. He kept thinking I was her. I didn't have the heart to correct him or tell him that he wasn't back home in his wife's orchard.

I surveyed the burned-out village in the dying light. We were pinned, outnumbered, and outgunned. Stranded in unfamiliar terrain. Worse, there was no way to radio for backup. And *everyone* was gravely wounded.

Kirk had lost an eye, his XO's skull had split open, and Richard's arms were so badly burned they were nothing but a mass of bubbly flesh. But worst of all, a bullet had passed through the tunnel rat's face, taking nearly all his teeth....Still, he was conscious, unlike the useless sniper. He'd shot up *mid-mission*.

Only Tyrian was still on his feet, pistol in hand. The most he could manage, since his broken arm hung uselessly in a splint he'd fashioned from the foliage. But the bone was still sticking out. His complexion was green. He wasn't shaking—probably in shock. Mother was right. I never should have come here.

Bleeding out, I weighed our odds of survival. It was tempting to take a picture of Tyrian, standing resolute over his bloodied comrades. The flash would give away our position. But the film would've been the final record of our existence. Our brief stay on earth.

My nose twitched. Among the earthy smells kicked up by the explosions and the stench of fire and burning flesh from bullet wounds, there was something else. Muck and sweat.

A rebel grabbed me through a hole in the wall before I could cry out. All I could do was stun him with the flash. Tyrian planted two shots in the guerrilla's head. That managed to rouse the sniper, so he ran off in a daze along with the rest.

The unit I'd spent the past few months embedded with broke and scattered, leaving me to fend for myself in the chaos. Gunfire erupted from all directions. Bullets whizzed by at various proximities, and the boys shouted, trading shots and war cries with the enemy.

Foreign curses hit a fever pitch, rising in the air alongside mangled bodies. People were getting thrown into the air. But there were no explosions. No landmines. No grenades. Nothing to launch them.

I peeked over the rubble, spotting a panicked donkey braying in the outskirts of the village. A glowing mass of twisted, red veins tore the animal's jaw out and beat Viet Cong soldiers with the bloody bones. Tore out their throats. Ripped them in half. I vomited as the Southern forces fell before the beast. I snapped a photo and passed out.

I woke in a field hospital alongside the bandaged men I'd come to know, chalking my memories of that night up to a nightmare. But then I had the negatives developed. I saw the beast. It was impossible to ignore the Ragnarok Unit's strange luck any longer. In that moment, I *knew*. One of the men I'd joined overseas was a demon.

Wherever they went, locals spoke of evil nghê sightings—of vengeful, tailless hồ ly tinh, and giant chó đội nón. But beneath their talk of folklore, their neighbors whispered of a far more sinister possibility. That these sightings had been of something far more terrible. Something *new*. The *chó săn máu. The Bloodhound.*

I didn't know how or what exactly was happening, but I swore to expose the demon in the Ragnarok Unit's ranks. *No matter the cost.*

ᚷᚱᚨᚠᛏᛁ ᛒᚢᛏ

CHAPTER 10: REVELATION

Olivia wandered into Zedd's in a daze and collapsed into a torn-up rotating stool by the counter, still clutching the overly stuffed folder. Her godmother was *gone*. And it was all her fault. She broke down, sobbing uncontrollably, painting the chair with frost. Her tears hit the floor as hail, and her breath lingered like a mist, stretching out through stacks of new tile and bins of damaged hair products.

"I'm so sorry," Jasmine said, wading through the foggy maze that seemed to go on for all eternity, reflected endlessly by the walls of cracked mirrors on either side of the salon.

"It's not your fault," Olivia said, looking away from the tall girl and the skeletal clown graffiti looming over them and the infinite labyrinth. "It's *mine*," she whispered.

The tall girl knelt down to look her in the eye. "Stop that right *now*. It's *not* your fault, and you *know* it."

Olivia squeezed her eyes shut. She hadn't been strong enough to save them both. Sister Paula had wanted this. She'd told her to save Jasmine. But Olivia *had* to look for a solution where there was none. She'd refused to make a choice. Disobeyed her godmother. Her dying request.

No, Sister Paula had asked for something even harder. She'd quoted Christ interceding on behalf of those crucifying him. Her former teacher wanted her to forgive the Blood Beast, or whatever man turned into it. But that person was an abomination! And how was she supposed to forgive someone who killed a *nun*? Her godmother. Her friend.

Olivia's teeth chattered until Jasmine hugged her.

"Do you think she'd want you to beat yourself up like this?"

Olivia sniffled in the warm embrace before breaking it.

"No," she said, wiping frozen tears and straightening up. "She'd want me to find whoever did this. Stop them from hurting anyone else."

The tall girl nodded and stood, but Olivia kept staring at the folder.

"You'd better be worth it," she muttered. "Man or monster, I'll *find* them."

The senior flinched, staring off at their distorted reflections. "All right," she whispered with a somber nod.

Olivia pumped up her stool and set the half-frozen folder on the counter by the computer.

"Looks like a stolen patient file for a V. Darr," Jasmine said.

"But it's not," Olivia gasped, when journal entries spilled out.

"Is that..." the tall girl began, glancing sideways at a photograph. "*Vietnam?*"

"Must be," Olivia said, flipping between paper-clipped portraits and soldier bios marked up with corrections.

"No way," she whispered, taking a closer look at images of the Blood Beast wreaking havoc on the battlefield.

Some papers hit the floor, but Jasmine scooped them up. "Looks like Darr was a journalist embedded with a unit overseas...suspected one of the soldiers of being that creature...and she was forcibly interned after repeatedly stalking vets."

Olivia looked away. "It's not fair. Being locked away for trying to stop something no one believes in."

"Yeah," Jasmine said, absentmindedly shuffling through papers. "Whoa, here are our suspects."

"Let me see," Olivia said, straining to get a better look at the men that might've murdered her godmother.

"First up's the overly redundant Commander Eric "Odin" Odenkirk," Jasmine said, setting his sheets down.

"They're reusing their call signs as aliases," Olivia mumbled.

"Yeah," the senior said. "Whoops, my bad. Darr had eyes on him during a beast sighting, so he's been cleared of suspicion."

Olivia frowned, glancing at Vivian's notes. "But that assumes there's only one of these guys..."

"You're right! We've got two specters, and now this *beast*."

"I don't see anything on ghosts," Olivia said, leafing through the documents.

"Me neither," Jasmine said, looking over her papers. "Maybe those were a later development. You see anything on simultaneous beast sightings?"

"Nope."

"All right. But the specters and the beast have to be connected. That *thing* showing up can't be a coincidence."

"Agreed," Olivia said, reading. "But was it on guard? Or did the ghosts sic it on us after I found the room number?"

Jasmine shuddered. "I *really* hope it's not the latter....But I'm kinda confident it's not, given all that graffiti."

"Good point. But the room number..." Olivia began, trying not to think about how she got that from what must have been Vivian's body. "That links them. Because the Ghost Giants killed her while she was looking into the Blood Beast, so if we can figure out who turns into the beast—"

"We *might* find the specters."

"And my mom."

Jasmine nodded, divvying up packets. "Axel "Jormungandr"— that's probably how you say it—Karsten was..."

"*Ruled out* for being in the brig during an attack," Olivia said, pointing.

"Benjamin "Baldr" Bond and Felix "Foxtrot" Traw were dismissed for the same reason," the senior said, setting them aside.

"Oh, wait, here we go. Anders "Njord" Berglin..." she said, powering up the computer.

"He look familiar?" Olivia asked, staring at his bandana and runic tattoos.

"No, but that name..." Jasmine said, doing a quick search. "Ha! He's the VP of a biker gang. *Berserkers*."

Olivia gasped at the logo, a one-eyed burning bear head. "That's the symbol on my gate!"

"Indeed," Jasmine said, scrolling through the leadership page. "Hang on a minute, their president's—"

"Commander Odenkirk," Olivia said, eyeing an old guy who had the same grim stare and eyepatch as his younger counterpart in recovery.

"Are they *all* on here?" Jasmine asked, flipping through rap sheets.

"Looks like it," Olivia said, looking back and forth between the screen and the old photographs. "Hey, why'd you recognize the VP but not the president?"

"My pops never found anything on 'im. Keeps a low profile. He thinks ole Kirk here delegated publicity to Berglin," she said, typing. "Speaking of, Berglin did an interview earlier *today*."

Olivia frowned at the name on the screen while the video buffered. "What's *Njord* mean anyway?"

"Good question," Jasmine said, opening a new tab. "Ah, Norse god of the sea. Guy's *clearly* humble."

Olivia snorted. "Explains the Viking etchings in Vivian's room."

Jasmine nodded. "She'd gone crazy, but not *that* crazy."

"Yes, come on out—" a man's voice said through old speakers.

The tall girl scrubbed through the video, checking the captions. "Looks like he was promoting tomorrow's food drive and an afterparty at the club....Scumbag's trying to make them look like the good guys. Ah, this aired live when we were attacked."

"So not him," Olivia said, setting his packet aside. "Tyrian "Tyr" Hansen is up next."

The senior snorted. "Named after a one-handed god of war."

"Sounds *useful*. Anything on *him*, though?"

"Yeah, that's where we get the term *Tuesday* from."

Olivia glared at Jasmine. "I meant the *suspect*."

"I know," the senior said, flashing her a smile. "Gimme a moment....He's the club secretary and attorney....Ah, been in court since this morning. Not him."

Olivia frowned, looking for guys that hadn't been dismissed. "Harold "Heimdall" Dahl, *ex*-sniper and raging alcoholic."

"Dead," Jasmine said, pulling up an obituary. "Looks like he finally kicked the habit when he kicked the bucket....Died in a car crash a few years back under *suspicious* circumstances."

"How *suspicious*?" Olivia asked.

"Newscaster asked a detective, Kurstin Wagner, whether she thought Dahl had died under the influence or if she suspected foul play. She just said their investigation was *ongoing*."

"Hmm," Olivia said, staring at the wall of text before going back to her folder. "What about Rupert "Jerv" Ratner? Says he was a *tunnel rat*, whatever that is."

"Means he's short," Jasmine said, typing away.

"Huh?"

"Tunnel rats were specialized soldiers tiny enough to fit in Viet Cong tunnels. But the passages were too narrow to afford them much gear."

"Which means...?" Olivia asked, hoping for something other than a continued textbook recitation.

"Guys usually went in with a pistol and a knife. Sometimes shirtless due to the humidity."

Olivia scrunched up her face, imagining fighting in those conditions without the aid of a bulletproof vest or a rifle. "That's...disturbing."

"Agreed," Jasmine said, shaking her head at the disappointing search results for Jerv. "But it gets worse. See, they got to decide if they wanted to wear a gas mask or leave it behind and be defenseless against gas traps."

"Why on earth would they even consider that?"

"Because it was too cramped to put it on down there, and wearing it made it hard to see stuff or hear ambushes. You know, increasing your odds of *death*."

Olivia shook her head. Based on her experience with the lead-rated respirator's foggy lenses, that checked out. But not having any protection from poison gas...that was a horrible choice. Just like how Sister Paula had told her to choose Jasmine...

The tall girl growled at the screen. "There's nothing on him. All I can find is that his nickname's Norwegian for *Wolverine*."

"Why doesn't he just go by that?" Olivia groaned, staring at a picture of the tiny creature lashing out at a bear.

Jasmine shrugged. "Who knows? They all seem *real* proud of their heritage. Bunch of racist sacks of—" She held her tongue, smiling sheepishly at Olivia.

Olivia's eyes widened, and she hurriedly shuffled through the old photos. Units were supposed to be desegregated in Vietnam, but all the men she saw were White—not that they had any control over that, though, in the modern-day photo on screen, all of the new faces were White as well. And Jasmine seemed convinced they were racist. Was it really that obvious? "Are they really—"

The tall girl nodded slowly. "Lotta gangs are divided along racial lines. So there's nothing special about these guys in that regard."

"I see..." Olivia said, feeling a tremor in her hands. She couldn't stand stupidity or bullies. And racists were *both*. They were so *irrational*. So *hateful*. They made everyone's lives *worse*. At best, they annoyed innocent people, and at worst, they killed them and made everyone else look—

"You good?" Jasmine asked, squeakily wiping moisture off the flickering monitor.

"Sorry," Olivia said, blushing at her frosty fist.

"*Anyway*," the senior began, "we can't exclude Jerv."

Olivia nodded at the old group photo. "He must be the only guy who didn't get a job in their gang."

"Yeah," Jasmine laughed, scrolling through. "Even Odenkirk's son and Dahl's ex were able to get a position....Wait, there he is! Look how tiny he looks next to—"

"Richard "Jotun" Rice," Olivia said, holding up the last rap sheet, glancing between an old army photo and the modern-day man on screen.

Jasmine whistled. "Dude's *huge*. And it looks like Jotun's a fitting name 'cause it means *giant*. But even after all these years, he's *still* jacked. Gotta be roids..."

Olivia skimmed his dossier. "Vivian says he and Jerv racked up extensive criminal records upon returning home....Charges range from aggravated assault, domestic abuse, possession of a controlled substance—"

"Yep, roids."

"—to first-, second-, and third-degree murder..."

Jasmine looked over Olivia's shoulder. "But most of those cases never go to trial due to a lack of evidence or people refusing to testify."

Olivia nodded, tapping a section marked *Witness Intimidation & Evidence Tampering*. It was circled and double-underlined on both Jotun's and Jerv's rap sheets.

Jasmine whistled at his official height. "Six and a half feet tall."

Olivia stared up at the senior. "And just how tall are *you* exactly?"

"Without hair, six-four. You?"

"Five, *flat*," she sighed. "Hope I grow soon."

"You will. Innit your mom tall?"

"Not compared to *you*."

The senior laughed, still typing. "Yeah, but that's *me*. Don't worry, you'll grow. You'll—"

"Jasmine?" Olivia glanced at the screen. She had an article on an old court case pulled up. Rice had been accused of killing his wife, Timberly Nahlia Rice, and burning down their house while their daughter was still inside. Despite overwhelming evidence, he was ultimately *not convicted* on account of the jury not finding his daughter's testimony *sufficiently compelling* on account of her age and recent blindness.

Olivia froze. Her mom's maiden name was Rice. "No, no, no..." Her burns, her blindness, her complexion—even the color of her hair and eyes matched Rice's. Olivia wept. That racist *monster* was her *grandfather*.

"I'm so sorry," Jasmine said, putting a hand on her shoulder.

Olivia stared down at broken floor tiles. There was no denying it. Even Jasmine could see it. The lights blinked overhead. These powers...had they come from exposure to the Ghost Giants, or were they genetic? Had they come from her mom? From *him*?

She stared at his photo, flickering on the screen. "The Ghost Giant was nearly seven feet tall.... "He has to be one of the Ghost Giants."

Jasmine shuddered. "I remember that specter in my house. It was taller than my pops, and he's six-eight." She stared at the photo of Rice and all the others posing by their bikes. "I just don't think boots'd make him that tall."

Olivia went transparent, sending the lights into a frenzy. "Do I look any bigger?"

The tall girl shook her head.

Olivia groaned and went solid. "Well, if he is the Ghost Giant, he grows somehow. Not that he needed to get any taller..."

"But if we assume the specters can grow, then why not this Jerv fellow? Heck, if they grow, they could be *any* of these guys!"

Olivia sighed, spinning in the receptionist's stool. "There's too much we don't know."

"Yeah, but...if they *do* grow, then aside from Rice, Jerv would be the most likely."

"How so?" Olivia asked, coming to a stop.

"Cause he's undoubtedly got short-man syndrome. Guy like that can't stand to be around taller dudes. What better way to get back at them than to be taller than all of them when he transforms?"

"Huh." If that were the case, it made sense, but, truth be told, Olivia didn't resent or envy Jasmine for her height. So clearly, not all short people felt that way. And the tall girl didn't seem convinced herself.

"But like you said," Jasmine began. "There's too much we don't know. And this Rice guy's the closest to the specters' height."

"Yeah, but how do you explain the *other* ghost?"

Jasmine stared at the keyboard, deep in thought. "Maybe we don't have to..."

"What do you mean?"

"Something's been bugging me about the way you described your parking garage scuffle."

"What?"

"You could only find your flashlight when you fell, not the knives."

"Your point?"

"You said that it grabbed you. That your vision *doubled*. But only *one* of your four hands disappeared when you touched the knives. That doesn't sound like doubled vision. And since we know that lead negates its powers—"

"You think it was the same ghost! That we were in two places at once! *Bilocation*! Just like Saint Martin de Porres!"

Jasmine blinked. "I don't know about that last part, but yeah. It sounds like you were in two places. So why not the specters? Maybe we only have one of them *and* the beast. Two suspects in total."

Olivia nodded slowly. "That could also explain why I saw the parking garage when it grabbed me at home."

"So maybe you were *bilocating* then too."

"Yeah, but we've got a lot of assumptions without anything to base them on..."

Jasmine looked at the phone. "Maybe we should call it in."

Olivia shook her head. "Are you crazy? If these things *are* human, then one of them's got my mom. They might hurt her if we go for help. And you saw the *photos*. These accounts," she said, holding up the papers. "At least one of them's got experience tearing through *soldiers*. What'll they do to *police*?"

Jasmine sighed. "Not really a fan of cops, but I wouldn't wish that on anyone. Still, your mom, your play. What do you want to do?"

Olivia frowned. "Wait...call it in!"

"Seriously? I thought you just—"

"No, gotta call my dad!"

"That's...actually a good idea," Jasmine said, watching her fly through a stack of ceiling tiles.

"Your call cannot be completed as dialed. Please hang up and try—"

Olivia tried each number three times before giving up. "I can't get through..."

The tall girl raised an eyebrow. "What's with all the numbers?"

"He's got a few cells for work."

Jasmine stared at her. "*Work*?"

"Yeah, he's a trucker."

The senior blinked.

"No network's got full coverage in Canada."

"*Oh*."

"What?"

"Nothing."

"*What?*"

"Look, for a moment, I was worried he was wrapped up in something shady."

Olivia scowled. "He's not a Berserker, if that's what you mean."

"I believe you," she said, holding up a hand.

The phone rang, and Olivia jumped.

Jasmine put a finger to her lips before answering. "Hello, Zedd's Hair Salon."

Olivia felt her dad's voice before the tall girl gave her the phone. "Dad?"

"Hey, kiddo....Why are you at a *hair salon?*"

"I—I'm with Jasmine," she said, eyes watering at what she had to tell him.

"That girl from the bus?"

"Yeah."

"Where's Paula?"

Tears welled up, and she sniffled. "Dad, she's *gone...*"

Jasmine put a hand on her shoulder, but neither that nor her dad's reassurances helped. Eventually, the senior rolled over a stool for her and held a hand out for the phone.

But Olivia shook her head with her hand over the receiver. "Thanks. But I need to do this."

The tall girl nodded and gave her a supportive smile.

"Dad," Olivia said, sitting up straighter. "We ran into a creepy beast made of glowing veins. It got her before we made it out with the evidence."

He took a deep breath. "I'm so sorry....That's terrible....How'd you escape?"

"I—I used my powers to fly us out. But I couldn't take two people," she sniffled.

"I see. But you were able to save...Jasmine?"

"Yeah," Olivia replied.

"And how'd she end up—"

"She was there at the library."

"Ah," he said. "And so she tagged along to Northville and saw the whole thing?"

"Yeah," Jasmine cut in. "I saw the beast, and your daughter rescued me."

"Okay..." he said. It was a long time before he spoke again. "This is hard, but if Paula's gone, we need to make sure that you two don't join her and that Ada doesn't suffer the same fate. It's what Paula'd want."

"I know."

"So, you said you found *evidence*?"

Olivia stared up at the busted ceiling. "Yeah, we found an old folder. It turns out that a wartime reporter was looking into the Blood Beast, and now her suspects are part of a biker gang, Berserkers."

"Son of a *gun*. That's too much of a coincidence."

"What is it?" Olivia asked, sitting on the edge of her seat as the tall girl leaned closer.

"Everything makes sense now."

"Why's that?"

"Because—the Berserkers have been trying to extort us. Ugh! I should have *seen* it!"

Jasmine stiffened. "Specters really are connected to the gang....That must've been why there was graffiti on your gate. It was a warning to pay up!"

The phone crackled. "What graffiti?"

Olivia froze. "It was a crappy version of their emblem. It showed up after you left. Dad, I'm sorry! I didn't know! I thought it was just more vandals!"

"It's not your fault," he said. "I should've told you what we were dealing with. But with everything going on your mother and I didn't want to worry you. All this time...how did I not see that your ghost and the extortion were connected?"

"There wasn't a pattern," Olivia said. "I tracked the sightings. We couldn't have known. But I should've mentioned the graffiti..."

Jasmine shook her head. "*I* should've told you what it was. Never occurred to me that you might not know, though. Or that your dad wasn't there to see it..."

"Not there to see it..." Olivia mumbled. Her eyes went wide.

"Come again?" her dad said.

"Dad! That thing we never got to the last two times we spoke—the Ghost Giant left a message on the painting! Said that it warned us and that we had two days!"

"Okay. Okay," he said. "This is good. They kidnapped her. Want us to pay up. Not that we could afford whatever they're asking..."

"Dad, it's okay—I'm going to get her back."

"Olivia, that *thing* has Paula's *blood* on its hands. I know she would've gladly given her life to keep you safe. But now she'd want us to go to the police."

"Dad, that *thing*, the Blood Beast—we have photos of it killing soldiers. What'll it do to cops? I'm the only one who can face it."

She stiffened, remembering how it had outmaneuvered her so easily, and she could *feel* Jasmine's discomfort from her reaction behind her back.

Her dad sighed. "What are you suggesting?"

"I..." What was she suggesting? "We've got two suspects for the Blood Beast, and I think one of them's the Ghost Giant."

"*The* Ghost Giant? I thought there were *two* of them."

"Long story..."

"Right now, our hunch is that the ghost's got bilocation," Jasmine chimed in.

Thanks, Olivia mouthed.

"*Okay*," the phone crackled. "So what are you two going to do? Run surveillance till I get back so I know where to go?"

Olivia turned to Jasmine, and she nodded.

"Yeah," Olivia said. "We can do that!"

"Okay. Ugh. I hate *all* of this. But I trust you, and it makes sense on paper. That said—*please*, for the love of God, *do not engage them*. Do you hear me?"

"Will do, Mr. Wade," Jasmine said. "We know how dangerous they are."

"Yeah," Olivia added. "I'll use the telescope to stay far away."

"Good....I'll try to get home sometime late tonight. I'm nearly through the worst of the storm. I love you."

Olivia's eyes watered. "Love you too. Be safe."

"You too. *Both* of you. And thank you, Jasmine."

"Happy to help, Mr. Wade."

"All right. Bye now."

The phone clicked, and the tall girl raised an eyebrow. "And just how's he supposed to deal with this when he gets back?"

"He was in the Army..." she shuddered. Just like those soldiers...

"Hey, chin up," the tall girl said. "I'm sure he's got better training than those guerrillas."

"Yeah..." Olivia said, watching her hand go transparent. "And he'll have me too."

Jasmine sighed. "In the meantime, we gotta figure out where to do a *stakeout*. This is so *not* how I imagined my day goin'," she mumbled, heading to the computer.

"*Same*," Olivia said, floating over while the senior clicked around on the Berserkers' website.

"Looks like this nightclub's their clubhouse—their local haunt," Jasmine said. "So to speak."

Olivia stared at the picture of all the gang members posing with their bikes. "Wait, that's the club by the parking garage!"

"You're right!"

Olivia pointed, hopping up and down. "And I've seen that bike before!"

"Which one?" Jasmine asked, zooming in.

"Jerv's! The antique! The army bike!"

Jasmine went slack-jawed, zooming in on a decal of a wolverine with whisker-like scars gripping a knife between its teeth. "It's certainly memorable. But you really saw *that*?"

Olivia blushed. "Actually, I don't remember the decal in particular."

Jasmine rolled her eyes.

"Come on, I was on the run!"

"Okay, okay," the senior said, holding up her hands. "Regardless, this is probably the best spot to do some scouting."

Olivia nodded. "Let's see what the other bikes look like in case they show up as well."

"Good idea."

They studied the screen, and, despite hating everything they stood for, Olivia had to appreciate their bikes. Sure, motorcycles were unsafe, but these were works of art! Odenkirk's sported twin ravens, Njord's a longship on the waves, and Hansen's a pair of wolves. But her grandfather's was arguably the most twisted, with its bloody, blackened skulls screaming in hellfire.

"Gonna be hard to miss that one," Jasmine said.

"Yeah....Ready?"

"Yeah, but lemme make a quick stop first."

Olivia followed her to the back office and watched her open a safe, feeling all the mechanisms click inside. It was a good thing thieves didn't have her powers. She even knew the contents before the door squeaked open. *Revolvers.*

"Wait, you grabbed a gun earlier! That's what took you so long!"

"Not that it helped..." Jasmine said, reloading.

Olivia's mouth twitched, but she kept her tears at bay.

"But yeah. Manager keeps a stash back here. Gave us the combination in case trouble comes knocking.

"But what if you...kill someone?"

"Rubber bullets," the senior said, squishing a tip. "Won't be lethal unless I shoot someone in the head point-blank. Still...they should've done *something* to that thing."

Olivia frowned. "I think they made it stronger."

"Yeah, like I could've known," Jasmine said, locking up and tucking the sidearm in her purse.

"Yeah," Olivia said, hanging her head.

"Hey, cheer up. We'll get 'em and bring your mom home. Deal?"

Olivia snorted. That wasn't something Jasmine could promise. Still, she smiled, for her sake. "Deal."

Saul sat in the driver's seat, and Froid handed him Park's file through the window. Now, where was the doc's résumé? Saul leafed through patient files while the Hawthorn psychologist looked around the parking lot warily, staring into the trees.

"If Anania finds out—"

"*Relax*," Saul said. "I protect my sources even more than my bottom line."

"Like a journalist?"

"*Exactly*." Whatever'd put the man at ease. Guy needed to see a shrink more than most.

"Listen..." Froid said, tapping his fingers together. "About my compensation..."

Saul snorted. And there it was. Why did people willing to bend the rules *always* have ulterior motives? Couldn't they just support the greater good pro bono, like him?

The psychologist cleared his throat. "You'll cut me in as your CI, right?"

"Yeah, sure." No, he wouldn't. This was an unsanctioned investigation. And any compensation would come directly from *his* pocket. But that'd be best, lest this guy talk to the department directly.

Froid wiped sweat from his brow. "Okay, phew. I mean, I'm taking a considerable risk here—"

"Aren't we all?" Saul muttered.

"I mean, my entire career could be in jeopardy if this ever—"

"Found it," Saul grunted. "Hey, I need to make some calls. Do you mind?"

"Oh, right! Guess I'll see you arou—"

"Yeah, thanks." Saul dialed the first number on his burner. Another thing he'd forked out cash for.

Froid turned to leave and paused mid-step. "Wait, the file—"

"Yes," Saul said, speaking to the automated phone menu. "May I speak to Doctor..." He squinted at the paper for effect. "How do you pronounce his name? Oh, her name! My bad..."

Embarrassed on his behalf, Froid wandered off.

"Excellent," Saul said with a smile. He could hang onto the file a little longer. He rolled up the window and studied the résumé. Interestingly, military service was indeed on there, but Park's record was *classified*. Saul would need to use that line in the future.

"If you know your party's extension—"

Saul entered the numbers and drove off, jamming out to the hold music.

"Hello?" a woman's voice asked.

"Yes, may I speak to Dr. Stevens? I had a question about a job candidate." Come on, buy the act.

"I'm...sorry, this isn't his extension."

Interesting. "Oh, my information must be outdated. Could you get Stevens's new number for me?"

"Um, sure. Hold on."

Saul grunted. More hold music.

"I'm sorry. I don't see him on our registry..."

Gotcha, you old fraud! "Okay, could you transfer me to records?"

"I don't—"

"I *really* need to get through five more of these before closing. Else my boss will be looking for *my* replacement."

The woman sighed. "Okay."

More hold music. Gosh, this song really sucked.

"Hello?" an older woman said.

"Yes, I'm trying to get ahold of a former employee, a Dr. Stevens. Extension number eight forty-seven."

"One moment..."

Saul waited for *many* moments *without* complementary music.

"I'm sorry, I don't have any record of a Dr. Stevens at that extension or any other."

Saul grinned. I have you now! Still, he sighed, pretending to be bummed. "Okay, thank you. Have a nice day."

"You too. G'bye now."

Saul grinned, dialing the next number. He would bet his paycheck that all the remaining calls would end similarly. The only question was, what was Park up to?

ᚹᚨᚾᛁᚱ ᛖᚳᛁᚱᛁᛏᛖ ᛟᚱ

Chapter 11: Stakeout

"Anything?" Jasmine yawned, leaning back in the driver's seat.

"Nope," Olivia replied for the umpteenth time, staring at parked bikes through her telescope. They still took up the whole sidewalk, and, as far as she could tell, they hadn't moved since she'd fled the museum. But now she recognized a few. Her grandfather'd parked by the door. Jerv's bike was next to the parking garage, and Foxtrot's was somewhere in the middle.

"Ugh, I still can't believe he has a decal of a fox killing a dog," she said.

"Well, you best believe. Because denial doesn't change *anything*," Jasmine mused, stomach rumbling.

"Sandwich?" Olivia asked, pulling two from her pack.

The senior shrugged. "Why not? Would you take an energy bar for it?"

"Sure," Olivia said, making the trade.

"Anything interesting inside?" Jasmine asked, glancing at the museum.

"Eh...everything, I guess," Olivia said, making a face at the energy bar. The senior had odd tastes.

The tall girl took a bite of the sandwich and frowned, probably thinking something similar about Olivia.

"*Everything*?" she asked. "We talking about paintings or *patrons*?"

Olivia blushed, reliving the sting of getting ditched, her later gratitude toward Harriet, and her disgust for Otto and for those guys bullying the Deaf dude. She shook her head. "Maybe both...but the paintings were less of a mixed bag."

Jasmine nodded. "I see." She set the sandwich aside and raised her energy bar like some rich person toasting at a fancy party. "Well, here's hoping things work out in the end. *Everything* included."

Olivia snorted and clinked their nutrition bars together. Jasmine was such a dork.

"Hey, we've got movement!" Olivia cried, when the club doors burst open.

As she raised the telescope, she could feel Jasmine's heart pumping, but she put it down with a sigh. "False alarm."

"Is it that pizza delivery guy?" the tall girl asked, squinting.

Olivia nodded, going back to her sandwich. They ate in silence until the senior settled back into her seat.

"So what brought you to the Cracks?" Jasmine asked between bites.

"Bad investments and Dad getting laid off," Olivia said, careful not to crumb. "You?"

"Same, though my folks didn't get laid off, per se. Their clientele just dried up."

"What'd they do?"

"Pops is a motivational speaker, and Mom's a personal trainer."

Olivia nearly choked on the remnants of her energy bar. The rich girl and her family *definitely* didn't belong in the Cracks. Then again, who did?

"We downsized to rebuild my college fund," Jasmine added, staring out into the distance.

After taking a sip from her water bottle to clear her throat, Olivia replied, "We did something similar for Mom's future meds."

She hoped her parents wouldn't sacrifice her mom's future for hers. She had to keep getting good grades and praying that their income bracket would land her a decent scholarship somewhere. Otherwise, she wouldn't be able to afford to go to college.

"*Future* meds?" Jasmine asked.

Olivia nodded, momentarily mistaking her reflection in the window for her mom's. She *had* to be okay. "We've been saving up for the immunosuppressants and steroids she'll need to prevent tissue rejection after she gets her sight back."

Olivia took a breath before adding, "We'd also need to pay for the follow-up appointments with all the specialists..."

Hopefully, her mom wouldn't be one of the 20 percent that rejected tissue regardless.

The senior blinked. "You're saying that she might be able to get her sight *back*, but you guys can't afford to *keep* it?"

"Yes. It's expensive without health insurance..."

Jasmine shook her head. "That ain't right. Your parent's employers don't offer benefits?"

"Dad can't find one that does, and Mom only gets freelancing gigs. They keep shopping around for a policy, but insurance companies keep rejecting her because of her *preexisting condition.*"

The tall girl hit the steering wheel. "How's our economy supposed to max out its talent pool if it's literally *handicapping* people?"

"Dunno," Olivia said, watching the still stationary bikes. "Dad thinks a lot of people are trapped in bad jobs because they're tied to their health care. *Hinders economic mobility* or something like that."

"Yeah....Well, with the ACA, relief should be on the way," the senior said.

"Hmm," Olivia replied. She didn't pay much attention to politics, but her dad didn't have any faith in politicians to get things done. By contrast, her mom was more charitable in her belief that those elected were simply serving a *different* constituency: *donors*, not *voters*.

"Say..." she began slowly. "You never called your parents back at Zedd's."

"Indeed, I did not. Thankfully, there's no point, seeing as they're off the grid for their anniversary. Only weekend off I get each year."

"Oh," Olivia said, wishing her dad was around as often as Jasmine's.

"'Sides, what would I tell 'em? Hey, Pop, I made a new friend, and you might think I've cracked, but trust me, she's got superpowers. And if you still think I've got it all together, I just wanted to let you and Mom know that we witnessed a murder and are tailing the people who might be responsible to find her mom. So if we disappear, blame it on the bikers!"

"It sounds kinda bad when you put it like that," Olivia replied, clinging to hope that they might be able to prevent her mom from suffering the same fate as her godmother. But it hurt so *much.*

Jasmine shifted in her seat and opened her mouth a few times before saying, "Hey, what sort of music do you like?"

Olivia shrugged. "I usually tuned into classical," she said, trying to keep her voice even.

"Hmm..." Jasmine said, pressing the volume knob.

"Scientists are calling for a geomagnetic storm—" an indistinct AM station crackled before the senior hit a preset.

The whole car shook as a deep voice came over the speakers. "You're listening to the Motown Madhouse."

Olivia frowned. Who named a radio station *that*?

"Earlier today," a female host began, "and nearly sixteen hours after the arrest of the *supposed* Exterminator, the DPD has *finally* released a statement—"

"And a photograph!" a guy interjected.

"And a photograph," the woman agreed. "And all it took was a sharp uptick in violent crime—"

"*Literally overnight*," the deep-voiced man said, causing his cohosts to burst into laughter.

"Oh, this oughta be good," Jasmine said, staring out the window.

Olivia nodded, supposing this was as good a way as any to pass the time.

The woman on air cleared her throat. "Let's see how residents reacted to their first look at the *vigilante* unmasked."

Camera flashes sounded, indicating a press conference.

"You expect us to believe that's *him*?" a voice clip of an angry woman said.

"What do you take us for?" a man cried. "You can't just dress up an anorexic guy in Kevlar and expect us to believe it's *him*."

"We tell you you can't police this community, and then you pull this? Put this on *us*? *Unbelievable*."

Olivia raised an eyebrow while the outrage continued.

"Oh, you hadn't heard they *got him*?" Jasmine asked, curling her fingers into air quotes.

Olivia frowned. "I heard that he got arrested, but that was it. The Ghost Giant broke my radio, so I didn't hear anything else."

"Oh..." the tall girl said. "Well, he's Black. But he's so scrawny he'd have trouble lifting a glass of milk, let alone a shotgun. No way he's the vigilante. Everyone thinks it's a setup."

"Hmm...then why would they say otherwise?"

Jasmine shrugged. "With all the backlash, that's a great question. Hopefully, they're trying to nab the real guy...*but* I doubt it."

The radio switched back to the female newscaster. "Lead detective Kurstin Wagner says the investigation is still *ongoing*."

"Wagner?" Olivia asked. "The detective from the Dhal case?"

"Probably a violent crime specialist," Jasmine said.

"*Ongoing*?" the deep-voiced commentator asked.

"Yeah, *right*," the guy piped in. "We all saw her. The only thing *ongoing* in her life is a continued search for her *soul* at the bottom of a cup o' joe."

Everyone on the radio laughed, but Jasmine winced. "I think anyone'd look tired on overtime, let alone if they were forced to push forward a puppet....They're usually better than this. You'll see."

"All right," Olivia said, freezing upon realizing that the tall girl had used the same excited tone her dad did when trying to tell her how awesome his favorite sci-fi characters were. And she'd used the exact same uninterested tone now as she did then. Wait! This was how her classmates reacted when she told them how cool the Lady Constance books were. Oh, no! Everyone thought she was lame!

"Aw, come on, guys," the woman on the radio said, "we haven't even got to the funny bit yet!"

The guy cleared his throat. "According to *authorities*, the name of the suspect they have in custody is..." He paused for dramatic effect. "*Vigil*."

Olivia blinked. "A vigilante named *Vigil*....Seriously?"

Jasmine frowned. "Sounds like a bad joke. But who thought that was a good idea? Guy's gotta be trolling or—"

"Next," the deep-voiced man wheezed, "they be tellin' us his last name's *Ante*."

The other guy chuckled. "You know what'd really up the *ante*? Huh, huh? See what I did there?"

It sounded like someone spit out their drink and slapped the table.

"*Shut up!*" the woman laughed, gasping for air.

But the guy continued. "Soon, we'll find they couldn't even *bother* coming up with a middle name. They'll just put down an *X* like Malcolm. Make it more *relatable—to us*."

"Now, hang on there," the woman said. "I think you're onto something. See, the police'll do that and high-five 'bout how smart they are, slipping a big-brained academic joke like that in there, thinking it'll go right over our heads. *Ex ante*, am I right, fellow grad students?"

"*Vigil X Ante*," the deep-voiced man said, mimicking a dramatic reading.

"Best name ever," the woman said.

"And *clearly* one of us," the guy concluded.

"We'll be right back after these messages," the other man said.

Jasmine was doing her best not to laugh. "C'mon. It is *kinda* funny."

Olivia gave Jasmine a pity chuckle when it dawned on her that she was desperately trying to make her laugh. To cheer her up. She nearly teared up at her kindness.

"Hey, we've got movement!" Jasmine cried.

Olivia whirled, raising her telescope as men in matching black leather jackets poured out of the club.

"Come on..." she mumbled, adjusting her grip. Where was her grandfather?

"Whaddaya see?" Jasmine asked, on the edge of her seat.

"Confirmation on short man syndrome," Olivia said.

Jerv kept pushing none too gently through the others on his way to his bike at the end of the line.

"Ugh, he's got a *rat tail*."

"*Gross*," Jasmine said. She gasped. "Whoa...I don't need a telescope to spot your grandfather."

Olivia spun, and her breath caught. He stood head and shoulders over everyone else, barking orders while adjusting a pair of red aviators.

"The dwarf and the giant," Jasmine whispered.

Olivia scowled but didn't take her eyes off her grandfather. "Dwarf at five-five? What's that make *me*?"

Her powers picked up on Jasmine's panicked reaction.

"*Petite?*" the tall girl offered.

Olivia shook her head—bad idea while looking down a telescope. Readjusting, she found everyone hopping on their bikes. Naturally, no one was wearing a helmet. Her grandfather popped a few pills and started his engine. The rest followed suit, flooding the streets with two or three per lane and no following distance. That had to be illegal.

"Here we go," Jasmine groaned, racing after them, trying not to get spotted while maintaining line of sight.

Olivia did her best to keep an eye on her grandfather at the front of the pack but couldn't see any more than a white dot amid the sea of giant one-eyed burning bear patches. Arched lettering wrapped around the tops and bottoms of the roaring beasts reading *Berserkers* and *Detroit*, respectively.

Her grandfather led the charge through a red light, and many of his fellow riders laughed obnoxiously. Meanwhile, other drivers slammed on their brakes and hammered away at their horns.

"Ugh! Why do they always put the tall guys in charge?" It didn't work out with King Saul and probably wouldn't end well here, either.

"Dunno," the tall girl said, staring down the light but not letting up on the gas. "Studies say they're more attractive."

"*Again* with the height thing?" Olivia asked, hoping the light would turn green.

"*Don't worry*," the senior said, squeezing the wheel and putting the pedal to the metal. "I think it works the other way around for us. No one's asked me out..."

Olivia shifted uneasily in her seat as the engine roared. "Hey, those guys are probably just too scared, right?" she asked, gripping the armrest. "Models are tall, aren't they?"

"Yeah, sure," Jasmine said.

The bustling intersection neared.

At last, the light turned green.

"Hallelujah," the tall girl muttered.

Olivia relaxed, but then the bikers started splitting up. "Crud!"

"Which way?" Jasmine asked, accelerating.

"Jerv and my grandfather are in different groups!"

"I can see that," the senior said, as the whole car shook into higher gear.

Olivia winced, unable to decide. Either way, they'd lose intel.

"*Olivia.*"

"Left! Go left!" she said, unable to take her eyes off her grandfather. She hoped she'd picked the right group to surveil but dreaded finding out which of the monsters he was.

Jasmine wiped sweat from her brow and looked around warily. "Keep your eyes peeled. If Jerv's group is doubling back to check for a tail, we are *screwed.*"

Olivia gulped and nodded, keeping her head on a swivel.

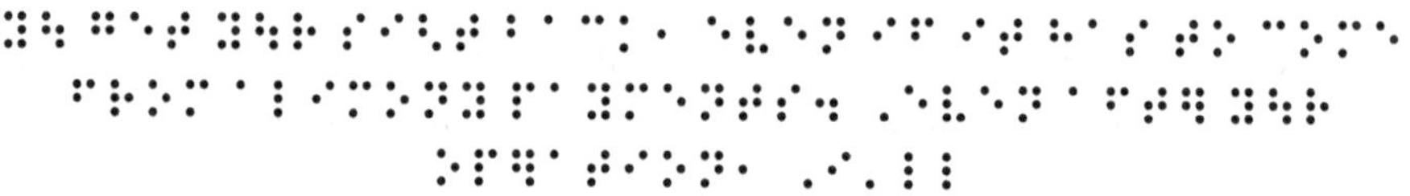

Saul sat back in his seat, pressing the cell between his shoulder and bearded cheek, listening to it ring. He took a bite of his coney[8] and got some on Park's résumé. *Whoops*. He wiped it off as best he could. But there was still a smudge. Oh, well. That was probably the most honest thing on the paper, given that *none* of Park's references existed. Either this document was a complete fabrication or—

"Hello, this is Dr. Junge."

Saul frowned. He'd thought it'd have been pronounced *young*, not *young-e*. Good thing he hadn't spoken first. "Hey, Doc, this is Detective Saul Omen of the Detroit PD."

"Oh—is everything all right, Detective Solomon?"

Saul snorted—everyone ran the syllables together. "Peachy," he said, continuing to chow down. This coney was definitely the highlight of his day.

[8] Coney: Detroit slang (derived from Coney Island) for hot dogs served with mustard, chili (beanless), and onions.

"Anyway, I just wanted to thank you for loaning Dr. Park to us on such short notice. He's been *real* helpful to our case."

"Oh, that's wonderful. He has such a way with the kids, but when your department called, I knew there was only one man for the job."

Saul nodded, hoping the Doc would expand on that. Naturally, he didn't. Expand on that—good Lord, he sounded like a shrink. Like Anania.

Saul cleared his throat. "Yeah, I was surprised myself. Initially, we were skeptical of reaching out to a child psychiatrist, but all our contacts kept pointing us in that direction."

Junge laughed. "You know, in the beginning, I, too, was a bit wary of hiring such a qualified candidate. I mean, *of course* I want the best quality care for our children, but, quite frankly, Dr. Park seemed *overqualified*. And to be blunt, I wasn't sure he'd have the best *bedside* manner. But I'm proud to admit that I couldn't have been more wrong. Everyone finds him, and his voice, quite charming."

"Yeah, I'll bet."

"Come again?"

Damn, he got some chili on his coat. "I mean, it seems like a leap of faith. He's either going to work out perfectly, or it's gonna be an unmitigated disaster."

"*Exactly.*"

Saul rolled his eyes. He'd just have to come out and say it. "So I'm just curious, what pushed you over the edge?"

"*Excuse me?*"

Saul frowned. Perhaps that was a poor choice of words, given the man's profession. "I mean, what made you pull the trigger on that initial hiring decision?"

"Oh, uh...I'd have to say I found his references quite *compelling*. They all spoke at length, vouching for just how good he was. Professionally and personally."

Saul frowned, doubting he'd get similar praise from his colleagues. But the good doctor seemed genuine—which was all he needed. "Thanks, Doc. Gotta go. Thanks again for the loan."

"My pleasure. Good—"

Saul slid his cell shut. Either that man was an expert liar, or Park really was a former or current spy who had contacts good enough to intercept calls or possibly plant agents in hospitals around the country. But which was more likely, highly competent people being competent or sloppy operatives trying to cover their tracks with a bribe?

Saul stroked his beard and leaned back in his seat, then he snapped his fingers. If Park's friends had resorted to a bribe, they probably wouldn't be smart enough to cover their tracks further. He raced back to Hawthorn Center, dialing his contact.

"Paging Dr. Froid," he said when the man picked up.

"Are you done with...you know..."

"Yeah," Saul said, rolling his eyes. He just needed to snap some pictures. Then he'd hand it right over. "Listen, I need another favor..."

"Oh...what—what is it?"

"Gonna need to take a look at last year's phone records." If Dr. Junge really had been on the phone with all Park's references, then he, Kurstin, and Johansen were up against some seriously shadowy figures.

ᛋᛉᛁᚱ �

Chapter 12: Covenant

Olivia let out a sigh of relief, and Jasmine released the steering wheel from her death grip, when the bikers stopped at a church.

"What on earth are they doing at a place of worship?" Jasmine asked, pulling into a wooded cemetery.

Olivia peered through her telescope and gasped at the adjoining building's broken windows and the absence of stained glass from the cathedral's arches. "It's abandoned."

"Huh..." Jasmine said, shutting off the vehicle.

The bikers filed in, and Olivia fidgeted in her seat. She didn't want to set foot on desanctified grounds, but.... "I want to know what they're up to."

The senior laughed. "Yeah, me too, but I like living. So I vote we stay on the sidelines. Follow when they drive off...just like we promised your pops."

Olivia turned to Jasmine with puppy-dog eyes. "But what if they've got my mom in there?"

Jasmine glared at her. "Don't give me that look!"

But Olivia didn't relent. Only her mom was able to resist such a look. Because, well...yeah.

The tall girl scowled. "S'pose it wouldn't be the *worst* place to stash someone....But we steer clear of them, got it?"

Olivia nodded.

"I mean it. We're gonna stay *far* away. Understand?"

"Yeah," Olivia said, leaning across the armrest and cupholders to hug Jasmine, bringing her into her song.

They flew through the windshield, and the tall girl groaned, looking back at the icy glass. "It's gonna take forever to scrape that off! Inside *and* out."

Olivia blushed, passing snowy trees and headstones in a blur. "My bad..."

Wait—her powers weren't cutting out in the cemetery. They worked on hallowed ground! They weren't demonic in nature! They were a gift from God! But if that were true, then why'd her grandfather have them? He was a criminal, *possibly* a racist, and, no matter which of the creatures he was, he was a murderer. It was just a matter of whether he'd killed the people in the parking garage or Sister Paula...

Jasmine shivered when they rematerialized outside the adjoining building, her hair raining down frost. "Anyone on the other side?"

Olivia turned her attention to the task at hand and touched the brick, feeling for vibrations beyond. The air was still. Or rather as still as oxygen and nitrogen molecules could be bouncing around CO_2 and dust particles. "Clear."

They slipped through the wall and flew down the corridors, hoping they'd finish searching before any bikers came through.

Weathered pencils and faded papers half-buried in rubble called out to Olivia, tugging on her heartstrings as they passed by in a blur.

"For once, I want a non-creepy abandoned building to search," Jasmine whispered, glancing at classrooms as they raced by.

Olivia nodded, flying through the ceiling at a dead end, continuing to feel out with her powers for any sign of people. But the only "person" she found was a chalkboard scribble of a nun dangling from a noose. She scowled, hoping that this sacrilege wouldn't be the fate of Spiritus Sanctus. It hurt to see a place of education and worship so thoroughly defiled. It would have broken Sister Paula's heart...

"Olivia," Jasmine whispered when they flickered solid, losing altitude.

"One...more..." Olivia groaned, phasing into the final room. She collapsed with the senior, barely canceling their momentum. And without her antigravity powers, the ancient floorboards groaned under the newfound strain.

"You all right?" the tall girl asked from between a rusty chair and a splintered desk.

Olivia nodded, trying to catch her breath. "So long as *that* thing doesn't show up," she said, pointing.

They stared at a chalkboard so overrun with a drawing of a many-eyed, sharp-toothed monster that it spilled out onto the metal frame and surrounding walls.

Jasmine's gaze lingered on it. "I've been thinking....Jerv spent years crawling around cramped tunnels. And the way the Blood Beast moved around on all fours....It's gotta be him."

Olivia nodded slowly. "Which'd make my grandfather the Ghost Giant." Somehow, that seemed preferable to him killing her godmother. But that only meant he'd broken her mom's legs. Why was her family so messed up?

"And if your grandfather's the specter, do you think he can feel distant stuff like you can?"

Olivia stiffened. She hadn't felt a basement or attic, so if her mom was here, she had to be in the church. With *him*. And if he could feel them coming... "Jasmine, if she's here, I can't just leave her....This might be our *one* chance to save her."

The tall girl sighed. "I know. But we gotta stay *far* away. We've got *no* idea how much range he's got."

Olivia frowned, shifting uneasily from toe to toe in the rubble before placing her hand on the adjoining wall. This high up, there was no one directly on the other side, but, given the cathedral's size, she had no way of knowing exactly where her grandfather and his goons were lurking.

"I have an idea," she said, "but you'll need to hold your breath."

The senior complied, and Olivia did the same before plunging them into the wall. Rather than passing through, they flew *inside* the bricks, traveling counterclockwise around the cross-shaped structure.

But Olivia couldn't feel anyone as they traced the right side of the transept. Nor was there anyone hiding or trapped inside the sacristy. And the sanctuary itself was just as devoid of life as the previous room's closets had been of altar linens, sacred vessels, and vestments. The bullet holes in the altar and ambo bore into her soul. Who shot up a church?

Heart racing, Olivia pressed on, flying through the empty baptistery to take a quick breath before tracing the wall again. Whizzing past the confessional, they wove their way to the back of the building, dodging arched window frames above and below by traveling alongside the interior wraparound balcony. Being one with the stone let Olivia feel a bit farther into the nave but still sensed no one. Nor was there a basement. It all felt as empty as the tabernacle. Aside from columns holding up what was left of the balcony, the place was barren, devoid even of pews.

Her heartbeat pulsed harder and harder, complicating her song. She was running out of air, but she could feel how weak the rear balcony timbers were. Fortunately, the bell tower was closer and sturdier. She raced up with Jasmine, past the broken stairs, and rematerialized, gasping for air as quietly as she could.

Naturally, the tall girl wasn't even winded. "That's so *creepy*," she said. "The way it feels....The lack of light."

Olivia nodded, trying to empathize and catch her breath, all the while lamenting that they would have been better off if Jasmine was the one with the powers. If only she had the tall girl's lung capacity.

"Any sign of your mom or the bikers?"

Olivia shook her head, slinking across the tiny chamber over boards that felt the least bit squeaky. Jasmine followed in her frosty footsteps to peer through a crack in the wall.

Looking down from on high, they finally got a glimpse of the Berserkers standing in the center of the transept with their backs to the shot-up altar.

"How come you didn't feel them?" Jasmine asked.

"This place is so big, and they were too quiet," Olivia said, pulling out her telescope. "If there's no sound waves for me to feel, I can't sense them. Besides, we were flying through *rock*. It's really hard to feel through when you're speeding by."

"Gotcha," Jasmine said, peering out of the corner of the window. "I count eight bikes, but only five inside."

Olivia frowned, pressing a hand to the wall and concentrating. Blessedly, she was more successful than she had been before, on account of ample movement. "There's one shuffling from foot to foot at the door below and another passing by."

"So they're on guard. Maybe the other's on patrol too?"

"Hopefully," Olivia said, staring down at her grandfather and his men through the telescope. Why were they just standing there? What were they waiting for?

She felt the answer before she heard or saw it. Raucous sound waves reverberated through the room, and motorcycles poured into the parking lot.

"We should get out of here," Jasmine whispered, peering out the window.

"Just because Jerv's back?" Olivia asked.

"That's not Jerv," Jasmine muttered.

Feeling Jasmine's heart rate spike, Olivia slunk over and peered through a hole in the wall. Her breath caught.

Instead of men in black leather, burly thugs in cutoff jean jackets dismounted, forming up behind a broad-shouldered, heavyset man with death in his eyes.

"Who are these guys?" Olivia whispered, staring through her telescope. Like the Berserkers, the newcomers all had diamond-shaped *1%er*[9] patches, and the big, auburn-bearded dude at the front even had the same *Sgt. at Arms* one her grandfather wore.

"Another biker gang—Wild Hunt," Jasmine whispered, tensing up as they neared.

They formed after the destruction of Poletown," she added, counting under her breath. "And right now, it's twelve to eight, and the group inside outnumbers the Berserkers more than two to one. We should play it safe and get out of here before things get—"

"If there's even a *one percent* chance they mention something about my mom, I can't afford to miss it," Olivia pleaded.

Jasmine growled, and her face passed through a range of emotions before relenting. "*Fine.*"

Olivia smiled and hugged her, but the tension in Jasmine's muscles lingered.

"Look," the tall girl sighed, "we'll stay for now, but, for the record, they're probably just here for a territory dispute."

"Why's that?" Olivia asked, feeling the Poles enter down below.

---

[9] The American Motorcycle Association once claimed that 99 percent of bikers are law-abiding citizens. Afterwards, Outlaw motorcycle clubs have referred to themselves as the 1 percent.

"Because rival gangs are meeting, but there's no one present who's got the authority to make deals. So they're probably here for a show of force."

Olivia nodded, watching the Wild Huntsmen stroll down the nave. Like the Berserkers, *Detroit* was printed on the back of their jackets, but *Wild Hunt* patches were sewn into the top. In place of the bear logo was one showing a motorcycle passing in front of a crescent moon, like a stylized bow and arrow, with tiny stars and bikes in the background.

She frowned. It was hard to tell from a distance, but the blonde beside the lead Wild Huntsman felt *different* from the others. "Who's that?"

Jasmine raised an eyebrow. "The guy that looks like a lineman is Bertholdt Merigold. He goes by Bear, and the thin dude's his half brother, Casimir Barring. Club secretary. People call him Cat, presumably because they're jerks pointing out that he's mute. You know, cat got your—"

"She's a woman," Olivia gasped.

"*What*? You *sure*?"

"*Positive*. Which is probably why she doesn't speak. Faking an appearance is one thing. But a voice—"

"If those sexist scum find out, she'll need more than nine lives....*Wait*, how can you tell that she's—"

"*Rice*," Bertholdt boomed, letting his voice echo through the Gothic ruin and off the few remaining organ pipes. "You wanna fill me in on why we came all this way?" he asked, stopping mere paces from the Berserkers.

Under the dusty rays slipping through gaps in the vaulted ceiling, his hair practically glowed like the fire in his eyes. And despite standing a full head shorter than his counterpart, he didn't seem to care that he had to crane his neck to stare the Berserker down.

Olivia watched, transfixed, as her grandfather crossed his massive arms and shook his head. "You came *all this way* so that we could invite you to a *party*," he sneered, his voice cutting through the room like ice. "A little gratitude'd go a long way."

Olivia winced. He sounded like a murderer muttering commands with a knife to his victim's throat.

"Pass," Bertholdt chuckled. "We don't associate with your kind," he said, turning to leave with the others.

"Which'd be?" Olivia's grandfather scoffed.

"Guys shaking down civvies," Bertholdt replied, continuing on his way.

"Desperate times call for desperate measures," the Berserker hissed. "And you can't *afford* to ignore *us*."

"And why's that?" Bertholdt asked, turning around and shaking his head, arms outstretched.

"Because you've fallen on hard times. Ever since you let that *cook* quit. Just before demand *spiked*."

"*Everyone's* fallen on hard times." Bertholdt laughed. "But humor me, Rice. Please, tell me how you plan to single-handedly *fix* the economy!"

The big man's lackeys laughed, but Olivia stood mesmerized as her grandfather ignored them. "For starters, we took care of the vigilante for you."

Jasmine gasped, as did the other bikers.

"But the police arrested him," Olivia whispered.

Bertholdt seemed to be thinking the same thing. "*Bull*," he spat. "If that's the case, then why's he still *breathing*?"

"*Because*," her grandfather hissed, "putting him behind bars gets him off the streets. And in case you haven't noticed, it's put the pigs through the wringer. Two birds, one stone. And as soon as he's outlived his usefulness...well, Baldr's Boys will take care of it."

Jasmine's eyes went wide. "They're planning to off him with a prison gang."

Bertholdt nodded slowly. "A clever scheme...far too clever for you. You're fortunate that we have a higher opinion of your betters. But we'll still need proof."

"And you'll have it," the giant said, ignoring Bertholdt's insult. "On one condition, though."

"Which'd be?"

"Bury the hatchet with the Grimm Guard."

Jasmine and the bikers gasped, but Olivia didn't understand. "What? What?"

"The Poles don't get along with the Germans," the senior said.

Rage spread through the Wild Huntsmen faster than paint through water, and many came close to drawing their weapons. But a mere look from Olivia's grandfather made both sides freeze.

Casimir flew into a flurry of signs.

"Dang," Jasmine said. "He—she's signing *fast*. Wish I knew what she's—"

"I *told* you this was a waste of time," Olivia translated. "Let's go before I *end* him."

The tall girl whirled. "You know ASL?"

"Yep."

Her grandfather eyed Bertholdt, and the Wild Huntsman just shook his head. "He thanks you for your hospitality, but we're out of here."

Olivia's grandfather momentarily smiled before becoming deadly serious, much as she assumed serial killers did before cutting up their victims. "Lie to me again, and that bulletproof vest *won't* save you," he hissed.

The Wild Huntsmen and Berserkers turned to one another, but none of them reached for their guns.

Olivia gasped when her grandfather signed back to Casimir, and the blood drained from the blonde's face. And, though her comrades didn't know what he'd said, it nonetheless chilled them all to the bone.

"What?" Jasmine said. "What'd he say? Uh, sign?"

Olivia gulped. "He told Casimir he'd burn her alive the next time she threatened him. But why does he know sign—"

"Now then," her grandfather said, pacing between each group, looming over them. "You're going to tell your old man that there's an opportunity to make peace. And you know that he's going to go for it. After all, it's what he did when he put your little band back together again."

Bertholdt's scowl seemed to imply that that outcome was possible.

"And then, you're going to join our alliance—"

"Like the old federation?"[10] Olivia said, translating Casimir's signs.

"Yes," her grandfather replied. "Only our alliance's bonds will be tighter. Naturally, you'll join alongside the Grimm Guard."

"Listen here, you illiterate *yooper*,"[11] Bertholdt spat. "Peace is one thing, but we will *never* work alongside the Germans."

"We're all trolls[12] here," Olivia's grandfather said through clenched teeth. "And you *will*."

"Do you have any idea what the Germans have done?" Bertholdt roared, causing bits of debris to fall from the ceiling.

"You sound like those stupid Southerners," the Berserker hissed. "You repeat the same damn thing over and over again. The Germans did this, the Germans did that. The South will rise again—well, *shut it*. Despite all the proclamations, I don't *see* any progress on *either* front. Neither of you do anything productive for your long-dead cause. But hey, at least you don't dress up in bedsheets or call yourselves dragons, wizards, and goblins. What a *joke*," he spat.

"*Wow*," Jasmine scoffed with a deadpan expression. "A man who hates the Klan. Truly an inspiration for us all."

Olivia winced, still hoping he wasn't actually racist. Not that she supposed it really mattered if he felt differently deep down. If all his actions and affiliations made him effectively as racist as Jasmine assumed him and his fellow riders to be, then what was the difference between him and *actual* bigots? Perhaps a similar rationale applied to Christianity without works? For if one lived like a nonbeliever, then what good was one's faith in the world at large?

Her grandfather stared Bertholdt down through his crimson aviators. "The Southerners don't *deserve* their reputation. But *we do*," he said, motioning to Berserkers and Wild Huntsmen alike. "We're a

---

[10] The Detroit Federation of Motorcycle Clubs was an organization created in the '70s to resolve territorial disputes between biker gangs.

[11] Michigan slang for someone who lives in the Upper Peninsula, which had the largest population of Scandinavian descent in the state at the time.

[12] Michigan slang for people who live in the Lower Peninsula, because the Upper Peninsula looks like a bridge, and trolls live under bridges in the tale of "Three Billy Goats Gruff."

different *breed* entirely. And you may *hate* the Germans. But I know who you hate *more*."

Bertholdt frowned. "The pigs?"

"No!" her grandfather said, throwing up his hands. "You're not thinking *big* enough. They're bossed around by spineless politicians who can barely run a campaign, let alone this *city*. No, the real threat's the *street gangs*. The sloppy, inconsiderate *filth* ruining our roads. The *people* whose idea of a *hit* is a *drive-by*. Shooting randomly, indiscriminately, without ever laying eyes on the target. Killing countless *civilians*. Crippling their communities!"

Bertholdt snorted. "They don't have the *balls* to face one another like men."

Jasmine and Olivia groaned. But her grandfather grinned like a murderer. "That's right," he said in a low voice. "They don't have the decency to *face* their foes one on one. They just hide behind one another's skirts like women, traveling in packs for a beat down, mowing down civilians for a single *shot* at hitting their intended target. This *collateral*, they write it off as the cost of doing *business*. See, that's the difference between them and *us*. We don't do collateral. We don't cap civvies. We aren't a bunch of *sissies*."

"Sexist and witty," Jasmine said dryly, much to Olivia's dismay.

Bertholdt crossed his arms. "They outnumber all of us sevenfold, but, without them, there'd be more than enough to stop living off table scraps."

"That's right," the Berserker said. "See, your hostility is misplaced. Sure, the Grimm Guard's a rival band, but we're all MCs.[13] Still heavy metal. But these rappers, they're a different genre entirely. So full of filth and simple beats it sounds like animal grunts."

"And there it is..." Jasmine said, popping her knuckles.

Olivia held her head, wishing that her grandfather just didn't like hip hop. But that animal beats part....There was no denying it. He *was* racist.

---

[13] Motorcycle Clubs, not to be confused with Master of Ceremonies (a term for rappers).

"Remember the real issues," he continued. "The ones that'll dog us today and tomorrow. Not the problems of the past. We MCs need to band together. Stand against the street gangs. So join us—Berserkers and Grimm Guard."

Olivia's powers picked up the tension in Jasmine's muscles all too well, so she put a hand on the tall girl's shoulder.

"I just wish they'd wipe each other all out," Jasmine said. "No more gangs, White or Black, bikers, or *otherwise*."

Olivia nodded, and so did Bertholdt. "Keep your friends close and your enemies closer..." he said. "The Grimm Guard are heretics, but the heathens are the real problem. A different *breed*. A kind that kills their own."

"*Exactly*," Olivia's grandfather said, contempt clear on his face. "Why, I remember when your father broke the hitman's code. Pulled the trigger on his own benefactor after offing the target. Seized *both* their thrones. United the Hunters and Wilders. Why? For money? Power? No. He did it for *peace*."

"Peace through conquest," Bertholdt said.

The Berserker nodded. "So convince him to live up to his own legacy. Help us end the bloodshed that's been spilling over into civilian casualties for so many years," he said, holding out a hand.

Olivia gulped, watching Bertholdt. Was this how fates changed? People agreeing to exchange one evil for another?

The doors flew open downstairs, and a short man sauntered in with six thugs at his side. "Which of you screwups got followed?" Jerv asked, twirling a switchblade.

Jasmine tensed, and Olivia paled. Was he talking about *them*? And if he was the Blood Beast, could he smell them? No....If they were mistaken and he was the Ghost Giant, then he was definitely close enough to feel them the way Olivia picked up on his metal teeth.

"What are you talking about?" her grandfather asked.

"There's a car in the cemetery," Jerv said.

"*Olivia*," Jasmine whispered.

"It's a *cemetery*," Bertholdt growled. "People *visit*."

"Hold on," Olivia said, feeling like she was missing something completely obvious.

"Then where are they?" Jerv asked, pointing a switchblade about. "Nowhere to be found....And yet, if they turned tail and ran, why didn't they drive off in a hurry?"

The bikers all went quiet.

"Permission to go and check if the engine's still warm, *sir*," Jerv spat.

"Olivia, we need to go *now*," Jasmine said.

Olivia nodded, unable to take her eyes off her grandfather and Jerv....She hadn't felt a gun on Jerv when he walked in. Just a pair of knives. But her grandfather...

"*Imbecile*," he growled, unholstering a pistol. "Fan out and find them!"

"My grandfather has a gun, but Jerv *doesn't*," she gasped.

"To arms!" Bertholdt roared, brandishing his sawed-off.

"C'mon, get your head in the game," Jasmine said, grabbing her as the bikers surged forward. "We gotta *go*."

"Jerv's the Ghost Giant," Olivia whispered. "And my grandfather....He's the...*beast*. He *killed* her."

"Olivia, now or never," the senior hissed. "If we don't—"

"Deep breath," Olivia said, taking the tall girl into her song and torpedoing through the wall, burrowing into the earth. This was all her fault! If she hadn't been so entranced by her grandfather—if she'd just left when Jasmine had asked earlier—Jerv would *never* have found the car. If there was any chance of them getting it out of there before the bikers traced it back to them, they had to take it.

Fortunately, Olivia didn't feel anyone around as they flew underneath the wooded cemetery, but—underground, she screamed, flying to the surface, gasping for air.

"What? What is it?" Jasmine whispered, looking around in wide-eyed panic.

"There's something *down* there!" Olivia shivered, hugging herself. "It *moved*. It—"

Something struck her, knocking her to the snowy ground.

"Olivia!" Jasmine cried, before getting hurled into a tree. She bounced off and hit the roots before rolling into a headstone. Groaning, the tall girl was barely able to force herself to stand.

"Jasmine!" Olivia called, struggling to her feet, desperately searching and feeling out for their assailant. Whatever it was sent her flying. She cried out and canceled her momentum, barely able to catch her breath, floating mere inches from the stone wall.

"What's *happening*?" the senior said unevenly, drawing her revolver and pointing it every which way. The weapon spun from her hands seconds before she joined it in hitting the ground.

"I don't know!" Olivia shrieked, desperately feeling out with her powers and watching for footprints in the frost. "I don't feel any—"

Tires screeched in the distance, and bikers cursed as police cars descended on the church.

She barely felt the next attack coming. "Invisible Man!" Olivia cried, trying to evade its barely perceptible strikes. She tried to match its song, but it was too erratic, too unpredictable for her to mimic and pass through. The creature knocked her into a headstone. Disoriented, she hit her arm before harmonizing with the rock to phase through. But her unseen foe kept coming.

"Forgive me," she said, shattering the tombstone. Rock, dust, and frost raced forward, but the Invisible Man backed off, vanishing entirely before debris could outline its form. But how? Olivia couldn't sense it at *all*.

She crept toward Jasmine, whispering, "I can only feel it when it gets close."

"*Great*," the tall girl hissed, pointing to misshapen footprints, waiting for more to appear.

They crouched there tensely, back to back, in search of any sign of movement. They flinched whenever the wind blew, assailing them with the cops' and bikers' shouts from the parking lot. They had to get out of here! But each time they tried, the Invisible Man knocked them down, harder and harder.

Jasmine eyed her fallen pistol, but Olivia shook her head. Faraway sirens sounded, and the tall girl dived. Struck in the gut midflight, she grunted and slammed into a cross-shaped headstone.

"Jasmine!" Olivia cried, feeling the air churn above her. She went transparent mid-somersault and felt the snow orbiting around her. And so, upon standing, she spun, going solid to fling it in every direction. Fingertips grazed the edge of the powdery cloud, and she evaded incorporeally—taking her early warning system with her, continually dodging foreseen attacks until her cloud dissipated.

The creature lunged from above, and Olivia sank into the frozen earth, realizing her mistake. One of the decomposing bodies was *moving* in its coffin. Impossible as it seemed, necromancy had been performed on sacred ground! She fled, rocketing out of the earth, to grab Jasmine. They passed through the rock wall just before *something* broke the surface.

They hit the ground running, fleeing from the Invisible Man and whatever *abomination* had risen. Tires screeched, and the stench of burning rubber filled the air before they reached the road. Jasmine jumped as a car skidded to a halt, and Olivia froze in the headlights like a deer.

The driver emerged, her dark ponytail and coat whipping about in the wind. "What are you two doing?" she snapped, keeping her gun pointed at the ground.

Olivia's eyes went wide when she saw the badge on the woman's belt. A cop! *Crud*!

"Nothing!" Jasmine stammered, while Olivia felt out for any sign of their pursuers.

She hoped and prayed the Invisible Man's camouflage was compensating for not being bulletproof.

The officer eyed the shouting match taking place in the parking lot. "You two know anything about that?"

They shook their heads, getting frost everywhere and blushing.

"*Uh-huh*," the woman said, rolling her dark green eyes.

Olivia looked down at her boots but couldn't think of anything to say. How were they supposed to get out of this?

"Never mind," the woman sighed, holstering her gun. "Are you two all right?"

"Yeah," Jasmine said, forcing a nod.

The officer took a deep breath. "Look, it isn't safe here. I'm taking you two back to school."

Olivia stiffened. They needed to be in the field, finding her mom! "But—"

"No buts, or I start asking questions. Are we clear?"

Olivia winced and nodded. They'd been caught running for their lives under suspicious circumstances, near two bands of known criminals, so this random act of kindness (and blatant violation of protocol) was probably the best they could hope for without further questioning.

The lady gestured toward the back seat, and Jasmine opened the door, taking one last, worried look at the woods as Olivia clambered in.

Crud, they'd left the car *and* the gun! But between the officer, the Invisible Man, and whatever *else* was lurking in those woods, it wasn't safe for them to go back. They'd just have to hope and pray that the cops would be the ones that found the evidence they'd left behind. Not the bikers.

Jasmine squeezed in the back and pulled up her knees. "Could you—"

"Yeah," the officer said, adjusting the passenger seat to give the tall girl more legroom. "Buckle up."

They complied, and the woman checked her rearview before heading out.

"Listen, two of the most dangerous gangs in the state were parked out there. You two weren't here. You saw nothing. You know nothing. *Understand*?"

"Yes, ma'am," Jasmine said.

Olivia simply nodded, gripping the creases of her fatigues as she would the folds of her skirts. With all the tracks they'd left, the odds of no one finding out they were here were *zero*.

"Good," the woman said, exchanging waves with a passing police car blaring its sirens at full blast.

Why were loud sounds so *painful*?

The cop handed Jasmine a business card. "If you remember *anything*, you call *me* at that number. No one else. Got it?"

The tall girl nodded while Olivia's mind raced. Why was this woman helping them? Did she suspect that the bikers had cops on their payroll? Could they even trust her?

"Now," the officer yawned. "Where to?"

Olivia and Jasmine inhaled sharply. Neither of them had planned on going to school today. And by now they'd be lucky to make it back for last period.

"Plymouth..." Jasmine said.

The woman sighed, no doubt realizing that it was a forty minute drive. "Well, I did say I'd take you. And a deal's a deal....Make yourselves comfortable."

Olivia shifted in her seat. But no matter what position she took, she couldn't get *comfortable*. She looked back at the distant church one last time, hoping the Invisible Man hadn't hitched a ride on that vehicle behind them.

But just who was their new adversary? Foxtrot? And that necromancy–how had it worked on hallowed ground? Did the Invisible Man raise people from the dead? Or did they have a Necromancer on their hands too?

⠀⠀⠀⠀⠀⠀⠀⠀⠀⠀⠀⠀⠀⠀⠀⠀⠀⠀⠀⠀⠀⠀⠀⠀⠀⠀⠀⠀⠀⠀⠀⠀⠀⠀⠀⠀

Sung-Min lowered his binoculars and took the battery out of his burner while police poured in, continuing to search the bikers for contraband. One call. An anonymous tip. That's all it had taken to preoccupy Subject A and the rest.

Had there been fewer armed men nearby, he would have ended things now, but preventing a bloodbath and further civilian casualties was the best he could do, given the situation. It had been presumptuous of him not to call for backup earlier, and he'd have to live with the nun's death. But grief wouldn't aid in his endeavor.

He pulled two circular drones the size of his palm from his coat and flung them into the sky like twin shuriken. The joint feed stabilized on his watch, and he double-tapped the car that Subject G and her friend were getting into, then did the same to the cemetery. One drone peeled off to follow, and the other remained stationary, high overhead, nigh invisible against the overcast sky.

When there was a break in the police cars, Sung-Min emerged from his hiding place to cross the street and slip into the woods before any officers or bikers broke off to search the area. By the time the shouting match died down, he'd already destroyed any footprints the girls or Subject A had left in the snow, retrieved the revolver, and unlocked the car.

Triple-tapping himself on the watch sent the drone overhead into a dive bomb, and its proximity to the watch caused it to land in his outstretched hand. Hot-wiring the vehicle took less than a minute. With that, he'd removed the last bit of evidence tying the girls to the scene, and he was back on the road without a trace.

ᚷᛟᛗᛖ ᚠᛏᛗ ᚷᛁᚠᛏᛏᛖ

Chapter 13: Omens Good and Ill

"What am I doing here?" Saul asked, surveying the abandoned psychiatric complex, pretending that he'd driven for quite some time instead of waiting mere minutes away at Hawthorn Center.

"Your *job*?" the young Northville officer asked.

Saul blinked. Despite Officer Kaydeem Jenkin's bow tie and glasses, he clearly *wasn't* the brains of this operation.

"Yeah, but half my department's grilling some bikers right now."

"I'm...sorry to hear that?" the rookie *said*, heading down an overgrown trail.

Saul sighed, following with his hands in his coat pockets. *Millennials.* Everything was always a question with them. The sooner he met with the kid's partner, the sooner he could get back to investigating Park.

But barring an enhanced interrogation with Dr. Junge, there was no way to tell just how big this conspiracy was. Either the doc was in on it and knew that the phone records Saul'd seen were fake, or Park really did have friends in high enough places to temporarily plant fake references around the country's top hospitals.

The competitive part of him hoped that Johansen had likewise run into a brick wall or was similarly down on her luck, but those outcomes wouldn't help Kurstin's investigation against seemingly impossible odds.

"Here we are," the rookie said, stopping by a ladder going up to the second floor of a crumbling building.

Saul glanced at the satanic graffiti inside. Stupid punks. "Seriously," he said, taking a mask from the rookie, "why am I here? Your partner seemed overly cryptic on the phone."

The kid scratched what little facial hair he had. "Oh, guess she wants me to fill you in. Residents reported hearing shouting and fireworks. We found a nun murdered inside. Given the grizzly nature of the scene, our chief wanted to spare the sisters from having to identify one of their own."

Saul scratched his beard. As much as he'd enjoy shaking down some bikers while waiting for Dr. Junge to get off work, tracking down a nun-killer would be more...*satisfying*. He donned his mask and began to climb.

"There was a cave-in between the crime scene and the stairs," Kaydeem called from below.

"Lovely," Saul grunted, squeezing into a room so tiny it'd be a miracle if any of its occupants *hadn't* gone insane. Which was probably why the prior tenant had drawn eyeballs all over the walls and tallied days like a prisoner.

Like a moth to a flame, he slipped into the narrow hall, toward the light streaming in from the giant hole above, but there were too many people packed in between him and the body to get a good look.

"Think the state'll let us use their lab, since it's literally next door?" A CSI tech laughed under his hazmat suit, stepping aside to let Saul pass.

"Detective Omen," a woman said, extending a hand. "Detective Willena Washington. We spoke over the phone."

"Pleasure to meet you," Saul said, noting subtle strands of gray that betrayed her age and marveling at her grip. Kaydeem would do well to take a page or two from her book.

"Wish it were under better circumstances," Willena said.

Saul shook his head, spotting a few shell casings glinting in the harsh tripod lighting. "Never is."

"I trust Kaydeem filled you in?" she asked, leading him through the caution tape.

"That he did. So tell me, who'd be stupid enough to—oh my God! Kateri!" he said, falling to his knees beside the ME.

"Detective!" Willena called. "Detective!"

Saul squeezed his eyes shut, unable to get Kateri's face out of his mind. At least she looked peaceful. But her blood-soaked white robes shattered the illusion.

"Legal name's Kateri Kimmerer. Goes by Sister Paula in the church," he said, head bowed.

"My condolences," Willena said, taking notes. "I take it you two were close?"

"We used to be," he said. She'd been the only one at the orphanage who hadn't hated him. He eyed the message she'd written in blood. "Luke 23:34. What does that mean?"

"Jesus said, 'Father, forgive them, for they do not know what they are doing,'" Kaydeem said, reciting from memory.

"Thanks," Saul mumbled, noting the lacerations on Kateri's back. They were too spaced apart to be real animal claws. Had to be faked. Amateurs. Her killers didn't deserve her kindness, nor she her fate.

"Do you know of anyone who'd wish to do her harm?" Willena asked, scribbling on her notepad.

"No." But that *young lady* Kateri had mentioned on the phone. She'd sounded worried. Was someone after *her*?

"All right," Willena said, tenderly putting a hand on his shoulder. "I know how difficult this must have been for you. But thank you for sparing the sisters some grief. If you need a moment to—"

"I've already said my goodbyes," Saul said, rising and striding away. There was nothing more he could do for her here. If he wanted to honor her memory, he'd have to ensure that the young lady wasn't in danger. He'd save her for Kateri. But that was something he had to do on his own. Time was of the essence, and Willena and Kaydeem would be hampered by protocol. Saul wouldn't.

"I'll contact the Sisters about funeral arrangements," Kaydeem said, holding out a hand for Saul's mask by the ladder.

"Thanks, kid," he said, handing it over and wiping the corner of his eye. Damn dust. He descended and strode back to his car on the warpath, trampling weeds underfoot while his coat billowed in the wind.

He drove to the library like a madman, letting the engine roar. Kateri wouldn't have set foot in that place without a reason. It had to be connected to that young lady.

"Hang on, kid," he said, pushing the accelerator to its limits— hoping that he wasn't already too late.

Tires screeched as he pulled into Woodward and hurried inside, crunching the remnants of salt and hailstones underfoot. Fortunately, Lady Luck was on his side. There was a nun up front.

Unless he missed his mark, it was Martha. Kateri'd never said anything bad about the woman, but it was more telling that she'd never said anything *good* about her either. He'd have to stay on his toes.

"Excuse me, Sister, you see another nun come by with a kid?"

"Humph! Sure did! Fool took pity on them–spare the rod, spoil the child's what I say."

Saul squeezed a fist below the counter until his busted knuckles nearly burst. No one called Kateri a *fool*. He'd done many things in his life, but striking a nun wouldn't be one of them. So he let the tension out, feigning relief with a deep breath.

"Wonderful, just trying to track the little *delinquents* down." She'd said *them*, after all. Were there multiple kids in trouble?

Martha grabbed the computer sign-in sheet and pointed to a name. "That brat here."

Olivia L. Wade.

Saul froze. He could've sworn he'd seen that name before. But where?

"And the Black one, Jasmine Jackson. As you can see, neither bothered to sign out."

Saul nodded. Now he had names. One of which was familiar. But why?

He glanced at the sign-in times, wagering that Olivia must've been the one Kateri had called about, due to her signing in mere minutes before she called. Interestingly, Olivia had come by earlier as well, and Jasmine had shown up between her visits.

"Do you know where they were headed?"

The nun shook her head, but a devilish grin unbefitting of her station came over her. "If I had to guess, I'd wager it was that scandalous place she had pulled up on that computer in the back. Real *satanic* looking."

Nuns weren't supposed to bet, gamble, or wager, but Saul wasn't going to bring that up. Still, her instinct had been right. "You mentioned a computer. Which one exactly?"

"The one in the *corner...*" the nun said, contempt as clear on her face as her wrinkles.

"Much obliged," Saul said, heading back.

"When you catch them, give them hell!" Martha called.

Saul chuckled, shaking his head at the strange sister. Her parents were probably big donors paying the church to keep her locked away. Seemed like a good investment on their part. This library, though....Sure, it was magnificent, but it seemed wasted on the bubbling cesspit that was Detroit. And, given how fast things were going downhill, he didn't know how much longer they'd be able to keep it open.

Luckily, the lights just needed to stay on long enough for him to pull the browser history. He sat down and frowned. *History. Patient history*! Yahtzee!

Cycling through snapshots of Park's file on his cell, Saul squinted, zooming in. It was grainy, but there she was. *Olivia Linda Wade*. Kid'd been a patient of Park's. Surely, it was a coincidence. But this *much* of a coincidence? Was Park *brainwashing* kids? *Blackmailing* them? Did he have Kateri killed?

Saul peered into the monitor's reflective glass to see if any bookworms were watching. Were Park's people *onto* him? Had he tipped them off? Was Kateri's death a warning? If it was, they wouldn't live long enough to regret it. And if this *was* Park's doing, this line of investigation would certainly be faster than stalking Junge.

Checking Internet Explorer's[14] history, Saul came up short, but he hit the jackpot with Firefox. Plenty of results—from both of Olivia's visits. Yes, she'd been looking into Northville Psychiatric, but her prior session had a ton of strange stuff ranging from rain to trains.

He didn't know what to think of that, but he didn't need to piece it together, because he had her final query: an address for an abandoned

---

[14] An extinct internet browser that once held the majority of market share despite being the least secure. In the end, it was responsible for vast amounts of human suffering by forcing developers to write bloated, outdated code, thereby slowing down the internet for the entire human race (at the time of publication, this "honor" now belongs to Safari).

parking garage in the heart of *biker country*. *Berserker* territory. Right around the area where he'd lost Park. Had Park met with Olivia there? Was the former spy really his prime suspect?

But how did Miss Jackson fit into this? Saul typed in a frenzy, uncertain of what he'd find without access to juvie records. He whistled–he wouldn't have found anything even if he had them.

Girl's stats were nearly as good as her grades, which was saying something. Admittedly, given her age, she'd likely been held back for a competitive advantage. But clearly, she'd put in the work, and that gamble had paid off, as she was primed for dual academic and athletic scholarships. A promising center if ever there was one. He'd put his money on her if she ever made it to the WNBA.

As for Olivia, Kateri usually gravitated towards goody two-shoes, and the search results proved that young Miss Wade was no exception. Her name appeared in the paper for honor rolls and perfect church attendance every quarter until eighth grade. Saul frowned until he saw the dates for seventh grade and freshman year. *Consecutive years.* She'd skipped a grade.

"Little prodigy," he chuckled, pushing the keyboard tray in and staring up at the high ceiling.

Impressive kids. The kind Park's people might've recruited one day. But would they really use minors in the field? It was hard to say what Olivia had gone through before, during, or after her hospitalization.

Actually, it wasn't. Saul checked the pixelated images on his phone. No criminal record...admitted for seeing a ghost...schizophrenia diagnosis: *negative*, 그러나 주제 D에 대한 우리의 관찰을 고려할 때 나는 아니오로 기울고 있습니다.

"Well played, Park. Well played..." he said. Even with translation sites, there was no way he could type those characters. Best move on to the parking garage before his luck ran out.

Saul hurried back to his car as quickly as he could in a fancy library. Even if he had a warrant, getting footage from the biker's club would've been impossible. But Saul was betting that he could talk his way into looking at a nearby establishment's tapes. He parked by a camera with the perfect angle and entered a museum, ignoring what passed for *art* these days.

"Hello," the receptionist—Ms. Maykov, according to her name tag—said in a Russian accent. "Are you eligible for our veterans discount?"

Saul shook his head and pulled out his badge. "Actually, I'm looking for some kids. Heard one might've come through this way. You see a short, pasty girl with green eyes and freckles?"

The woman gasped, nearly spilling her water. "As a matter of fact, I did! She was on my tour this morning! Snuck in and broke in upstairs, leading poor Peta on a rooftop chase!"

"Wow," Saul said. That didn't sound like Olivia at all. Something was definitely off here. "Mind if I take a look at the security footage?"

"Be my guest," Ms. Maykov said, leading him to a side room. "Oh, Peta–this man's here to find the girl that caused the *incident* this morning."

"Oh, thank goodness!" the round security guard said, pulling up a rolling chair and the relevant footage.

Saul grinned, happy that these Good Samaritans hadn't needed the legal system to get involved to do the right thing.

"Well, I'll leave you two to it," the receptionist said on her way out.

Peta nodded, pointing. "Here she is, entering the building. Showed up before the other kids and slipped in during the rush."

Saul frowned, watching the students funnel in. Time to establish rapport. "Sure hard to police all that chaos in the moment."

"You've no idea," Peta said, fast-forwarding. "Weekends and school tours are the worst. Why, once, we even had a boarding school tour on a weekend on *Museum Lover's Day*."

Saul nodded in a display of mock empathy. "That right? I had no idea." Honestly, he hadn't known there *was* a Museum Lover's Day.

"Yeah," Peta said, tracking Olivia through the sped-up footage. "Most people think we just sit around all day staring at screens and paintings, telling people not to touch them or reminding them to throw their food or drink away, but when something comes up, it's rough, I tell you."

Saul sighed, feeling sorry for the poor guy. Kid had no idea how easy his job was. Then again, with hedonic adaptation, or *adaptive difficulty*, as Kurstin liked to call it—what a nerd—everyone had a psychological upper bound on how good or bad things could get. Given enough time, even refugees in war-torn areas would think bombings were no more of an inconvenience than traffic.

Saul shuddered. Good lord, he was thinking like Anania....But he wouldn't call her. She'd just be *disappointed* he'd been drinking. *Again.* Things were better this way.

"Here she is slipping away with these two," Peta said, scrubbing through footage from multiple cameras.

Saul frowned. Olivia seemed even more interested in the exhibit upstairs than in the goth boy who'd ditched her for the other girl. Women had such terrible taste in men. Especially Anania. Saul shook his head. "What is this exhibit?"

"It's a Lady Constance thing," Peta said, holding up a pamphlet with a blonde in an overcoat on the front.

"A what now?"

"Bit of a supernatural detective chick-lit thing with a blend of fantasy in an alt-history Victorian Era. The stories are really well written. And the characters are pretty—pretty compelling," he said, blushing and twiddling his thumbs before looking away. "Opens tomorrow for Halloween."

Saul sighed. The boy needed to man up. Own his interests. Why, he should advertise them, for Christ's sake! Chicks'd dig a guy into this Constance crap! He'd practically be a chick magnet if he just opened up. He had a lot of *potential*. But, like the footage, Peta had a *long* way to go...

"*Say*," Saul said, frowning. "She's been looking at that display for a while now."

"Oh! Sorry! I must've bumped the pause button," he said, pressing play.

Saul grunted. Why was it that whenever he tried to see the best in people, something inevitably made him question the faith he'd placed in them?

"Wait, go back!" he said.

Peta complied with stunning reflexes, just like he had when he gave chase on a different screen.

Saul scooted closer, squinting. Olivia'd pulled out a telescope. And were those *night-vision goggles*? For the love of God, she was even *dressed* like a soldier under that old coat! Had the girl completely lost her mind? Or was Park just catering to her fantasies to use her for his own end?

"What's out that window?"

"Just the parking garage," Peta said, while footage of the girl jamming the radios played.

Whatever was going on, she still seemed to have her wits about her.

"At first," Peta began, "I thought she was scoping the garage out, but see here–she looks reluctant to go in further after hiding from me."

Saul frowned. "*Hiding*? Oh..." Peta finally lumbered on screen. Poor guy needed to get into better shape. At least his bulk made him more intimidating to rambunctious schoolchildren. But he was right. Olivia did look hesitant to venture in. "Think you're onto something."

"You—you think so?" the kid said, seemingly apprehensive about the praise, as if it would be rescinded at any moment. Boy needed confidence.

"Of course," Saul said. "Maybe you picked something up from those novels after all."

Peta blushed. "Oh, I didn't say I—oh, look, there she is! Oh, she doesn't look so good."

Saul grimaced. That was an understatement. Olivia looked *traumatized*. Something had happened in there, but she ran off camera before giving any clue as to what.

"Have anything from a different angle?"

Peta shook his head and second chin. "Afraid not. And—and we were going to file a police report, but—"

"That's okay, I'll take care of it," Saul said, shaking Peta's hand. "Firm up that grip, and hold your head high. You've done a great service today."

"Oh—oh, thank you, sir!" Peta said, following his instructions to the letter.

"Attaboy," Saul said, slapping him on the back on his way out. Might be hope for the kid yet if he could keep that up.

"Did you find what you were looking for?" Ms. Maykov asked.

Saul nodded, noting her resemblance to the attractive blonde beside her and the lack of a wedding ring on the latter's finger. Why, unless he missed his mark, she was about Peta's age and clearly as much of a Constance fan, given her T-shirt. Maybe the boy just needed a little *push* to get his life in order.

"I did indeed," Saul replied. "Peta was *spectacularly* helpful. Truly amazing. And his knowledge of the exhibits upstairs is top-notch."

"*Really?*" the younger woman said, perking up.

Saul nodded. "Praised the well-written storylines and compelling characters."

Her eyes lit up so much they almost glowed. Yep, total fangirl.

"Well, I best be off," Saul said, heading out.

"So long," Ms. Maykov called.

"Farewell!" her relative said, waving with the biggest smile.

Saul nodded to himself. "All up to you now, kid." If Kurstin could find a spouse, so could the boy.

Turning his attention to the task at hand, he crossed the street, listening to the grating sound of the distant car crusher, behind Helvete, compacting whatever the Berserkers had wanted disappeared. There was nothing to be done about that, but he hoped that the girls weren't an equally lost cause. He shook his head, sloshing through the runoff spilling out of the parking garage. Sure, it had rained, but water was pouring out like Niagara Falls.

"What on earth?" he muttered, stepping over the condemned sign. Not only had the temperature dropped, but every inch of the interior was coated in rapidly melting ice. Something fishy was going on.

Trudging up the ramps with a flashlight, Saul continued until he came across a massive pile of frozen rubble under a gaping black void. Nothing but distant ice shone up there. *"Freaky."*

"Do you have a warrant, Detective?" a familiar voice asked in an even tone.

Saul whirled, finding the dark-haired lawyer dressed in his trademark suit and glasses. Curse his luck—the runoff must've masked the man's approach.

Still, Saul grinned, trying to recover. "Ah, Tyrian. Was hoping it'd be you. Don't get the chance to talk to middle management enough these days."

In that overdressed getup, the clean-shaven Berserker looked like he belonged here even less than the ice, but Saul tried to keep his emotions in check. Grudging respect. Too much would lead to admiration as surely as too little would lead to him underestimating the man. And despite the lawyer's appearance, Saul knew this was one of the most dangerous men he'd ever met.

Tyrian shook his head. "I'd say it's a pleasure, but it never is."

"*Ha,* good old Tyrian!" Saul said half-heartedly. "Say, what's with all the ice?" he asked, sweeping an arm around.

"We had a rat problem," the lawyer said, adjusting his glasses.

"Biped or quadruped?"

The secretary just stared at him.

Saul laughed. He hadn't expected an answer. But one of these days, Tyrian would slip up. They all did in the end—everyone was only human, after all. "Say, I've got a similar problem back at my place—"

"Somehow, that doesn't surprise me."

"Funny, but do you recommend liquid nitrogen or dry ice?"

Tyrian merely checked his watch. "Detective, *why* are you *here?*"

"'Cause I heard that kid I put in the hospital cracked," he said, concealing his motives by holding out a hand.

Tyrian frowned, passing over a crisp Benjamin. "That reminds me. The *twins* came back. Guess you owe *me.*"

"*What?*" Saul scowled, digging in his wallet for enough bills to make up the difference. He was supposed to be bleeding the bikers dry, not lining their pockets. He'd have to sit on those two. Beat them down so hard they'd put the life behind them—for real this time.

"Pleasure doing business with you," Tyrian said, taking the cash. "Now I'm going to have to ask you to leave."

"Yeah, yeah," Saul said, slinking off with his hands in his coat pockets. "Shame, though. I was starting to warm up to the place."

"Detective, as much as I enjoy taking your money, might I suggest a better use of your time? A drink, perhaps. Or a woman, even. One you don't have to ever see again—because we both know how that ends for you."

"*Fuck you,*" Saul growled with a grin, squeezing his fists so hard his busted knuckles bled. "One day, Tyrian, you're going to get what's coming to you."

"Mm-hmm. Well, until then, have a nice day, *Detective.*"

Saul seethed, leaving in a fury. That manipulative *psychopath* wanted him in a blind rage because he wanted him to overlook something. But Saul wasn't going to fall for that. Even without the red flag that was Tyrian's presence, an *idiot* could see that something was up with all the ice.

Unorthodox as it was, their cleanup method would certainly dilute, destroy, and dispose of any evidence down the storm drains by the time he could get a warrant.

Saul shook his head, splashing onto the sidewalk. He still might not've known why Kateri had gone to Northville, but, clearly, Olivia had seen something she should'nt have. And that did *not* bode well for her future. The only question was, did the bikers already have her?

Saul hopped in his car and called Kurstin. "Need a favor," he said, driving off.

"Shoot."

Saul scratched his beard, unsure of how Jasmine fit into things, but went on anyway. "I think some girls are in trouble, but I've only got the address for one. I know this is really more of a Johansen thing, but can you pull one for me?"

"Sure. Who am I looking for?"

"Jasmine Jessica Jackson. Age nineteen. Probably lives in Plymouth."

"One second," Kurstin said, typing on the other end. She cursed. She never did that.

"What is it?"

"Her face....You said someone else was in danger. *Who*?"

"Olivia Linda—"

Kurstin cursed *again*, and keys jangled on the other end.

"What's going on?"

A door slammed over the speakers. "She's my *niece*! I dropped them off earlier! And school's nearly out!"

Saul hit the gas and flipped on his sirens, cursing his luck. The precinct was closer to Plymouth than to downtown, but win or lose, he still had to try.

"I'll meet you there as soon as I can!" he said. "Just focus on getting there! I'll get Johansen to call the school!"

"Thanks!"

"Godspeed."

Olivia rushed out of the locker room when the last bell rang, joining the mad dash for the exit, still toweling off her hair. She had to find Jasmine and figure out a way to get the Berserkers to lead her to her mom. And find a way to avenge Sister Paula. But so far she'd come up with *nothing*.

Despite all the commotion, a shrill wolf whistle, amplified by her powers, cut through the noise and into her very core.

"Same clothes two days in a row, Wade?" Devin called, pushing through the crowded halls. "If you want, I could show you how to shower sometime..."

Olivia suppressed a gag at his offer and cigarette breath, relieved by the frigid outdoor air. "By the look of that greasy mop on your head, you're the one who needs help," she spat.

Her tormentor went redder than his hair and nearly as bright as the bloody war paint he'd smeared on his face, along with the rest of Canton, for School Color Day. But he didn't get the hint or head back to his own building.

Olivia sighed, counting her blessings. At least he'd followed the dress code by wearing his hockey uniform instead of a revealing mismatch of clothes that no single Indian tribe had ever worn together. However, those who had adopted such attire were now plagued by goosebumps and hurrying away.

The Plymouth students passing by at the buses had much better sense, with their pilgrim outfits' higher fabric-to-skin ratio. Though Olivia wished she didn't have to see–or *feel*–how skintight the girls' cat-eared black panther costumes were.

"Salem sucks!" someone dressed as a political activist cried.

"You're going down!" a Salem athlete in witch-hunter garb called back, strolling hand in hand with a girl whose high boots weren't anywhere near tall enough to reach her scandalously short miniskirt, which everyone in their school seemed to think *witches* wore.

Olivia stared at her boots. If they hadn't had the lamest mascot of the three, the Rocks, fewer people would have jumped at the Witch Trial theme. As it was, she stuck out like a sore, green thumb in her army-brat attire, funneling into Salem High and up the short set of stairs. Posters for homecoming and voices bouncing off lockers assailed her with metallic twangs.

"So she does own green."

"*Wrong* day."

"Bialy was *livid* when he heard about her hair."

"Teacher's pet."

"Looks like we're in for another snowy Halloween."

"No! Then we won't be able to see the Northern—"

"Last chance, Wade," Devin said with a nauseating grin. "If you don't go with me to the game tonight, then no one will take you to the dance or afterparty..."

"*Hard pass*," she said, relieved to see Jasmine wading through a crowd of freshmen.

"No means no–now get lost, *twerp*," she said, scaring him off with a glare.

"Thanks," Olivia said, falling into step beside the tall girl, immensely grateful that she didn't have to keep dealing with Devin or zigzagging around everyone.

"Look," Jasmine said, clearing a path to her locker. "We need to *talk*."

"*That's* an understatement," Olivia mumbled, feeling around with her powers to make sure that no one watched her enter the combination.

"Pft," the senior said, blowing on her curls as the door squeaked open. "Don't I know—it..."

Olivia shook her head at the tiny locker mirror and the pastel rainbow streaks still marring her hair. But she froze upon feeling the tall girl's expression and something that didn't belong on the top shelf. Backing away to follow the senior's gaze, Olivia gasped at an old-timey milk bottle labeled The Coward's Way.

And that scent....It wasn't milk. It was *bleach*. Paired with the Redemption hair spray, it was clear that it was for her hair, but the surface cleaner would burn right through her scalp—scarring her for life. But the double meaning derived from the container....Her hands trembled in sync with the hall lights. Someone had broken into her locker and wanted her to kill herself!

"*Olivia*," Jasmine whispered.

Upon feeling everyone stop to stare at the flickering bulbs, she got her shaking under control before frost formed.

"Shoulda went out with me when you had the chance," Devin laughed under the buzzing lights. "Cause now you'll be drinking *alone*."

Olivia made a fist, but Jasmine stepped between them while everyone looked on.

"Listen close, you little *punk*. I'm going to call the cops, and then you're going to be arrested for attempted murder. Got it?"

"Oh, yeah?" Devin laughed. "You can't prove it was me."

Olivia snorted. "Aside from the fact that you're here, what you said, and the handwriting, you left a *fingerprint* on the *glass*," she said, feeling it from afar.

The blood drained from Devin's face, and a triumphant smile spread over Olivia's. "Now you'll never torment anyone ever again."

Devin gulped, lunging for her, but Jasmine shoved him back, slamming him into a locker.

"*Enough*," Mr. Bialy snapped. Everyone jumped, parting like the Red Sea before cowering by their lockers.

The chemist advanced with a scowl on full display between his glasses and dark goatee. Usually, his grim expression was there to catch students off guard when he cracked jokes in his classroom, but it was clear that he was out for blood today.

Olivia gulped when he stopped by Devin, hoping that he wouldn't look at them the same way he did the second-year freshman.

"What's the meaning of this?" he asked.

"Devin put bleach in my locker and left this on my doorstep," Olivia said, quickly holding out the hair spray. "I'm sure you'll find fingerprints."

Mr. Bialy turned with a slightly less stern expression and took the canister before running a hand through his long, dreamy hair and turning on Devin, letting him writhe under his gaze. "Office, *now*."

"Olivia Wade," the principal said over the PA system. "Please report to the northeast exit immediately. I repeat, Olivia Wade, please report to the northeast exit immediately."

"What *now*?" she groaned, grabbing her puffy white coat and book bag, struggling under the weight of all her textbooks and makeup assignments.

"Now *that's* an understatement," Jasmine mumbled, taking the weight from her shoulders. "Guess your dad's back."

"Go," Mr. Bialy sighed. "I'll get this *mess* straightened out. Miss Jackson, if you'll accompany me to provide your side of events..."

The tall girl nodded, and Olivia waved goodbye, clipping on her military pack while walking backwards. "Meet you back at your place?"

"Sure," Jasmine said. "Your books will be waiting for you."

⠄⠇⠌⠒⠏⠉⠞⠆⠏⠀⠆⠗⠙⠃⠲⠀⠏⠀⠎⠏⠗⠙⠒⠓⠒⠆⠗⠏⠶⠀⠈⠇⠴⠒⠏⠆⠎

Jasmine exhaled, waiting in the office beside the small girl's bookbag. She tried not to look like she was watching or enjoying Mr. Bialy yelling at Devin from inside the principal's office, but there wasn't much else to do.

"*No*, your son can't attend the dance if he's been *suspended*," the secretary said, hanging up on yet another caller and answering the next in the queue.

Having taken whatever call had led to Miss White calling Olivia away, Jasmine wished that the woman would stop keeping her in the dark as to the reason. Though, admittedly, she was probably being overly cautious after saying too much when Mr. Bialy dragged Devin in. "What is it this time? Roids again?" she'd asked.

"I don't care if you've been on hold for five minutes or half an hour," the secretary said, arguing with a peppy caller. "Nothing—"

Someone burst in and nearly collapsed on the secretary's desk, barely holding herself up.

Jasmine blinked. It was that cop who'd dropped them off! What had her business card said her name was?

"I need to pick up my niece," the woman said between breaths.

"Hang on," the secretary said, holding the phone away from her ear while the peppy caller yelled. "Name?"

"Olivia Wade. Family emergency," the woman with the ponytail panted.

Jasmine blinked, but the secretary's next words pierced her soul like nails in a coffin.

"I'm sorry, but her grandfather's already picked her up."

ᛣᛐᚩᛈᛘ ᛉᛃ

Chapter 14: Sit Down

"There you are!" a panicked security guard with a graying stache said. "Your granddad's here. Said something happened to your mother."

Olivia stiffened, going white as a sheet. That monster was *here*.

"Miss Wade..."

"I'm fine," she said, mind racing. It had to be *him*. Her dad's side wasn't in her life, and the Berserkers were the ones who'd taken her mom. If she didn't go, they might hurt her!

"Where is he?" she asked quickly.

"Right this way," the guard said, leading her to the bustling parking lot.

Olivia tried to steel her resolve, but her stomach churned at the sight of the man who'd murdered her godmother.

"Took you long enough," he said, stepping out from under a tree and rising to his full height. Salt and cinders crunched beneath his combat boots, and his dog tags shifted, clinking together with every breath and step.

Olivia's heart fluttered when her powers picked up on scar tissue hidden beneath his jacket sleeves. Like her mom's, his arms were covered in it—admittedly his scarring was far more extensive—and her skin crawled at the twisted sneer on his face.

"Hope your mom's okay," the guard said, trotting off.

"Thanks," Olivia mumbled, turning her nose up at her grandfather. He reeked of exhaust fumes and gasoline. Still, she lifted her chin to look him in the eye, but the light glinted off his sunglasses, making them shine red like the Blood Beast's.

She couldn't stop feeling the pistol tucked away in his jacket pocket. The weapon that proved he wasn't the Ghost Giant. But surely he wouldn't use it or transform in broad daylight with everyone staring.

"*Dang*," people whistled, looking up at him in passing. Car horns sounded until gawking drivers moved on, then the whole process started up again when more drivers spotted him.

"Hop on, *runt*," he said, strolling over to his bike.

"Where's my *mom*?" Olivia hissed, standing her ground.

"You're a brave one. But I won't ask twice," he said, clicking the safety off and pointing the hidden pistol at her.

Olivia froze, and something inside her *broke*. Dread, unlike anything she'd ever felt, *consumed* her, changing her world in an instant. She didn't understand how Lady Constance could stare down the barrel of a gun without flinching. Only, she did....It was because Lady Constance wasn't real.

Olivia bowed her head, feeling shame at her admiration of a fictional character, the frost beneath her boots, and how *small* she felt in her grandfather's shadow.

"*Sit*," he hissed, as if she were a disobedient dog, not his granddaughter.

"Where?" Olivia cried. "I don't see a *sidecar*!"

"On the back." He scoffed. "For a runt who skipped a grade, you're pretty *stupid*. But at least you're pretty. Gotta be one or the other, since you can't be tall and strong."

Olivia glared up at him, fighting back tears. Why did his words hurt so much? She didn't want his approval or *anything* to do with him! He was a monster!

"I *hate* you," she said, hopping on, loathing the decals of bloody, blackened skulls screaming in hellfire.

"Wonderful. Now, safety first," he said, sitting down without a helmet. The suspension groaned under his weight, and Olivia backed away, trying not to touch him, but the seat was just too tiny.

"Go on, stash your little pack of horrors on the side," he said, with a gesture of the concealed gun.

Olivia complied and donned the girly helmet covered in pink hearts and flowers that had been hanging there.

"Hope you like your present. Now, hold on *tight*."

The bike roared to life, and the whole thing *shook*. Vibrations flowed off the engine, digging into her bones, and the helmet did little to dampen the noise as they throttled out of the parking lot, racing past students, parents, and teachers in old beaters and shiny sports cars.

She tried not to cling to him, but there was nothing else to hold onto. So Olivia pressed her helmeted head into the giant patch on his back, simultaneously wanting to hide it and get as far away from it as she could.

"You're listening to the Desecration Nation station," a demonic voice said over the speakers. Her grandfather kicked it into high gear, and a death metal track blared while they raced through the streets. The screams were so harsh that the singer must've spewed up blood and profanities in equal measure.

Olivia held on for dear life at every sharp turn. Despite her grandfather's age, he'd never learned to stay within the lines. They wove through honking cars and nearly hit a pedestrian while cutting a corner at an intersection. She prayed to God and all the saints, begging for help, pleading for her life.

The city whizzed by, and she only tried to shut her eyes once, forcing them open to reduce the nausea. Unable to see over his broad shoulders to find a stable horizon without unbalancing the bike, she focused on her powers, feeling the speedometer continue to climb, knowing that if they crashed, there'd be no recovery.

She shook with terror, and then practicality, to go partially intangible. Frosty buildup burned off in the wind, streaming behind them in a trail of mist.

"Cut it out, or I'll put a bullet in your head!" her grandfather called over his shoulder.

So Olivia went solid and hunkered down, song after song, hoping that she wouldn't throw up in her helmet, that the lyrics wouldn't scar her for life, and that he wouldn't crash. For better or worse, they pulled into a retro diner before two out of the three happened.

Speedy's neon sign buzzed overhead with a sickly hum, and the *p* flickered when her grandfather parked under the striped awning. Olivia stumbled off on wobbly legs and tore off her helmet, momentarily holding it like a barf bag.

"Come along," her grandfather said, strolling by with her Indestructible pack. He flipped the *open* sign to *closed* and didn't even bother holding the door for her.

"What a *gentleman*," she muttered, stumbling past the shiny row of bikes before pushing the stiff thing open.

A rusty bell overhead greeted her along with beefy and flabby bikers with a blend of scars and tattoos, glancing over their shoulders.

Olivia looked away to avoid eye contact or tripping over missing floor tiles. But she could feel them leering down at her from atop their counter-side stools.

Since they were the only other patrons, the place felt empty, much like the backs of their jackets, since most of them lacked the complete set of patches her grandfather wore.

"Pick up the pace," he called from a booth opposite the far end of the counter.

Olivia groaned, ignoring the feeling of the thugs' weapons as she passed by. Those didn't worry her, since she had powers, but the man snickering at the end from his perch did. *Foxtrot.*

She glared at him, taking her seat in the booth nearest the redhead, across from her grandfather. She hated being penned in with the Blood Beast and, quite possibly, the Invisible Man or the Necromancer. At least she'd be able to phase out the window if it came to that, but, in the meantime, her powers forced her to endure the nauseating lights pulsing unevenly above. Dirty power felt *so* wrong.

"Cheery place," she said dryly, eying the bloodstained Lions jersey above the jukebox and feeling her grandfather going through her things.

"What are you doing?" she cried, snatching sketches from his hands and going red at the one of a shirtless guy.

"Weapons check," he said, studying her telescope, flashlight, and water bottle with careful scrutiny. "And stay away from boys. Can't have you *screwing around.* Ruining the family name."

Olivia's cheeks burned. "I would never—"

"You've got guts, coming here unarmed," he said, giving her things back. "But lay off the smokes," he said, shaking the lighter and rattling the magnesium powder within. "They'll ruin your pretty face."

"It's *camping gear,*" she hissed, sitting and feeling her pack to make sure nothing had been taken or added.

"Like the radios and goggles?" he asked.

"*Yeah.*"

"Uh-huh," he snorted, sliding them over.

Olivia belted the pack around her hips and jumped when the back door banged open. A plump middle-aged waitress skated out around the chrome counter and set down two platters full of greasy burgers; eggs, bacon, and sausage; and an assortment of French, curly, and waffle fries next to a pitcher of pop and two milkshakes with cherries on top.

"Little faster next time, Melinda," Olivia's grandfather said, making it sound more like a death threat than an idle remark.

The woman stiffened and gave Olivia a pained look of sympathy before skating off and tripping on a missing tile.

Olivia gasped and hopped up to help, only to freeze at her grandfather's icy tone.

"*Sit.*"

Reluctantly, she complied, hating the goon who muttered, "Typical women, always tripping over their own feet," as Melinda skated with a grimy cut that was sure to get infected if it wasn't cleaned right away.

"I'd eat that before it goes cold," her grandfather said, popping pills.

She eyed the tiny burger beside the small portion of fries and the fruity, carbonated drink.

"Don't worry–in my house, the man pays."

"How *chivalrous*," Olivia muttered, watching him slide *both* milkshakes next to his plate. Still, she stood on principle for only a moment, because food was food.

Blessedly, the burger tasted *way* better than Jasmine's energy bars. She devoured the kid's meal and reached for some of her grandfather's, slapping his hand away when he tried to fend her off.

"You have spirit, runt. But tread lightly," he said, slapping something tiny and metallic on the table. "Best not wear out your welcome."

Olivia blinked. It was a flattened bullet. The one from her water bottle! Had he pulled it out or—no, she couldn't have fallen through the parking garage with it on her. It must've come loose during her fight with the Ghost Giant!

The hair on the back of her neck rose when she felt Foxtrot's grin. That smugness....Was *he* the Ghost Giant, not Jerv? Just which monsters was she trapped in here with?

Her grandfather tapped the table, pointing. "You'll be taking that with your meal if you lie or refuse to answer."

Olivia paled. That would give her lead poisoning! But with her powers cut off, she'd be dead long before then.

Her grandfather cleared his throat. "Now then, what do you know about your family's *situation*?"

Olivia scowled. "Your gang—"

"*Club.*"

"*Whatever*. You've been extorting us. And now, you're holding my mom *hostage* because we didn't pay."

"Close enough."

"Is she alive?" she asked, trying to hide her nerves.

He shrugged. "Last I heard. My turn. Your powers—what can you do?"

"That's *it*?" Olivia snapped, alarmed by his indifference. "*That's* your level of concern for her wellbeing?"

"*Powers*," he hissed, tapping the bullet and downing the pitcher like it was a massive mug.

Olivia glared out the window. Dampened by the glass, she could barely feel the distant cars driving by the barren parking lot. "I can feel vibrations from a distance. Walk through things. Make them incorporeal. *Shatter* them."

Her grandfather slammed the plastic pitcher down, rattling the ice inside, and nodded, as if that was the expected answer.

"Can you project?" Foxtrot asked.

Olivia turned on him and the others down the line. "*Project*?"

"Obviously not," her grandfather snorted. "Not that it matters, since she's a girl."

Olivia whirled. "What are you talking about? And why's it matter that I'm a—"

"If that goes on the floor, you'll eat it anyway."

Olivia gasped and grabbed the bullet before it rolled off the table, gagging at a dead roach beneath her dangling boots. How'd she miss that? She shuddered, not flickering the lights because of the bullet in hand before sinking into the cushions, feeling truly powerless.

"Foxtrot," her grandfather said between bites.

The man nodded. "*Projecting*, being in two places at once—"

"You mean bilocation."

"*Whatever*. You'd probably be good at it, given that you can't even keep your head in one place."

Olivia scowled. "And just what's that supposed to mean? Why would you—"

"Isn't it obvious?" her grandfather said. "You can't even focus on a single question before asking another."

She glared at him. "And just how is me being a girl *relevant*?"

Foxtrot shook his head. "You're short and nearly as thin as an exhaust pipe. 'Bout as noisy and, given your attitude, as foul as one too."

Olivia slapped the bullet on the table and plummeted the temperature. "*Relevance?*" she hissed, letting the frost forming at her fingertips orbit around her.

Under the flickering lights, Foxtrot and his flunkies shied back, but her grandfather was clearly unphased and unimpressed.

"*Relevance,*" he muttered. "You sound like Tyrian."

"Sure do like attracting attention. Don't you?" Foxtrot laughed, trying to cover his elevated heart rate. "Guess it's only natural, you being a girl and all. You *like* it."

"You sexist sack of—"

"Fix the lights, or that goes down your throat," her grandfather said, sliding a steaming burger away from the advancing frost.

Olivia growled and snatched up the bullet, letting the floating frost drop. "Why's it matter if I'm a girl?"

"If you're in two places at once," her grandfather began, setting his hands on the table. "It means you're running at half-strength. Sure, if you were like me, you could bat someone aside one-handed throttled like that. But as you are, you wouldn't even make a dent."

"Hmm. That *actually* makes sense."

"'Course it does. Now—apparently, you can fly. Tell me about it."

Olivia frowned. She could only *float*. Push off things like astronauts in zero gravity to build up momentum and change her trajectory. But the conviction in his voice. That certainty he was right. Did he not know that she couldn't truly *fly*? Did she know something they didn't?

"I'm waiting," he said.

"Why?" she asked, ready to test her theory. Determine whether she had an advantage. "Can none of you sorry excuses for soldiers fly?"

"Ha. None of us were dishonorably discharged. No, that'd be your degenerate *father*."

Olivia flinched as if slapped. "*Liar*!"

He shook his head. "Ever wonder why he can't find jobs or keep work?"

She winced. No, it wasn't true! It couldn't be! But her heart sank, knowing it explained everything. The jobs, his admiration for the military...that distant gaze he got whenever it came up.

"Huh," her grandfather said. "Guess if you can see it, you aren't as blind as your mother."

"Oh, yeah?" Olivia cried, pounding the table and leaning on her fists to glare at him at eye level. "Well, everyone can see that you're a sexist piece of filth that killed your *wife*!"

"*Sit down*," he spat.

Olivia recoiled, shrinking back in her seat when he leaned over, mere inches from her face.

"*I* didn't kill Timberly," he hissed. "Your *mother* did."

"Liar!" Olivia cried, tears streaming down her face. "She's not a *murderer* like you!"

"Oh, but she *is*." Her grandfather laughed, cold breath hanging in the air under the intermittent lights.

Olivia tried to get her shaking under control, until she noticed the bullet. It was still in her hand. The hair on the back of her neck rose, and her breath caught. She wasn't shaking in fear. *He* was. In *anger*. "It's *you*."

"What are you talking about?" he hissed, venom clear in his voice as he leaned back in the booth.

"The lights, the cold. This talk of projecting. It's *you. You're* the Ghost Giant."

"Ghost Giant, huh?" He shook his head. "For a kid that's supposed to be so bright, you sure are slow."

"What do you—"

"*Fool girl*! Where did you *think* your powers came from? Nearly as stupid as your parents!"

"They're not—I'm not....But your gun—your bullets! Lead negates our powers!"

"*Almost* an intelligent observation," he scoffed. "But not every bullet's made of lead."

"What are they, then? Rubber?"

"Do I look like a *sissy*?" he asked, whipping out his pistol and ejecting a round from the chamber. "See, these're copper. Now, *pay attention*! You see the hole in the top? These are hollow-points. Armor piercers."

"Sounds illegal."

"They *aren't*. And they're better this way. The tip mushrooms on impact. Packs more of a punch when it flattens. Less likely to pass through the target. Less chance of collateral. They're *safer*."

Olivia shook her head. Bullets would never be *safe*. "And that red ring on the base?"

"*Extra* fun," he snorted, rechambering it before stiffly reholstering the gun.

Clearly, he was done sharing his hobby, but Olivia's eyes widened at the faintest feeling of a bandage beneath his fingerless glove. Obviously, that was for a stab wound, not a bruise like the Blood Beast would have. The clues had been there all along, if she hadn't been too distracted to see them.

"What are you grinning about?"

"Because," she said, feeling the stab wound in his shoulder pulse with what had to be pain. "You're not invincible. Men are fallible. And *you* got knifed by a *little girl*."

"Hmm. You mistake stupidity for *bravery*," he chided. "Your mother did the same. Right up until the moment she *screamed*."

"WHAT DID YOU DO?" Olivia cried, slapping the bullet down and lunging *through* the table with a sharpened pencil.

Her grandfather grabbed her one-handed, forcing her to solidify. *Every* fiber of her being screamed at the forced materialization, and she gasped in pain. He shoved the bullet in her mouth and threw her into the booth, letting the blow force it halfway down. She collapsed on the frosty table, choking, while her pencil rolled away.

"*Swallow*," he said, leering down at her.

Tears flowed freely, and fear swept over her. He'd let her suffocate.

"*No*," she sobbed. No more dead brain cells. No more helplessness.

Olivia forced herself to stand and drove a fist into her stomach by leaning over the table, careful to keep it below the sharp bone at the base of her rib cage to perform a self-Heimlich.

The thugs at the counter laughed, but her grandfather just stared while she repeated the motion. At last, the bullet went flying. She gasped for air and collapsed in her seat.

"Well done, *runt*," he said. "But your attack was childish, predictable, and ineffective. The next time you pull something like that, I'll melt the skin off your hand so that you'll remember never to raise a weapon against me ever again. Got it?"

Olivia squirmed, knowing he meant every word, but forced a brave face and threw his icy tone back at him. "*Yes*," she hissed.

"Good. Now, per my message, you have a day to pay up. But given your *interference*, we've raised the rate. Unfortunately, even with your newfound *talents*, you don't have the spine to rob a bank. So I recommend bringing the deed to that *house* you're staying in to Helvete by midnight tomorrow."

Olivia scowled. He wanted to force them out onto the streets. "And if I *refuse*?"

He shrugged. "Then we'll find some *other* way for your mom to work off your *debts*..."

Olivia balled up her fists, letting rage consume her. "You won't *touch* her," she growled.

"And why's that?"

"Because if you do, I'll *kill* you."

"That right?" he asked, setting his sunglasses aside. He stared down at her through bloodshot eyes, icy blue irises full of malice. "See now, that's funny because that's what I told my stepdad every time he *beat* us..." He squeezed his fist so hard that his knuckles popped. "But you best believe that when I grew, I put him in the *ground*."

Olivia's lip twitched. Sister Paula's dad had done the same to her, but she hadn't turned into a monster. Yet here Olivia was, threatening to kill her own grandfather against her godmother's wishes.

"You lack *resolve*," he spat.

Olivia glared up at him, unwavering, as their knuckles frosted over.

"But I *understand*," he said, breath lingering in the air. "I know what it's like to fight even though you don't stand a *ghost* of a chance," he hissed, eyes igniting.

The light overhead burst, raining sparks and glass down on the table. Foxtrot and the other goons shifted in their seats, terror evident in their racing hearts, but Olivia stared into the face of evil, undaunted. Red light poured from his eyes, thrumming in sync with the glowing veins radiating out from his eye sockets. Just like the Blood Beast's. In that moment, she *knew*.

"You're all of them. Aren't you?"

"That's right," he hissed, cold breath pouring from his mouth like a dragon's.

It was clear now that those glowing eyes belonged to both the Ghost Giant and the Blood Beast—that the Invisible Man was simply more transparent than the Beast's translucent skin. Her inability to match its song—that was just him changing his tune, like she did whenever she passed through objects. Her failure to detect it from afar —he was just fading away whenever he stopped bilocating. And that *thing* writhing in the ground—it was him, holding his breath.

"You can't fly, but you have something else, don't you?" she said, unable to see how bilocating alone could render him invisible.

He nodded. "The flickering lights, the cold—they're all a side effect of our powers. But there's always *another*. Something unique. You mess with gravity. I alter *light*," he said, dimming his eyes.

The entry bell rang.

"Can't you read?" he hissed. "Sign says closed."

"I know," laughed a familiar voice with a hint of an accent. "Place should be shut down for false advertising!"

Olivia paled. "*Rafe?*"

Tyrian "Tyr" Hansen sat, hands folded, across from three imbeciles in a drafty party barn the Grimm Guardians had deigned to make their clubhouse in this climate.

"He did *what?*" Jaeger rasped into the phone, revealing dental work even worse than Jerv's. "Blood or not, no son of mine's getting arrested for something so *stupid*! Bail him out!"

"Anything I can help with?" Tyrian asked, checking his watch and using the reflection to confirm that the thugs behind him were still holding their shotguns and hunting rifles incorrectly. If their enforcer, Braun, the so-called *Beast*, paid half as much attention to them as he did the serving girls passing by, their security would be world class.

Jaeger smashed his cell to pieces on the table, which was ridden with burn holes. "*No*," he growled, blowing smoke from his nostrils as if he were eager to uphold his street name. Blood and dirt clung to his brown leather jacket in scalelike patches.

Supposedly, the redneck prided himself on doing an *honest day's work*. But even if that were true, it was clear he didn't know how to delegate. A crucial trait for any *president*.

"*Look*," the hothead said. "Even if we were open to working with the *Poles*, what am I supposed to make of *this*? A lone *secretary* deep in the heart of my territory, without any backup? What sort of message does that send? That the Grimm Guard's not dangerous? That we'll just *roll over* when you come calling? And you're not even in uniform! Where's your vest?"

Tyrian didn't blink. He was *always* in uniform.

The Grimm Guard's leader cleared his throat, probably hacking up part of his remaining lung, waiting for him to respond. But rather than speaking when prompted, Tyrian took a moment to adjust his tie before eyeing Jaeger's broken and missing teeth and bloodshot eyes.

"We both know that my organization is...*unconventional* relative to yours. Our president is often away on *business*, and our VP has been *compartmentalized* for plausible deniability in our legitimate holdings. Which leaves me running much of the day-to-day operations. But you already know the respect we've shown you through my presence. So why, then, am I met with these *grumblings*?"

Jaeger spat on the chew-stained floor. "You're just a janitor, cleaning up the messes Rice fails to fix. And if he were a mechanic...well, I wouldn't hire him."

Tyrian said nothing. Childish taunts had never gotten a rise out of him, even in his youth. But these fools had never grown up. They were tools to be used and nothing more.

Jaeger smirked, mistaking silence for compliance, and slapped something on the table under a chapped hand caked with dried blood. "Since we're talking about things we already know, I'm sure you're aware of how much you're asking, given the *gifts* they've given us over the years—"

"Yeah," Weiss, the Wiccan, said, sitting up. "Like my—"

"Quiet!" Jaeger roared, backhanding his dandruff-covered secretary to the floor.

Tyrian eyed the fallen apple farmer's muddy prosthetics. He couldn't understand why anyone would constantly remind people that a Huntsman had burned their legs off, nor could he comprehend why the dwarf's masochistic boss had decided to pay more attention to the blood oozing from his overly dry skin rather than to checking to see if his grumpy subordinate was sufficiently cowed. *Amateurs.*

"Like I was saying," Jaeger said, pushing a pack of smokes and a bit of soot across the sorry excuse for furniture. "This is what the big man gave us last year."

"Newports," Tyrian said. "Are you really so thin-skinned?"

"Watch your mouth," Braun growled, finally looking away from the women. He flinched when his boss slammed a brick on the desk, tossing up dust and ash.

Tyrian just frowned, wondering if this was something Jaeger's idiot stepson had put through a window.

"Ever heard the Polack phrase, *Would you like to buy a brick*?" the head hick asked.

"Can't say that I have," Tyrian said, wondering what sort of multicultural lesson he'd receive from a high-school dropout.

Jaeger chuckled. "Post-war Poland had lots of rubble. Plenty of bricks. But not enough to go around," he said, rubbing his fingers together. "Especially in the *capital*."

"Warsaw saw war," Braun snickered.

The Grimm Guardians laughed, but Tyrian just sat there. Such children. He wouldn't question his boss, but he so wished that Richard had been assigned this lot so that he could have negotiated with the Wild Hunt instead.

Their leader took a long drag from his cigar before blowing smoke rings and continuing. "Anyway, *enterprising* young folks would approach anyone too well off, asking if they'd like to buy a brick."

Tyrian kept a straight face, wondering what relevance this had to their current negotiations.

"Naturally, most folks said *no*. Who wants a *brick*? Plenty on the side of the road! But that's where things got *interesting*. See, the young'uns'd strike the stingy fellow in the head with the very 'merchandise' he refused!"

Jaeger slammed a fist on the table, flinging blood all over the place. Bones showed through his overly tight skin, highlighting his heartbeat whenever his flesh lightened and darkened with each pulse of his arteries. Richard would have laughed at the pale imitation of his more menacing effect. But Tyrian just eyed the chain smoker.

"Why are you telling me this?" he asked when his phone buzzed. "Excuse me," he said, checking it. Four missed calls. *Why* had these backwater louts set up shop in an area with such spotty reception?

The lead Grimm Guardian leaned in, extinguishing his cigar on the table with a hiss. "Oh, you can go, because here's my final offer and the conclusion of my tale, all in one. After all these years, I want to *finally* return the favor. Give the big man a taste of his own medicine," he said, hefting the brick.

"If you want me to join your little *alliance*, that's my price," the Dragon said, barring his cracked and jagged fangs in a twisted grin.

ᚾᛟᚹ ᚦᛖᛋ ᚱᚨᚱᛖᚢ

Chapter 15: Sidelines

Olivia peered over the top of the booth, and Rafe lit up on spotting her.

"Oh, hey, Liv!" he said, hurrying past half the counter-side bikers before they could move.

"Don't serve your kind," a bald biker with face tats said, trying to bar his way.

"Eh, the feeling's mutual," Rafe replied, adjusting the guitar strap on his shoulder and slipping past with ease.

"These guys bothering you?" he asked, setting his hands on the frosty table.

"You should leave," Olivia mumbled, sliding her eyes toward her grandfather. Rafe had *no idea* how much danger he was in.

"Agreed," he and her grandfather said in unison. They turned to one another with a smile and a scowl, respectively.

But Rafe just laughed, turning back to Olivia. "We should go together! Come back when the place is renovated. Why, I know a place with sundaes so great you'll—"

"You talk too much," her grandfather cut in. "Make yourself useful and get the dishes," he said, scooting some over.

"Racist hellion!" Olivia growled.

He ignored her, but Rafe just kept smiling. "Oh, jolly giant—as I just explained, I don't serve your kind."

"Gotta big mouth, *Rafe*," her grandfather said, snapping his fingers.

Bikers jumped down, pulling lead pipes, knives, and chains from their jackets.

"Only my friends call me that." Rafe laughed, backing away toward the jukebox. "But you may address me as *Raphael*."

Olivia gulped. So long as none of the goons pulled a gun, dispatching them wouldn't be a problem. But if she entered the fray, her grandfather also would. And she doubted that she could protect Rafe— or even herself—from him.

"Make it quick," her grandfather hissed.

"If you insist," Rafe said, scratching the *XIII:II* tattoo on his left collarbone and plunking a coin into the jukebox.

"*Rafe*, it's ten to one," Olivia mumbled, fidgeting in her seat.

"Relax and enjoy the show," he said with a wink, selecting an old-timey tune. Tapping his foot to the beat, he rolled up his sleeves, revealing the green whale and school of fish on one arm and an old staff crossed with a tarnished trumpet playing throughout the ages on the other. But he didn't bother taking off his wrist weights or the guitar case.

Bikers looked at him in befuddlement, but he just smiled, egging them on. "Whenever you're ready."

Naturally, they rushed him.

Olivia prayed he would be okay, while she and her grandfather looked on. But Rafe just kept smiling. He was *always* smiling.

He deftly dodged Foxtrot's chain-wrapped fists, and the jukebox glass gave way to metal, exacting its revenge by cutting into the redhead's arms each time he failed to learn his lesson.

"Uno," Rafe said, pinballing the Berserker's head off what was left of the machine and watching him fall.

Olivia gasped. Did he actually stand a chance? With the narrow aisle, it was hard for more than one to face him at a time, and he didn't seem concerned in the slightest.

The tables began to turn, much like the turntable in the background, and debris scratched the spinning track into a remix while Rafe danced away from the second goon's brass knuckles. A third man lunged in with a serrated pocket knife, but Rafe redirected it into the second biker with a wince. A knee and back kick to the bikers' groins in sync with the song put them both down.

"Dos. Tres."

Olivia's eyes bulged, and her grandfather growled.

A guy with a box cutter clambered over the counter and rushed Rafe from behind while he dealt with a dude wielding a pipe. But he spun, hefting the guitar case over his shoulder to hit each of them in the face whenever he faced the other. They soon fell to an overhead blow and a baseball bat–like swing with the case.

"Quatro, cinco!"

Olivia's jaw dropped. He made it look so easy!

"Get in there!" her grandfather roared.

A berserker with a wrench charged, tripping over the same tile the waitress had, holding up his comrades' advance.

Rafe raced forward, stomping all over the downed man and twisting away from a crowbar.

"Seis," he said, landing and redirecting blows with the guitar case as if it were a quarterstaff, using the shoulder strap and handle for extra leverage. In no time, Siete and his crowbar fell with a clang.

"What on earth?" Olivia mumbled.

"The hell!" her grandfather shouted.

The track kept skipping in the background while Rafe hopped around Ocho. He choked the biker with the case, standing back to back, and somehow did a backflip with his foe in tow, sending him face-first into the ground, cracking a tile.

The madman even blocked a sheath knife with his wrist weights and took his opponent to the ground with a breakdancing headspin, knocking him out with an elbow to the temple.

"Nueve," Rafe said, doing a kip-up.

The bald guy with face tats dropped his tire iron with a clatter and ran out the door.

"Diez," Rafe said with a bow over the groaning bikers. "Quick enough for you, *señor*?"

Olivia stiffened, feeling the jukebox speakers crackle in sync with her grandfather's writhing form. He pushed the table forward, pinning her to the booth, and stood.

"Dance away from this!" he hissed, throwing a ghostly punch.

Rafe blocked it with his wrist weights and chuckled.

Olivia gasped. Of course—they were made of lead!

Her friend backhanded her grandfather before tripping him. Man and table hit the floor with a thud, and Rafe fastened his foe to the fallen furniture using a set of ankle weights.

Olivia stared, wide-eyed, and he grabbed her wrist.

"Time to go!" he said, dragging her away.

"But he's got my mom!"

Rafe paused and met her eyes.

"Get down!" Olivia cried, feeling her grandfather tear himself free and hurl the table at them. Plates fell with a clatter while she tried to bring Rafe into her song, but his weights held him more firmly than any anchor.

Thankfully, he ducked. The table flew overhead and slammed into the glass door, shattering it and spilling glass shards everywhere.

"Follow my lead," Rafe said, springing forward, jumping off tables, walls, the counter, and even the ceiling. Olivia went incorporeal and followed suit in zero G under intermittent lights.

The scratched track skipped along to its new beat when they descended on her grandfather. He threw more tables, shattering them into a hail of splinters midflight. Rafe spun, shielding himself with his guitar case, and Olivia phased through the wooden fragments, matching their songs in rapid succession. In retaliation, she blew up booths, clouding the room in a shower of stuffing.

Cracked tiles, broken plates, and food frosted over when her grandfather charged. His form blurred and slowly split into two, lashing out at both of them. Rafe hopped around groaning bikers and vaulted over the counter, but his pursuer passed right through, freezing everything.

Olivia flew through booths and tables, spraying her grandfather with wood, plastic, ceramic, and drywall. She could feel how difficult it was for him to match each material's unique song while fighting Rafe— who blocked blows with his weights and continually slid back across the icy floor under the impact of every attack.

As her assailant closed in, Olivia screamed and balled up her fist, striking with every bit of force she could muster, knowing it wouldn't be enough. But it *was*. Her grandfather grunted, flew across the room, and slammed into the wall, momentarily floating above the floor before dropping down.

"Zero-G punches," Olivia whispered, eying her frosty fist. She grinned, launching herself into the chaos, and lashed out with antigravity strikes. But each time she sent him flying, he'd vanish and slowly rematerialize, dangerously close behind her. She retaliated with her telescope bat, but each swing struck only mist when he disappeared, tiring her out.

A blow to the gut sent her through the ceiling. Breathing hurt more than crashing through gypsum, and, thankfully, she managed to match the song of wooden framing before it broke her back. Among the falling debris below, she saw icy footsteps creeping toward Rafe.

"Oh, no, you don't!" She canceled her momentum and rained down wood, drywall, and lightbulb glass. Dust outlined the Invisible Man quite plainly, giving Rafe enough time to skate away.

Shattering a rafter at the joints, Olivia dove, bringing the broken beam with her, unleashing it in a spray of splinters.

The Ghost Giant tore off the icy countertop to block the blast, while the Invisible Man lobbed stools at them. Rafe bounced off every flat surface available, delivering kicks and karate chops to his foes over downed bikers. Each figure he struck became more and more solid while its twin faded more and more.

In the chaos, Olivia eyed the fallen ankle weights and grinned. With her grandfather preoccupied, she pushed off the ceiling, canceled her momentum at the floor, and lobbed the weights at one of his many feet. They wrapped around his ankles like a bola, making him materialize in full—banishing the copy that was flanking Rafe.

Now solid, he staggered back under direct blows, falling into a booth. He kicked the weights and Rafe off with a roar. "Dodge this!" he said, rising and pressing a hand to the ceiling.

The roof came down in an instant, and the sudden shift in pressure blew out the windows. Rafe swept jagged glass from the frame with his guitar case and backflipped out. Meanwhile, Olivia, like a musician in an orchestra, kept shifting her song midair under the onslaught of debris, never once getting hit, unlike the moaning thugs now buried in the rubble.

Glowing eyes painted the dust red, and Olivia gasped. With no more ceiling and the window frame out of reach, she could only fall, hoping to kick off the table—but he grabbed her midflight.

Their songs collided, battling for control in a chaotic clash of tones. Olivia strained against the onslaught, trying to slip away while her grandfather fought to make her solid. His overpowering rhythm lost ground when Rafe forced him to split in two in order to defend himself.

Chaos reigned while her friend whipped a velcroed chain of weights around, latching onto the fallen set of weights and increasing his range farther. At last, Olivia got away, only to dodge *three* snarling Blood Beasts.

"Ugh!" she growled, swinging her telescope bat at the now-empty air. Just how many places could he be at once?

As if in answer, multitudes descended on them, becoming ever more solid when they were about to land blows and fading faster than they'd formed whenever Olivia and Rafe tried to retaliate. They fought back to back, fending off wave after wave of creatures on uneven ground blanketed with icy rubble.

Twinkling frost formed like glitter on the stirred-up dust, shining in the mist that concealed Ghost Giants. They sprang out of the swirling fog with ghostly claws alongside Blood Beasts, which leaped off what little remained of the crumbling walls and counter, jaws wide. The air began to clear as Olivia and Rafe beat back the monsters, but that only invited Invisible Men into the fray.

She felt out the hidden ones with her powers, and Rafe seamlessly slipped off his coat in the mix. He waved it around like a mad matador, churning up dust to silhouette foes. To help him out, Olivia did the same, albeit less gracefully, with her puffy coat, and she shrieked when undead hands broke through the rubble, threatening to drag them into the earth itself.

Sweat froze on her brow as she floated above their grasp, and her stamina wavered with her powers. He was trying to wear her down! Hiding a grin, Olivia flickered her form more erratically before falling to the ground, solid, pretending to be more winded than she was.

In response, intertwined skeletons with forms so unstable it looked like they were shivering formed between her and Rafe, lashing out with their many arms and jaws all jumbled together in a single, writhing mass. Olivia swung, feeling out with her powers to see which limbs were an illusion, and flinched. They were *all* real. He was in the same place multiple times! He was overlapping his ghostly forms with no blind spots!

"Rafe, look out!"

He whirled, velcroing his weighted whip around an Invisible Man sneaking up behind them. The Shivering Skeletons vanished before they could grab Olivia, and she floated there, staring in awe.

Rafe had thrown his coat over her grandfather to block his sight, and now, unencumbered by the weights, he let loose a series of rapid punches so fast that his toned arms appeared nearly as blurry as a Ghost Giant's indistinct form.

A gunshot split the air. Unlike with Jasmine's revolver, Olivia went partially solid under the sheer power of the sound and paled, barely feeling the flaming copper bullet race by. There was no way she'd ever be able to match their song at that speed! *How* in God's name had her grandfather dealt with Jasmine's shots?

Rafe tackled her out of a broken window when the pistol flashed again. Beams of light erupted from the barrel, whizzing past, and a burning stench radiated from the fiery chemical trails. Olivia and Rafe hit the ground, grunting and skidded away on his guitar case with a horrid grating sound that dug into her bones.

She groaned, feeling her grandfather step forward while the incendiary rounds sizzled in their craters. He raised his gun one-handed.

"Step away from the girl."

"*No*," Rafe said, unwavering.

"Have it your way," he said, turning his gun on the bikes.

"WAIT! STOP!" Olivia cried, feeling a gas line underneath.

But he pulled the trigger.

Rafe spun, shielding her, as a fuel tank exploded. It set off a chain reaction down the row with massive blasts, and the buried gas line ruptured, engulfing the building in flames.

Olivia tried desperately to phase, to protect him from the incoming debris, but he still had an extra weight in his pocket. Burning shrapnel flew into the guitar case, severing strings with a twang before cutting into the wood with an echoing crack. But worst of all was the sound and feeling it made when fiery fragments broke through the second layer of plastic, nailing the instrument to Rafe's back with a hiss.

But no matter how hard or fast it struck, he didn't cry out. With every hit, he just wrapped his arms around her tighter. The pink helmet bounced off the ground like a smoldering meteor before breaking apart, blackened and broken.

The odor of burnt flesh hung in the air when Rafe broke their embrace and rolled away to extinguish himself, straining as he drove debris further into his skin. The guitar and case had taken the brunt of the attack and saved his spine, but his left shoulder had been left vulnerable.

Burn holes in his scrubs revealed blackened metal sticking out among feather tattoos and charred skin. Her heart wavered at the blood and seared flesh, feeling the latter pulse with pain.

"You *monster*!" she cried, picking up a chunk of asphalt. But her grandfather had vanished from the building. The hairs on the back of her neck stood on end, and she whirled as Rafe's wounds and shrapnel frosted over.

"Get away!" she cried, shattering rock after rock as her grandfather tried to attack. Asphalt chunks exploded like shotgun blasts, and icy fragments raced out, passing through him. Distant sirens sounded.

He rematerialized inside the burning building, but her frosty, long-ranged strikes merely hissed on contact with the flames. She could feel him shifting his song to match the alien tune of fire as his red eyes burned back at her. But no matter how hard she tried, she couldn't match the erratic beat. She couldn't venture into the inferno.

"Midnight. Tomorrow," he growled, receding into the flames. "And if either of you breathe a word of this to the cops, your mother's *dead*."

Olivia fell to the ground in tears, weeping for the mom she couldn't save, the friend she couldn't protect, and the bikers she couldn't help, pinned under the rubble as the flames raged toward them. She pressed her hand to the ground, trying to feel through all the interference, but there was no trace of her grandfather. He'd left his goons for dead.

"Rafe!" she cried, feeling him shuffle forward through the pain of inflamed and punctured tissue.

"I am fine, chica. 'Tis far less severe than it looks," he said, eyeing the burning building. "You know what you need to do. I would do it myself, but—"

"I *can't*," she whispered, unable to harden her heart to condemn the wicked men to a death she couldn't save the bikers from.

"Yes. You *can*. I believe in *you*. Your grandfather stood in there, and so can you. Like Shadrach, Meshach, and Abednego, all those centuries ago."

"I don't know *how*," Olivia wept, feeling and hearing their screams as the flames advanced.

"*Focus*, chica. *Breathe*. Feel the air within your lungs, the blood coursing through your veins, the bones beneath your skin, and the ground beneath your feet. The sweat on your brow and the air *all* around you. These are but three of your four states of matter. This, you *know*."

She nodded, wiping her tears.

"But now you must go *beyond*—beyond mere solids, liquids, and gasses. Reach *out* and deep within. Feel the cardiac cells in your heart —the neurons in your brain. *Feel* the electricity within. The electricity that has *always* been there. Now, reach out to the flames and embrace the song of *plasma*! *Unleash* the sound of chaos! Let it give way to *order*. Cast off your lack of understanding and *feel*! *Dance* with the beat! Now *go*! Race through the fire unscathed!"

Olivia kicked off and felt her whole world change. She didn't understand how she did what she did, but she phased with the beat, passing through burning walls in a blur. Flames hissed on contact with frost. Scorching songs screamed as if wounded, adding further complexity to their music, but their shrieks couldn't drown out Foxtrot's cries.

She grabbed him, shattering his gun holster and his hidden pouches containing extra ammo. Extinguishing his wounds, Olivia took him into her song and threw him outside weightlessly, feeling Rafe pull him down to the pavement.

The fiery song screamed, pretending it was the only thing in existence, but Olivia felt past it in her molecular dance, focusing on the faint sounds and breathing underneath it all. She barreled through the sizzling flames, hurling the other bikers and Rafe's fireproof coat outside.

"Why?" Olivia felt a biker groan when Rafe caught one of his companions as she searched for more.

"Why save us?" he coughed.

"*Because*," Rafe said. "I hope that *none* of you burn in this life or the next."

"But...we *hate* you," he croaked.

"Ah, then I suppose you will have to live with that until you change," he said, tending to another's wounds.

Veins pounded in Olivia's head as she ran low on air. Even with the oxygen conserved from weightless movements, she still hadn't found Melinda or the ninth biker. Roller-skate tracks showed that the waitress had fled long ago, but there was no way the wounded man could have managed the same feat.

She froze upon finding him. He was *still*. She flew to Rafe with the unresponsive biker in her comparatively tiny arms, crying, "His heart stopped!"

"Let me see him," Rafe said, quickly starting chest compressions.

As the unresponsive man gasped, squealing tires bore through Olivia, and Jasmine leaped out of the passenger seat.

"Olivia! Thank God you're okay!" she cried, throwing her arms around her and whispering, "You're like the little sister I always wanted. I thought—I thought we'd lost you!" she wept.

Olivia hugged the tall girl tighter, unable to keep it together anymore. She'd stopped asking her parents for a sibling long ago. And even though Jasmine wasn't the long-lost sister she'd had pictured, no amount of imagination could ever have come up with someone as cool and kind as her.

"I missed you too," she said, sobbing into her shoulder.
The car honked.
"We need to *go*!" a familiar voice called.

Olivia blinked. Why was the woman who'd picked them up earlier here?

Flashing lights lit up in the distance, and Rafe nodded, helping the previously unconscious man sit up. "Go, chica. You've done your part. Now let me do mine."

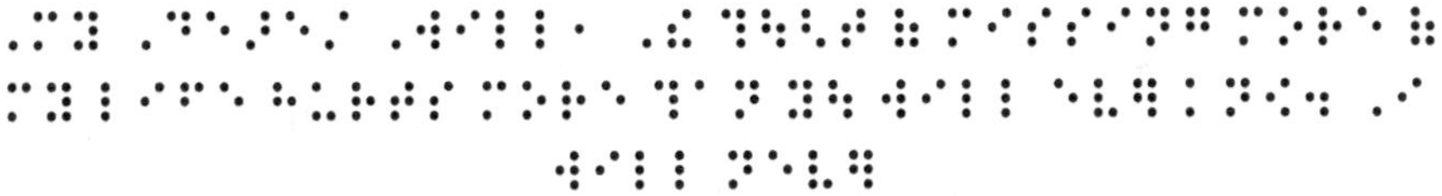

Distant Memories: Sisters

Olivia lay on her stomach with her feet in the air, trying to sketch Lady Constance's hunchbacked reaper on one of the sketchbooks Victoria's mom had bought for them. Thanks to the natural light streaming through the window, they didn't need to turn on the harsh fluorescents.

Across from her, Victoria tapped her matching sketchbook to get her attention, signing, *That bag looks heavy.*

Olivia nodded at her drawing, signing back, *It's a bag of souls*, spelling out the last word since she didn't know how to sign it.

Victoria showed her how before holding up her paper. Instead of the usual jumble of math equations, a massive, robed figure took up the page. In contrast to the giant wizard with the pointy hat she usually doodled whenever she did draw, this one's hood was pulled so low that only his beard was visible. And in his massive, tattooed arm, he hefted a giant metal staff that looked more like an oversized mace no man could ever hope to wield.

He works with souls too, Victoria replied.

Olivia nodded. *That staff's a lot bigger than his paintbrush wand.*

Her roommate laughed, shaking her head. *That's someone else. This one's*—she began, devolving into a seizure.

"Victoria! Victoria!" Olivia cried, rushing over to grab her friend's shoulders. She struggled to hold her down, trying to prevent her from falling or hitting her head.

"HELP! HELP!" Olivia cried, while her friend's heart monitor blared intermittently amid the thrashing.

Someone barged in while she clung to her frigid, flailing friend, trying to gently keep her jaw still so she didn't bite her tongue.

"Li—vi—ah—" Dr. Park's throat mic cut in and out before devolving into static.

Victoria went still, and Olivia wept at the anklet's flatline sound.

"No! No! No! Stay with me!" she said, squeezing her friend's hand while Dr. Park started chest compressions.

ᛗᛈᚠᚱᚹᛗᛊ ᛒᚢᛏ

CHAPTER 16: CONFESSION

"How'd you find me?" Olivia whispered, wiping her tears and buckling up beside Jasmine while the officer with the ponytail hit the gas.

"The police put out an Amber alert, and a waitress called in," Jasmine said.

Olivia blinked, imagining her and her grandfather's faces plastered on TVs and hoping that he wouldn't find out Melinda had made the call.

"They're taking us into protective custody," Jasmine added.

"Wait, *us*?" Olivia whispered. "Why are they taking—"

"Any idea why I can't get ahold of your mom?" the woman asked, staring at them in the rearview.

Olivia gulped and lowered her head. "I...I can't say anything." She couldn't risk her mom's life.

"*Olivia*," the senior mumbled.

Leaning over to whisper in the tall girl's ear, she forced the words out unevenly. "He'll kill her if I talk,"

Jasmine gasped and put an arm around her, awkwardly hugging her through the seatbelt.

The officer narrowed her eyes and turned her reflective gaze on the tall girl.

"Still not my place," the senior said.

"Hmm," the lady said, tapping her nails on the steering wheel while stopping at a light. "Did he *threaten* you? Is that why you're keeping quiet? Is it blackmail? Does he have photos of you—"

"NO!" Olivia said, going red and staring down at her boots. Thank God it wasn't like that!

"Okay," the woman said, changing lanes and tactics. "Then they have some *other* type of leverage on you. I'm gonna go out on a limb and guess it's your mom."

Olivia and Jasmine stiffened, and the driver nodded, reaching for her radio.

"No!" they cried.

"Dispatch, this is Wagner—"

Shaking her foot to make it incorporeal and jam the signal, Olivia cried out, "Please, he'll kill her!"

"*What?*" Wagner asked.

"He said he'd kill her if I talked to the police. *Please* don't call it in!"

"Wagner, this is Dispatch," the radio crackled. "You cut out there for a moment. Please repeat."

"Uh—where are we at on the crime scene?" she asked quickly.

"We're on site," someone else said.

"Turn up your radio!" a guy sang. "Don't blast your *stereooo*."

"Acknowledged," Wagner groaned.

"Or at least play something other than chiptunes," the singer snickered between laughs.

"That's enough, Jim," Dispatch said. "Now, cut the chatter."

Wagner muted the radio. "All right, tell me everything," she said, squeezing the wheel when her cell rang.

It might have been rude, but Olivia's powers forced her to feel the conversation.

"Hey," a gruff voice said. "There's been *another* explosion..."

"*Where?*"

"Wade Residence. Burned to the ground."

Olivia stiffened, holding back tears. Her house was *gone*?

Jasmine glanced at her with concern, but Olivia looked away.

"*Dang it,*" the woman said, hitting the wheel. "Meet me at the safehouse ASAP."

"But what about—"

"Don't wait around for a body. Just hurry!"

"Aye," he grunted, hanging up.

"What is it?" Jasmine asked, clearly unnerved by the *body* part.

The driver sighed. "Olivia, I'm so sorry, but your house burned down."

Jasmine held her tighter, and Olivia wept. Surely he didn't kill her mom in the fire! She hadn't said anything—anything more than she had to. No, he couldn't have known she'd talked. He must have set the blaze earlier if the authorities had just found out. Her mom *had* to be safe. But now there was no home for her to come back to, and all their stuff...the scrapbook of everything her mom had missed....Olivia made a fist. If that was gone, her grandfather was going to *pay*.

She must not have hidden her anger very well, because no one spoke on the way. Or maybe Jasmine, like her, was trying to figure out where on earth they were going with all the convoluted turns. Hopefully, their driver was taking extra precautions to make sure they weren't being followed. Or they were completely lost. Olivia was starting to lose faith until they pulled into a fancy apartment complex whose concrete exterior had long since taken on the color of aged bones.

"All right," Wagner said, shutting off the vehicle. "Keep your hoods up and your heads down. Got it?"

They nodded, venturing into the cold with their heavy backpacks in tow, lugging them into the heated lobby. Olivia set hers down by the elevator, and the senior snatched it up while they waited, refusing to give it back.

Olivia crossed her arms and sighed, not wanting to make a scene. If the tall girl really wanted to carry it up like a bellboy, so be it. But she'd better not be expecting a tip.

Pacing back and forth while the elevator's internals whirred, she tried not to draw attention to herself, but, despite her best efforts, a gruff, bearded man's gaze fell on them as soon as he entered the lobby. His heart rate rose and fell and spiked again as he made his way over.

Olivia didn't look up, lest she let him know that she was onto him, but she could feel his subtly accelerated footsteps, the giant trash bag stuffed full of clothes, and the long coat trailing behind him. But worst of all, she felt the gun hidden underneath. And there was something else tucked away on his belt too. Something *familiar*. Wagner had it too....A police badge!

Her unease subsided as he waited for the elevator, pretending he didn't know them. Jasmine kept staring up at the numbered floor lights, but Olivia could feel the electricity shift within, changing which ones lit up. And she could feel it race through the speaker and door wires before they slid open with a ding.

They piled in, and Wagner hit a button, only speaking when the doors closed. "This is my partner, Saul. Saul—"

"Olivia and Jasmine," he said, nodding to them. "Pleasure to meet you."

"Likewise," Olivia said, uneasy about the state of his attire. Unlike her mom's coat, the cuts and stains on his didn't strike her as the hallmarks of poverty. Rather, they stuck out like red flags for someone who didn't care if things fell apart. And his busted knuckles....With that bag over his shoulder, he looked like a drifter who'd stolen everyone's Halloween candy.

"Hey, thanks for picking up my stuff," Jasmine said, hefting the stolen backpack.

"Don't mention it," Saul chuckled. "Seriously, *don't*. The guys'll give me crap to no end if they—"

"I'll find some outfits for you tonight, okay?" Wagner whispered to Olivia.

"Thanks," she said, wishing that she'd brought her gym clothes with her. That her wardrobe hadn't gone up in smoke. And that so many other things had gone differently.

The elevators dinged open, and Wagner led them to a room at the end of the hall. But before she could knock, a giddy woman threw the door open.

"Hi!" the overly peppy lady said. "Come on in!"

Unfortunately, with the five of them standing there, the narrow yet expensive-looking entryway felt quite cramped. But the bright white walls practically glowed under the LED bulbs and the natural light streaming in from around the corner, highlighting the abundance of greenery and *paintings*.

"Whoa," Olivia said, studying Impressionist, Realist, and Baroque landscapes. "This must've cost a fortune."

"Actually, they're as fake as the plants," Saul chuckled, shutting the door and locking all four locks.

"Used to be an art forger's den," Wagner said, hanging up her coat.

"*But,*" the other woman began, "pending liquidation, it's an *awesome* place to crash. I hope we keep it!"

Olivia frowned. Something seemed *different* about the new woman's face. Her skin tone looked closer to Wagner's, but her nose and cheekbones appeared more similar to Jasmine's than—Olivia stopped staring and blushed. She was biracial. Perfectly normal.

"This is Jada—" Wagner began.

"Johansen," her colleague cut in, shaking Olivia's hand harder and faster than anyone ever had.

"But you can call me Jada," she said, turning her death grip on the tall girl.

"Everyone does—'cept Kay, here," she added, throwing an arm around Wagner's shoulders. "'Cause we're *besties.*"

"*Right,*" Kay said, pushing her *friend* away. "And you're totally *not* making me regret rooming with you in college."

"Anyway," Saul said, clearing his throat. "Jada'll be your *den mother* for the weekend," he said with a dark smile.

"Try not to choke on her bubbly personality," Wagner added.

"Oh, *stop,*" Jada laughed, playfully slapping her *bestie*'s arm.

"Okay, tour time!" Jada said, clapping her hands together so hard that Olivia winced at the resulting spike in sound.

"So it's a two bedroom, two bath, and this is the *entryway.* You can put your shoes on there and sink your toes into this *luxurious* carpet," she said, doing just that.

"Or keep 'em on," she added. "You know, in case we've gotta run for our lives!"

"So many options!" Jasmine laughed, kicking her sneakers off.

"Exactly!" Jada said, leading her down the hall.

"Is she always like this?" Olivia mumbled, unlacing her boots.

"Unfortunately," Saul muttered, following with his shoes still on.

Wagner stayed behind with Olivia. "Forgive her," she said. "She's trying to overcompensate with humor to make you feel at home. If you want her to stop, just let me know, and I'll have a talk with her."

"No, it's fine," Olivia said, ready to head on in.

"Actually," Wagner said, putting a hand on her shoulder. "There's something I need to talk to you about."

"Okay," Olivia said, feeling and hearing Jada's words from afar.

"Kitchen comes with marble countertops and an island, and because this is an open concept, you can eat at the island, on the couch while watching satellite, or out on the balcony with a scenic view of the Ren Cen,"[15] she said, sliding open the French doors.

"Look," Wagner said. "*Technically*, I'm not supposed to be on this assignment, but the chief gave me special clearance."

"Why's that?" Olivia asked, staring into the woman's dark green eyes.

"Well, for one, Saul stumbled on this, and—" She sighed. "The chief thinks that no one's more invested in keeping you safe because we're *related*."

"What do you—" Olivia gasped, recoiling. Wagner's eye and hair color, skin tone, and facial features were all remarkably similar to her dad's! "You're my aunt, aren't you?"

Wagner nodded somberly.

"Then *why*?" Olivia sniffled, backing away. "Why show up *now*? After *all* these *years*?"

Wagner—Kay—looked away, whispering, "Because I was a *coward*. There were so many times I wanted to. I even drove to your house a few times...but I was always too afraid to get out. Too scared to knock. I thought Will—your dad—would *hate* me."

"Why?" Olivia asked. Kay said nothing, and so Olivia's shoulders slumped, and she took a shot in the dark. "It's because he got dishonorably discharged, isn't it?"

Her powers picked up on Kay's heart rate spiking.

"Who told you that?"

"So it's true? Isn't it?" Olivia asked, on the verge of tears. Not again! Why was *everything* falling apart?

Her aunt held her while she cried. Her grandfather had been right. And if what he'd said about her mom was also true...

---

[15] A series of seven interconnected building's serving as GM's global HQ.

"Look," Kay said, "I spoke with him on the phone earlier, when we were looking for you."

"How?" Olivia gasped.

"Jay looked up his numbers for me," she said, shaking her head. "Look, he didn't say much before the signal dropped, but he wanted you to know that he wanted to tell you himself when you were older. But, given the circumstances, he trusted me to explain in case you had questions."

Olivia nodded slowly. She couldn't let this gnaw at the back of her mind. She *had* to know. No matter how terrible it was. "Why was he discharged?"

⠶⠿⠄ ⠰⠮⠄ ⠰⠽ ⠶ ⠒⠓ ⠶⠶⠄ ⠶ ⠼⠶ ⠶⠄

Kurstin sighed, staring into her niece's light green eyes, and sat down against the wall, motioning for Olivia to join her. Still, she stared up at the ceiling, unable to face her even peripherally as she brought the girl's whole world down around her.

"He tried to do the right thing. But he went about it the wrong way," she said, hesitant to rip off the bandage. Hating herself for telling Will that she'd answer his daughter's questions.

"In short, he heard that the quartermaster was stealing equipment and selling it on the side. Everyone knew, but no one could prove it. Guy was too careful. So your dad took matters into his own hands and got caught breaking into the barracks. He got a dishonorable discharge and time behind bars with a commuted sentence for good behavior."

"Was he right?" Olivia murmured, holding onto her last shred of hope like a parent, unable to refute overwhelming evidence, wishing their child had committed a crime for a *good reason.*

Kurstin closed her eyes, remembering freshman year. Dad had shouted Will out of the house and forbade her from going to his court-martial, visiting him in prison, or ever seeing him again. Being in high school at the time, she hadn't had a choice. Nor had she had any way of learning if he was right.

"Yes," she whispered. "He was right."

"Then *why*..." Olivia sniffled.

"I only found out a couple of years ago after the Exterminator torched the guy's operation. But by then, I thought it was too late, and I didn't want to reopen old wounds..."

Olivia hugged her, sobbing into her sleeve. "I'm sure he wants to see you. *I* want to see you..."

Kurstin held her niece, failing to understand how this girl now meant the world to her.

"Thank you," she whispered, waiting for the tension to fall from Olivia's shoulders, but it never did.

When Olivia got her tears under control, Kay helped her up, saying, "We should join the others.

"Yeah," Olivia said, following her long-lost aunt down the narrow hall, past paintings of lakeside lilies, flower gardens, and otherworldly orchards. But the scenery didn't help. She just hoped her mom wasn't a murderer like her grandfather.

"Do you know what cops have in common with vampires?" Jasmine asked, lounging between Jada and Saul on the couch with her long legs propped up on the fancy, glass coffee table beside a laptop.

"No," Jada said.

"You both have to be invited inside."

Saul groaned, and the peppy woman slapped her knee. "Ha! Unless we've gotta warrant! But you know what? I think you're onto something—'cause we're both always on the hunt for fresh *blood*!"

Olivia and her aunt inhaled sharply, but Jasmine couldn't stop laughing. "I see what you did there! New recruits—"

"And crime scenes!" they said together.

"Oh, joy," Olivia mumbled. "Now there are two of them..."

"God help us..." Wagner muttered.

"Kill me now," Saul grunted, rising.

"*Hey*, why the long face, Kay?" Jada asked with a grin. "This topic hasn't gotten *that* long in the *tooth*."

"*Jadalynn Aliyah*," Kay said. "So help me, I will—"

"Really, Kay? You wanna go there? Break out the middle names?" she asked with a smirk.

Olivia turned to her aunt. "What *is* your middle name? Scratch that. Is *Kay* actually your first name?"

"Kurstin Wilma," Jada snickered with a wink before her friend could speak. "Which is funny for *so many reasons*, not the least of which is because your dad's William Kurtis and your grand—" she gasped under Saul's glare.

"Nice goin'," he muttered.

"Relax," Kurstin said dryly, motioning for Olivia to sit beside Jasmine. "I already told her."

"Phew!" Jada said, getting up. "'Cause that would've been *awkward*," she said, punctuating the last word with a high-pitched tone.

"You knew. Didn't you?" Olivia whispered, nestling in beside Jasmine.

"I *may* have overheard stuff while we were searching for you..."

"And you didn't say anything?"

"Wasn't my place," the senior retorted. "Speaking of not saying anything, what happened at the diner?"

Olivia felt out with her powers to make sure that the adults were preoccupied in the kitchen and that there were no hidden listening devices before whispering, "He's got my mom, and he's *everything*."

"*Everything*?"

Olivia nodded. "Ghost Giant, Blood Beast, Invisible Man, and others."

The tall girl's eyes went wide. "How'd you get *away*? Did you set the fire?"

Olivia shuddered, remembering the bullet she'd nearly choked on and momentarily flickering the lights. "No, he did that, and I had a little help from that guy that led me to the museum."

"*Rafe*?"

"Yeah," Olivia said, wrinkling her nose at the smell. Whatever the cops were cooking, it smelled *fishy*.

"Anyway," she said, "he took down nine bikers *single-handedly* and even held his own against my grandfather."

"*How?*" Jasmine asked. "Does *he* have powers?"

Olivia shrugged. "I don't know, but he had a pair of wrist and ankle weights and knew something about my *abilities*."

Jasmine whistled. "Sounds like someone we *need* on our team."

"Yeah, but unless he just *shows* up again—"

The senior snorted. "You said he's a med student, right?"

"Yeah, so?"

"So he'll be in the system. And Jada says this place's got Wi-Fi," she added, eyeing the laptop at her feet.

"Did your new BFF give you the password?"

"Aw, your jealousy's cute, but you're still my fave," she said, ruffling her hair.

"Cut it out," Olivia said, fending off the senior's hand. "Seriously, do you have the password?"

"No, but we've got a *hilarious* tech wiz, a grumpy beat cop, and your aunt, the straight woman. I'm sure they'll have no trouble finding him."

"Hmm—after what my grandfather said, Rafe probably needs police protection too. Though we still need to find my mom..."

Jasmine motioned to the cops. "Uh, three detectives."

"*Right*," Olivia said, lightly hitting her head. "But unless we can keep them quiet, we're risking my mom's life. And even if we can trust them, there's no way they'll believe what we're up against."

"So show 'em," Jasmine said.

Olivia blinked. "Are you *serious*? My grandfather could be anywhere."

"Do you *feel* him anywhere?"

Olivia felt out with her powers but didn't feel anyone in the units above or below, outside or inside the walls. Just a pair of birds on the balcony. "No, but does *he* look trustworthy?" she asked, glancing at Saul.

"Touché. But at least tell your aunt—you can't just leave her hanging after what you said in the car, 'specially if she's filling her colleagues in as we speak..."

Olivia's eyes went wide, and she shuddered. That was *exactly* what they were discussing.

"So we've gotta poke around without alerting Rice..." Saul said, frowning up at the flickering lights.

"Hey, Kurstin," Olivia said a bit hesitantly.

"One moment," her aunt said before heading over. "What is it?" she asked.

Olivia gulped. "Did you tell them about what we...discussed in the car..." she asked, looking up in desperation.

Kurstin grimaced.

"They can't tell a *soul*!" Olivia pleaded.

"*Relax*," her aunt said. "They won't do anything to endanger—"

"No," Olivia said. "You don't understand what we're up against!"

"On the contrary, we do," Kurstin said, as if patiently explaining the obvious to a small child. "Saul and I have been trying to nab your grandfather for years, and Jay's crossed paths with him as well."

"If they already know," Jasmine said so quietly that no one other than Olivia would be able to hear—or rather *feel*. "Then we need to *buy* their silence. And if your grandfather's *everything*, we need *all* the help we can get."

Olivia sighed and nodded. Logically, it made sense. If her aunt truly wanted what was best for her and trusted her colleagues enough to tell them that her mom's life hung in the balance, then Olivia needed to trust them, too. "Can you call them over?" she asked, unzipping her backpack.

"Sure," her aunt said, eyeing the overly stuffed folder. "Saul! Jay!"

"What's this about?" Saul asked, drying his bloody knuckles on a dish towel while Jada made a face and doused her hands in sanitizer.

The three of them stared at Olivia when she set the folder on the table. "Can the three of you keep a secret until my mom's safe?" she asked, hoping they'd keep it indefinitely after she showed them what she and her grandfather could do. Still, her heart raced at the possibility she'd get locked up again or studied in a lab for the rest of her life if word got out about what she could do. But that was a risk she had to take.

Jada frowned and Saul shrugged. "If there's a valid reason, sure."

"Eff it," Jada said. "I wanna know. Count me in."

But Kurstin didn't say anything.

Olivia looked up at her aunt and whispered, "*Please.*"

The woman sighed. "I'll keep quiet until your mom's safe. But no promises after that."

Olivia nodded, hoping that she wasn't trading her freedom for her mom's, but no price was too steep.

"No matter what happens," Jasmine whispered, "I've got your back."

"Thanks," Olivia mumbled, taking a deep breath and a leap of faith, floating translucently.

"HOLY!" Jada cried, jumping back and knocking into Saul when his fingers twitched.

"Jesus H.—" he muttered, nearly tripping over Kurstin's foot.

"Mmm-mmm, divine retribution is swift today," Jada said, letting out a nervous laugh.

But it was her aunt's gaze that Olivia couldn't look away from. Kurstin just stood there, frozen, until she smiled. "Cool."

Relief and warmth flooded through Olivia as she descended into a pile of frost.

"Earth to Olivia," Jasmine whispered.

Olivia blushed, realizing she'd been staring at her aunt, wishing that she could hug her, eternally thankful that she'd accepted her instead of turning her back on her or shying back in fright.

"Right," she muttered, before glancing at the rest of them. "My grandfather has similar powers."

"Say what now?" Jada asked.

"In what way?" Kurstin asked, narrowing her eyes.

"He can't float," Olivia said, "but he can pass through things. Manipulate light to make illusions and go invisible."

Saul grunted. "Explains how he gave us the slip all these years. Game's rigged."

"Well, now it's time to level the playing field," Jasmine said, spreading the dossier out on the coffee table.

The cops leaned in close, and Olivia pushed a photograph of the Blood Beast toward them. "Here's proof my grandfather has had these abilities for a *long* time. *And* that he's used them on the battlefield."

"Hence," Jasmine began, "a SWAT team might not be the *best* idea."

The officers poured over the material long enough for the stove timer to go off.

"I've got it," Kurstin said, hopping up and returning with five plates perfectly balanced on her arms like a waitress.

"Bon appétit," Jada said with a flourish, waving a napkin.

Olivia dug into the seasoned tilapia and broccoli, and Jasmine sampled the mashed potatoes and steaming rolls. Saul set down a bowl of pears.

"Almost like that painting," he muttered, eyeing a forgery.

"It's delicious," Olivia said.

"My compliments to the chef," Jasmine said between bites.

"Thanks," he grunted.

"Wait," Jasmine said. "*You* made *this*?"

"Yeah," he said. "Don't act so surprised."

"He's too modest," Kurstin said.

"Such humility," Jada laughed.

"All right, enough," he said, still chewing. "Were it not for your little *display*, I'd have thought these photos were faker than the paintings."

Jada nodded, meticulously wiping her mouth. "But now we need to know what we're up against."

"Tell us *everything*," Kurstin said.

Richard "Jotun" Rice receded into the flames and slowly projected an invisible copy of himself high into the sky. He banished his original form below, letting wind rush through his jacket in the familiar skydiving sensation. With the bird's-eye view and prescription sunglasses, he projected as far as he could see—above Helvete and through the sunroof into his private office.

The phone rang. It had to be One-Eye. His timing was always uncanny.

"Yeah?" Richard asked, picking up.

"They're on their way to the girl's house. Take care of it."

The line went dead, and Richard growled. Even after all these years, the old man was still pulling him out of the fire like he had that night in Nam. *Damn it all, he* was supposed to put out other people's fires, not *start* them like some *amateur*! But...another blaze would solve this problem. And Devil's Night would be the perfect cover.

Projecting himself back into the sky invisibly, he split in two. One copy descended into the generator room while the other kept splitting off copies to chain projections toward Plymouth—into the runt's house. From those forms, he oversaw the joint operation, splitting off further copies to gather gas cans in Helvete and rematerialize them in the Cracks.

He flipped on all the burners, careful not to ignite them, while simultaneously tracking frost through the house as he doused curtains, carpets, and wallpaper with gasoline. The sweet smell of chilled fuel mixed with the artificial scent of natural gas as the former seeped through the floorboards into the basement and the latter drifted up toward the ceiling and drafty attic. But the traces of lead oxide and the gas mask by the stove ruined the moment.

None of this would have happened if the vigilante hadn't gotten arrested. If One-Eye had let *him* deal with the situation, he'd never have lost his cool or taken that hit of snow and ice. But because he was a *worthless addict*, he'd *relapsed*, seen his *daughter*, and got saddled with a blind *cripple*.

Richard punched the refrigerator, shattering it into a million pieces and simultaneously destroyed that *revolting* painting. His *worthless* spawn would *never* get her sight back. And he wouldn't let Baldr deal with the Exterminator when the time came. The vigilante would burn just like this mask and house.

The doorbell rang, and all his forms froze, going invisible. A pair of cops were at the door. And he'd forgotten to deal with Jerv's *stupid* street art. What in the hell had possessed that fool to stoop to street-gang tactics? Oh, well, no time like the present to fix it. All of hisselves shifted their mass to converge at the stove for precision.

"Mrs. Wade!" an officer called, pounding on the door.

Time to shut him up. Richard turned the dials. Gas *ignited*, rippling out in an explosion. Near-weightless, interlinked copies of himself rode the shock wave toward the door and blew it off, phasing his various vocal cords to let out an unholy roar.

The pigs panicked and fell to the ground, screaming and burning as Richard swooped low overhead with leathery wings. But best of all, the bloody skin, sharp teeth, claws, horns, and hooves, all reflected his glowing eyes, amplifying the effect.

He crashed into the gate, demolishing it and the infernal markings in an instant, vanishing with a puff of illusory smoke. Still, he lingered invisibly, listening to the pigs squeal.

"De—demon!" one cried.

"Monster!" the other shouted.

"SATAN!"

"*Devil*!" they screamed, running for their lives.

An evil smile spread over Richard's face. It was good to know that he'd destroyed their potential testimony and sanity in one blow. Oh, how he'd missed this, using his powers to the fullest. Making those who deserved it *suffer*. And now that months of roughhousing with the runt had *finally* paid off and unlocked her abilities...he was so looking forward to their inevitable rematch.

ᛜᚱ‹ᛊ ᚨ┼ᛗ

Chapter 17: Purgatory

Olivia finished walking everyone through her encounters with the monsters, her failed experiments, and her discoveries along the way before quenching her thirst with a glass of milk—thankful that she'd been able to omit her stay at Hawthorn Center.

"Still can't believe Park had nothing to do with this," Saul mumbled, so quietly that Olivia hoped she was the only one who could hear.

How'd he know about Dr. Park?

"So," Kurstin said, pushing her plate forward, "vacuums and flashlights don't work, but *lead* does."

"Thank God for bullets," Jada said, adjusting her utensils until they were perfectly parallel.

"Yeah, real fortunate for us," Saul said, tossing a napkin on his plate.

"Yeah..." Olivia mumbled. She was still *plenty* vulnerable to the stuff. At least Saul didn't seem keen on sharing whatever he knew about Park.

"Still a net gain," Jasmine said. "You could get shot before and after you got your powers, so you know, be grateful. At least you can dodge everything else."

"Right..." Olivia said.

"And you don't have any idea how to bilocate," Kurstin asked.

Olivia shook her head. "I can only make things float," she said, holding up the napkin she'd folded into a cube and making it do just that.

"Feel them from a distance, pass through them, or *shatter* them," she added, demonstrating everything with a ghostly hand.

Everyone winced when the napkin disintegrated, raining down frosty powder onto her plate.

"So..." Jasmine said, wadding up her own napkin and tossing it into the trash can with perfect form. "Anyone got a game plan?"

"Hmm," Jada said, squinting at her laptop while Kurstin looked over her shoulder.

"Looks like your friend didn't stick around after stabilizing those Berserkers," Jada said.

"And forensics didn't find any bullet casings either," her aunt added.

"How far'd the blaze spread?" Saul asked. "Maybe they burned up in the fire."

"No," Olivia said, shaking her head. "Copper's melting point is three times that of lead. They should still be there."

Everyone turned to her, except for Jada, who typed away. "So it is," she said, giving her a wink.

"Unless," Jasmine began, "your grandfather got rid of them. Maybe that's what he was doing when he 'attacked' you," she said with air quotes. "After he injured Rafe."

Olivia groaned. How could she have been so blind? Of course! She'd barely held her own against him with Rafe's help, yet she'd managed to *fend him off* once Rafe was down.

"Wait!" she said. "What about the bullet that triggered the explosion? Unlike the others, it wasn't embedded in the pavement. It might've gotten launched somewhere during all the explosions."

Saul stroked his beard while his colleagues stared up at the ceiling.

"Fair point," Jasmine said.

But Jada shook her head. "Rice has been at this a long time. He must have a way to find and dispose of the bullets—otherwise, we'd have found proof of his pyro tendencies long ago."

Olivia sighed.

"Chin up," Kurstin said. "We don't need a bullet to tie him to the scene, since we can charge him with your testimony once your mom's safe. But right now, we need to find her."

"Yeah," Olivia said, head down. She needed to save her. Free her from the Berserkers. Free her from blindness and bankers. Make sure that she was finally *free* to *finally* live her life.

"My money's on Helvete," Saul began. "Odds are they're playing it close to the chest and stashing her there, since Rice can hide her in places we can't look."

"Yep," Jada said. "But we still need to rely on more than just your gut."

"Not to mention figure out *where* she'd be in the club," Kurstin added. "It's a big place."

"I'd fly through," Olivia began. "But if he feels me doing that..."

"Then it's game over," Jasmine and Kurstin said in unison.

"*Yeah*," Olivia said, a bit weirded out by that outburst. "Regardless, we need a better plan."

"Wait a minute," Saul began. "You said your mom's legs were broken."

Olivia nodded uneasily, hoping her mom wasn't in too much pain.

"Well," he said, "given the severity of her injuries, I'd wager they *outsourced* her treatment."

Jada snapped her fingers. "That's right! And given that they'd want to avoid hospitals, they probably brought in—"

"*Decker*," Kurstin said, disapproval clear on her face.

"Who's Decker?" Olivia and Jasmine asked.

"A freelancer," Saul said.

"All the gangs use him," Kurstin said.

"Used to be a trauma surgeon until he lost a few too many patients," Jada added.

Jasmine frowned. "Don't they have insurance for that?"

"He lost his practice after his premiums got too high," Kurstin said.

Olivia stiffened. "Wait, you think they took her to a doctor that *kills* people?"

"Why'd you leave a guy like *that* on the streets?" Jasmine asked with a scowl.

"Let's just say he's *mobile*," Saul muttered.

"Besides," Jada began, "his clientele's not just gangsters. He helps their victims and the uninsured. You shut him down, you cut off their lifeline."

Olivia looked away. What kind of a choice was that? Go to the hospital and get saddled with debt, or visit a doctor who might *kill* you? And her mom hadn't even had a *choice*.

She tightened her fists. "So you think this doctor might have her?"

Kurstin put a hand on her shoulder. "I doubt they'd have turned her over to his care. Probably made a house call."

Jasmine nodded. "Would've been a bad idea to move her in her condition."

"So," Olivia began, "if we find *Decker*, he'll point us in the right direction."

"But if you don't know where he is," Jasmine said, "how are we supposed to find him?"

Jada frowned. "We can check some of his old haunts."

"*Or*," Saul said, popping his neck, "I can go crack some skulls. See where the roaches run."

"*Saul*," Kurstin groaned, while Jada glared at him.

"Don't even *joke* about that," she said.

"Relax," he said, taking everyone's dishes over to the sink. "I won't overplay my hand. Besides, it's less suspicious than me doing *nothing*. There's no way they'd buy that I'm just *sitting* on my hands after hearing they kidnapped my partner's *niece*. Not to mention, it's clear her mom's missing, given that there wasn't a body at the house fire."

"How's that even supposed to work?" Olivia asked. "Isn't it wrong —uh, suspicious, to just start shaking people down."

Jasmine nodded, crossing her arms. "Yeah, that'd be police brutality."

"Sheesh," Saul scoffed. "You approach a scumbag with probable cause. If he runs, it's your duty to give chase. And if he resists and gets hurt in the resulting scuffle, so be it."

Of the four of them, only Jada seemed to lessen her scowl, but she didn't look convinced.

"*Look*," he said, "I'm not going to lose sleep over roughing up a guy who drowns puppies or sells stock to dog fighters. For Christ's sake, a woman's life is at stake. But if you *want*, I can try *asking nicely* first and see if these 'charitable souls' will point us in the right direction," he added, grabbing his coat and heading out.

"Well, that was *enlightening*," Jasmine said when the door shut.

"That's one way to put it," Jada said.

Olivia nodded, stomach still churning. Wrong as it was, she couldn't deny that some dark part of her wanted to unleash holy vengeance on people who abused animals, but she doubted she'd have the stomach for it in reality.

"Trust me, not everyone on the force is like that," Kurstin said, pushing her empty plate away and massaging the creases between her brows.

"*Anyway*," Jada said, shutting her laptop, "I can use far less *invasive* methods at the hospital."

Jasmine turned to her. "You wanna draft Rafe for the inevitable rematch?"

Olivia nodded quickly. "That would be *wonderful*." She was dying to talk to him further. And who knew what other powers and things he might teach her.

Kurstin nodded slowly. "He did seem to know more about your abilities than any of us, and he even managed to go toe to toe with your grandfather."

"Wait," Jasmine said. "I hate to play into stereotypes, but what if he didn't stick around because he was concerned about deportation..."

Olivia's shoulders slumped. It wasn't *fair* that people like him weren't allowed in when people like her grandfather were. If only they could *make room* by kicking the latter out for the former.

"She's right, Jay," Kurstin said. "A badge might spook him."

Jada grinned and spoke in an annoying, high-pitched voice that Olivia had only heard snobbish cheerleaders use, saying, "Then I'll just ask around and see if anyone can help me find my friend. You know, my *friend friend*, not my boyfriend."

Kurstin groaned, and Jasmine laughed.

Olivia sighed. "So we have one guy beating the truth out of people and another *seducing* hospital staff."

"It sounds kinda bad when you put it like that," Jada said.

Kurstin sighed. "And given that both of you might not succeed, I guess I'm on Decker duty."

"Yep," Jada said, whipping out a fancy new smartphone and typing away on the touchscreen. "Here's a list of past locations you can try."

Olivia turned to Jasmine, and, even though she didn't have telepathy, the tall girl's expression made it clear that, given how short on time they were, she didn't like the idea of sitting still just because the bikers were after them. Unfortunately, with the Amber alert they'd issued, Olivia couldn't even show her face to the general public without getting called in.

Kurstin's phone chimed and rang. "Yeah, Chief?" she asked.

"Warrant's signed," an elderly voice said. "Thought you might want to head up the raid."

"Yes. Thank you. I'll be right there," she said, hanging up.

"Raid?" Olivia asked.

Her aunt nodded. "Chief's ordered a raid on Helvete, since Rice is still at large—standard procedure, nothing to worry about."

"Ooh, take this!" Jada said, sticking a pen in Kurstin's shirt pocket.

"Jay—"

"Spy pen!" Jada cried. "If your sister-in-law's being held there, you'll be providing *valuable* intel!"

Olivia made a face and stared at her aunt's wedding ring, wishing they hadn't been alienated from her dad's side of the family all these years—or at least from Kurstin and her husband. Who knew what her other grandfather was like. Given her current track record, she was in no hurry to find out.

"So, since all three of you'll be busy..." Jasmine said slowly.

"*No*," Kurstin said.

Olivia blinked. "Wait—"

"We're on the clock here," Jasmine added.

Olivia turned her puppy-dog eyes on her aunt, but the woman infuriatingly closed her eyes and massaged the bridge of her nose.

"We can't just sit around when we're running out of time!" Olivia whined.

But her aunt just sighed.

They were silent until Jada spoke. "Kay, realistically, we can't risk sending anyone else. If any of the gangs get wind of us asking around…"

"*Fine*," Kurstin groaned, taking a deep breath. "But you're strictly recon. Call it in. Do *not* engage. Understand?"

"*Yes*," Olivia said, high-fiving the senior.

"Hey, do you have a phone we could borrow?" she asked sheepishly, not feeling one on the tall girl.

"Have a burner!" Jada said, tossing her a flip phone.

Olivia caught it with a start, holding it with reverence as it vibrated with a new message.

"There's my number and the list," Jada said, grabbing her purse. "Keep it off until you find the place. Otherwise, your location data is going to look *pretty strange*."

Olivia nodded, thankful for the phone—no matter how temporary it was—and the advice. She didn't want her powers raising any red flags before she really got to use them.

"And remember," her aunt said, heading down the hall. "Call us when you find Decker. *Don't* go in. They might have guns."

"Oh, Decker's got a *ton*," Jada laughed.

Kurstin shook her head. "*Not* helping."

"*Relax*, Kay. They'll be *fine*."

"Yeah," Jasmine said, following them to the entryway. "We'll be fine, *Mom*."

Olivia stifled a laugh and looked away. Unlike the tall girl's joke, her aunt's expression was *hilarious*.

"*Mom*? I don't look—"

"That old?" Jada asked, ignoring the obvious. "Keep frowning like that and you will. Why, those wrinkles'll settle in faster than a vampire on a—"

"*Okay*," Kurstin said, "*we get it*."

"Oh, well," Jasmine sighed. "We had a good run."

"Yeah," Jada replied. "We took a good idea and ran it into the ground."

"Six feet under," Jasmine added.

Jada grinned. "With a stake in its heart."

Olivia and her aunt groaned, donning their coats, prompting the tall girl to turn to them. "Don't worry, it's truly dead and buried."

Kurstin sighed, hugging her niece. "Be careful out there. And try to stay *sane*."

"You too," Olivia replied.

"Happy *hunting*," Jada said, giving Jasmine a fist bump. Seeing Olivia smile, she added, "Yeah, there's those teeth!"

Maybe she'd been too hard on Jada. Perhaps she did tell a good joke now and then after all the bad ones had lowered her guard.

"And remember," Kurstin said, "you're supposed to be in our custody, so don't get caught—"

"Or spotted," Olivia said, rolling her eyes.

"Or killed," Jasmine snorted.

"Or take candy from strangers," Jada said. "They might be pyros."

Kurstin glared at her while Olivia mumbled, "That doesn't make— *wait*, Devil's Night."

Her aunt nodded. "Steer clear of fires and arsonists."

"Will do," Olivia said, feeling the tall girl's heart rate spike.

"By the way, since you're going out, can you get my car back...?" she asked, holding out her keys.

Kurstin sighed. "I'll drop you off, Jay."

"And I'll grab that gun you're *totally* allowed to carry," Jada said, snatching the keys up.

"I took classes..." the senior said, looking away. "And it usually doesn't leave the store..."

"Still can't believe everyone *missed* that," Kurstin muttered on her way out.

"I know, right," Jada said, shutting the door. "An entire *vehicle*. Must not've been able to see the forest for the—"

"*Enough*," Kurstin groaned.

"Ready?" Olivia asked, holding out a hand as the adults' footsteps receded.

"Ready," the senior said, taking it.

Olivia glanced at the text and powered the phone off. She took a deep breath and Jasmine into her song. They flew through the walls and plunged down the side of the building, cheering like she imagined people did on roller coasters.

Will Wade pulled his rig over by the exit, now buried in snow, barely able to keep his head up or see out of the windshield. He checked his cells and found that, despite the distance he'd traveled, they still didn't have any signal. After all these years, Kurstin had called out of the blue to tell him that Olivia had been *taken*.

Hundreds of miles from home, there was *nothing* he could do to save his little girl or Ade. Out here in the wilderness, nature had robbed him of even the chance to keep hearing his long-lost sister's voice.

He pulled down his ski mask and kicked the frozen cab door open, cracking the ice that held it shut. Hopping down into knee-deep snow in his coveralls, he braved the blizzard by lantern light. Exhaustion and the storm had forced him to take a nap earlier, but if he stopped again now he'd have to defrost all eighteen tires with the sledgehammer *again*. And he had no desire to adjust the chains either. Instead, he waged war on the snowed-in road with a pickaxe and shovel to clear the way, praying he'd make it in time.

Each swing grew heavier and heavier, wearing him down like past mistakes. He hated himself for getting caught all those years ago and forcing Kurstin to bear the burden of breaking the news to Olivia. She was far too curious not to ask. And Ada...poor Ade. She really was *missing*.

Tears and sweat froze his mask to his face and beard as he took his frustration out on the remnants of the storm. He hated himself for his inability to be there for them. His inability to provide for them. To give them all they wanted—all he wanted for them. And most of all, he hated himself for his stupidity. The foolishness that had cost Ade years, if not decades, more of her sight.

The wind picked up as he hacked away at winter's second volley. Despite his progress, the elements forced him to backtrack to unearth his rig. And when he returned, the snowdrift had grown taller than him. Taller even than that monster that tormented his daughter. He screamed over the howling tempest, hammering away at the impasse as the walls rose farther around him, filling in the path he'd worked so hard to clear.

When the shovel slipped from his frozen fingers for the fourth time, he finally decided to face the facts and throw in the towel. He wasn't up for the task, like so many other things. His head hung low, and his tools grated on the ice as he dragged them back on numb feet and unsteady legs. The temperature cut right through his hood, hat, mask, and scarf, burning his face. Meanwhile, frozen breath clinging to his beard pricked his skin with every shiver.

He slipped and nearly fell in his attempt to clamber back up to the driver's seat, then he pulled the door shut and collapsed from exhaustion. The last thing he saw through the frozen windshield was the erratic maze he'd carved collapsing like his long-dead dreams.

ᛗᛚᚹᛗᛖ ᚠᛏᛒ ᚹᛊᚱᛁᛗᛖ

Chapter 18: Devil's Night

When her lungs couldn't take it anymore, Olivia resurfaced for air in a back alley. They checked their bearings like they had so many times before in their search for Decker, but the sun had long since set. And without street lights, the clouds in front of the moon kept everything shrouded in darkness. She stumbled forward, barely able to see or *feel* anything since her powers were on the verge of giving out from exhaustion.

She shivered in her puffy coat, barely going transparent, staring at the indistinct silhouette of an old building across the street. "Think that's it?" she asked between breaths.

"Hope so," Jasmine said, rubbing her arms and stepping out of the alley.

"Yeah," she said, when a beam of light illuminated a rusty sign. *Second Chance Animal Shelter.*

"*Last Chance* would've been more accurate," Olivia muttered, following in her footsteps. According to the list, it was a *kill* shelter.

"Try not to think about that," Jasmine whispered, climbing the concrete stairs.

"This place is even sketchier than the last one," Olivia said, trying to keep up.

The tall girl snorted. "The last place was a *morgue.*"

"I *know*," Olivia said.

"Well, this place doesn't hold a candle to the crematorium," she said, looking through the dusty boarded-up window.

Olivia shook her head, wondering if Jasmine even realized what pun she'd made at this point.

"Regardless, it looks equally abandoned," the senior continued. "Feel anything inside?"

Olivia frowned, putting a hand against the cool bricks, and froze. "The glass has been painted over..."

With her powers on the fritz, she could barely pick that up—or the grin spreading across the tall girl's face.

"So they just want us to *think* it's abandoned. Guess we gotta see who to award squatter's rights to."

"Right," Olivia said, not wanting to call in a false alarm. She pushed through exhaustion and rock to get them through the wall. It was even darker inside.

"Mind if I borrow your goggles?" Jasmine asked, voice echoing off the concrete floor.

"Sure, but what am *I* supposed to do?" Olivia asked, pushing down on her pack's zipper to open it noiselessly.

"You've got lighter eyes, so you'll see better in the dark," the senior said, claiming her prize.

"Really?" Olivia asked. She'd have thought the difference in light absorption between iris colors would be negligible with their pupils dilated, but maybe the senior simply had fewer rod cells.

"Hang on a minute," Olivia said. "I'm the one with experience leading the blind."

"Shh," Jasmine whispered, so quietly that Olivia could barely feel it in her current state. "That may be, but you can't communicate with me as quietly as I can with you, so just follow my lead."

Olivia felt more like a child being taken by the hand than a blind woman being led around with dignity, but at least no one was there to see them traverse the winding halls.

"Door up ahead," the senior mumbled.

Olivia tapped the ancient timbers and felt rusty hinges alongside a myriad of locks, so she pushed through, nearly depleting her powers.

Light poured in from the room at the end of the dim hall, forcing their eyes to readjust while the stench of sweat overwhelmed them.

Olivia blinked, looking around uneasily. Bedridden people groaned in their sleep on stretchers inside chain-link cages that must once have been kennels. But now they'd been converted to makeshift patient rooms. They even had clipboards wired to the open doors.

A bark-like cough echoed throughout the hall.

"Swine flu," Jasmine hissed, pointing to a quarantine sign.

They rushed through as quietly as they could, thankful that UV air filters were running on full blast, simultaneously warding off potential infection and masking their echoing steps.

They slunk into a spacious room with a high ceiling where a man in a lab coat was working underneath a bright, industrial light hanging in the center. Overturned gym equipment surrounding a series of fences interlinked into a giant octagon with massive, rolling toolboxes inside. Between all the obstructions, it was hard to tell what he was doing, but Olivia felt she'd soon have an idea as her powers returned.

"That must be Decker," she whispered. "But who converted the kill shelter to a fight club?" she asked.

"Dunno, but it's more cinematic than that *operating theater*," the senior mumbled.

"Yeah," Olivia said, faintly feeling the doctor stitching up someone's face. She shuddered at the sensation of the needle passing through flesh and barely put down any frost.

"I'm going to call it in," Jasmine said, pulling out the phone. "Crap, there's no signal..." she muttered, snapping the cell shut.

A voice echoed through the chamber over hurried footsteps. "Come on, *Becky*, the boys are in the lead!"

Olivia and Jasmine froze, and the doctor looked up from his work as a thin girl dressed in black and white raced in.

"I'm *trying*!" a similarly dressed shorter girl said, lugging a gas can inside.

Jasmine cursed. "*Jesters.*"

"Those creepy clowns from Northville and Zedd's?"

The tall girl nodded. "On Devil's Night, no less. Come on. We can't let them—"

"Stand down," Decker said, brandishing a shotgun.

"I think he has things well in hand," Olivia mumbled, continuing to hide as she felt more footsteps.

A tall Jester in a trench coat stepped in, alongside a bigger woman in a sleeveless striped shirt.

"Well, well, well," the tall one said in an accent muffled beneath her bandana. "The boys might be a few buildings ahead, but they'll be three victims down."

"Three?" Olivia mumbled, until a scrawny guy on the operating table hopped up and shrieked, darting behind a toolbox inside the ring with a bag of half-thawed peas pressed to his face—dragging along an oblivious child playing a video game.

But Decker just paced around the interior of the cage calmly, taking aim at the Jesters before they could pour any fuel.

"That accent," he said to the tall one. "You're Kiwi. We don't get many New Zealanders through here..."

The bandanaed girl sneered.

"What did you tell your friends?" he asked.

"That we can score big!" the giant Jester sneered in a Hispanic accent, dropping her gas cans and hefting a sledgehammer.

Olivia scowled. Was this all just a *sick game* to them? Judging by the laughs and how they all followed suit, pulling out their weapons even though there was a *gun* pointed at them, it was. Olivia had worried she'd been crazy before she got her powers, but these people were just *insane*.

"Really?" Decker asked dryly.

But Olivia froze, detecting a subtle, growing tremor in his hands.

"That's right," the short one said, twirling a section of broken pipe. "But we'll settle for drugs instead of points, so hand 'em over or we'll take *both*."

"A pity," Decker said, looking down the barrel of his gun with unsteady hands.

The girls just laughed at him and the swaying gun with sickening grins on their painted faces.

Jasmine cursed, slinking off behind him around the octagon toward the tallest one, muttering, "He doesn't have it in him." She held a finger to her lips as she passed the cowering dude and the kid.

The tallest Jester kicked over a gas can, and the cap fell off, spilling fuel as she lit a lighter and circled around to put a toolbox between her and the gun.

"He can't take us all," her larger companion sneered, sliding a can around the floor with her foot as she moved.

"Last chance," Decker said, continually switching between targets. "One more step and I open fire."

But he *didn't*.

Fueled by adrenaline and the desire to protect the patients down the hall, Olivia pulled her puffy faux-fur hood low and crept toward the shortest of the four menaces with her flashlight and telescope bat ready. She shuddered upon feeling the void that was her opponent's weapon. *Lead* pipe.

Creeping around a treadmill, she got a better glimpse of her foe's skeletal clown face paint. The shorter girl, *Becky*, had the same bloodshot eyes and overly pale skin as her companions, highlighted by the small amount of dark, revealing clothing they'd chosen to wear.

Olivia shuddered. Did none of them have any decency or common sense? It was freezing outside!

Someone screamed on the other side of the room, and Olivia whirled as someone crashed into a weight bench.

"Oh, you little..." the tall Jester groaned, bleeding through her skeletal bandana and onto her low-cut top. "Dora, get the giant!"

Decker fired a warning shot at the big Jester's feet, and, even though the deafening blast echoed throughout the chamber, everyone sprang into action as if the bell had rung at the start of a cage match.

Dora fled from the leaking gas can she'd been kicking along and dived for cover.

"There's another one!" the thin Jester cried, pointing at Olivia. True to her fishnet and one-piece swimsuit theme, she used protective gloves to draw wicked tangles of fishing line covered in hooks from her sleeveless jacket.

"Come on, Lu," Becky said, swinging her pipe experimentally. "Let's get the runt."

"Who are you calling *runt*?" Olivia growled, tightening her grip on the flashlight. Hoodie girl couldn't be any taller than her. And her hair....That fake blood was an even crappier dye job than her own.

Olivia dodged razor-whip strikes and pipe swings while feeling Jasmine evade the masked leader's knife and Dora's sledgehammer. Hammer blows and shotgun blasts tore into the wall and everyone's eardrums. Had Olivia been using her powers, she was confident the resulting thunderclaps would have forced her solid.

Hearing came and went in rhythm with the shotgun blasts, and, through the ringing in her ears, she could barely pick up on the Jesters' taunts, which were gradually devolving into frustrated groans, while quarantined patients shrieked down the hall.

When the opportunity presented itself, Olivia blinded Becky with the flashlight and set her sights on Lu. Momentarily flickering her form while Decker reloaded, she went barely semisolid. But with the instant weight loss, she launched off with inhuman speed. She collided with the skinny girl, and, with a bit more of her antigravity powers, she sent Lu flying into the fence, wincing at the sensation of hooks digging into the girl's skin.

Lashed to the octagon, the Jester let out a horrific cry, unsettling everyone and bleeding everywhere. Decker whirled and took aim but held his fire as Olivia wound up for a final attack. Using a smidge of her remaining powers to make the telescope weightless, she *swung*. Becky blocked with her pipe, but that only restored the telescope's weight. And Olivia had already swung it as fast as she could—without air resistance—maximizing the force. The metallic clang hit like an auditory slap, rattling through their bones, and the pipe went *flying*. The short girl stared up as it bounced off the ceiling and walls.

Olivia deadlegged her foe with the bat, and the girl cried out as she hit the ground along with her clattering weapon.

"My leg!" she screamed.

Her thinner companion on the fence shrieked, pulling a needle from her rain boots. She jammed it into her thigh and powered through the pain to tear herself free.

Olivia stared in horror as an evil smile spread over Lu's face. She clung to the chain-link for support as her bleeding slowed.

A defibrillator made a charging sound, and Lu turned in time to see Decker shock her through the fence. She writhed, collapsing on the concrete.

"Don't even think about it," Olivia said quickly, trying not to show her exhaustion or fear when Becky attempted to pull a syringe from her pocket.

Knives clattered to the floor, and all eyes turned to Jasmine as she bumped into a punching bag with *both* her foes in headlocks. The masked Jester was on the verge of passing out, and, though Olivia couldn't feel it, it was clear that Dora's head was badly swollen beneath her sugar skull face paint. At last, the tall one went limp, and the other tapped out.

"You have my thanks," Decker said, emerging from the ring while his patient fled with the child.

Olivia leaned against a broken exercise bike to catch her breath as Decker checked the big Jester's wounds and searched her for weapons. All he found was a syringe identical to the one her thinner companion had used before breaking free of the wire.

"Search them," he said, adjusting his glasses. "I don't want any more surprises."

Jasmine checked the stirring leader and shook her head, and Becky just threw her syringe at Olivia's feet, shaking—terrified out of her mind.

Not feeling anything else on her, Olivia picked up the needle but couldn't read the strange language. Was it adrenaline? Was that how Lu had managed to detangle herself? No—adrenaline would have increased the heart rate and, by extension, bleeding. Platelets? No—that would have resulted in an instant clot and a heart attack.

"I'll take that," Decker said, holding out a hand, the shotgun slung over his shoulder.

Olivia kept her head down to conceal her face and pulled out her radios. Whispering into one to speak through the other, she used the last trickle of her powers to distort the output and conceal her voice.

"Before I hand it over," her radio crackled. "You treated a blind woman with broken legs..."

"And if I did?" he asked, heart rate accelerating.

"Where is she?" Olivia asked.

Decker eyed Becky and Lu as the latter stirred and pulled a notepad from his jacket.

"I'm afraid that's privileged information," he said, clicking a pen and jotting something down before tearing off the page.

"Ask for this at the pharmacy. It'll help treat your skin condition."

Olivia stiffened. She didn't have a skin condition! Still, she glanced at her hands self-consciously but didn't see anything. Eyeing the paper, she hoped it was a hidden message and traded the syringe for it. They were going to have a *long* talk if it wasn't. She squinted, deciphering the sloppy handwriting.

> *Junkyard behind Helvete. Bunker under a pile of scrap.*
> *You'll need the crane to lift it.*

The *junkyard*! She'd been so close this whole *time*. "Thank you," Olivia said with the last of her powers.

He nodded to her. "I'll take it from here," he said, bending down to tend to the tall one's wounds.

Jasmine nodded to him and helped Olivia shuffle out the door the Jesters had come from.

"Thanks," Olivia mumbled, handing her the note before she collapsed.

Dr. Roy Decker tended to the masked girl's wounds after handcuffing her companions to various posts around the ring.

"You killed her! You killed her!" the girl shrieked, high out of her mind.

"I did the best I could," he whispered, remembering the Kiwi patient he'd once treated. "I'm sorry that it wasn't enough."

"But she was my mom..." the girl cried.

"I know," he said, hugging her.

"I know," he repeated when she hugged him back, sobbing into his shoulder.

"And now, I need you to tell me where you got those syringes," he whispered, running a hand through her sticky hair.

"Otherwise, I won't know how to help your friend," he lied, feeling the tremors returning, hoping that whatever mystery drugs he had in his pocket could cure him before he ran out of time.

⠠⠺⠓⠁⠞ ⠙⠊⠙ ⠽⠕⠥ ⠙⠕ ⠞⠕ ⠛⠑⠞ ⠓⠊⠍ ⠞⠕ ⠞⠑⠇⠇ ⠽⠕⠥
⠞⠓⠁⠞⠦

Jada trudged down the hospital's east wing in heels. She'd only had to flirt with four guys—three of whom were twice her age—and leave one button undone to make it this far. And she hadn't even had to give out a fake number yet!

"Excuse me," she said in her sorority girl voice.

"Yes? How can I help you?" a guy in scrubs asked with a hint of an accent as he turned around outside a patient room.

"Hi, handsome, I'm looking for my friend," she said, smiling.

"Do you have a name?" he asked, smiling with perfectly white teeth.

"Rafe Ramírez. He's got *dreamy* dark hair and *gorgeous* green eyes and, you know, *lots* of tattoos," she whispered.

"Interesante, I am he."

Jada frowned at him and shook her head with a wry smile. "Ha, good one! Now, seriously, if you could just point me in the right—"

"Would you like to see a magic trick?" he asked.

She shrugged with mock enthusiasm. "Sure." As long as it led to the elusive med student, why not? And if it didn't, then she'd tug on his sense of decency, because he'd *owe* her.

"Please take a photo of me and tell me what you think."

"*Okay*," she said, pulling out her new phone and doing just that.

"That's him!" she gasped, looking up and failing to see the resemblance. "But how did you—"

"Hold on to this *feeling*," he said. "For it will be hard for you to believe otherwise."

"What do you..." she blinked, and her mouth fell open. It was *him*! "*Rafe?*"

"Sí, señorita. As I said before, I am he," he said with a flourish and a humble bow.

"But *how?*" she asked, glancing at the photo and failing to comprehend how she couldn't see the obvious a moment ago.

He shrugged. "I can prevent people from recognizing me."

She tilted her head and smiled with narrowed eyes. "That's an *oddly specific* and *really random* ability."

"Is it?"

She nodded.

"'Tis outlined quite clearly in scripture," he said, reciting from memory: "They picked up stones, seeking to stone him, and yet he walked through the crowd.....Believing him to be the gardener, she asked where he had taken him, and he said, *Mary*....Then, two of them walked alongside him on the road to Emmaus but were kept from *recognizing* him."

Jada blinked, recalling those stories from Sunday school. "I've never thought about it that way before....Are you..."

He laughed. "Do you see trumpets announcing His return? No, I am not He, but I suppose that we are alike in this small way."

Jada nodded, somewhat alarmed at being in the presence of someone with such a biblical ability. Olivia's talents were incredible, but there was something off about Rafe she couldn't quite put her finger on. "Can you do anything else?"

"I can sing and dance and tend to the wounded, if that's what you mean." He laughed.

"That's not—never mind." Despite his limited powers, she found herself a tad envious, given that she had to go to great lengths to accomplish similar feats with a disguise. Then again, if she were like him, she'd miss picking out her clothes, doing her makeup, choosing her posture, and changing her voice.

"Would you mind coming with me? I think you'd be invaluable in helping us rescue a friend of a mutual friend."

"I would be honored to join you in this endeavor," he said. "Could you pick me up after my shift?"

"Absolutely!" Jada said, whipping out her phone. "Here's my number," she added, stopping dead in her tracks at the sound of a familiar voice coming from a patient's room across the hall.

"Absolutely *disgraceful*."

She stuck her head in and glared at the TV while the occupant dozed. *Hansen*.

"Detroit's finest stormed into our places of business," the evil biker lawyer began. "On their *witch hunt*, and what do they have to show for it? *Nothing*."

"Oh, no, not again," Jada whispered.

The cameras cut toward officers in bulletproof vests coming out of Helvete empty-handed. And at their head was poor Kay.

"Detective Wagner, Detective Wagner!" the reporters clamored, ambushing her with microphones and flashing cameras.

"No comment," she said, holding up a hand to block the photos while pushing through the mob with startled police dogs.

Jada's heart trembled. Twice in one day....She wasn't sure how much more bad press Kay could take. She'd never liked the attention. But now...

The feed cut back to Hansen. "You see? The detective has no words to defend the actions of her department. No way to justify its *harassment* and *defamation* of my clients. We're gearing up for the biggest charity ride in the county, and all law enforcement can do is treat my brothers-in-arms like common criminals. Enterprising veterans who've brought jobs and prosperity to our community during this city's darkest hour."

He shook his head. "As the old saying goes, when we do right, nobody remembers."

"Mr. Hansen! Mr. Hansen! Is it true your club's hiding the kidnapper?"

"What would you say to your colleague as he continues to elude the authorities?"

"Do you think he's behind the fires?"

"He's still at large!"

"If Richard "Jotun" Rice is as innocent as you seem to imply, why don't you encourage him to come forward?"

Hansen raised his hand to quiet the crowd and adjusted his glasses. "I shan't deign to speculate—"

"Then *don't*," Jada growled.

"But I can't help noticing similarities between this most recent house fire and the one the legal system once tried to pin on my friend Richard. Hopefully, they'll acquit him of this one as well, and of the tragic diner fire that nearly took the lives of several motorcycle enthusiasts."

Jada glared up at the screen until Rafe put a hand on her shoulder, but that didn't make it much better.

"Now, as his lawyer, I would encourage him to turn himself in and cooperate with the investigation. After all, what he's doing makes my job harder, and him look guilty. But Richard, if you're watching this program, I want you to know that I *understand*. I want you to know that even though I may not agree with what you're doing—"

"Evading capture!" a heckler cried.

"Eluding arrest!" another said.

Hansen cleared his throat.

"As your friend, I can understand why you'd choose to go it alone when a system that's so often failed us has set its sights on you. Singled you out during this trying time. *Hounded* you at a time when it seems that reconciliation with your daughter may no longer be—"

"You little," Jada hissed as he paused to wipe a nonexistent tear from his eyes. The media were just *eating* it up.

"Richard," he said, clearing his throat, "I want you to know that I understand why you'd choose to flee after your daughter's fate has been entrusted to those who've consistently failed to find the truth. Unjustly determined us to be guilty before hearing the facts. We've been burned too many times.

"And so I understand why you would refuse to cooperate with a system that's so often failed you and those you've cared for. I understand why you would risk everything—not to clear your name, but to find her. All the while holding out hope that she might still be alive.

"And I know that you do this knowing full well that your good deeds will be punished. But you will do it anyway. Your behavior tonight should come as a surprise to no one. Because that's what you've always done. You've risked your neck time and again to protect your family, blood or otherwise—estranged or not. Why, if you hadn't defied those in authority all those years ago to save another...I wouldn't be standing here today.

"And so, even though I know that it will not change your mind, know this: the board has unanimously approved donating a portion of our proceeds to help locate your daughter. So, to everyone else, come on out, join the manhunt, or help with your wallets. Come to Helvete and stand with us in solidarity. Help us celebrate the community others would seek to tear down. And contribute to our efforts to bring Mrs. Ada Wade home!"

The camera cut to the audience, cheering with thunderous applause.

"No more questions," Hansen said, turning away.

"What a load of bull," Jada sneered, storming off.

"Do you think anyone will actually believe that?" Rafe asked.

Jada snorted. "Only the *public*'s dumb enough to buy it."

ᚹᚨᛚᛚᛖᚾ ᛟᚹ

Chapter 19: Halloween Heist

Saturday, October 31st, 2009 (Halloween)

Olivia woke in yesterday's clothes with the faint warmth of the sun on her face. Yawning, uncertain of where she was, her sense of touch informed her that she'd slept on a giant comfy bed with pillows far softer than anything she could have ever imagined. Farther out, her molecular echolocation detected Jasmine dozing on the other side with her *revolver* beneath her pillow.

Jada must've gotten it back for her. Still, Olivia shied away from the weapon and froze when Jasmine turned in her sleep. Not wanting to wake her, she waited until the senior's breathing resumed its normal rhythm, staring at the large painting of a rising or setting sun. They must be in the safehouse guest room.

In desperate need of a shower, Olivia rose and nearly stepped on giant shopping bags fuller than any she'd ever carried. Her new clothes had come in! Rummaging through as quietly as she could, her fingers passed over the softest nightgowns she'd ever felt, and she lit up at the beautiful Constance and art-themed tees, as well as the elegant dress clothes and shoes. Her aunt rocked!

Eager to try them on, she grabbed a few outfits and tiptoed out, stopping upon feeling Jasmine's feet hanging over the edge of the bed. She didn't need her powers to know that they were cold, so she gently pulled the blanket over them before sneaking out.

No one was sitting on the couch, and Saul was on the balcony with his back turned to her, seemingly arguing with someone over the phone. Before she hopped in the shower, her powers picked up on the glass subtly shaking with his voice.

"No, Willena, I did not inter—"

Rejoicing under the warm water, Olivia shook with delight, instantly regretting her decision when the water chilled, kicking off a vicious cycle. Blessedly, the water heater was more than up to the challenge. And after several minutes of vigorous scrubbing, she reached for the towel and grinned, feeling the water clinging to her—and, more importantly, its *shatter song*. Moisture evaporated with a hiss before she tried on her first outfit. She'd save *so* much time now that she didn't need to bother with towels or hair dryers!

Rubbing the steamy mirror and turning to admire her new attire, she beamed with glee. She absolutely *loved* this new button-down top and the way the skirt and tights complemented one another. They felt classy like her old uniforms but didn't restrict her breathing, since she wasn't on the verge of outgrowing them. Kurstin was the best!

But her hair was still the *worst*. Even after all that effort, she'd only reduced the hair spray to faint splotches. But, astoundingly, her powers were keen enough to pick up on the faint coloring still left. Maybe she could phase it out....She tried and shrieked.

Outside, footsteps raced, and doors flew open.

"Olivia!" Kurstin cried, pounding at the door.

From the other side, Olivia could feel her aunt's wild hair and pistol, as well as Jada drawing her sidearm.

"Are you all right in there?" Jasmine called, revolver in hand.

Did *everyone* sleep with a gun?

"*Yeah.*" Olivia blushed, opening the door.

"*What happened?*" Saul asked, reholstering along with Jada.

"I...I tried shattering the dye with my powers. But this happened..." she said, holding up her split ends. "And it felt like if I pushed any further, my hair would have shattered down to the roots—leaving me bald forever."

"*Okay,*" Jada said. "I recommend *not* doing that, then."

"I'll fix those later," Jasmine yawned, clad in athletic shorts and some tee of Cinderella running away from a basketball toward a mustachioed pumpkin.

"*Saul,*" Kurstin snapped, catching him staring at her backside.

Olivia went red. Not wanting to stick around for this conversation, she tried to covertly slip away with Jasmine. But with everything her powers had given her, they'd taken away her peace.

"Sorry," Saul chuckled. "I get the 8-Bit shirt, but those sleeping shorts....I just didn't peg you for a *Double O'Eleven* fan."

"Those are mine!" Jada said, with an Irish accent, shooting up a hand and beaming with pride.

"If you *must* know," Kurstin growled, "I forgot my go bag in the car and didn't feel like going back down to get it last night."

Sadly, shutting the guest room door did little to dampen their voices.

"So Little Miss Undercover lent them to you," he said.

"*Yep,*" Jada said.

"Truly the greatest detective," Kurstin mumbled. "And you're more than welcome to grab my stuff for me," she added, thrusting her keys at him while Olivia searched for something made of lead.

"Eh, maybe on my way back. Had to hang up on someone. And now that you two are up, I think I should go smooth that over in person."

"Well, that was *exciting,*" Jasmine laughed, untying the bandana holding her Afro back and adjusting her curls in the mirror.

"*Yeah,*" Olivia mumbled. "By the way, how'd I get here?"

"I carried you up," the tall girl said with a grin.

Olivia blushed. Her dad hadn't done that in years. "Oh..."

"How much you weigh, anyway?"

"It's *rude* to ask a *lady* her weight," Olivia retorted.

"Not in sports," Jasmine laughed. "I'm one-ninety, in case you were wondering."

Olivia's eyes bulged. "I wasn't."

"So, how heavy?" the senior asked. "Or should I say, how *light*?"

Olivia crossed her arms and looked away, mumbling, "Half of you."

"Ha! I knew it," she said, poking her in the side. "Not even triple digits!"

Olivia squirmed away and felt a knock at the door before hearing it.

"It's Jada," she whispered.

"Come in," Jasmine called.

Jada stuck her head in and laughed. "As you can see, I'm not Saul, so breakfast is either going to be cereal and eggs or whatever takeout you can find on this map within a three-block radius."

"Uh, I'm fine with cereal," Olivia said, turning her nose up at the pigtails on MacKenzie's red-headed clown logo before turning to Jasmine.

The tall girl nodded. "Eggs are great."

Jada stared up at her. "Lemme guess—you want five, and you'd like two?"

They nodded, and Jada grinned. "Coming right up. Now follow me, children! We have much to discuss before Kay wakes," she added with a whisper and a maniacal laugh.

"She went back to bed?" Olivia asked, crossing the living room.

"Kay's pulled two all-nighters in a row, so I think she could use some beauty sleep."

"And we need her at her best, unless you've decided to take up your granddad's offer," Jasmine added.

"Do thieves get refunds for returning stolen goods?" Olivia asked, hopping up on the island stool, unable to touch the ground like the tall girl.

"Nope," the senior said, passing down name-brand cereals.

"Then that's still my answer," Olivia said, grabbing a box of Hex Mix. "We're *rescuing* her."

The senior nodded, pouring a bowl of almond flakes.

"So what'd we need to discuss?" she asked.

"First," Jada began, sliding down a jug of 2%. "I need to know if either of you can convert video footage to a 3D map."

"Uhh..." Olivia said, letting her mouth fall open.

"*No*," Jasmine said.

"That being the case," Jada said, firing up the burners, "I'll start working on Kay's raid footage while you two stop by the courthouse and get the blueprints to speed up my work."

Jasmine frowned as the electric stovetop heated up. "Shouldn't someone *else* do that, if we're supposed to be lying low?"

"Like who?" Jada asked. "Saul's out fixing whatever he screwed up, and Kay and Rafe are resting."

"You found Rafe?" Olivia said, going red when she realized she'd asked a bit too loudly.

"Yeah," Jada said. "He volunteered to help with our little heist as soon as he's rested up from the night shift."

Olivia smiled, confident he'd be a godsend in getting her mom back.

"Anyway," Jada said, cracking some eggs, "with time being of the essence and the courthouse opening soon, you two are the logical choice, seeing as weekend traffic won't slow you down, and I don't have to worry about you leaking what we're looking into like I would if I asked someone at the department to do this for us."

Olivia and Jasmine nodded, crunching on their cereals.

"So eat up," Jada said, passing the fruit bowl over. "And we'll work on a plan when you get back."

"*Wait*," Olivia said, wide-eyed. "Shouldn't I *not* be showing my face after that Amber alert?"

A creepy smile spread over Jada's face while the skillet sizzled. "Are you sure you're not clairvoyant? Because that was my next point. You'll need a *disguise*. Luckily, I've got a wig that you can borrow."

Olivia froze. "Wait, you want me to wear a *wig*?"

"They're not so bad," Jasmine said. "We just need to braid your hair to hide it under the cap."

"I *hate* braids," Olivia mumbled. She couldn't stand how tight they felt or how they looked. But Jada didn't seem to hear her as she fussed over Olivia's clothes.

"I think we can work with this outfit....We just need to turn the watch face to the outside—"

"But this is how my dad wears it," Olivia said.

"While that protects the lens from scratching, that's a military thing, honey," Jada said, adjusting it for her. "And right now, it draws attention. So, since you don't have to worry about the potential glare giving you away to snipers, outside it goes. Now, your ring is *perfect*, and what do you have tucked away under there?"

"My necklace?" Olivia asked, pulling out the simple wooden cross that Sister Paula had given her for her First Communion and holding it close.

"Hmm...as much as it fits our aesthetic, you can continue tucking it away if you like. Makes you more *mysterious* if people spot the string and wonder what's on the other end—instead of focusing on your pretty face and the resemblance to that girl in the Amber alert. Speaking of, a pair of fake glasses and piercing blue contacts, will keep everyone fixated on your eyes, so there's no chance they'll recognize you."

Olivia shuddered, covering her seat and cereal in frost. "Hold on, there's no way I'm wearing *contacts*."

Naturally, this made Jasmine laugh. "Do I get a complimentary beauty consult as well?"

Jada took one look at the tall girl and grinned. "Let's see what Saul gave us to work with!"

⠐⠎⠑⠦ ⠯ ⠤⠐⠕⠩⠞⠦⠞ ⠽⠂ ⠕⠝⠢⠦⠾ ⠠⠏⠒⠄⠐⠉⠄ ⠳⠌⠐⠦ ⠿ ⠗⠄ ⠄⠄
⠝⠒ ⠡⠄⠐⠆⠦

Olivia flew underneath the courthouse foundation and surfaced with Jasmine in an empty restroom.

"For what it's worth, I agree with Jada. You look *adorable* in this shawl," the tall girl said, adjusting the evil wig for her in the mirror.

"Shut up," Olivia grumbled, hating the way her braids were packed in under a tight cap and how the artificial wig strands tickled her face. And her *eyes*. No matter how many times she blinked, she couldn't get rid of that *horrid* sensation underneath her lids.

Jasmine, by contrast, had gotten a full-service makeover, with Jada fawning over her, lavishing makeup and trendy clothes on her. She'd even loaned the tall girl a top that was a tad too short on her, only emphasizing her midriff and abs—which Jada claimed *accentuated* her style.

"Can't forget your glasses," Jasmine said, kneeling to put them on her.

"I'm not some *doll* you can play dress up with," Olivia said, grabbing them and clearing the infernal foggy lenses.

"I *know*. I never had to sit on any of my dolls and hold them down while someone else put drops in their eyes. Thank the Lord Almighty Jada thought to give me one of her bullets."

"*Not helping*," Olivia growled, straightening her skirt. At least they didn't know about the time a doctor had to administer eye drops to flush out a splinter from her eye when she was little. Her mom and a nurse had to hold her down throughout the whole ordeal. Blinking was infinitely less painful now than it had been then. But both times it felt equally strange, demanding her attention each time she did it.

"So, can I put your pigtails in?" the senior asked with a mischievous smile.

"No!" Olivia snapped, stomping out of the restroom. The moment she could free herself from these *horrendous* things, she would. And she'd shatter off the infernal makeup hiding her freckles. But she immediately regretted that thought, recalling how Jada'd grinned with glee over her handiwork. The extra color the makeup had lent her had, in Jada's words, made her look just like her aunt had at her age—save for the eyes. She'd even snapped a photo to show Kurstin when she woke up.

"It'll look strange if *you're* the one leading the way," the tall girl whispered, easily overtaking her.

"*Fine*," Olivia said, falling into step alongside her and trying to stick to the plan. Her new shoes were cute but, not broken in, still awkward to walk in. She felt like she was clomping around like a horse every time her footsteps echoed off the polished granite walls and floors.

Her distorted reflection stared back at her from every surface as they crossed the empty lobby, and though both she and it wobbled on unsteady feet, the dark hair and eyes made it seem more like a cheap knockoff whose creator hadn't even bothered to get the basic details right. Despite the discomfort, she took solace in the fact that others wouldn't be able to identify her, given that she couldn't recognize the alien face staring back at her. If only Jada had had a pair of dark green contacts, so she could at least have gotten a better picture of how her aunt had looked when she was young.

"'Scuse me, ma'am," Jasmine said, stopping by the only staffed window, "I've got a school project and wanted to look at the plans for the Helvete Nightclub."

The elderly woman glanced at them, and, sure enough, her gaze lingered on the colored contacts. "That's the building on the corner of Stantz and Spengler, where the old Lycan plant used to be, right?"

Jasmine nodded.

"Wait here a moment." The teller yawned, disappearing into the maze of shelves packed with folders.

Olivia adjusted her glasses, ever aware of how they felt on the bridge of her nose, and stood on tiptoe to glance over the counter before relying on her powers to paint the picture for her. Interestingly enough, they picked up on the grooves in distant placards, helping her truly understand why the blind community had switched from raised letters to Braille. Lowercase *l*'s, *i*'s, and *t*'s felt *very* similar, and capital *C*'s, *G*'s, *O*'s, and *Q*'s were just evil. Arch-i-tect-ural Plans, Bu-sin-ess Fi-lings, Court *Cases*.

Her eyes widened. Just because her grandfather had been right about her dad being dishonorably discharged didn't mean that he was right about her mom being a murderer. After all, *he* was the one who had been charged, and, unlike him, the records wouldn't lie.

Feeling around for lingering eyes and cameras, she said, "Cover for me."

"What are you *doing*?" Jasmine growled, looking around in panic when Olivia went transparent.

She vaulted the counter in ghostly form and sailed down an aisle under flickering lights.

"What on earth?" the receptionist called, staring up at the ceiling.

Olivia carried on, unfazed, feeling that the woman didn't have a line of sight on her. And each camera's little red dot flickered when she flew past.

"Best infiltration powers *ever*!" she whispered, going through a wall separating the new documents up front from those from prior centuries. The nineties went by in a blur, and she canceled her momentum in '87—the year her mom lost her sight. The year the grandmother she'd never met had burned to death.

Modulating her trajectory with a partially tangible fingertip in order to leave behind the smallest possible amount of frost, Olivia navigated the shelves alphabetically.

"Need to get maintenance down here," the woman mumbled in the other room, carrying a few tubes back to the counter.

"People, people, people," Olivia muttered, floating by the *R*'s like an astronaut. *People v Reed, People v Reynolds, People v Reynolds* —again...

She frowned, coming to the last folder on the shelf, and felt a security camera around the corner, past the ring of flickering lights. That had to go.

Weaving her way through shelving and blind spots, she sneaked up on the camera in question and lingered until the lens frosted and iced over. It made an unholy zapping sound, and Olivia went red when the little light went out.

"Whoops," she said, hurrying back to her search and not wanting to tell Jasmine that she had wasted taxpayer dollars.

"Didn't find the most recent plans, but I brought you everything we had on file," she felt the receptionist say, her distant voice echoing into the back room.

"*Wait*...where's the kid?" she asked, picking up the phone. It was weird how Olivia could *feel* the suspicion in the woman's face *and* voice.

"Pft! Studying architecture in the *little women's room*. Always wants to go on trips until she's *gotta go*."

Olivia rolled her eyes at the not-too-subtle hint.

"Yes!" she said, finally finding *People v Rice*, before groaning at just how many of them there were for *one year*.

"Babysitting can be hard—" the clerk began, dialing.

Babysitting?! Just how old did they think she was?

"My kids made us stop every—Matthew, what are you doing here?"

"Camera's on the fritz," a man sighed, adjusting a belt laden with jangling keys, an unloaded sidearm, and two hefty batons. "Protocol says I gotta check it out."

"*There*," Olivia whispered, finding a sealed file. That had to be it. Her mom had been a minor at the time.

Footsteps echoed through the back until Matthew stopped to gape at the frosty wall she'd passed through.

"What the..." he mumbled.

"*Crud*," Olivia whispered. Maybe these *weren't* the *best* infiltration powers ever, with all the clues she left behind. Still, she used the distraction to fly through the ceiling.

"The hell?" he said, spotting the frozen camera.

Olivia blushed, soaring through the maze of wires and supports between levels. Lead piping made it way more difficult than it should have been, but at least she wasn't towing the tall girl or a bulky backpack. Still, she had to do her best to avoid gas and water mains. She didn't want a sudden shift in temperature or pressure to blow the old fixtures.

Keeping her distance, she traced the plumbing to a cluster of pipes and, feeling a urinal, shuddered. Wrong room! Retreating to the adjacent group, she descended into an empty women's room and hurried out with the frosty folder tucked under her shawl.

"'Bout time," the tall girl grumbled, tapping her foot in sync with the copier sounds. "*What* were you thinking?"

"Needed to *borrow* something," Olivia muttered, moving her shawl a bit to show the corner of the folder.

"Unbelievable," the senior hissed. "You look at that *outside*."

Olivia glared at her. Of course she wasn't going to look at stolen—*borrowed*—goods out in the open.

A frustrated maintenance man trudged past with a ladder and a cloth-covered bucket of tools. "Lynn."

"Frank," the receptionist replied, returning with a giant roll of papers hot off the presses. They smelled *divine*.

"Best of luck with your *project*," she said, staring at Olivia as she handed the senior the rubber banded bundle.

Olivia narrowed her eyes at the subtext, and the tall girl grinned, putting a hand on her shoulder and steering her away like a child.

"Thanks," she said, waving goodbye before whispering, "Let's go, little one. Before you get caught *shoplifting*."

"I never—"

"Aw man, it's dripping!" the maintenance guy cried. "We're gonna have to replace the whole unit!"

Olivia winced, and Jasmine clearly picked up on her guilty conscience, shooting her a glare harsher than any expression her mom had ever given her.

"Unbelievable," the senior grumbled. "Theft and destruction of public property and it's not even *noon*."

⠃⠄⠀⠆⠀⠒⠆⠆⠀⠃⠂⠆⠄⠶⠀⠿⠀⠃⠄⠐⠶⠃⠐⠶⠄⠢⠀⠔⠂⠆⠀⠶⠂⠆⠄⠆⠀⠶⠀⠄⠀⠒⠶⠶
⠆⠄⠆⠀⠿⠶⠶⠃⠄⠀⠲⠆⠶⠄

"She did *what*?" Jada laughed, unfurling the blueprints on the coffee table.

"It's not funny!" Jasmine said, snipping away at the last of Olivia's split ends while the first-year looked over her ill-gotten gains.

Still, part of her was thankful that she wasn't getting in as much trouble as she had when she'd filled Kurstin in on last night's Jester encounter. *You're an adult! You're supposed to be the responsible one! Why didn't you call?* She imagined her folks would say similar things when they discovered that she'd spent her homecoming weekend differently than they'd imagined. But that was a problem for tomorrow, and this morning's *incident* was still fresh in her mind. "I nearly had a heart attack!"

"I assure you, you *didn't*," the small girl said from her island-side perch.

Jasmine grinned, confident that that comment warranted a free shot with the spray bottle. She squeezed the trigger with glee.

"*Hey!*" Olivia protested. "That wasn't even *close* to my hair!"

"It wasn't? *My bad*," she chuckled, doing it again and hoping that her efforts to distract Olivia from her pregame jitters were working.

"*Jasmine!*" she hissed, spitting water.

Yep, totally working.

"By the way," Jasmine said, glancing back at Jada. "Can you work your magic and wipe the security tapes in case they take a closer look and notice the miraculous disappearing girl?"

"Bah," the hacker said, clicking away on her laptop. "They don't get paid enough for that. 'Sides, they'll wipe 'em Monday morning to make room for the next day's footage. Budget cuts and all."

"*See*," Olivia said, poring over her new documents. "We're in the clear."

"I feel safer already," Jasmine muttered, wondering what other safety measures had been compromised in the name of cutting costs. In an effort to cheer herself up and take the little menace down a notch, Jasmine lined up another shot. Unfortunately, the small girl went incorporeal, so the water passed through her and broke apart on the island countertop as ice.

"That's *cheating*," Jasmine said, grinning at the chilled bottle. "Now hold still!"

Olivia tried to suppress her giggles and evade in solid form, but she was no match for Jasmine's years of experience. She held the chair still and kept switching the nozzle settings to make it act more like a tiny fog machine or a squirt gun, arcing shots up for the first-year to dodge into.

"Scooore!" she called, catching Olivia in the ear with just such a shot.

"Hey, that's *cold*!"

"And whose fault is that?" Jasmine asked, rattling the ice chunks inside the bottle.

Jada muttered something under her breath, and Jasmine frowned.

"What'd she say?" she whispered.

"Remind me to never let you touch *my* hair," Olivia said, a bit too smugly.

"*Harsh.*"

"I don't think so." Olivia giggled.

"Sit up, please," Jasmine replied, spraying her on the neck to get her to jolt upright.

"Evil," the small girl muttered.

"Evil? You wanna see *evil*?" she asked, pretending to aim at the folder, then turning the bottle to get Olivia in the eyes when she went to defend the documents.

"Well played," the first-year spat, blinking to clear her vision as water dripped down her chin.

"Now there's a good sport," Jasmine said, ruffling her hair before working the product into her stained locks.

"Hey, what's wrong?" she asked when the small girl's shoulders tensed up.

"Couldn't use my powers for a second there."

Jasmine frowned. "Maybe you were too distracted?"

"Yeah...probably..."

Jasmine continued to lather her hair as the small girl turned the page, wrinkling her nose.

"This shampoo smells *odd*..."

Jasmine snorted. "Yeah, I stopped noticing that after a while. But if you'd prefer, we can use *this*," she said, pulling a canister from her bag and clanking it on the table.

Olivia gasped at the can of white hair spray and the *Retribution* lettering on the side.

"Where did you get this?"

"Was thinking about dying my hair like the others for class color day, but didn't feel like washing it out. So I asked Saul to pick it up for me when he went to get our things. Thought you might want your flamethrower back."

"You're the *best*!" she said.

"I know," Jasmine said, using the spray bottle as intended to start rinsing the cleanser and dye out.

"Hey, you're much more accurate than before!" The small girl snickered.

"*Really*?" Jasmine asked. "'Cause I think I made all my shots."

Olivia snorted. "You treat all your customers this way?"

"Just the difficult ones who can't sit still."

"*Difficult*? I've *never* been *difficult* in my life!"

"Really—'cause you act like you're five."

"*Five?*"

Jasmine raised an eyebrow. "Oh, are we just repeating words now? 'Cause I thought your use of *customer* was interesting. Didn't know I was getting paid."

"My presence is gift enough. And, obviously, you could use the *practice*."

"Speaking of, if you wanna do your thing now."

Moisture hissed and evaporated like steam, drying her hair in an instant.

Jasmine shook her head in wonder, wishing she could do that as she brushed the resulting frost away. She didn't know if she'd ever stop being surprised at her friend's powers or just how soft her hair was. Sure, she'd worked with plenty of White clients before, but Olivia's hair was far silkier than the rest.

But that made sense, given that the follicle count and fineness increased with lighter-colored hair. Still, despite months at Zedd's, that texture felt unnatural. So *delicate*. There was no hint of coarseness and the accompanying sturdiness. The small girl's hair was fragile, just like...well, just like the first-year herself appeared.

"So, we wash the dye out? 'Cause I can't feel any."

"*We?*" Jasmine asked. "I'm not sure what *you* did, but yeah, that's certainly what *I* did."

"You know what I—"

"What is it?" Jasmine asked, looking over Olivia's slumping shoulders.

The small girl's eyes watered.

"What is it?" Jasmine whispered.

Her friend pointed to a single word on the page: *shaking*.

"My mom has *powers*..." she sniffled. "It was all her fault."

ᚠᚨᛉ ᚦᛖ

293

PART THREE

INTERLUDE: DETECTIVE FREAMON'S REPORT

The origin of the fire was traced to the kitchen on the first floor, specifically the skillet on the front burner (right-hand side of the gas stove). Evidence supports both witnesses' testimony that the deceased was preparing sausages prior to her time of death and the outbreak.

It is Fire Inspector Jose Rigger's opinion that the catalyst was indeed the grease catching fire while the stove top was left unattended during the alleged verbal argument and later physical altercation. However, while the pattern was consistent with that of a grease fire, there were no signs of chemical accelerants.

Thus, neither the inspector nor I can fathom how such a blaze could have gotten out of hand <u>without</u> the presence of moisture, causing the flames to flare up (as adding water to a grease fire is both dangerous and counterproductive). And while the Fire Investigation Division's preliminary findings are indeed consistent with the defendant's new argument, I personally find it preposterous that he's amended his initial testimony to try to pin it all on his little girl. And calling for expert witnesses to look into this <u>ludicrous</u> "repressed memories" theory is beyond <u>insulting</u>.

Given the defendant's extensive criminal record, this detective would humbly suggest a simpler explanation: he <u>lied</u>. And now that he's found a more <u>plausible</u> explanation, he's latching onto it in one last desperate attempt to blame <u>her</u>.

Richard "Jotun" Rice has shown us <u>exactly</u> the kind of man he is by attempting to sacrifice his own daughter's wellbeing in his inane attempt to avoid prison time.

But I'll have no part of it. I interviewed his daughter shortly after the blaze and found no <u>hint</u> of forgetfulness. For God's sake, the girl lost her sight. Every moment of that horrific experience is seared into her mind and skin. I've already submitted the recording of our interview into evidence, but I've attached a transcript below for your convenience.

Sincerely,

Detective Jordan Sylvester Freamon

F: Can you state your name for the record?
R: Ada Augusta Rice.
F: And how old are you?
R: Thirteen.
F: Thank you, Miss Rice.
R: Please...call me Ada. I want nothing to do with <u>him</u>.
F: All right, Ada. Now, I know this may be difficult, but can you tell me what happened as clearly as you can remember?
<u>R nodded</u>.
R: I was cooking breakfast with Mom when <u>he</u> came home...
F: That's okay—take your time.
R: I—I think he was <u>intoxicated</u>.
F: What makes you say that?

R: It's what I heard mom say once when he
came home like that before. But I don't know.
But he was always in a bad mood when he came
home like that. So mom told me to go to my room
and listen to the new CD she bought me.

F: And was that a normal thing for you to do
in these types of situations?

R: Yes. I think she wanted me to listen
to music so that I couldn't hear them
arguing, but...

F: But what?

R: But I heard her <u>fall</u>. She hit the ground
so hard, and I just couldn't take it anymore. I
ran out of my room to try and get to her.

F: And then what? What did you see?

<u>R sobbed</u>.

R: I saw <u>him</u> standing over her. Yelling at
her. I don't remember what he said. But I was
too scared to come closer. He was standing
between us, and I just stopped by the stove.
I remember grabbing a <u>knife</u>. I—I didn't want
to hurt him, but I was just so scared. I'm
so ashamed.

F: It's okay.

R: No it's <u>not</u>! She's dead, and he hit her!
I heard him hit her! He broke her arm. And then
she landed...broke the other one. The blood—the
bones....They were—they were—

F: Miss Ada, we can stop here. There's no
need for us to—

R: <u>No</u>. I can keep going. I just need
a moment.

<u>R took a few deep breaths</u>.

R: I was too scared to approach him. So I
screamed at him. Told him to get away from her.

F: And then?

R: He turned on me, and I was just so scared
and angry, and I started shaking.

F: And then?

R: And then I heard this <u>sound</u> building. I
saw the glow. Smelled the smoke. Burnt sausages.
I turned, and the flames jumped out at me...set
me on <u>fire</u>....That was the last thing I
ever <u>saw</u>.

ᛟᚠ ᚦᛖ ᚺᚠᛟᛖᛞ

Chapter 20: Unity

"What are you talking about?" Jasmine asked.

"Don't you see?" Olivia wept. "The shaking—it's linked to our powers. My grandfather said they came from him. They're *genetic*. And she was my age when this happened. How could I have been so *blind*? They didn't *skip* a generation. My mom has them. That's how water got in the grease that started the fire. She shook, and the frost melted, setting off the blaze."

The tall girl put a hand on her shoulder to comfort her, but it didn't help.

"Look," she whispered, "your mom didn't know about the specter. That means she didn't know about her dad or the powers you think she has. Which means he didn't tell her. It's *his* fault that she didn't know about *any* of that."

It took a while for the words to sink in, but Olivia couldn't find any flaws in the argument. With no way to disprove her, she forced herself to nod. *Everything* was *his* fault. Her grandmother's suffering. Her mom's. Sister Paula's death. The reporter's. The man she failed to save in the parking garage, and who knew how many more.

"Jay, *where* did you get those?" her aunt asked, staring at the blueprints on the coffee table.

"Huh, funny story," Jada giggled.

"Ah, home sweet home," Saul grunted, lumbering in.

"Welcome back," Olivia said, covertly wiping her tears and plastering a fake smile on her face. No one ever asked if she was okay when she was smiling. She'd learned that lesson soon after the Ghost Giant had come into her life, and she'd used it to the fullest to get people to stop asking if she was okay. She wasn't, they wouldn't understand, and she didn't want to talk about it.

"Did you get Rafe?" Jada asked.

"He did indeed, señorita," he said, right next to her on the couch.

Olivia whirled, as did everyone else. "How did you...?"

"I am good at masking my presence," he said, winking at her. "Now you see me. Now you don't."

Jasmine and Kurstin had jumped, much to Saul's and Jada's amusement.

Meanwhile, Olivia strained out with her powers. He'd been there just a moment ago, and she could *feel* him there, but her eyes didn't seem to be working. She could see his shadow and a break in the couch, but she just couldn't focus on the void where he should be.

"Are you invisible?" Jasmine asked.

"No, señorita," he said, miraculously reappearing, "I can simply prevent people from recognizing me as me or as a *person* altogether. But one such as your friend can still sense me, and this wonder does not work on security cameras. Hence, I'd exercise caution when devising whatever part I might play in our rescue efforts."

"You knew about this, *didn't* you?" Kurstin said, scowling at her colleagues.

"Some things must be seen in order to be believed." Jada laughed. "And you should have seen your *face*!"

"Anyway," Saul grunted, suddenly becoming deadly serious. "Feels good to have a wild card up our sleeve. So what's our strategy?"

"Strategy?" Kurstin asked. "I just woke up."

"Aw, it's cute that you think you're in charge," Jada said. "Come, gather 'round! We've much to discuss!"

"Guess it's time to huddle up," Jasmine muttered, heading over.

Olivia floated over and sat beside her on the divinely soft carpet.

Saul dragged over two island chairs and nodded to Olivia and Jasmine, but Olivia shook her head. "Carpet's comfy."

Jasmine nodded. "I'm with her," she said, sprawling out.

"Suit yourselves," he said, hopping up on one.

"Okay," Jada said, clapping her hands together and spinning her laptop around to show a satellite view of the club and the adjoining scrapyard.

"A trusted source told us that the Berserkers are holding Olivia's mom in an underground bunker under a pile of scrap."

"My money's on that one," Saul said, pointing to the biggest one in the center.

"That's what I'm thinking, too," Jada said, holding a copy of an ancient set of blueprints. "It lines up *perfectly* with the old boiler that was there before this section of the old Lycan factory burned down. Wouldn't even've had to dig."

Kurstin shook her head. "Just because that's the most likely spot to stash her doesn't mean she's there. We may not know the full extent of what Rice is capable of, but I don't think we can rule out him tunneling."

Olivia nodded. "But even if she's somewhere else, I'll be able to feel whatever heap they've got her under."

"Fair enough," Jada said, grabbing another set of blueprints. "But let the record show that I agree with Saul on this one. See, after good ole Henry Fjord bought the place, he retrofitted it with electricity and swapped the boiler for a generator. He even dug a maintenance tunnel underneath it all the way to here."

"*Exactly* where the modern building still stands," Jasmine said, craning her neck to spy a newer rendition of the floorplan.

"Yep," Jada said. "And if it were me, I'd hook that up to the ventilation system so as not to compromise the bunker's integrity with air holes."

"Makes sense if they planned to weigh it down with a literal ton of scrap," Saul muttered.

Kurstin nodded. "It could also double as an escape route."

"Unfortunately," Jada said, picking up a photocopied letter, "the Berserkers' remodel plans seemed to have gotten *lost in the shuffle*, so we can't confirm whether it's hooked up to the ducts."

"Why am I not surprised?" Saul said. "They treat that place like a fortress. Who knows what other modifications they've made."

Olivia frowned, staring at the scale on the blueprints. The ducts were practically big enough for someone to crawl through. "They're really *that* big?"

Jasmine shrugged. "It's a big building that's gotta move a lot of air. I'm sure it got hot in the summer when it was a factory, not to mention now, when they pack so many people in."

"Back to the point at hand," Kurstin said. "I agree with our resident tinfoil hat—"

"*Privacy and emergency preparedness advocate,*" Jada interjected.

"Regardless of title," Kurstin continued, "the logic's sound. We can check the central pile first."

"And if she's not there," Rafe began, "Miss Liv can figure out whichever pile they put her under."

"I just need to get inside," Olivia said. "Fortunately, there are so many ways for me to do that."

"Well, I wouldn't recommend flying over," her aunt cautioned. "They've had snipers out since the raid."

"Yep," Jada said, pulling up photos.

Olivia stared at the silhouetted men stationed on the rooftops and parking garage. Their goggles and shotgun scopes glowed red in the moonlight. "Lemme guess, those are thermals."

"Probably," Saul grunted.

Olivia nodded, knowing that her powers would make her stand out like a neon sign on those. "So I go *through*."

"Not so fast," Jada said, bringing up stills of twelve-foot fences topped with barbed wire that gleamed under the towering lamp posts.

Jasmine whistled. "Those bulbs are brighter than Friday night lights."

"And they leave zero blind spots for snipers," Saul said.

"And eliminate the possibility of me entering unnoticed," Olivia added, flickering the screens and lights overhead.

Her aunt and Jada nodded. "And, since they've welded sheet metal to the chain-link and lined it with aluminum for extra *privacy*," Jada said, pointing out the shiny spots sticking out from under the weathered paint, "it's likely the whole area's a dead zone."

"So you'll lose radio contact with me once I get in," Olivia said.

Kurstin sighed, crossing her arms. "Why'd they even bother with the foil? All that metal accomplishes the same effect."

"Ha," Saul chuckled. "Well, if they've got all that money to throw around, I'm glad they're spending it on redundant stuff like that instead of attack dogs. Those'd be more difficult to deal with, and, thankfully, I don't see any paw prints."

Olivia nodded, relieved there were no mistreated canines to contend with. "Okay, so I go *under* the fence."

Jasmine frowned. "Any idea how deep the wiring goes?"

"Who knows how they've got it rigged up," Jada said, scowling at the *missing documents* letter.

"But if they're aware of Rice's powers," Kurstin began, "then, worst case, there's a significant radius for you to avoid..."

Jasmine groaned. "Too bad we can't just cut their power without tipping them off."

Saul nodded. "And since they've got a backup generator, such a move would be *less than ideal*."

"So I dive *deep*." Olivia said.

Everyone grinned, then her aunt frowned. "Thanks to the snipers, you'd only be able to resurface on the far sides of those junk heaps to break line of sight."

"Assuming that they don't have patrols out watching for that very possibility," Saul grunted.

"Or motion sensors," Jada said, zooming around the 3D map. "It's what I'd do, though I never saw any when I was splicing this together."

Saul chuckled at a blurry section. "Given the shaky cam footage you pulled this from, I don't think we can bank on them not being there."

"It was a *hidden camera*," Kurstin growled. "How *stable* did you expect it to be when I was *running* around?"

"We all know you did your best, hon," Jada said, flipping back to the aerial view. "We'd better print this out so that you don't get lost in there—however you manage to get in there."

Jasmine nodded. "Looks like it's twice the size of the club."

"Lot of ground to cover," Olivia said.

"*Without* surfacing," her aunt added.

"Can I get one of those little oxygen tanks old people use?" Olivia asked to blank stares.

Rafe chuckled and all eyes turned to him. "We've an old dive instructor that calls his tank *mini scuba gear*. But I digress. New divers often get lightheaded on pure oxygen till they build up a tolerance."

"Same for athletes on oxygen therapy," Jasmine said.

Rafe nodded. "And if you go for a more natural mixture, the tank'll be bulkier. *Heavier*."

Olivia frowned, imagining herself lugging around a massive tank like a firefighter. "But I *could* lighten it."

"Ya could. Ya surely could," Jada said in a pirate accent. She opened a new tab and switched to a normal voice. "But liquid oxygen can be smaller and more condensed....But I don't know what the fault tolerance is on those devices....Your powers might lower the temperature too much for the regulator to convert it to gas..."

"Best not to drown on supercooled oxygen or die of internal frostbite," Rafe said.

"We'll look into it more next time," Jada said, closing the tab.

"Next time?" Kurstin asked.

"There better not be a *next time*," Olivia mumbled, confident that being kidnapped once was enough for her mom.

Jasmine tilted her head at the map. "Maybe you can swim around under there if you start from the club and double back to breathe."

Saul stroked his beard. "Might be our best bet for beating their countermeasures."

Olivia frowned, reaching out with her powers. "I can feel farther than the radius of things I disrupt. So I can check whether they've got shallow wires on the lights. And if they don't, plan B will be to start in the club if I can't go through the back."

"We'd just have to get you into the club," Jasmine muttered.

"Which will be easy if I can go in under the street," Olivia said.

"But it's an old building..." Kurstin said.

"So there might be a lot of lead paint..." Olivia muttered, as everyone fell into deep thought.

Saul shrugged. "Worst case, the front door's our only option."

"Easy for you, perhaps," Jada said. "But for them..."

"There's no way I'm not getting carded," Jasmine said.

"Or identified on sight," Olivia muttered.

"Unless..." Saul began.

"Go on," Kurstin said.

"It's a terrible idea," he said. "But if we've got no other options, we can pull a jacket from lockup, and I can escort them in as a biker."

Jasmine snorted, rapidly tapping her fingers to the beat of some song. "We'd just need to make sure I'm not showing any skin and she's completely hidden."

"Surely you're not going to stuff me in a backpack?" Olivia asked.

Kurstin shook her head at Saul. "Are you kidding? They know your *face*."

"Not if we trim up or dye that beard," Jada said, grinning. "And with a bandana and some sunglasses, you'd look the part even more than you already do."

"Thanks," he grunted.

"Don't they all have *name tags*?" Rafe asked.

Jasmine snapped her fingers. "They're even sewn into the jackets!"

"Who would you impersonate?" Olivia asked.

Saul frowned. "Not someone who went MIA. Might've been capped by their own people..."

"Someone from one of the out-of-town chapters'd be best," Jada offered.

"Aye," he said. "I'm sure we can intercept one during the charity ride and detain him overnight..."

Jasmine crossed her arms. "You'll have probable cause for that, right?"

Olivia winced. "It'd be suspicious if there wasn't, right?"

"*Yes*," her aunt sighed, massaging the bridge of her nose.

"'Course we'll have probable cause." Saul snorted. "Not risking my hide by tipping them off. Harassing a suspect about a cold case would be the safest bet."

"Then there should be plenty to choose from," the tall girl said, shooting him a half-smile. "You know, since they're gangsters and all."

"*Exactly*," he replied.

Kurstin nodded slowly. "We'll take some more heat in the press for snatching them from a charity ride."

"But they'll jump at the opportunity to get in another dig at us," Jada said.

Olivia lowered her head, hating how complicated this was becoming. "So if we go this route," she began, "who makes the arrest?"

"After the raid, they'll be on high alert if it's either of us," Kurstin said to Saul.

"Agreed," he said.

"And if they have someone on payroll..." Jasmine began.

"Then I'd be under extra scrutiny if they know I've been detailed to the safe house," Jada said.

"No biggie," Saul said. "I'll have someone who owes me a favor haul a guy in, and we'll go from there."

Rafe stroked the stubble on his chin. "And since it'll be someone from another chapter, the doorman should be less familiar with him and, by extension, make your job easier."

Saul nodded. "And I've never seen a one-percenter get stuck with door duty. So I'll just get a vest with one of those patches and pull rank if the door guy questions anything."

"And if he calls it in?" Jada asked.

"If he's sneaking us inside," Olivia said, "I can jam their comms."

"Bingo," Saul said.

"Great," Kurstin said. "Let's hope it doesn't come to that. Now we just have to figure out a way to sneak the rest of us in..."

"Uh, *hello*," Jada said. "It's *Halloween. Costume party*," she said, pointing to the biker's website.

"And I can just waltz right through," Rafe chuckled.

"If you want," Jada chuckled. "Though no one in their right mind would ever turn you down."

"Ha, you jest!" he laughed.

Olivia blinked. Was Jada *hitting on* Rafe? Or was she just a flirt?

"But seriously," Kurstin said, "we can play lookout while you stage your *expeditions* from a safe place."

"Which'd be where exactly?" Olivia asked, eager to move on.

"Let's see..." Jada said, unfurling a giant printout of the floor plan on the coffee table.

"All right, men, listen up," Richard said, pacing through the ranks of his brothers-in-arms standing at attention alongside the hang-arounds and the vets they'd picked up off the streets.

"Thanks to the pigs, I won't be able to ride alongside you, but I'll be keeping an eye on the operation nonetheless. Now, I won't lie to you. Tonight *will* be rougher than years past. Not only will we need to keep our brothers safe, but we'll also have to stop the Grimm Guardians and Wild Huntsmen from duking it out—or getting too chummy. Our future *hinges* on tonight. Tonight, we need to be prepared for *anything*."

He didn't look down to see it, but he felt many nod subtly, all staring ahead dead-eyed with grim determination. He took his place at the front and stood tall to address his security team as one.

"I know the *pain* you suffered. The *friends* you lost. The flesh and limbs you sacrificed. Wounds you *endured*. Visible or not. And I know the greeting you received upon returning home. *Some* thanked you for your service. Maybe a few even saluted you.

"But others spat on you. Mocked you. Hippies and college kids. For those of you joining us for the first time, I know what they told you. That you fought for *oil* instead of freedom. That you were *degenerates*, like the scum in Abu Ghraib and My Lai."

Their heart rates all told him what he'd already known. That what he'd said was true.

"Well, *no more*. Our country may have turned its back on *us*. But I will *not*."

"Hooah," the men shouted as one.

"*We* will not."

"Hooah."

"The Berserkers will *never* abandon you."

"Hooah."

"Jarheads or Army dogs—it doesn't matter anymore."

"Hooah."

"We were all soldiers here."

"Hooah."

"And we're still brothers-in-arms!"

"Hooah."

"So stand tall and keep your chin up," he roared.

"Hooah!"

"Stand beside us tonight and take your first step on the road to reclaiming your life!" he shouted with a raised fist.

"Hooah! Hooah! Hooah!" they chanted.

He saluted them, and they saluted back, filled with purpose once more.

"*Dismissed*," he cried, turning to leave as they filed out.

"Give me your tired, your poor," he muttered. "Your huddled masses yearning to breathe free, the wretched refuse of your teeming shore. Send these, the homeless, tempest-tossed to me. I lift my lamp beside the golden door," he hissed, igniting his eyes in the dark.

ᚺᚠᛞ ᛖᚲᛟᚲᛗᛏ

Chapter 21: Division

Olivia frowned, looking over Helvete's schematics for a quiet place inside to stage her search. "The dance floor's too crowded, and there're too many eyes on stage and backstage," she added, glancing at the footage of her aunt racing past audio engineers during the raid.

"Too many VIPs in the balcony," Kurstin added.

Saul shook his head. "Private biker bar and chop shop'd be crawling with gangsters."

"Kitchens and storage rooms are probably bustling," Rafe said.

"So that leaves the restrooms and the dressing rooms," Jasmine began.

"And the private offices," Olivia said, hating how her grandfather's was right next to the hall of women's rooms backstage. Surely he was mature enough not to walk through those walls and spy on women invisibly...

"We can't forget the basement and generator area," Jada said.

Olivia nodded at the eerie winding halls and their extrusive pipes bathed in red overhead lights. "If those are lead, there's probably not much I can do in there."

Jada navigated to a vast, creepy space devoid of everything save for concrete pillars all too reminiscent of those her grandfather had trapped his victims in.

Kurstin shook her head. "Those cameras in the corners are capable of showing them the whole room, so if security notices movement..."

"Game, set, match," Jasmine muttered.

"So restrooms and dressing rooms sound like the most appealing candidates," Rafe said.

"That's *one way* to put it," Saul muttered.

"'Least ours are cleaner than yours," Jada said.

"Yeah," Saul chuckled, "but ours have fewer hidden cameras. I wouldn't put anything past these *scumbags*."

Olivia shuddered, and all eyes turned to the flickering lights and then her. "Sorry," she said. "But I should be able to feel if there are cameras, and maybe I could use a stall as a launch point to sneak into a dressing room."

Kurstin nodded. "That's right—at least one of them will be unoccupied by whoever's on stage."

"Great," Jada said. "So if she can find her mom from that point, we just need to extract her from there."

Olivia bowed her head. "She won't be able to walk."

Also, Jasmine mouthed. *She's blind.*

When she looked up, Olivia didn't let on that she'd felt that. "We'd have more options for getting her out if we took care of my grandfather."

"That's what we'll be on-site for," Kurstin said.

"We've got lead," Saul said, patting his pocket.

"And stun guns," Jada said, whipping hers out. "Do you think this has enough juice to disrupt him?" she asked, pressing a button.

Electricity crackled with a menacing light and Olivia winced, feeling the energy. "I think so..."

Saul snorted. "Then we just need to hope it's strong enough to bring a guy his size down. Even without mystical abilities, he's *huge*."

Kurstin nodded. "If it devolves into a fistfight, *don't* let him grab you."

"Aside from the obvious," Jasmine began, "why not?"

"He's got enough grip strength to fire high-caliber pistols one-handed," Saul said.

"If he gets you," Kurstin said, "he will *not* let go."

"Kinda like a pit bull," Jada added.

"*Wonderful*," Olivia said, hoping that analogy hadn't ruined the breed for her.

Rafe leaned back and stretched his arms. "So if our goal is to spot the jolly giant and neutralize him before he does either of those things to us, what areas would be best for us to cover while Miss Liv surveys the scrapyard?"

"Well, I should probably stick close to her," Jasmine said. "You know, keep a lookout, in case the situation changes before she comes back for air."

Olivia nodded. It'd be reassuring not to be racing into a trap during her mad dash for oxygen.

"Good idea," Kurstin said, gesturing to Jasmine's revolver. "You don't have lead bullets for her to deal with, so I think that'd be ideal."

Saul snorted. "Well, if I have to dress up as a degenerate anyway, I might as well make the most of it and take the biker bar. I can even stick around by the chop shop to cover both fronts."

"Yes," Kurstin said, "but what if they *recognize* you?"

"Oh, he'll be *fine*," Jada said, dismissing her concerns with a wave of her hand. "They'll all be too drunk or high to focus on anything other than the *entertainment*."

"Or whatever rivals happen to cross their path," Kurstin added.

Saul grinned an evil smile. "I still can't believe the Grimm Guard and Wild Hunt will be partying under the same roof, but I can light that powder keg if I need to."

"And whether or not you set it off, it's the *perfect* distraction!" Jada cried. "With the Berserkers preoccupied with keeping the peace, Kay and I can sip margaritas at the cocktail lounge on the other side, ready to rush in and lay down the law if things go south!"

"Somebody's been watching too many movies," Kurstin muttered. "But yes—we can lend a hand and manage the spillover."

"And keep an eye on the dance floor until then!" Jada cried.

"But hopefully it won't come to a shootout," Kurstin said. "Because everyone in the private party'll be *armed to the teeth*," she said, like a teacher explaining the obvious to a particularly dense pupil.

"Well, I'm sure I can mingle up front or in the back with the serving staff," Rafe said. "I'll just stick to the crowds, lest the jolly giant sense something amiss by my presence or that of the earpiece I'm sure to end up with."

"Earpieces'd be nice," Jasmine said.

"Oh, we'll definitely be using some," Kurstin said.

"They'll even be *encrypted*," Jada added with a giant smile. "Unlike our competition's open radios, which we'll *totally* be listening in on."

"Just like they do with our police bands," Saul muttered.

"That's great and all, but I'm not sure how often ours'll be *operational*," Olivia added, wishing there were compact analog ways of swiftly communicating.

"I'm sure we'll manage," Jasmine said.

Kurstin nodded. "We can check in on a regular schedule and before and after you start ghosting through things."

"Yep," Jada said. "But now it's time for contingencies. Because no plan survives first contact."

"I think we're good," Saul said, motioning to himself and Rafe. "He can just disappear into the crowd, and I can ditch the biker getup."

"But you two will need a little more *work*," Jada said, staring across the coffee table.

"*Us?*" Olivia asked.

"Oh yeah," Jada said.

"How?" Jasmine asked. "If we get caught, we're kinda screwed no matter what."

"Not necessarily," Jada said, pulling up images of prior parties.

Olivia scowled at posters of skimpy racing girls at the starting lines hanging above actual women who'd been forced to dress in such attire.

"Thanks to anti-discrimination laws," Jada began, "they'll hire people like us and happily take our money." She flipped through photos of a crowded dance floor with plenty of non-White customers and servers.

"Men of *principle*," Jasmine muttered.

"Plus, this uniform'd be the logical choice, since it'd give you near-universal access," Jada added.

"*Uniform*," Olivia muttered. There was barely enough fabric there to stitch into a top for herself, and she was *short*.

"Just don't try the biker bar," Saul grunted.

"Wouldn't dream of it," Jasmine laughed.

"*Anyway*," Kurstin said, staring at a group photo, "it looks like some of them bring their kids to work all dressed up."

Olivia crossed her arms, not liking where this was going. "And how exactly do you propose that *I* blend in? I'm too old to hang out with them.”

“Precisely what a grumpy teen would say!” Jada cried. “You’re a natural in the part! And given your prior performance at the courthouse, you’ve had plenty of practice acting disgruntled!”

Kurstin sighed, covering her eyes with a hand. “Trust her. Undercover’s her forte.”

“That’s right. It’s my forte. And this’ll *totally* work.”

“*Fine*,” Olivia said. If it helped get her mom back, she’d do it. “But what about Jasmine? Do you honestly expect her to go around showing that much skin?”

The tall girl shrugged. “I’m fine showing my abs and legs, but even if my height doesn’t raise a red flag—”

“Models are tall,” Jada said.

“Told you,” Olivia added, eliciting an eye roll from the senior.

“I’m more concerned about my *face*. Her granddad’s *seen* me. You told me I was in *danger* when you picked me up,” she said, turning to Kurstin.

She nodded, and Jada frowned. “The bikers might be on the lookout for you, but I doubt they told the ladies anything.”

“Still,” Saul said, “even if this is a contingency, it pays to play it safe.”

Rafe nodded. “So Miss Jackson needs an outfit that conforms to the *dress code* and plausibly obscures her face.”

“Any suggestions?” Jasmine said, scratching her head.

No one said anything until Olivia grinned and flew into the guest room. If she had to wear a stupid costume *just in case*, then so did the tall girl.

“*Olivia*,” Jasmine called, “what are you doing?”

She flew back with Jasmine’s giant bag of clothes and stuck her hand inside incorporeally, pulling out exactly what she needed each time by feeling the general shape of everything without looking.

“Since blue’s clearly your favorite, we can work with that,” she said, tossing black sweatpants back in. Sadly, her powers didn’t pick up on color.

"I don't get it," Jasmine said, watching her lay out a hoodie, workout wristbands, and a zip-up sports bra. "Am I supposed to be some sorta *eighties* backup dancer?"

Olivia grinned. "Well, if you wear the jacket around your hips and the wristbands up here..."

The tall girl's eyes bulged. "*Jasmine*. You're making me look like *Jasmine! Princess Jasmine*."

"Haha!" Jada cried. "And a veil or some hair extensions would really tie this updated athleisure look together!"

Olivia shot the groaning girl a smile, only to get a scowl in return.

"Since you've picked out my costume, it's only fair I do the same. I'm thinking *pigtails*."

Olivia paled. "You wouldn't."

"Oh, yes!" Jada said.

"Stop fanning the flames!" Olivia cried. She turned on her aunt, feeling her try to hide a laugh with her hand.

"Oh, I don't know why you're laughing, Kay!"

"*Me?*" Kurstin grimaced. "We're just keeping an eye on things from the dance floor."

"And we'll need *costumes*," Jada grinned.

"We're posing as *customers*. That's *our* disguise."

Jada groaned. "Does *anybody* pay attention to what I say? It's *Halloween*," she added, flipping her laptop around and pointing to the Berserkers' site. "See—costume party. *Everybody*—"

"Aside from the bikers," Saul muttered.

"No, they're pretending to be masculine men," Jasmine snickered.

Saul let out a hearty chuckle, and Jada high-fived the tall girl before continuing. "See, Kay, *everybody* dresses up. *Especially* the patrons."

Kurstin covered her face with her hand. "Is it not enough that we're going *clubbing*?"

"Oh, no, Kay. We'll stand out if we don't blend in."

"By standing out," Jasmine said, high-fiving Jada. *Again.*

Olivia gave her aunt a sympathetic smile. She could only imagine what Jada had in mind.

"*And,*" the crazy woman began. "Since we're *undercover...*"

"You'll be taking the lead..." Kurstin groaned.

Jada nodded. "Like you said, it's my *forte.*"

Kurstin winced at that word, heart rate steadily climbing. "I just blew my last paycheck on—"

"Don't worry. I *know* you still have that elf costume I bought you. You know, the one you promised *not to get rid of.*"

Kurstin blushed. "That was *years* ago, and I also said I'd never *wear* it."

"Oh, you totally are!"

"I've grown since then! And I doubt the *tunic* would even go past my—"

"You didn't grow *that* much. Besides, we can get you some tights! And it'd look *perfect* with your old archery bow!"

Olivia's heart went out to her aunt, and she opened her mouth to object, but Saul had the misfortune of laughing.

"*Saul,*" Kurstin growled.

"I think I'm going to make a call." He chuckled, heading for the balcony.

But his interruption didn't deter Jada. "Throw on some knee-high boots, a quiver, and pointy ears—it'll be great! Heck, I'll even pick them out and get them for you! My treat. No tricks!"

Kurstin sighed as if resigned to her fate.

"I'm sure you'll make a stunning elf," Jasmine said.

"Thanks," Kurstin sighed.

"*Well,*" Olivia began, "if she picked out *your* costume..."

"It doesn't matter—the woman has no *shame.*"

"Cover her up, then," Jasmine offered.

"Oh, yes!" Jada said. "I can get one of those little masquerade masks!"

"I've got a better idea," Kurstin said with a wry smile.

Jasmine grinned. "Oh, you've got a better way to score some payback?"

"Do tell!" Jada said.

But Kurstin just shook her head. "It's a surprise."

"Kay, I love you to death, but your surprises *suck*."

Jasmine raised an eyebrow. "Worse than a vampire going for the *jugular*?"

"Oh, much worse!" Jada cried, high-fiving the tall girl *yet again*.

"Stop *encouraging* her," Kurstin groaned. "And if you must know, you'll be wearing a *dress*."

"But, Kay, I already picked out a spy suit!"

"Well, Jay, that's tough, but if you want to keep insisting that I wear tights, I'm sure you'll make it work."

Olivia turned to Rafe while her aunt and Jada bickered. "Back at the diner, you seemed to know a lot about my powers."

He nodded, a twinkle in his eye. "What of it?"

"Could you..."

"Tell you more about them? I'm afraid not, Miss Liv."

"Why not?" Olivia asked, rejection cutting through her. What reason could he *possibly* have for not sharing vital info that might save her mom's life?

"Miss Liv, do you know why pros start to lose their edge?"

"Age?"

"Yes, chica, that can be one factor. But another is that they begin to acquire many tools and techniques throughout their years of practice. And while these things—when used properly—lead to far greater results than they ever thought possible at the start, they often begin to lose their edge with each individual component."

Olivia frowned. "Because their attention is diluted?"

"Exactamente," he said. "And let's just say that I've known people like you and your grandfather throughout my travels. It never ends well when novices are overwhelmed with options at the start. Thus, providing further hints at this stage would be but a distraction that'd rob you of the joy of discovery."

Olivia hung her head, wishing that she'd been more grateful for the gifts she'd been given instead of being impatient to receive even more.

"Besides," he said, putting a hand on her shoulder, "I saw what your grandfather can do, so trust me when I say that you already have everything you need to succeed." He gestured to the three women laughing across from them.

"Thanks, Rafe," Olivia said, hoping he was right.

"Any time, chica."

"By the way—I know that you don't need to, but will you be dressing up?"

"I've an outfit that's served me well in the past." He laughed.

"*Outfit*," Olivia mumbled, spinning to her aunt in alarm.

"By the way, thanks for the clothes," she said, looking away. "They're really nice." Far nicer than anything she used to own. Far nicer than anything her parents could afford while saving up for her mom's future.

"See!" Jada cried. "I told you she'd love them!"

"Yeah, thanks for the tips," Kurstin said.

"*Tips*?" Jada protested.

"So it was more of a sixty-forty endeavor."

"*Sixty-forty*. In *whose* favor?" Jada said, hands on hips.

Jasmine hid a laugh behind her hand when Kurstin whirled on her.

A bittersweet smile overcame Olivia as she watched the merry band bicker. "Hang on a little longer, Mom. Help is coming," she whispered.

"So we'll sneak past the snipers in the car and set up in the strip mall behind the noodle shop to avoid their line of sight," Miss Wade's voice said over the speakers as Sung-Min cleaned one of his guns in a dingy hotel room in preparation for tonight's mission.

"Caw! Caw!"

While he was thankful that the directional mic was sensitive enough to detect the subtle vibrations of voices resonating through the glass on the French doors across the street, it also picked up the incessant chatter of the two ravens perched on the balcony. Regrettably, sniping them was *not* an option.

"Yes," Detective Wagner said. "And if you can't get through underground—"

"Meet up with Saul at the museum," Miss Jackson said. "Yeah, we got it."

Youths. Always so impatient. He popped a briefcase open and donned the bulletproof digi-shadow camo within before slipping a turtleneck over it. Once, the American government had resorted to black magic when all else failed. *The Black Magic Unit.*

Those days were gone, but he and the others still wore their old gear and the upside-down flag patches with pride. Though, unlike the rest, he had a South Korean flag patch sewn into the other sleeve to represent his dual citizenship.

The old unit patch from his days in his birth country's military hung below, opposite the patch for his current unit. After funding had been cut off, they'd never changed the emblem—a laughing skull in a top hat—and Sung-Min saw no reason to. Those who knew what it represented would be properly terrified.

His phone chimed.

Backup's on the way

Who'd you send?

Myself

Sung-Min raised an eyebrow. War was coming *here*. Interesting.

Acknowledged. Death out.

ᚠᚼᛖᛁᛗᚼᛏ ᛏᛁᛗᛗᛖ ᚦᛗᛋ

Chapter 22: The Gates of Hell

"Still won't go through?" Jasmine asked, checking her costume jewelry in the rearview.

"Unfortunately, no," Olivia sighed, powering off the burner and hoping her dad was okay. He should have been back by now, but no one had heard from him since her aunt's call got disconnected yesterday.

"Mic check!" their earpieces cried, sending Jada's shrill tone directly into their skulls via bone conduction.

"Oh, no," Olivia groaned, feeling Jada's voice reverberate through the artificial pigtails that everyone was sure to see, thanks to the neon green hair ties Jasmine'd picked out for her. "Is she gonna use that accent all—"

"*Dryad?*" the woman asked, putting a French twist on it, as she emerged from Dana's Deals in a vibrant red dress she'd worn over her skin tight "spy suit." It was rather astounding how her outfit managed to look less modest than all the others on display despite containing more fabric than all of them combined.

"Here," Kurstin groaned, stepping out in a woodland tunic and tights. She pulled up her hood to cover her earpiece and pointy prosthetics, seeming to wish she could disappear into it. In contrast to her bow and quiver, Jada had opted to conceal her weapons in stiletto boots and wore her earpiece openly, *claiming* that it went with her costume and masquerade mask.

"*Ifrit* in position," Jasmine radioed in, signaling for them to approach. "Still don't see why I couldn't have gone by *Genie* or *Djinn*, if you wanted to be all *authentic.*"

"You get an absurd name because you made me go by *Ghost Girl,*" she said, radioing in and adding, "Present and accounted for."

"Messenger's inside," Rafe said, barely audible over the music.

"Saul standing by," the man grunted from some distant rooftop.

"*King of Clubs.* Your code name is *King of Clubs,*" Jada corrected him. "I picked it out to flatter you. So *use* it."

"You said this channel's encrypted. So it doesn't matter what I call myself. They won't hear it."

"Should've gone with *spades*," she muttered, hopping in the backseat with Kurstin.

"Do you really have to keep talking like *that*?" the unenthusiastic elf asked.

"I can talk like this if you'd like!" Jada retorted in a Swedish accent. "Dad taught me these to help *conceal my identity*," she added, switching back to the French one.

"Is *concealing your identity* why you stuffed your bra?" Jasmine muttered.

"Of course!" Jada said without skipping a beat. "Do it all the time in undercover. First dates too! Tells me what kinda guy I'm dealing with on the second round," she added with a wink.

Olivia shuddered at the callousness of it all, dispelling the heat rising in her face with frost. Still, the analytical part of her wondered if guys'd stare at *that* or the bright contacts Jada had opted for. But her suspicions aligned with the kind of clientele she thought the nightclub attracted.

"Stop *corrupting* her!" her aunt cried.

"Road's clear," Saul said. "And someone's mic's stuck on."

"*Whoops*," Jada said, clicking hers off.

"Here we go..." Jasmine mumbled beneath her sparkly veil. As they drove along their preplanned route, taller buildings hid them from the snipers' lines of sight.

"Hold!" Saul called.

Moments before a Berserker patrol rode by, Jasmine hit the brakes and pulled out a map.

"Go."

A few more rounds of *Red Light Green Light* and close calls later, they parked at a smoke shop hidden from Helvete by a Vietnamese restaurant across the street from the museum.

Olivia's eyes bulged wider than the creepy eyeball on the palm reader's sign next door. She was surprised that *anyone* could afford the advertised prices plastered over the liquor store's windows, much less the *quantity* of alcohol that impoverished-looking folks walked out with.

The lights at the psychic's place went off on the hour, and Jada hopped out to stretch her legs while the proprietress locked up.

"Think she's going as a gypsy?" Jasmine asked when the woman strode by in a gaudy headscarf and red skirt.

"*Nope*," Olivia said just before the lady took her curly wig off. With such *commitment to craft*, she was probably just a scam artist and not in contact with actual demons.

"The lack of signage denouncing the vigilante was what gave it away," her aunt said, hopping out for phase two. "Be safe."

"You too," Olivia replied, leaning out the window to hug her aunt goodbye before watching her follow Jada. Soon, the two of them were lost in the jumbled procession of costumed masses heading for the end of the line wrapping around the block. Unable to see the end, Olivia had no idea how long it would take for them to get in position by the scrapyard.

Throngs of red queens and pirates in long coats passed alongside people dressed as dalmatians and cheerleaders, shuffling along with costumed chain-gang prisoners on their pilgrimage while Olivia and Jasmine waited in the car. From their spot behind the crystal ball shop, Olivia couldn't see or feel the distant junkyard, but she knew it was there as assuredly as she knew the car battery accounted for the empty space in the engine.

"Still don't know how they're supposed to help if things go sideways when there's a twelve-foot metal wall between them and the snipers," Jasmine muttered.

"I know," Olivia said, thankful that she wasn't freezing like the women parading around in schoolgirl costumes with tied-off tops and miniskirts.

"Wonder what they got in there!" Jada said over the background noise, indicating that she and Kurstin had made it to the edge of the yard.

"That's our cue," the senior said, hopping out.

Olivia nodded, making the sign of the cross. God, *please* help me get her back and keep everyone safe. Amen. She trudged behind the tall girl with her backpack, feeling Indestructible gear jostle around inside.

Sneaking into the narrow alley between the shops, they hid behind a revolting dumpster.

"Operation Hail Mary is a go," Olivia radioed in, forcing herself to take a deep breath before pulling Jasmine into her song and the pavement. They raced under the street and went *deep*, pushing past the foundations and the sewer system to bedrock. Olivia swam toward the scrapyard and nearly gasped.

The original foundation was still intact, but beyond lay nothing but aluminum and *dead* zones. She raced around underneath, like a swimmer trapped beneath the ice, desperately looking for a way up, but found the same lining over nearly every inch.

Her heart pounded, and her lungs burned, begging for air as she retraced their route and broke the surface.

"Operation Hail Mary is a no go," she gasped.

"What happened?" Kurstin radioed.

"It's *all* covered in lead," Olivia said, "*and* aluminum."

"Just like the—" Jada radioed in before pausing. "*Privacy fence?*"

She must've been tapping the comms in between phrases that wouldn't alert the others waiting in line, a mental task Olivia didn't envy.

"Yes," she said.

"And shattering—surrounding—material's—breaking through—manually—in—air bubble—out of the question?" Jada asked.

Olivia frowned. "Without knowing what's on the other side....No, I won't risk my mom's life."

"What about the sewer and utility pipes?" Saul asked.

"Same problem," Olivia said. "They're either made of lead or too narrow for us to squeeze through the gaps."

"'Tis time for plan B then," Rafe said from a quieter location with sizzling sounds.

Saul grunted. "Give me five minutes, and I'll meet you by the museum."

"And there goes our overwatch," Olivia mumbled, hoping they'd get in without needing it.

"Got it," Jasmine radioed, heading back to the car and popping the trunk to grab her trash bag of clothes, which they'd packed fuller with whatever her dad had left in the vehicle.

"Hope this beats you standing on my shoulders in a trenchcoat," she said, lugging the hockey stick.

"Lady Constance's hunchbacked reaper is a *way* better disguise," Olivia hissed, reentering the alley. "And we didn't even have to spend a *dime*!"

"If you say so," the tall girl said, donning her dad's hockey mask and gloves before slipping on a *giant* hoodie. Olivia was sure it would've been a dress on her. She hopped up for a piggyback ride so the senior could drape a torn, inside-out *Go Wildcats!* blanket around her as part of the fake robe. It took a little finagling to stuff her backpack through the giant tear, but when they got it, that part of Jasmine's costume was securely in place.

"Ready?" the senior asked, hefting the trash bag over her shoulder.

"Yeah," Olivia said, using an incorporeal arm to rearrange the bag, hiding herself underneath and freezing it to her backpack.

"*Bag of Souls* in place," she said. "Time to descend into the underworld!"

"*Oh, joy,*" Jasmine groaned, sinking into the concrete.

Olivia inhaled before the pavement closed around her, thankful that the body spray–infused hoodie masked the dumpster's odor. They raced underneath the streets and emerged behind the museum.

"Not gonna lie, that's kinda *freaky*," Saul said, looking up at the tall girl as she rose before leading them across the street. Even with the robe muffling and distorting the sound waves, Olivia could still feel him rubbing at the dye in his beard.

"Remember," he said, "you're my date, and you don't speak—"

"English," the senior said. "Yeah, I know. Jag talar inte engelska," she said, reciting the line of Swedish Jada'd given her.

Supposedly, Jada's dad was half-Swedish and half-French, but Kurstin couldn't vouch for the authenticity of either accent Jada put forward.

"Yeah, but more *arrogantly*," Saul said. "Like you're a model some *commoner* isn't worthy of laying eyes on. *Jag talar inte engelska.*"

"*Jag talar inte engelska.*"

"Eh, good enough," he said, while she continued reciting the phrase like a spell.

"You sound like those girls on the bus," Olivia whispered.

"So I do," Jasmine whispered, walking with the aid of Saul's arm and her hockey-stick scythe.

"Oh my *God*," Jada hissed in their ears, spotting them from around the corner.

"They'll never buy this," Kurstin groaned.

"*Relax*," Saul radioed back. "Given the hand we've been dealt, it's the best move we can make."

"Operation Waltz through the Front Door is a go!" Jada cried, much to the bemusement of everyone around her.

"Wait," the bouncer said to a man in a Godzilla costume, letting two women behind him through.

"Hope I'm cute enough to get in," Jada giggled.

"*Shut up*," Kurstin hissed, shuffling forward.

The bouncer thinned the herd by turning most of the geekier-looking men away, until Saul strode by.

"*Barlow?*" the bouncer asked, eyeing a bloody patch on Saul's stolen jacket and gaping up at Jasmine.

"Yeah, step aside, *Francis*," Saul said, covertly eyeing the man's name patch through his sunglasses.

"Thought the cops picked you up or something."

"Couldn't make the charges stick," Saul said, pushing by.

"Wait," he laughed, reaching for Jasmine's robe. "What are you hiding under—"

"*Jag talar inte engelska!*" the senior snapped.

"Hands off the *merchandise*," Saul growled, squeezing the man's arm. "You wanna look or *touch*, get a promotion. *Got it?*"

Olivia canceled her momentum to stifle a gag, and Jasmine popped her knuckles.

"Yessir," Francis gasped when Saul released him.

Olivia breathed a sigh of relief as the door swung open. Music louder than anything she'd ever heard assailed her, bearing into her bones. It felt as if the air itself was *screaming*. Everyone and every*thing* was dancing to it—the costumed masses, the shaking walls, the rippling cocktails. *Everything* bowed to the overwhelming sound waves.

"Too...loud..." she groaned.

"*In*," Jada laughed over comms, sauntering up behind them.

"Excelente," Rafe said over the radio.

"They let you bring the bow in?" Jasmine asked.

"In exchange for my *number*," Kurstin groaned.

"Wonder how bad he's gonna get *thrashed* when he starts texting that *drug lord*," Jada cackled.

"Ha," Saul grunted, heading for the biker bar. "Best be on my way."

Kurstin nodded. "I'll keep an eye on all *this* with Jay—"

"*Electric Rose*—" Jada insisted.

"While you two get *changed*," Kurstin continued.

"You doing okay?" Jasmine whispered, working her way through the dance floor to the restroom.

"Hanging in there..." Olivia said between clenched teeth. The air was in a constant state of flux, writhing under the onslaught of sounds that were far too loud.

She held onto Jasmine for dear life, trying not to falter under the music or all the people pressing in around them. Blessedly, no one noticed the tall girl's extra-bony *back*, thanks to the trash bag's padding.

"Sorry," the tall girl said, nearly knocking over a guy in a fish costume.

"No apology needed, *gorgeous*."

Olivia groaned, feeling Jasmine blush, while all the sounds threatened to crush her.

"You could do better," she whispered.

"Yeah, yeah," the senior said, joining the line for the women's room.

"*Wow*," an old guy with a mustache and glasses said, staring up at her. "You're *tall*."

"Thanks," Jasmine said, eyeing his name tag. "Mister E! *Mystery*! Ha, that's so clever!"

"*Thanks*!" he said, sipping his drink and shuffling forward.

"This must be what Hell is like," Olivia groaned, hating that she was trapped under all this *noise* between *two* people with terrible senses of humor.

"So what are you supposed to be?" the man asked, adjusting the glasses he'd worn over his domino mask.

"The Hunchback Reaper from those Con Lady books," Jasmine said, tapping her hockey-stick *scythe* on the floor.

"*Con Lady*?" Olivia growled. She still couldn't believe that the senior's only exposure to those books was her teammate's academic dishonesty. Apparently, they got a *nerdier* girl to go on and on about them in the locker room for book reports.

"Oh, why are you stooped over?" the man asked.

"Huh..."

Olivia sighed, whispering in Jasmine's ear so she could recite her answer.

"Because I'm bent and broken from old age, weighed down by the bag of souls I've carried for so long."

"Huh," the guy said. "So it's like Santa, but Halloween?"

"Exactly!" the tall girl said.

"*No*! It's *nothing* like that!" Olivia snapped.

"Well, nice meeting you," Jasmine said, ignoring her when they were *finally* able to enter the crowded restroom.

"You can do your thing now," she whispered, backing into a stall and locking it.

Olivia tried and *failed* to phase. "Oh no....It's too *loud*. The vibrations are disrupting my powers!"

"*Crap*," Jasmine growled, lowering her onto the tank. "This is a *nightclub*. Are they going to work *anywhere*?"

"I don't know!" Olivia groaned, trying to keep her voice down and leaning back so the tall girl could try and get out of her reaper garb in the tight space.

"We've hit a snag," Jasmine said over the radio.

"We'll have to proceed on *foot*, over," Olivia added.

"Acknowledged," Rafe said.

"*What*?" Kurstin asked.

"*It's* not *working*..." Olivia replied, only able to get her hands to flicker with all the sound waves pounding at her.

"Copy that," Jada replied. "If you can make your way to the dressing rooms, you might be able to squeeze into a vent there."

"And pray they're actually hooked up to the bunker," Saul said.

"On it," Olivia said. One way or another, she was getting her mom out of here. Being powerless didn't change *anything*.

"Hold it," Rafe said. "Some bikers are helping themselves to the kitchen's finest."

"Got it," Jasmine whispered, stuffing reaper garb into the bag.

"Oh—hey, *handsome*," Jada said.

"Guess her mic's stuck on," Olivia mumbled.

"*Again*," Jasmine muttered.

"'Scuse me, ma'am, but wutta you got on underneath that little dress, there?" a guy drawled.

"My *spy suit*," Jada giggled, switching to the voice of a Southern belle. "I'm a *secret agent*."

Kurstin groaned, but Saul snorted.

"And what's a pretty li'l *thang* like you doin' covering up that pretty li'l face?"

"Well," she whispered, "I haven't tanned in a while for work, but I was worried I wouldn't be able to pass for *White*."

"Say wut now?"

"See, here's a pic of me and my ma. See the resemblance?"

"Aw, *hell*!"

"Well played," Jasmine and Saul radioed in.

"You best believe I turned that Turncoat away faster than a Yankee at a *Lycan* campaign rally!" Jada cried.

"Oh Lord," Kurstin replied.

"Turncoat?" Jasmine muttered.

"What's that?" Olivia asked.

"Confederate-themed wannabe biker gang," Jasmine replied. "They sell pirated goods and are probably milling around up front, wishing they were invited to the back with the big boys."

"Coast is clear," Rafe said.

The tall girl hurried out before anyone saw them together, and Olivia counted four pairs of flats and heels passing by before rushing out.

The senior grabbed her hand like an overprotective babysitter, and Olivia kept her head down, hoping that everyone thought that she was just short or even younger than she was.

They stepped out of the restroom, and, between the unrelenting notes, Olivia caught sporadic feelings of the strange looks patrons shot them and the trash bag under the strobe lights.

Jasmine just raised the hockey stick to them in greeting, as if that explained everything.

"Status," Kurstin asked.

"Nearly there," the senior groaned.

"I'm at the bar with *Dryad*," Jada giggled. "And we've got eyes on you two—easy to pick you out of a crowd."

"And I'm in the back," Saul said amid a rougher set of background music. "It's *wild* back here."

"Oh! Sounds like my kinda place!" Jada cried. "Come get me!"

"*No*," he said firmly.

"I can take that for you," Rafe said, gently grabbing the trash bag when they reached the kitchen door.

"Thanks," Jasmine whispered.

Olivia frowned up at him, still uncertain of how his green tweed detective getup could ever have helped him, since it was over a century out of date. She squinted under the kitchen's bright white lights, noting how they reflected off the pristine tiles and shiny shelving all too reminiscent of Hawthorn Center. At least it smelled far better, with the divine scents of steak, burgers, and shrimp. Still, everything shook with the same omnipresent beat, but at least the staff were too busy grilling, frying, and cooking to pay them much mind.

"We've got some Civil War *reenactors* up front," Kurstin said. "Any surprises in the invite-only section?"

"Not really. Ninevites sent an old wine bottle, but no representatives. And aside from the new trinity, we've got a few Frontiersmen, some ex–Militia Men, and a low-level Bratva guy."

"Bratva?" Olivia whispered.

"Russian mob," Jasmine replied, entering the waitresses' lounge.

"Now stay back here this time," she said, scolding her with the same tone she'd used at the courthouse as a group of waitresses painting their nails looked over.

"*New girl*," a woman in a barmaid outfit said.

"Me?" the tall girl asked, pointing.

"Managed to convince them the boss had neglected to mention a new hire," Rafe chuckled, heading off with the bag and hockey stick.

"Yes, *you*," the barmaid said. "Do you have shorts under those sweatpants?"

"Yeah," the tall girl said. "Do you want me to change here or—"

"*Yes*," the woman groaned, directing her to the many light-up makeup mirrors.

Olivia slunk after her, trying to keep Jasmine between her and the grumpy lady.

"This one's open," a tan woman in a mime costume said in an accent identical to Jada's. Apparently, her impression *was* authentic.

"Thanks," the tall girl said, taking a seat.

"It'll be a little chilly on the upper levels," the woman added, adjusting her red ascot and suspenders. "But you'll be more than happy with the tips, since those are *inversely* correlated with thread count," she added, continuing to powder her face.

"Good to know," Jasmine said, slipping her sweatpants off and turning to Olivia.

"Come on, you can talk to the kid *later*," the barmaid snapped. "We don't have all night!" she growled. "Chop chop!"

Jasmine shot Olivia a distressed look before departing.

"Ifrit's gone," she radioed in.

"Be careful," her aunt said.

"You've got this," Jasmine muttered, as if talking to herself.

So close to backstage, Olivia still couldn't phase, and her echolocation was completely overwhelmed. Wandering down the rows of light-up makeup mirrors, she could only see vents way up high by the ceiling. And journeying to the outer edges only revealed cocktail waitresses congregated around the ducts on the floor. Perfumes wafted to her nostrils while the women touched up their costumes and eyeliner. There was no way she'd get by them—or into the manager's office in the back—unseen.

"Ugh—who let the kid in!" an Asian woman in a clawed-up tiger costume cried. "I thought we agreed, no kids this year!"

Olivia froze. Crud!

"Who's your mom, huh?" the tiger lady asked, hands on hips.

"Siggy's kid can't talk," a lady in an autumn floral crown said, adjusting her picnic blanket–patterned bikini wrap and skirt.

Olivia held back a smile. What a wonderful coincidence! But who was *Siggy*?

"Ugh!" the tigress growled, stalking off and muttering to herself about double standards and favorites.

"Don't mind my sister," said a woman in a pink catgirl costume and headband, leaning forward to adjust Olivia's pigtails.

Crud—some of her *real* hair was sticking out! But the lady just adjusted her wig to conceal it. Olivia politely closed her eyes, like she did at the dentist, when the woman's chest strayed too close for comfort.

"Cute costume, kiddo," she said with a warm smile, kneeling to eye level to smooth Olivia's collar before adjusting her own.

It seemed that there were kind people everywhere, even in the unlikeliest places and outfits.

"K.T., drinks at forty!" the barmaid boss lady called.

"On it!" the catgirl replied, taking Olivia by the hand and hurriedly leading her backstage.

"If you're looking for your mom, she just went on stage, but you can wait for her in her room. Last door on the left," she said, pointing before running off, a set of white pawprints moving up and down on her tight short shorts.

"Strange place," Olivia mumbled, keeping her head down and her hands on her backpack straps. She walked past techs working on audio equipment, lights, and fog machines with high-voltage wires. All of that electricity would cut through her whether she could use her powers or not.

"I'm heading for the dressing room at the end of the hall," she whispered over comms.

"The one by your granddad's office?" Jada gasped.

"I think so..."

"Be *careful*," her aunt and Jasmine said.

"Of course," Olivia replied with as much confidence as she could muster. But worry blossomed in her as she passed Freyja's and Brunhilda's rooms. Siggy's was indeed right next to her grandfather's office, separated only by an all-too-thin wall. Her hand trembled without going incorporeal on *Sigfried's* door.

Entering quickly, she flipped the lights on and gasped. The room was packed full with a maze of overburdened rolling racks stuffed with fur-lined coats, dazzling dresses, and revealing outfits. Siggy had *way* too many clothes. Olivia navigated the labyrinth, past boxes of plastic-wrapped costumes, feeling the vent cover in the back.

Olivia froze upon passing the massive lighted mirror and stared at a family photo she hadn't seen since she'd left Hawthorn. She'd never met the thin boy or his broad-shouldered brother, but she wept when she recognized the white-haired girl and her mom. Siggy was *Victoria's mom.*

Olivia sat by Victoria's hospital bed late at night, listening to the heart monitor's slow beeping until footsteps sounded at the door.

"Hello, Olivia," the rich girl's mom said, putting a hand on her shoulder.

"Hey," she said.

"Any improvement?"

"No," Olivia said, getting up to offer her seat to Ms. Sigfried.

"You know there's no need for that. Please, sit. I'm sure you're tired," Ms. Sigfried said gently, running a hand through her daughter's hair—through albino locks identical to the woman's own. But Victoria didn't stir.

"She's getting worse, isn't she?" Olivia asked.

The woman nodded and knelt before her. "Vic wanted you to have this," she said, pulling out a silver friendship bracelet with her daughter's name engraved on the beads.

"No matter what happens," she said, "promise me you'll remember her how she was. Not as whatever she might *become*."

Tears welled up in Olivia's eyes as she let Victoria's mom slip the bracelet over her watch. What was that supposed to mean? *Become*? Did they think she had *brain damage*?

"Olivia," Dr. Park called from the hall.

"I gotta go," she said.

Ms. Sigfried hugged her. "Thank you for helping her. For always being there for her."

Olivia nodded, trying to be strong, as she headed for the door.

"Wait, you forgot your sketch pad," Victoria's mom called.

Olivia stopped in her tracks and sighed, knowing there were still plenty of blank pages to work with. But it didn't matter.

"She always liked my drawings. I think that's why she started making her own....I want her to have it. So she can look at them when she wakes up," she said, *hoping* she'd wake up.

Ms. Sigfried smiled, tearing up a bit. "I'm sure she'll love them."

Olivia nodded, whispering, "Goodbye," before following Dr. Park back to her room.

"That was very kind," he said through his throat mic.

"Hmm..." she said, mind elsewhere.

"What is it?" he asked.

"She's dying, isn't she?" Olivia asked.

Dr. Park stopped outside another patient's room and motioned for her to sit.

"Do you want a snack or something?" he asked.

Olivia shook her head and pulled her knees up to hug them.

He frowned, sitting down beside her, and put a hand on her shoulder. "We don't know if she's dying."

"It takes her longer and longer to wake up each time," Olivia wept. She couldn't take it anymore. Watching her friend die. Witnessing the other patients' outbursts without anyone at her side. Being trapped in here. All alone.

"I can't watch her die. I can't. I just can't."

"Well, maybe you don't have to," Dr. Park said. "Maybe you'll come back to visit, and she'll be all better."

"Back to visit," Olivia mumbled. "I spend all day—I'm going home, aren't I?"

Dr. Park smiled. "Not much gets past you. The paperwork is almost finalized. Just promise me you'll act surprised when your dad comes to get you. You know how he loves his surprises."

The next day came and went, and Olivia left without the courage to ask to visit her friend. Or even find out whether her friend had *died*. Something she'd *hated* herself for ever since.

ᛗᚨᚠᛊᛏᛗᚱ ᛁᚺ

Chapter 23: Belly of the Beast

"I promise I'll come see you," she whispered to Victoria's photo, signing *wherever you are* and donning the friendship bracelet she wasn't worthy of from her pack. Some mistakes deserved constant reminders. Had to be faced. No matter how painful.

"Miss Liv!" Rafe radioed.

"What is it?" she asked.

"Two Berserkers inbound."

Saul and Jasmine cursed.

"They probably saw you on camera," Jada hissed.

"Get out of there!" Kurstin cried.

"Come on," Olivia whispered, racing to the vent and flickering her hands. "Shatter. Shatter. Shatter." But the rattling screws and cover wouldn't give, consumed by the overwhelming music.

The doorknob turned, and Olivia hid in a thick fur coat hanging from a rolling rack.

"Lights are on," a burly man said into his radio.

"Hello?" his flabby friend called, lumbering in. "Anyone in here?"

Olivia frowned at her sporadic echolocation. They felt *familiar.* Bruised. Had she saved them at the diner?

"She's gotta be in there," Foxtrot's voice crackled. "Saw her go in on the feed."

Clearly, like these two, he'd squandered his second chance. As soon as she got her mom back, they were all going behind bars.

"Yeah," the burly one replied, rummaging through nearby racks. "Well, she's not now."

Olivia tried her best to keep her breathing steady, sweat pouring down her face. Please don't let them find me, she prayed. Please don't let them find me.

The flabby man grunted, scouring the place, looking under and over each rack in the maze.

"Have you *idiots* found my granddaughter yet?" the radios crackled.

When the burly guy stopped in front of her hiding spot, Olivia stifled a gasp. Sure, her coat reached to the floor, but if he just ran his hand through like he had the other outfits...

He gulped and reached for his radio. "Uh, no, boss."

"*Imbeciles*," he hissed. "*All* you had to do was have a faster response time than the cops. And you couldn't even manage that! I swear, you're all even less worthy of a bailout than Wall Street and the Big Three. Next time you get picked up, I'll see to it that Tyrian lets you *rot*."

"Yes, boss," the flabby guy said, wiping sweat from his brow. "Do you want us to—"

"Get to my office!" he hissed. "You know what she can do! Don't let her poke around in there! And the rest of you, keep your heads on a swivel for a *schoolgirl*. How hard can it be?"

"Yes, boss," a multitude said, while the distraught duo hurried out and flipped off the lights.

Olivia breathed a sigh of relief in the dark, mouthing *thanks, God* to the ceiling.

Shadowed footsteps rushed by outside, disrupting the faint light coming in from under the door, but straining her ears and powers didn't tell her anything. There was just too much interference from the infernal music.

"Are they gone?" she whispered into the earpiece, hoping this hadn't been a ruse to lure her outside into the waiting arms of a firing squad.

"Sí, chica," Rafe replied.

"But your cover's been blown," Kurstin said.

"We heard it over their comms," Jada said.

"I know," Olivia said, stepping out into the darkened maze, eyes adjusting to the faint light.

Wherever her grandfather was, she felt infinitely blessed that he was inexplicably too busy to rush in and deal with her himself. Perhaps the club hampered his abilities as well, if so they might have a chance to take him down after all.

"We should've put another outfit in the bag for you," Saul grunted.

"Shoulda coulda woulda," Jada said. "But, thankfully, she's in a *dressing room*."

"Yeah, but Ms. Sigfried's taller than me," Olivia said, heading for the vent and pausing. If the ducts weren't connected to the bunker, she'd have to leave the safety of the vents and get spotted for sure, unless she picked out another outfit here and now.

"Hmm..." the senior said. "Going by what the women are wearing on stage, maybe you can find something *stretchy*? Something that's *already* your size."

"Okay," Olivia said, swapping her fake glasses for night-vision goggles. "I'll see what I can do." She started digging through the nearest rack.

"And at this point," Jada began, "you might as well go all out and try to cover up *completely*."

"So as not to leave any forensic evidence behind," Kurstin added. "Be careful about fingerprints, hair, *and* skin flakes."

"Okay," Olivia whispered, squeezing into a dark catsuit that went up to her neck. But it was too long in the limbs and *way* too tight everywhere else. Shuddering to think of how it would cling to Victoria's mom, she failed to put down any frost.

"Great," she mumbled. Without phasing, there was no way she was getting out of the garment. So she cut off the excess material around the wrists and ankles with her shuriken compact.

If she were more like Jada, she could probably go out in something like this without undermining her confidence or performance. But she wasn't, and she doubted her parents or teachers would approve of such attire.

Thankfully, slipping a sleeveless leotard over it fixed the problem. Even through her night-vision goggles, she could tell that the material was too thin and transparent. But the underlying layer remedied that issue, just as the new addition fixed the other's problems.

An impractical glow-in-the-dark army outfit stood out to her, so she tried on the boots to see if Ms. Sigfried's footwear would fit. Despite a difference of several inches in height, they wore similar shoe sizes. And while luminescent soles *weren't* the best idea, she didn't see any alternatives, so she shoved her dress shoes in her backpack and pulled on the long, matching socks for comfort and to help tuck in the material bunching up around her boots.

She turned her nose up at a skimpy bridal costume but pulled on the pair of long gloves that made up most of the material. They went past her elbows and kept slipping down, but her hair ties solved that problem while simultaneously eliminating her pigtails.

All that was left to hide was her face, so she pulled on an arctic balaclava with a giant hole in the top and adjusted her wig to look more normal. Unfortunately, the mask was a little too big, but wearing her night-vision goggles on the outside held it in place. A hooded cape tied the outfit together, and a rugged-looking thigh pack complemented the Indestructible one belted around her waist, making the whole ensemble look a tad more militaristic.

Knowing that Victoria's mom wouldn't mind, Olivia helped herself to an unopened bag of earplugs, thankful that Jada's earpiece transmitted sound directly into her skull, so she could dampen the music.

She glanced at her dim night-vision reflection but felt something was missing. There was too much negative space on the front. And given that her new disguise looked pretty superhero-y already, she might as well lean into that theme completely.

"Jasmine had better appreciate this," she mumbled, drawing an adorable little ghost emblem with big green eyes on her chest with the aid of colored lipsticks. It even looked like it had a little skirt!

"Progress report," her aunt said over comms.

"Heading out now," Olivia said, hauling her backpack over to the vent in the corner and searching for something to unscrew the cover with. The edge of her contact case would do. Speaking of, she tried to remove the lenses but flinched every time her finger neared her long lashes.

"Wow," Jada said, "you take even longer than your aunt to get ready."

"I'm not even going to respond to that," Kurstin muttered.

"You try finding stuff in the dark," Olivia groaned, empathizing with what her mom went through every day. Sadly, she couldn't bring herself to remove the vile contacts or phase them out. Obviously, she was *stuck* with them, so she unscrewed the dusty cover instead.

"I've infiltrated the vents," she said, crawling forward.

"I take it your stuff's *still* not working," Saul said.

"Nope," Olivia said, staring up a vertical shaft and knowing she'd have to leave her backpack behind.

"In fact, it's worse in here with all the echoes," she said, feeling the music dig deeper into her bones while she braced her back and legs against either side of the duct, eternally grateful for the cape's extra padding on the way up.

"I'm faring better in the VIP section," Jasmine replied. "Made over a hundred bucks so far."

"Good for you," Olivia groaned, hauling herself over the edge.

"Dang, gurl," Jada whistled.

"*Focus*, Jay," Kurstin said.

"Going radio silent," Olivia said, feeling computer beeps mixed in with the music ahead. Fans and hard drives whirled while she glanced through the cell bar–like cover.

"Cleanup on table forty," Foxtrot said, watching a monitor. "That dude in the Lycan vampire hunter costume just hurled again."

"A were*wolf* that can't hold his whiskey?" someone snickered, panning through footage. "Sounds like a certain Grimm Guardian we know."

They all laughed as Olivia crept past, wishing she could've done something about their fragile electronics. A distant fan came on, and her cape billowed in the breeze, prompting Foxtrot to turn.

Crud, crud, crud! Olivia crawled away, trying not to make too much noise as he got up to check the duct.

"Think we got a rat or something," he said.

"Jerv, that you?" someone asked, to resounding laughter.

"He better not be in here," Olivia muttered, turning the only way she could.

"What are you *doing*?" she hissed, rounding the corner and spotting Jasmine setting drinks on fire for a heavyset blond she recognized from the Berserker's site. "That's the president's *son*!"

"Yeah, he and the VP are actually kinda nice," Jasmine said, tucking the lighter away and clearing another table. "Even let me change back into sweatpants when they saw my goosebumps."

"Probably didn't want to see *your* skin," Saul grunted.

"Nah," Jasmine replied, "I think Junior likes my legs."

"How *progressive* of him," Jada laughed.

Olivia shuddered, barely putting down any frost.

"Please be careful," she whispered, crawling past an open vent by Jasmine and eyeing the flabby blond. "I can't lose my *sister*."

"Right back atcha," she whispered with a touching smile before replying on the open line. "And don't worry. There's a method to my madness. Inner circle's supposed to meet after Odenkirk arrives, but Junior and Njord still haven't been summoned."

"Good to know the leadership'll be busy," Saul said.

"Keep us posted," Kurstin replied.

Olivia crawled out over the edge of the balcony, suspended two stories above the dancefloor. The vents groaned beneath her weight but, blessedly, held. Costumed patrons danced below under ever-shifting lights that made them look like the damned writhing in hellfire. The whole structure pulsed with the same infernal movement until ethereal vocals pierced the ruckus.

Despite the pleasant change, the earplugs did little to dampen the speakers at point-blank range. Seeking to avoid hearing loss, Olivia went down a branch leading toward the entrance and glanced back at the singer emerging from the fog on stage. There was no mistaking that voice. She hadn't known Victoria's mom could sing, but it was definitely her.

But the *Siggy* before her bore little resemblance to the *Ms. Sigfried* she'd known. Red contacts and that spiky vampire costume made her seem as inhuman as her heavenly voice. But the lettering on the back of her jacket clashed with her angelic vocals. Private Property had to be one of the worst band names ever.

Olivia shook her head. It all felt so surreal—being confronted with what her best friend's mom did for a living, crawling up here high above a nightclub on Halloween to save her mom instead of attending weekend Mass.

Sliding down a vertical section of duct by the front door brought her back to reality with a muffled clang.

"*Ow*," she groaned.

"What was that?" a guy dressed as a snake asked.

"Beats me," a chick in an eel outfit replied.

Olivia shook her head, heading past their crocodile, lizard, and turtle companions toward the cocktail lounge. She'd never drink, but some of the bottles on the lighted shelves admittedly looked like works of art, with their imaginative shapes and logos. But did the patrons know just what sort of monsters they were giving their money to? Did they even care?

Peeking through a slotted vent cover, she spied Jada batting her lashes at a couple of guys at the bar. The magician hitting on her seemed oblivious to the mounting fury of his dove and rabbit assistants.

Meanwhile, her aunt grumpily waved a pickle-suited admirer away, taking off a leather glove to flash her wedding ring at him.

"I'm in the vent by the bar," Olivia said over comms.

Jada briefly made eye contact with her and bumped into a guy dressed as either an alien or a frog. "Oh, what're you doing over there, *gorgeous*?" she asked, giggling.

"Got blocked by a *fan*. Entering your domain now, Saul," Olivia said.

Siggy's divine vocals soon gave way to doom metal, and the mixture of cologne and perfume was replaced by dusty carpets that stank of spilled booze.

"Eh, welcome to the lion's den. Keep your eyes forward," Saul said, hurriedly stepping in front of the cover to obscure her from view and probably prevent her from seeing whatever the bikers were gawking at.

"Okay," Olivia said, trusting his judgment as catcalls broke out. Still, she sensed flashes of the decor, feeling it shift from the sleek metallic furnishings out front to rougher wooden fixtures. The patrons likewise changed. Gone were the costumed men. In their place, she felt only leather or denim jackets on the ones nearby. And in addition to Detroit at the top, she also felt cities like Grand Rapids, Ann Arbor, and Lansing spelled out.

But the women's jackets didn't have giant, intricate patches on the back. Theirs simply said *Property of* one of the gangs or of some man. Rage bubbled up at feeling a third vest proclaiming the wearer to be Ragnar's property. What could have possibly possessed them to wear such things? And was Siggy's *band name* a sign of rebellion or conformity?

A knot formed in the pit of her stomach while she crawled on, turning her head to look away from the scantily clad women dancing on stage. Some might've said that such performances were *empowering*, but no argument could convince Olivia that they were anything other than *degrading*, yet another way the women sold out their dignity for the amusement of leering men. Olivia wished that she could've helped them. That they'd sought jobs *elsewhere*. Places where they weren't sexualized or *objectified*. She made a fist and wished the bikers would *burn*, *sooner* rather than later.

Snippets of conversations and lyrics assailed her on her way to the garage:

Ich komme, um dich zu holen, alter Mann.

"Think the patriot guard'd ride at our funerals?"

Egal, wie weit du rennen kannst...

"Got the Grim Reaper *and* a coffin on your colors. What are you, *sixteen*?"

Wie gut du glaubst, dich verstecken zu können.

"Let's bounce, too many *prospects*."
"*Seriously*? Didn't you *just* start paying dues?"

"Got my rockers faster than anyone!"

Ich werde da sein.

"I would've had the Huntsmen stand *brideside*," Jerv mumbled over his drink at an empty table by the garage. "Can't stand them and their literal blue collars..."

Und sie sagen, ich bin der Verrückte!

"Oh, what's wrong, Jerv?" a Berserker playing pool asked. "Couldn't *afford* her *company*?"

Olivia went red, and the shorter man chucked a knife across the room, cutting a dart in half to score a bull's-eye.

"Am I just some *joke* to you?" he growled, lunging for his tormentor with another blade.

Bystanders cheered them on, waving dollar bills at them as wildly as their companions threw money at the dancers. These people were *despicable*. They should be thankful that she didn't have her powers right now. Otherwise, she'd bring the whole place crashing down on them.

"Where are you?" her aunt asked.

"About to enter the garage," Olivia whispered, crawling past massive speakers cranked up so high that they shuffled around inches at a time, jostling bins of loose screws, nails, and bolts. Drinks danced along with the tune, as did the dust falling from swaying light fixtures, shifting the lighting more frequently than the dance floor's strobe lights and the deafening power saws shooting sparks alongside blowtorches.

Her earpiece cut out among the power tools, and she froze when someone in heeled boots trod past, scoffing at racy calendars that had very little to do with cars.

"How's my cousin's bike coming?" the redhead asked. Unlike the other women, her jacket looked like a man's, marking her as the club's sole female member: Valerie *something...*

The power tools wound down, and, with all eyes fixed on Valerie, Olivia hurried past.

"We'll get to his as soon as we finish Jotun's," a big man hissed, crossing his beefy arms in such a way that the giant snake tattoo enveloping them looked as if it wanted to squeeze the life from someone in a bear hug. "And before you ask, my sister's condition *hasn't* improved."

"I *didn't*," Valerie said, taking a seat beside a vent and forcing Olivia to wait.

"But while we're on the topic," Valerie began, "I guess your brother's not coming back. Something about a *figurehead* at the front of the *pack*?"

"Yeah," the big guy spat. "You know, Val, the rest of the guys might've enjoyed the *view* these past few years, but we both know the only reason you're in charge is because the old man didn't have the *guts* to pick between my brother and me. He just went with Dahl's little ole lady in *memory* of him. But I guess he's right. Who better to follow in one failure's footsteps than another?"

"Profound, Ax. Profound," she said, striding over and pistol-whipping him across the face.

Olivia winced when Ax hit the concrete, feeling teeth crack.

Valerie pressed her revolver to his head. "Any ideas on what sorta *failure'd* best fill your boots if I pull the trigger?"

Olivia gulped, crawling forward as silently as she could while their backs were turned.

"No," Ax hissed, dripping blood into a grease pit like venom.

"Good," she said. "Now, remember—if you *ever* question our *boss* again...I'll throw you to the dogs. Just like your brother. *Got it*?"

Ax nodded.

"Excellent," she said, standing. "Now get back to work!" she snapped, heading for the junkyard.

Ax lashed out at the table with the radio, knocking it and all the beer bottles to the ground with a chorus of breaking glass.

"Come on!" someone cried when the speakers cut out.

"Yes!" Olivia said, feeling her powers return and all eyes look elsewhere. Finally, a use for drunken stupidity! She flew past a stack of tires, feeling their words trailing behind her.

"Just 'cause Valkyrie's got more bite to her bark than your brother," a mechanic laughed.

"And you may have an *ax* to grind, but I recommend burying the *hatchet*," an old geezer chuckled.

Gosh, Jada and Jasmine would fit in great with these guys, if it weren't for *everything* else.

Olivia frowned, feeling a vent branching off through the old maintenance tunnel ahead. She canceled her momentum, whispering over the radio, "I found the tunnel!" But she got nothing but static in reply. Stupid interference. Jada'd warned her this might happen. But with the throbbing foundations on her right and no cover from sniper fire or patrols on her left, there didn't seem to be any options for reestablishing communication. So Olivia crept forward with a scowl, feeling a *double* lead lining along the maintenance tunnel vent.

"You've got to be kidding me," she muttered, taking a deep breath and swimming out toward the giant dome at the end, unable to determine what was inside thanks to the same lining. Finding no fissures to widen, she hurried back to the *normal* part of the vents, gasping for air.

"These guys are more paranoid than a doomsday cult," she muttered, angling herself before kicking off to fly down the passage without touching the walls, thankful that her powers didn't disrupt her analog goggles.

Everything went smoothly until she felt something ahead. Canceling her momentum, she found herself floating mere inches above a tripwire hooked up to a grenade.

Crud! With no momentum to get past it and unable to push or kick off the walls, she was *stranded*. And ice was building up, weighing down the tripwire. Even if her powers didn't give out before it snapped, she'd have to phase past the initial shock wave and shrapnel. At which point she'd be covered in lead dust, making her a sitting duck for whoever heard the explosion from the bunker.

There had to be a way to move forward *without* losing her powers. She needed an *insulator*. Something that could give her time to push off before the lead made her solid. Her flashlight and telescope would have to do. But with her arms pinned to her sides in the tight confines, she had to slowly move her shoulders up and *really* bend her hands to pull them out of her Indestructible pack incorporeally.

"Here goes nothing," she mumbled, briefly tapping her gear against the walls. Solid atoms shot through her equipment like mercury through a thermometer about to burst before she broke contact and felt them recede just as quickly. Little by little, she started floating forward.

"I can do this," she said, navigating like a fish subtly moving its fins to float around, constantly racing against the forced solidification.

Horizontal, vertical, and diagonal tripwires barred her way, so she floated around them whenever she could and *through* them when she *had* to, ever conscious of the frosty buildup left behind and the cold grenades waiting to burst.

Rat and bear traps adorned the sides, ceiling, and floor alongside landmines in alternating patterns, forcing her to twist and spin around them before canceling her momentum to avoid knocking into the walls, mined or otherwise.

"I'm coming, Mom. Just hold on a little longer," she said through gritted teeth.

⠐⠦�⠎⠀�⠙⠀⠺⠕⠗⠅⠀⠞⠕⠀⠙⠕⠲

Richard sat at the round table in the center of the bunker with the meth lab at his back and the security feed playing out on the TV wedged between the armory and treasury safes opposite him, doing his best to ignore the other seated officeholders and the high-ranking members standing behind them.

Still, with Jerv leering at Foxtrot's cousin, it was hard for Richard to tune out his subordinate's glare when Foxtrot was standing at his shoulder. Richard just drummed his fingers on the table faster, focusing on the distant security camera footage. He still couldn't believe his men had let the runt slip through their fingers. He'd given them advance warning and everything. But because of them, he was stuck in here watching Delilah perform *without* the audio.

"Vice president's report," One-Eye said over the landline setup in front of his empty seat.

"Record attendance and door donations tonight," Njord said. "And with Tyrian's spin control, our proceeds are up from last year."

Richard rolled his eyes. None of that mattered, least of all Njord. The man was a shadow of his former self. He'd never been the same since that horrible night. Then again, *none* of them had.

"That true?" the phone crackled.

"Yes," One-Eye's disgrace of a son said, sifting through spreadsheets. "Based on my projections, I'd say that a 52 percent increase would be a *conservative* estimate, not counting the sizable bump in public opinion we're about to enjoy."

No matter how good the boy was with numbers, he should never have been allowed to waddle into their ranks. The nerdy frat boy made one-percenters everywhere look like a *joke*.

"Excellent," the president said. "Road captain's report."

"Preparations for tomorrow's joint ride have been finalized," Valerie said, pushing forward highlighted maps, heart beating like a jackhammer. Credit where credit was due, she kept doing her best to live up to the impossible task she should've never been assigned.

"Tyrian," One-Eye said. "Anything to add regarding the ongoing peace process?"

"Given the time," he said, checking his watch, "I'd say the Dragon and the Wolf will meet any minute now. I'll debrief you when I find out how it went."

"Wonderful. That brings us to our most urgent order of business. Ninety-nines, leave us."

Njord headed out with some others, but Valerie didn't move.

"Sir—"

"I told you," Jerv laughed. "If you wanna join the boys, just show up with a chick next time."

A few of the men laughed, but Richard wasn't amused.

"Shut it," he growled at the little man. Of all the women in his life, Val was one of the only *two* he'd never had any problems with. And

Jerv was mistaken if he thought he'd get her job if she was forced out or quit.

He could feel Jerv turn his beady eyes on him, but, outwardly, he ignored him in favor of the distant screen.

"Enough," Tyrian said in an even tone as Njord helped Valerie up the steps. The blast door creaked open, briefly letting in the night air, and the ninety-nines filed out before it banged shut.

"Richard," One-Eye said. "We've managed to get ahead despite each of your *setbacks*, but our outreach with the Wild Hunt nearly failed after that Amber alert. And we've had to concede that it's past time for your *extortion* racket to end."

"I agree," he said, leaning back. "I just think it's a shame that a certain someone had to go and *advertise* what we were up to."

"If you've got something to say, then *say it*," Jerv spat.

"Oh, I will," Richard said, finally looking him in the eye now that Hilda had taken Delilah's place on stage.

"Your *street art* just cost us that *subdivision*. Properties we could've snapped up and flipped—we could have brought in *boatloads* of cash and goodwill as we stemmed the tide of urban decay. But no, you thought it would be *funny* to act *unprofessional*. Like a *gangster*!"

"*Richard*," Tyrian whispered, far too quietly for any ordinary individual to hear.

"Oh, yeah?" Jerv growled, baring his silver teeth. "I'm not the one who got high and *flipped out* over not getting the chance to *off the vigilante*. Grow up and drink yourself to death like the rest of us," he spat, sliding a beer bottle over.

Richard backhanded it off the table. Everyone except Tyrian flinched when the glass shattered. He hadn't *touched* the stuff since Timberly had passed, and that son of a gun knew that full well.

Richard felt his blood pressure rising as Tyrian cleared his throat, but Jerv kept running his mouth. "All these years, I've had to put up with this crap. The constant disrespect. But no more! I'm tired of serving under a *woman*. Riding in the back with all the dust, tar, dirt, fumes, and *hang-arounds*! I want an actual *seat* at the table!" he said, kicking Valerie's chair.

"Are you finished?" Tyrian asked in an even tone.

"*No*," the little man growled. "No matter how many times *he* screws up, you just keep *rewarding* him. Even if he goes too far and nearly kills his own flesh and blood. You all let him just try and pass it off as a *ransom*! Well, I'm *sick* of it!"

"I make things *easier*," Richard scoffed, leaning forward. "I *destroy* evidence, make witnesses *disappear*. And ensure that *none* of us have to take a *pay cut*. What do *you* do? *Other* than run your *mouth*?"

"*Nothing*," Jerv spat. "Because none of *you* let me. Well, I'm tired of it. I *deserve* better. I *demand* better," he said, slamming his fists on the table he wasn't supposed to touch.

"Richard," the phone crackled, "tolerating this insolence would set a poor precedent."

"I agree," he said with a sinister smile, materializing behind the fool by slowly splitting apart and dismissing his original self with ease.

"No, wait!" Jerv said, whirling.

But Richard struck him with a blackout punch, bouncing his head off the table with a metallic clang that echoed through the chamber alongside everyone's inhalations.

"Cheap shot," the little man muttered, spitting out a fake tooth and blinking, as if that'd help him see.

"Next hit's all yours," Richard said, spreading his arms wide. "*If* you can *reach* it."

Jerv lashed out in a blind rage, coating a knife with frost with every strike, trying in vain to stab him in the heart. So Richard shattered the blade on impact and listened to the fool shriek as blood poured from the shrapnel in his arm.

"Always so quick to resort to weapons," he said, tossing Jerv across the room.

He hit a gun safe with a loud clang before landing on the concrete.

"Can't you fight like a man?" he asked, punching Jerv back to the floor when he got up. "Or do you need to use your *compensators*?"

"Give me my sight back, and I'll make you eat your words," the man hissed, making a bloody fist.

"Bring it, *short stuff*," Richard said, tapping a safe in the treasury to make it look like him before going invisible to restore the man's sight.

Jerv screamed at the illusion and put his full body into the punch. Amped up on adrenaline and holding nothing back, his bones split on contact with the safe, and he shrieked all the more. The others looked away. *Weaklings*. They didn't have the *stomach* for this line of work.

"That'll do," Tyrian said.

Richard nodded, kicking Jerv into the wash area between the meth lab and the armory. "Clean up your *mess*," he said, gesturing at all the blood.

"Oh, and if you even *think* about touching her, I'll tear you in half. *By hand*."

⠻⠄⠳⠦⠃⠄⠄⠒⠉⠒⠀⠖⠀⠃⠄⠄⠆⠳⠖⠓⠀⠖⠆⠀⠳⠎⠀⠒⠄⠁⠀⠠⠒⠆⠀⠍⠄⠀⠶⠖⠶⠒
⠆⠄⠀⠶⠀⠠⠩⠖⠆⠎⠄

Ada sat on a wash bucket with a hand on the shower dial she'd been chained to, ready to scald whoever was pulling back the curtains, if it came to that.

The man gasped, and his footwear squeaked as he slipped. There was a thud and a groan from down low, confirming her suspicions that he'd hit his head.

Naturally, laughter echoed through the chamber until the temperature plummeted and a cold voice cut through the chill.

"Pathetic," a harsh voice hissed from nearby, up high. "She didn't even have to turn the water on to spook you. You've lost your *edge*. Not sure what further use you'll be to us if you let a blind *cripple* get the best of you," he growled.

The man on the floor cried out in agony, and Ada hurriedly turned the dial when she heard popping sounds from down low. She groaned as the monster she'd once called *Dad* pointed the shower head away from himself and turned off the steaming water.

"Let go of me," Ada said through clenched teeth, turning her nose up at the stench of exhaust fumes drawing near. When he leaned in, she forced herself not to shy back at the chill he gave off in place of the body heat everyone else radiated in such close proximity.

"I keep you fed, clothed, and housed—and got you blood transfusions—and *this* is how you repay me?" he asked. "Even after I went through all the trouble of having your legs patched up?"

"You're the one who *broke* them," Ada spat, trying to keep her voice steady despite the pain in her wrist.

"You broke into my home and took me from my *daughter!*" she spat.

At last, he relinquished his death grip with a sinister chuckle.

"What if I told you that she's on her way here?" he whispered in her ear.

Ada squirmed, feeling the blood drain from her face, and her eyes instinctively watered. "Liar."

"No, it's true," he said.

"Then it's because you *took* her."

"No, see—she's coming of her own *free will*. Thinks she's going to *rescue* you."

Ada tried not to react, not understanding why Olivia would ever attempt something so foolhardy, but, with her heart racing, he knew. Somehow, he *knew* she was worried. He laughed that awful laugh, like he had when she was little, making her feel so small, weak, and pathetic.

"Almost feel bad for the poor thing," he said. "But as soon as she joins us, the three of us'll accomplish more than you can *possibly* imagine."

None of that made any sense. "You're *insane*."

"Nah, just better informed. But don't worry, you'll help—for her sake. And she for yours."

Ada bowed her head. If there was even a *shred* of truth to what he'd said.... "You're a *monster*."

"Funny—she said the same thing. But if she doesn't get out of that vent *right now*, she's going to get a demonstration of what happens when *either* of you disobeys."

Ada stiffened and heard a bang with a metallic echo before something screeched and clattered to the floor. A softer thud sounded beside it, and Ada's heart raced as tears formed.

"Olivia?" she whispered.

Distant men wolf-whistled before crying out in pain when the temperature dropped.

"Get away from her," a staticky voice crackled from the same height Olivia's voice would have come from.

Ada wept, and the room went *silent*. Something tiny dropped at her daughter's feet. It almost sounded like a *pin*.

ᚠᚨᚾ ᚺᛖᚱᚨ ᛏᛟ ᚦᛖᛁᚱ

Chapter 24: All Hell Breaks Loose

"Get away from her," Olivia said, distorting her voice through the radios and pulling the pin from a grenade. The whole chamber fell silent when the pin dropped.

Her heart melted at the sight of her mom weeping. She was *alive*. But Olivia's blood boiled at the monster looming over her. He even pressed his foot into Jerv's back like he had that guy in the parking garage moments before he'd murdered him.

"Everyone out, nice and orderly," the lawyer that'd *humiliated* her aunt on TV said, setting a phone on the receiver.

The bunker doors banged open and the evacuation proceeded as calmly as it could. Olivia stared her grandfather down.

"Cute costume," he sneered. "But what are you going to do, *runt*?"

"I'm taking her home. Now *get away* from her."

"Or else what?" the lawyer asked, calmly striding over. "You'll take us with you?"

He shook his head. "It was quite *resourceful* of you to procure that from Jerv's death trap, but we all know that Richard can get us to safety in time. So, since you haven't thought it through, why don't you put the pin back in so we can commence negotiations?"

Olivia grinned beneath her mask. She hadn't felt his heart rate falter in the slightest, but that only meant he was an expert *liar*. "*Pass*. Also, you're *wrong*. I *have* thought it through. I can shatter the firing mechanism at any time. No delay—unlike his *projecting*. So why don't you ask *him* if *either* of you'll survive the blast."

Jerv writhed under her grandfather's foot. "It's got lead in it, doesn't it? Let me go! Let me go!"

"*Silence*," her grandfather growled, pushing down until the former tunnel rat stopped squirming.

The lawyer adjusted his glasses. "You're Catholic. Taking a life is a sin."

"*Murder*'s a sin. But that requires the taking of an innocent life. And *none* of you are *innocent*."

"Does that include your mother?" he asked.

Olivia's heart skipped a beat, and tears formed under her night-vision goggles.

"I would *gladly* lay down my life for the greater good," her mom spat, breaking Olivia's heart.

"And that of your daughter?" the lawyer asked, letting the question linger to torment them.

"No," her grandfather said. "No matter how rational you pretend to be, there are *always* limits. You won't let her throw her life away."

The lawyer nodded. "Or commit a mortal—"

Click. Olivia tossed the grenade over her shoulder. She felt all eyes on it as it bounced into the armory. The three Berserkers' hearts skipped a beat, and she *lunged*, kicking off the concrete with zero-G during their moment of hesitation. She grabbed her mom and sailed into the concrete wall while her grandfather tackled the lawyer into the floor.

"NO! NO! N—" Jerv cried as the grenade went off. Stored munitions exploded in rapid succession like firecrackers, blasting open safes and causing their contents to combust. Bullets and shrapnel zipped through the air alongside gun and safe parts, racing after the shock waves.

Even within the wall, Olivia pressed her eyes shut, weeping at the feeling of Jerv crashing into the lab. The shock wave had liquefied his organs, killing him instantly. But the debris and flames were disfiguring him further. According to his file, he'd been a truly nasty person, but she still couldn't stomach his death. How on earth was she supposed to force herself to do what had to be done? The one thing that would ensure her and her mom's safety.

Her mom gasped for air in the rock, and Olivia raced out into the lab. "Hang on, Mom," she said, choking on the stench of burning flesh while she knelt beside her, rubbing her shoulders.

Where there had once been safes on the other side of the bunker, now there were flames, misshapen hunks of twisted metal, and burning bills fluttering in the air. Beams of moonlight broke through ever-shifting gaps in the lead-laden smoke from a giant crack in the dome, illuminating the overturned table in the center.

Her grandfather emerged from the charred rubble with the lawyer, unscathed. "You're going to regret that."

"Olivia," her mom whispered, putting a protective arm in front of her. "*What* is *happening?*"

"I promise I'll explain everything when we get out of here," she said, mind racing as the lead particles dissipated with the smoke on the other side.

The lawyer dusted himself off and departed up the stairs while her grandfather stalked forward, slowly splitting off into multiple Ghost Giants standing shoulder to shoulder, closing in around them.

Olivia whirled, feeling them in the walls, lying in wait if she backed up. She glanced around at her foes and covertly eyed the lab equipment and chemicals. Red phosphorus and lithium were explosive, but she wasn't sure about the barrels of methylamine. Coolant tanks adorned with a hockey logo caught her eye. *Ammonia.* That would do.

"Back off!" she said, drawing her telescope bat and circling protectively around her mom to "accidentally" knock into a canister pierced with debris, feeling its quiet hissing, dampened by her outburst, and its metal exterior rolling over the rough concrete.

"Or else *what?*" he asked, voices echoing in unison as the tank bumped into Jerv's burning corpse.

"Or else, I'll—I'll...I'll think of something!" she snapped.

"You're *stalling*," he said, forms pausing mere feet away. "But why—"

The tank ruptured, setting off a chain reaction through the lab. Olivia held onto her mom and clamped a hand over her nose and mouth, riding the shock wave, to rocket toward the gaping hole on the other side.

"Hold your breath!" she cried, releasing her hand and kicking off the top of the chasm to dive through the earth under the cover of smoke.

Swimming for the club, she felt projections dive into the dirt ahead and behind. But despite her grandfather's multipresence, he *didn't* have antigravity powers. Thus, she outpaced him easily, even with her mom in tow. And all he could do was awkwardly crawl after her and keep diving—never materializing *beneath* the ground. He could only project where he could *see*, not where he could *feel*! And given the time it took for his copies to form, it was clear who held the advantage.

Olivia grinned, then scowled at the shaking walls ahead. Darting toward the stablest section, she shattered the earth in an explosion of dust and dirt to block her grandfather's line of sight. Non-incendiary shots rang out behind as she powered through the walls. Club music raged, forcing her to materialize alongside her mom, knocking them into a desk and a rolling chair.

"Olivia," her mom groaned.

"We're in the manager's office!" she cried over the radio, feeling the lettering etched into the nameplate. "But my grandfather's—"

Her earpiece cut out when he broke through the wall with an army of Ghost Giants that rapidly encircled Olivia and her mom. He didn't seem to have any trouble maintaining his forms under the onslaught, but that's when it hit her—she could feel *exactly* how he did it. He wasn't resisting the music. He was dancing *with* it!

Olivia grinned beneath her mask, embracing the beat, finding it far easier to phase with it than without it. *"Bring it."*

His projections lunged, but she shattered the desk, phasing her mom and the rolly chair through the splinters. Discordant growls of pain altered the wall's song, but Olivia matched the altered beat, flying her mom and the chair through the wall and into the waitresses' lounge.

Servers screamed and fled when Blood Beasts broke through behind her, but Jasmine threw open the door on the far end in full reaper garb. The tall girl opened fire on the creatures more successfully than she had in Northville. They scattered like the ladies but soon converged to more accurately phase through her bullets.

That's when she felt how he did it. He was shifting *before* the bullets even left the chamber! He felt their song from *afar* and preemptively changed his tune to shatter them on contact. That must've been how he'd detected those copper rounds at the diner as well!

"Ghost Girl!" Jasmine called.

"Get her out of here!" Olivia cried, rolling her mom weightlessly to Jasmine before *obliterating* the carpet behind her.

"Olivia!" her mom called as a massive curtain of shattered thread and glitter rose up to block her and Jasmine from her grandfather's view.

Her heart twinged when she turned to face him, but she knew what had to be done. *None* of them would be safe until she brought him down. And so her cape rose alongside frost while she floated up.

"Just you and me," she said, drawing her telescope bat.

"*Pass*," he said.

Armed Berserkers flooded the room, pouring in from backstage and the gaping hole in the manager's office.

"Bring me the reaper and the cripple," he said over his radio.

"Have it your way," Olivia said, trusting the others to get her mom out safely.

⠰⠺⠀⠊⠀⠲⠗⠐

"Hey, Mrs. Wade," Jasmine said, pushing the rolling chair through fleeing cooks. "My name's Jasmine, and I'm going to get you out of here."

"Thank—you—" she said, holding on for dear life on the bumpy, tiled floor.

Bikers charged in from the private bar before getting thrown out and beaten back by a bloody man in a red bandana.

⠶⠄⠀⠊⠀⠐⠾⠄⠀⠿⠂

"Go!" Saul roared, kicking over a mop bucket. Plastered bikers slipped, tripping those behind them up in a pile, clogging the entrance.

A Grimm Guardian clambered over the fallen, so Saul blinded him with a martini. After the first explosion had sounded, he'd started the bar fight in the back in a similar fashion, but there was no one else to sheepishly point to this time. Instead, he slammed the blinded man into a vat of boiling oil, evading another's blade.

He grunted, hearing the rolly chair depart for the dance floor, and threw a Wild Huntsman into a flooded sink. That's when *the twins* emerged. If they recognized him through his disguise, all bets were off. And it looked like they'd been working out. He didn't like his odds, but charged anyway, praying that he'd buy the ladies enough time.

⠒�⠆

Jasmine burst into the women's room to a bunch of patrons screaming over the shots ringing out and helped Mrs. Wade out of the rolling chair.

"Just hold on, now," she said, covering her with her cloak like she had Olivia. Surprisingly, despite her height, Mrs. Wade was only a little heavier than her daughter.

"Status?" Mrs. Wagner asked.

"Inbound," Jasmine replied, stepping into the club.

⠒�⠆

"*Busy*," Olivia said, evading bullets by going through the floor of the waitresses' lounge. Bikers fired at her icy trail before getting cut by her ghostly compact shuriken, pulled through into the basement, batted across the room, or torn up when the flooring shattered beneath them.

Her grandfather never stopped to help them, instead choosing to lash out at her with his projections' various claws, hands, teeth, and fists. Olivia bounced off makeup tables, sending their lights into a frenzy among the chaos. Demonic forms glided after her, and undead hands reached out from the floor.

Rocketing upward, she rained down glass and sparks from overhead lights and demolished walls, bursting water pipes to flood the room before letting live wires spill into the mess. Bikers fled the electrified torrent in a panic while her grandfather chased her upward, through the ceiling of the VIP lounge.

"Go, go, go!" Wolfgang cried over the gunfire breaking out downstairs, pushing his youngest son forward. "Make sure Cash and the rest are safe," he told his eldest.

"But, Dad!" Griffin protested.

"I'll be fine," Wolfgang said, exchanging an amber-eyed nod with Bertholdt as he rushed Griffin downstairs with the Grimm Guardians they'd been negotiating with.

"No, you won't," he heard Jaeger rasp during a break in the music and the gunshots.

Despite his aching joints, Wolfgang stopped ambling after his sons and turned to face the lone German.

"I've waited a long time for this," the Dragon said, hefting a brick by their balcony-side table and exhaling smoke.

"I'm sure you have," Wolfgang said, pulling an allergy rescue syringe from his pocket while what few patrons remained fled downstairs.

Jaeger laughed, squeezing the brick that had taken his teeth long ago. "That won't save you," the man wheezed.

"Won't it?" Wolfgang asked, injecting epinephrine—or, as it was more commonly known, *adrenaline*—into his thigh. He felt his pupils dilate and upped his pacemaker, preparing to face a man half his age. His final quarry.

He hefted the vintage he'd been saving for the end of their negotiations. *The Last Wish: A Death Wish. A drink to die for.* "A toast to your retirement," he said, raising the black bottle. "And to my finally joining you."

The Dragon gritted his teeth. "Foolish old man! Only one of us is dying here tonight!" he roared.

"All right then, show me," Wolfgang said, grinning as he raised his fists. His opponent charged, but Wolfgang sprang faster, lower. He took the man he should never have spared in the gut and over the edge, feeling the exhilaration of the hunt one last time as he carved a brighter future for his children.

· ·. ·. ·.· ·· ·· ··

"Yahoo!" Jada cried, jumping at the sound of a loud thud but nonetheless ripping off her tearaway dress and snapping off her breakaway heels behind the bar to unveil her spy suit.

"Eyes on me, boys!" she called as Jasmine hid among the masses fleeing the restrooms.

"What are you doing?" Kay snapped, trading gunfire with one-percenters and wannabes while stray bullets shattered glass bottles.

"What I was born to do!" Jada replied, frying a man leaping over the counter with her stun gun.

"We had a deal!" Kay growled, trading fire with Confederates.

"You can rip off your tights any time, hon," Jada said, drawing shock batons from her high boots and zapping a gangster coming around the corner to stop him dead in his tracks.

Her friend growled, and the kitchen doors banged open. Saul stumbled back with gritted teeth, trying to wipe blood and something else from his eyes while he did his best to slow the advance of two muscular guys whaling on him.

"King of Hearts, get down!" Jada radioed, tossing a baton. It took a biker in the head, and he writhed on the ground with it stuck on his chest, shocking the other with a flailing limb.

"I prefer Diamonds," Saul grunted, blinking wildly and trying to crawl to the bar under gunfire.

"I'm pinned!" Jasmine called from around the corner of the stage.

.· ·. ·· ·· ·· ·· ··

"Gotcha covered!" Olivia radioed in, shattering a massive section of the roof underfoot, bringing it down on the men firing at her mom and friend. Snipers fled as the hole continued to widen.

Club music swelled from below along with pistol and shotgun blasts, forcing Olivia to hit the notes of their shock waves in time to zip around old chimneys to avoid burning bullets and scattershot rounds. Bikers cried out when she jammed their goggles on approach and they ripped them off in time to get blinded by her flickering flashlight.

She winced whenever they blasted one another and shrieked whenever her grandfather got too close. Given his unrelenting pursuit, his thermals had to be analog like hers.

Chimneys exploded under his fists. But Olivia just phased with them and batted bricks into snipers before the dust cleared. Evading gunfire, she melded into the blackened rooftop and frosted it over, zigzagging from biker to biker—alternating with the public bar's divine tune and the abyssal arrangement of the private clubhouse's beat along the way.

She dodged her grandfather's lunging forms and lost weightlessness whenever she sent more than one person flying—which rarely ended up being her grandfather, given that few of her swings actually connected, and even fewer ended up doing anything, between his phasing and subsequent momentum canceling. Turning his trick on him, she negated the impact of his strikes on contact and stopped a sniper in his tracks.

The man screamed in sheer terror among the faded planet murals atop the parking garage, unable to pull the trigger or even move as ice built up. Momentum stealing was *definitely* going to come in handy. Olivia bounced him off the crumbling ruins, forcing her grandfather to shift his approach amongst the frosty, painted stars twinkling in the moonlight.

∴ ⁖

"What are you doing?" Jay called under the moonlight streaming through the broken ceiling and the gunsmoke when Kurstin drew four arrows from her quiver.

363

"Changing tactics! I'm out of bullets!" she yelled, nocking an arrow diagonally and trying to line up a trick shot in the mirror behind the bar.

"Take mine!" Saul shouted, sliding his gun over and squeezing his bloodshot eyes shut.

Kurstin eyed the revolver but still loosed her arrow. It arched over the counter, scaring a Turncoat half to death.

"Donelson, get down!" said a man with a Southern twang while his companion fled behind a downed table.

"I told you the bow would come in handy!" Jay called, double-kneecapping a Berserker with a shock baton and felling him with a blow to the chin.

"Yeah, yeah," Kurstin said, launching more turning arrows. Archery was like riding a bike. Still, she grabbed Saul's gun and checked the mirror to make sure it was safe to return fire, catching a glimpse of Jasmine and Ada crawling under the stage.

She fired at a Turncoat before he discovered her allies and spun when the doors banged open. Two Berserkers stumbled out of the private bar with death in their eyes, but a man in an oni mask and a trench coat charged, tackling them back inside.

⁙

Aiden "War" Todd threw the bikers to the floor and traded blows with their brethren, using a blend of orthodox and southpaw strikes to fell them like those he'd defeated in hundred-man brawls. He fought against instinct to avoid throat, temple, and sternum shots. Instead, he shattered ribs and joints with brass knuckles to stem the tide. He prayed that his foes would stick to melee weapons so long as he kept their comrades alive.

Men writhing in agony piled up at his feet while he held the line. Death rarely called for backup, and now that he had, there was no way Aiden would let his old friend down. As soon as Subject F and her rescuers were clear, he and Death would assist in A's apprehension if need be.

Someone yanked at the back of Aiden's coat mid–roundhouse kick, throwing him to the floor. Rather than roll to evade the raised foot, he twisted the man's ankle with a snap before his foe could stomp. His opponent roared but didn't topple.

"Little Green Beret," the man hissed in a thick accent, swinging his blade when Aiden hopped back up.

"Spetsnaz," he muttered beneath his mask, recognizing the fighting style while deflecting blows with his brass knuckles.

"Always wanted to go toe to toe with one of you," the Russian spat, pulling the trigger on his ballistic knife.

Aiden winced as the spring-loaded blade cut through his body armor—into his shoulder. But he grinned, since his foe had taken the opening. Pushing through the pain, he made good on his windup and broke the man's jaw.

"Till next time," Aiden said through gritted teeth, fending off others one-handed.

At last, the former Spetsnaz fell, knocking over a pitcher of ice before hitting the ground, out cold.

⁙

Snipers slipped on ice and screamed when Olivia descended on them atop the parking garage. Then her grandfather grabbed her. She demolished the floor, forcing him to shift his song and letting her slip through his fingers while he reduced the rock to powder. They crashed down into the murals of Earth below and fought from Moscow to Berlin and London. Going deeper, they carved a path through DC to New Orleans and Seattle and waged war throughout Detroit's painted landmarks until they plunged into the flooded level below.

Being incorporeal, they didn't splash down, but frost and ice formed in the depths, rising to the surface, forming an ever-shifting playing field bobbing on the water. Blood Beasts scrambled across the unstable isles, leaping off before the floes capsized or Olivia demolished them.

Twisting, crystalline structures formed beneath the waves, tracing their trajectories, giving Olivia and her grandfather more and more things to push off of as they spiraled through the ever-growing tunnels. She broke the surface and a frosty painting of machinery to cave in a wall.

Water flooded into the club's basement, leaving their ice sculptures behind as a monument to their struggle, while they raced perilously close to live wires, feeling the chaos unfolding above.

⠒ ⠈⠄ ⠒⠶⠒⠿⠄

Jasmine crawled out from under the stage and hid Mrs. Wade behind her cape-blanket as they sneaked past a door marked *Private Offices* toward the front door, far from the chaos at the bar on the other end.

"There she is!" a Turncoat cried.

Crap! Jasmine dropped him with two rubber rounds and exchanged gunfire with his compatriots behind a fallen table until she ran out of ammo.

"What is this?" Mrs. Wade asked, grabbing disinfectant spray from beside a fallen top hat and table card. *Number 40.*

"*Flammable*," Jasmine said, pulling out her drink lighter and unleashing a blue flamethrower on a charging foe. Thank you, *Olivia.*

"Custer!" a Turncoat cried as the man burned.

Jasmine drove him and his allies out of cover until they fled past her range.

"And this?" Olivia's mom asked, holding up a bottle of whiskey.

"*Perfect*," Jasmine said, stuffing a napkin in it and lighting it to toss her Molotov. Turncoats broke ranks and scattered faster than the spreading flames.

"Gotcha!" a man who stank of drink drawled, grabbing Mrs. Wade.

Crap, they'd been flanked! Jasmine tackled him away and pummeled him with bulky rings, which cut into his face with every strike. Still, he threw her off and rose to his feet alongside her, wiping blood from his eyes.

She sneered at the *Stonewall* nametag on his coat and raised her fists. Testosterone may have given him an edge, but Jasmine knew how to even the odds. Unfortunately, he'd anticipated her below-the-belt strike and grabbed her leg. However, neither of them expected Mrs. Wade to stab him in the heel with a fork.

The Confederate screamed, and Jasmine drove him back with ringed punches, dodging wild knife strikes or blocking them with her metal bracelets. Finally, she delivered a *devastating*, long-legged kick to his jaw, breaking it entirely. He toppled alongside a table and stayed down.

"Yes!" she cried, turning to Mrs. Wade as she took a bullet in the thigh.

Jasmine screamed, barely able to hear Mrs. Wade over her own howling.

"No, it can't end like this," she mumbled through the pain, trying to keep the warm liquid in. They were so *close*. The door was right *there*! She wouldn't let her friends down. And she *refused* to end up with a cane like her pops.

She pulled out the syringe she'd found before leaving Decker's. If it gave that Jester enough strength to tear herself free from the fence, then it should be more than enough to get her back in the game. She rammed the needle into her thigh and screamed as its contents burned through her veins.

⠃⠄⠒⠆⠰⠆

"Miss Jackson is down," Sung-Min radioed beneath his Frankenstein mask, slitting a Turncoat's throat from behind.

The man's allies never heard their comrade fall, just as they hadn't any of the others. Nor did they hear Sung-Min's approach in the chaos.

But if they *had* listened, they would have heard the gunfire dying out, snuffed out like their comrades' heartbeats.

"*Lee*," a Turncoat whispered, desperately searching among the tables for aid.

"Here," Sung-Min whispered in a Confederate's voice.

The lone man turned, and *Lee* became his final word.

Sung-Min crept toward Miss Jackson and Subject F's last known position, hoping that he hadn't failed again. Using his lab coat to blend in with the tablecloths, he readied his medical equipment as he went. But he found nothing but a trail of blood and an empty *syringe*.

"Oh, no," he whispered upon recognizing the markings.

"What have you done?" he asked, watching Miss Jackson bolt out the door with F while a guy in a green tweed suit strolled past.

⠀⠒⠒⠉⠒⠒

"There," Zachery Zinderman said, hobbling at the head of the Grimm Guardians as they passed the AV equipment.

Wulf raced ahead, like he did on their rides, to reach the door to the dance floor and more importantly *the stairs*. It'd been too long since they'd heard from Jaeger, and, with the ongoing shootout, it was too hot to try the other set.

"Lo siento, but the upper and lower levels are closed off," a man in a green Victorian getup said, stepping through with an open book while scratching a *Hebreos* tattoo on his right collarbone. "Please proceed to the nearest exit," he continued, gesturing back to the way they came.

"Wulf," Zachery said, eliciting chuckles from his underlings.

The mad dog grinned, pulling his prized hunting knife from his jacket—the very same blade his daughter had nearly disemboweled him with after Wulf'd attacked his mother-in-law.

"My apologies, gentlemen," the scrawny weirdo said, pulling a book from his newspaper-laden satchel and hitting a button on the sound system. "But I really must insist. Ye shall not pass and all that."

Wulf grinned, taking aim as the music swelled.

"*Let's go*," the stranger said in sync with the song.

Wulf chucked the knife, and the mysterious man snapped his book shut, *catching* the blade between the pages.

"A *novel* strategy." He tossed the weapon aside with a clatter. "But I urge you to *reconsider*," he said, holding up his copy of *Sir Gawain and the Green Knight*. "You stand even less of a chance than the knights in this tale."

Zachery scowled. He so did *not* enjoy being insulted. "A hundred bucks to the man who brings me his head."

Wulf and Braun, along with the rest of his underlings, lunged at the opportunity as the music swelled. They fell to a barrage of alternating punches that struck so fast it looked like their foe was practically *swimming*.

"Gotta real Don Quixote over here!" the stranger said, batting aside Braun's beefy fists. "Swinging for the fences!"

The hairy man growled as the speakers blared something about church and bleach before proclaiming someone to be the truth. Wulf pulled a gun but dropped it when the stranger tossed his book at it.

"I don't even need to be a *judge* to throw the book at 'em!" he laughed, retrieving his tome and dropping the big and scrawny men with blows to the temple.

"Not bad, eh, old friend?" the freak chuckled, dusting off the old volume and felling the rest of Zachary's men.

As the last Grimm Guardian standing, Zachary removed his jacket and took up an old boxing stance with sloppier footwork than he'd have liked.

"If you want something done right," he muttered, repeating a lesson he'd learned long ago on his pumpkin patch.

He threw the first punch, but the stranger batted it aside before bashing him over the head and backing out the door.

Zachary rushed out, ready to deliver a left cross, but found only another stranger reading. "Did you see a Hispanic guy run by?"

The man sighed, swapping his book for a newspaper from his satchel. "I *strongly* recommend you take up another quest," he said, straightening the edge of a page.

⠐⠂⠄⠡⠒⠐⠅⠄⠂⠒⠄⠅⠐⠂

"I wouldn't," Olivia said, warning her grandfather.

But he pulled the trigger anyway.

She phased to the song of copper and let the flaming round pass through her. It slammed into a sniper's bulletproof vest, knocking him from his perch atop the scrap heap. He tumbled down and bowled into his colleagues, sending them into one of the frosty trenches she'd carved in the vehicular graveyard.

"Told you," she said, racing through the pile, shifting through weathered songs in rapid succession. Gunfire from all sides pinged off the frigid metal as she evaded dead zones and her grandfather. Fiery tracer rounds hissed on frost as standard bullets bounced off like hail, cracking ice with metallic clangs, forcing her to take increasingly complex paths. She retaliated with icy shatter-storm explosions and buried her foes in rusty avalanches, saving one from a wicked spike before pinning him under another heap of twisted metal.

Olivia demolished the frost floating around her to unleash a frigid burst of smoke screen and pinballed another contingent in the mist among the hail of bullets. Felling bikers and lampposts alike in droves, Olivia plunged the yard into darkness. A darkness only broken by sporadic muzzle flashes and the illumination from her grandfather's glowing eyes, both of which glinted off the ever-growing frost.

Bikers screamed in the dark with racing hearts when she lunged at them like her grandfather leaped at her. But, unlike her prey, she could feel him vibrating excitedly with the molecules in the air, before he had the chance to fully materialize. And no one needed special powers to hear the cops closing in. Sirens encircled the scrapyard like her trenches surrounded the last men standing.

She burrowed like a worm, springing scrap heaps on them like metal waterfalls, damming up their escape routes—funneling them into the dark. She even brought down the crane when they swung its payload at her like a wrecking ball. And she blew up the forklifts while phasing their drivers to safety.

Her grandfather grabbed a magazine from one of his men and tossed his gun around, catching it midair with his projections to fire from different angles, raining bullets down like a meteor shower. But Olivia evaded and chased his men off like a comet, tearing them up with ice and jagged metal orbiting in her wake.

"Fall back!" Foxtrot cried, climbing over scrap.

"Coward!" Olivia's grandfather yelled, setting him on fire with a single shot.

He screamed, and Olivia hurried to extinguish his burns, but her grandfather *shattered* him.

"NO!" she cried, phasing through bony shrapnel and frozen blood.

At last, he grabbed her in a death grip. Stealing momentum dulled the pain, but his song *slammed* into hers, attempting to make her go solid. She plunged them into the earth to force him to stop, hoping he still wanted her alive. But he raged against her, multiplying into that entangled-skeleton thing to try to tear her apart from every angle. Olivia strained to steal his momentum but couldn't hold him off for long. Every fiber of her being felt like it was about to split.

But she wouldn't let him win. She'd never let him take her mom again. He'd never hurt anyone else.

"Goodbye," Olivia whispered, hurling them toward the lead-lined foundation below.

"NO!" her grandfather roared.

ᚺᚠᛗ ᛖᛗᛗᛏ

Chapter 25: Salvation and Damnation

Olivia closed her eyes, trying to make peace with what was about to happen, until her grandfather canceled their momentum and kicked off sideways, rocketing them into the club. She struggled to match the rapidly shifting song of the earth, unable to change course. They tumbled through a brick wall and searing hot pipes with a hiss before striking lead and disentangling.

She hit the ground and rolled to a stop down a corridor lit by ominous crimson lights. Copper and lead pipes filled with gas and water lined the winding halls, spreading out from the boiler room like a fungal infection.

Frost formed and hissed further down as her grandfather stumbled to his feet, chest heaving. His dog tags clinked together, and the fiery silhouette of a Viking head on his shirt rose and fell as if enraged. Its long, bloody beard curled like a spirit's tail and began to glow along with the rest of the image and his thermals.

"Well, you got your wish," he sneered. "Just you and me now."

"Pass," Olivia said, between breaths, flickering the lights and reaching out to frost over the pipes. Steam erupted, flooding the halls with a hiss while she sneaked away, trying to avoid touching the scalding pipes and come up with a plan. There was too much interference for her to radio in to see if her mom was in the clear. If she was, then she could flee. But they'd probably spend the rest of their lives on the run until her grandfather was *dealt with.*

"Even if I couldn't feel you," he said, voice echoing off the metallic piping, "you'd have to do better than steam to mask your heat signature."

"I know," Olivia said, dumping magnesium from her lighter on the floor and running back with her Retribution hair spray.

"And what's that supposed to do?" he asked, rounding the corner.

"This," Olivia said, looking away before unleashing her flamethrower. Magnesium exploded in a ball of light, frying the sensitive components inside his thermals while he phased.

"*Clever*," he said, taking the goggles off. "Unfortunately, those were *expensive*. But don't worry. You'll soon earn *more than enough* to replace them."

"I will *never* work with you!" she spat, feeling sweat soak through her mask while the pipes continued radiating heat.

"Not really up to you," he said.

"My mom's *free*. You have no *leverage*."

"Heh. There's nowhere she can run where we can't find her. But you were the real prize all along. Why do you think we let you get this far? Let you stray so far from the pack..."

"*Liar*," she said, heart racing, terrified at how she felt no fluctuation in his pulse. "If that were true, why'd your *plan* involve me taking down all your goons? Tearing up your property?"

"Insurance will pay for the damages and renovations. Besides, that was a *field test*. As expected, you passed with flying colors. *No one* will be able to stand against the two of us," he said, grabbing a magazine hidden between two pipes and reloading.

"But I'll let you walk away if you can dodge this bullet," he said, taking aim.

Reaching out to feel inside the chamber, Olivia felt nothing but dead zones. *Lead.* He had her in his sights, and there was no way out. One hit from those hollow-points, and the bullet would be stuck in her. There'd be no escape, even if they had Decker pull it out.

"So, what do you say?" he asked, clicking the safety off.

"No," Olivia whispered, feeling the gas rushing through pipes all around her. She matched the song of copper and unleashed a torrent of *ghost fire*. Pipes burst, and explosions *engulfed* the maze. She embraced the song of destruction, riding the shock waves tearing the place apart, feeling her grandfather toss the weapon away before the gunpowder ignited point-blank.

She rolled into the flooded basement and phased through a pillar to shield herself from the ball of flame. Fire hissed as her grandfather stepped through, devoid of any weapons.

"You're *really* going to wish you hadn't done that," he sneered, tearing off tattered jacket sleeves to unveil muscular arms covered in screaming-skull and hellfire tattoos in the same pattern as his bike.

Infernal forms materialized around the flaming, flooded wreckage, battling for control of the temperature. Blood Beasts, Lion Dogs, and Tiger Demons sprang at her while decaying, bubbly, and skeletal hands reached for her from the walls, ceiling, floor, and pillars.

Olivia flew away while demons reached for her with leathery outstretched wings like hands. Frost evaporated with a hiss on hot ash and embers as headless horsemen made of multiple entangled projections gave chase. She dodged Ghost Giants and Invisible Men and evaded False Flames that emitted cold instead of heat and Living Shadows that didn't match up with the lighting. But an undead hand broke through the ice and leaped out with the rest of its body to tackle her like a beast.

No—he'd tricked her! Conditioned her to dodge each form in a certain way! He'd stuck to the same patterns so she'd ignore the obvious—they were all *him*. And he could move however he wanted to.

She tried to fend him off, but he became her mom and Sister Paula. In that moment of hesitation, he forced her solid. Pain shot through her, and blackness enveloped her vision.

Olivia skidded across the ice and bounced off a support post. Feeling heat nearby, she retreated, trying to match the song of fire, but she couldn't tap into her powers.

"What did you do to me?" she screamed, unable to feel vibrations in the sound waves as she removed her goggles to no avail. She stumbled around, blindly trying to keep her balance on the ice and avoid the encroaching flames melting it to slush beneath her boots. Shivers ran down her spine.

"You alter gravity," he said directly behind her.

"I control *light*," he added from somewhere else.

"Which means," he said, circling her, causing fire to hiss.

"I can stop it from reaching *you*," he said above.

Olivia gasped. "Our powers don't work without *sight*." It's why her mom didn't have any!

"Obviously," he sneered.

"But—but we can go through walls, underground. There's no light—"

"Did you ever *trigger* your powers in there? Or did you just keep using them once you got started?"

Olivia gulped. She hadn't.

"Didn't you ever notice how your senses were subdued in the *dark*? That you never woke up in a block of ice after shivering in a cold bed?"

Her sightless eyes went wide. She hadn't been able to use her powers when Jasmine had gotten water in her eyes. And they'd been on the fritz at Decker's, because she was exhausted *and* because it was *dark*. And she hadn't even noticed in the dressing room, because she'd put her goggles on when the lights went off. But the bus stop she'd sheltered in when she first got her powers—her hand hadn't gone through the glass the final time because she'd *shut* her *eyes*.

"*Anything* that affects our vision affects our powers. And unlike me, you can't emit infrared light to boost your goggles."

Olivia stiffened. In her contempt, she'd underestimated him.

"Migraines and double vision from drinking are the *worst*."

"That's why you couldn't save her," she whispered. "You came home drunk the day of the—"

He grabbed her by the throat with frigid fingers and lifted her into the air like he had when he'd taken her mom. Only this time, he held her over the flames.

"Your *mother's* the reason Timberly's dead. *Not me*," he hissed.

Olivia's mind raced as she struggled to breathe. There had to be a way out. All she had to do was blind him, and she'd be free. She dug in her pack, feeling the heat worm its way through her boots.

Hair spray? It was flammable, but he'd phase with it. Her compact? Nope, she'd lost that in the chaos earlier. Telescope bat? Nope. Flashlight? Would it even *flicker* with his powers raging? And, despite the cold radiating from him, it was so *hot*. Was her cape on fire?

Her shaky fingers closed on the lighter. There were just a few grains of magnesium left inside. All she had to do was *light* them.

"*No*," she choked out through the smoke and his death grip, opening the side compartment. "It *is* your fault. *None* of this would've happened if you'd just told her about what the two of you could do," she spat, trying to mace him with the hair spray.

He grabbed her arm so hard it felt like it would snap, but she smiled beneath her mask.

"Wrong hand," she whispered.

No doubt, he whirled, whether attracted by motion or her warning, so she opened her fingers, setting the grains inside alight when the glove caught fire.

The burst of light must've worked, because her sight and powers surged to life. But the reaction released enough energy to split the water molecules into oxygen and hydrogen, fanning the flames and exploding in her hand.

Her nerves cried out in agony, but she pushed past the pain and phased through the flames, simultaneously soothing her burned skin with frost and extinguishing her cape. She went for the flashlight, but he batted it aside in a blind rage. His form blurred in and out of solidity as he struggled to restart his song with impaired vision. Olivia slammed him into a pillar, cutting him off from the light, but he shattered chunks of rock to powder and threw her off, somehow overcoming her momentum stealing. She evaded the dust and froze midair as he roared, imprisoned in steel and concrete like the people in the parking garage. But he blinked and shook wildly, clinging to his song and struggling to build it up.

His pupils were already reacting to light. If he got free, there would be no second chance. Seeing no other way, she maced him with incorporeal hair spray. He screamed as she tried to tear him from the pillar. But he devolved into a Ghost Giant–like blur with a roar, coating it in icy spikes.

The pillar cracked, and bones snapped before Olivia pulled him free. Concrete and metal gave way, along with the ceiling and the balcony above. Wood, timbers, metal, and curtains cascaded down.

Olivia fled, trying to drag him along and match the shock wave's song while it rippled through the dancefloor like a tidal wave, bringing down the whole level. But he threw her off and fell into the flames with a flicker. He screamed as the hair spray caught fire, and his eyes burned.

"NO!" she cried. Even after everything he'd done, she *still* couldn't force herself to let him burn—to suffer a fate *worse* than her mom's. She plunged into the inferno to save him, chilling charred skin while the stage and remaining balconies gave way. They flew out as the parking garage came down and landed when the rooftop cracked further open, caving in completely.

"The songs," he whispered. "They're gone..."

Olivia wept over him with her head bowed. They were finally *safe* from him, but at a terrible cost.

"Ghost Girl," Jasmine whispered through her earpiece, "you're not alone."

Olivia stiffened upon feeling a *crowd* of stunned people staring at her, mouths agape. She pulled down her goggles, confident that they hadn't seen her eyes, but was ever thankful that the infernal contacts and wig were both the wrong color—and, more importantly, that she was wearing a *mask*.

It was only then that she heard the screams in the wreckage. The people she'd trapped by trading their lives for hers. She turned her back on the crowd and her grandfather's milky eyes, singed cape billowing behind her. She knew what she had to do.

The flames hissed, and people in the rubble wept and screamed as she descended and pulled them free before carrying them to safety. They flew through debris and twisted metal, dodging lead pipes, scattered bullets, and vibrationless clouds of lead oxide–filled smoke.

"Help!"

"Save me!"

"A—angel."

"I'm alive!"

All these voices and more rejoiced whenever she delivered another to the crowd, to the firefighters and paramedics. But disarmed bikers just knelt in silence as cops cuffed them.

Icy tears built up beneath Olivia's mask and goggles for every still body she passed while seeking out the remaining coughs, breaths, and heartbeats.

"I'll come back for you, I promise," she whispered, hoping there'd be enough left for grieving families to identify.

She descended on an old man in a faded jean jacket, surrounded by the flames, feeling his scars and carbon fiber collarbone.

"Gravity," he coughed, drinking from a black bottle beside a dead Grimm Guardian with a broken back and teeth. "The great equalizer."

Olivia flinched back upon feeling his pacemaker. But it had already shorted out.

"No, no, no!" she cried, grabbing him and *racing* for the paramedics. "I'm so sorry!"

"Not your fault," he gasped. "Pushed it too hard. Can't save *everyone*. Sooner you learn that...the *better*."

"His heart and pacemaker stopped," she cried through her voice-changer, setting him in a stretcher.

"Start compressions," a paramedic said to another before pulling out a syringe.

"*Go*," the old man whispered. "Save who you can."

Olivia wept and nodded, hoping she hadn't cut his life short or cost others theirs by wasting precious seconds. Tears flowed freely as he smiled up at her. She sobbed, saving others in a daze and trying to find solace in the fact that whatever happened, he was at peace.

But it hurt *so* much. She'd been partly responsible for this, yet everyone thanked her when she saved them and reunited them with friends waiting with open arms. Her heart throbbed with pain like everyone's burns and the survivors' wounds as they were subjected to disinfectant. She scoured the flames in search of human remains, dousing the fire with frost while the firefighters battled the inferno.

Kurstin cuffed Olivia's grandfather and hauled him off, while Jasmine and Jada helped bystanders carry the wounded to the first responders. Of course, they remained in disguise as a veil-wearing, robed giant and a hockey-masked *secret agent*, respectively. Saul, meanwhile, resisted paramedics' attempts to tend to his wounds and helped cover the dead she brought back.

High-ranking Grimm Guardians stared at the final body she set down. The patches were charred, but they might once have said *President*.

"All up to you now," said a man by the name of Miller with a misshapen face, putting his hand on a guy covered in paper cuts with cauliflower ears and missing toes.

A hairy beast of a man bowed his head alongside a dwarf with prosthetics and a dude with a colostomy bag.

Olivia's heart broke at the stretcher rolling in. The man with the pacemaker had *not* survived. The big bearded guy from the church put his massive arms around his sister and some other amber-eyed guy with a curly-haired version of Mr. Bialy's haircut while two thin older men patted them on the back.

She'd failed to save plenty of others, gangsters and non-gangsters alike, but by failing to save these two—well, the glares she was getting from the Grimm Guardians made it clear how they felt, though the Wild Huntsmen seemed more appreciative.

Thank you, the blonde woman mouthed.

Guilt swelled in Olivia's heart, knowing she'd hate her like the rest if she knew she was *responsible* for her dad's death. But Olivia couldn't find the words.

"It's not working!" people groaned, hitting the sides of their phones and cameras while trying to take pictures and videos as she floated.

The Berserker's lawyer stepped through the crowd and adjusted his tie. "Thank you for all you've done here tonight," he said with a fake smile in front of the nonworking cameras.

"Stay out of our business, and we'll stay out of yours," he added in a whisper too quiet for anyone else to hear.

Olivia's stomach churned, and her anger burned. She had no idea what he'd do but couldn't risk her friends or family. She wished she could have done more. Saved more. Stopped her grandfather from bringing the building down. From killing all the others: Foxtrot, Jerv,

Sister Paula, the man in the garage, the reporter, Cisco. The grandma she'd never met. And everyone else he and his fellow thugs had murdered. But now, with this threat, it was unlikely she'd be able to prevent further killings without repercussions.

"I'm sure the papers will have their own opinions," the lawyer continued. "But what should we call you?"

Despite who had asked, she couldn't bring herself to let down all the people pressing forward to hear her answer, least of all the tall girl glaring at the lawyer beneath her out-of-place veil. Perhaps it was her turn to cheer Jasmine up.

Olivia sighed, readying herself and her improvised voice-changer to appease her friend.

"Ghost Girl," she crackled through the speakers, taking flight to hide in the clouds. She dispelled soot and ash clinging to her costume better than any camo pattern she could have made herself, trailing particles in her wake like a comet.

The clouds parted, and she gazed up in awe, taking in the sheer beauty of the full moon and the dancing auroras—feeling their electromagnetic power from miles away. The crowd gasped below while light shone through her. So much for keeping a low profile.

She sailed through the moonlit clouds, unsure of where to go, taking in the northern lights above and the city lights below. Dark patches in depopulated districts tugged at her heartstrings, as did the bystanders. They'd come together as one to help the survivors.

Snow fell, mingling with ash and smoke, and the breeze blew her along until a familiar voice and guitar reached her ears:

> Come gather round, and let me tell you the tale of the
> Spirit of Success and Sacrifice. You see, there were once
> three travelers who roused a spirit from a lamp.

Olivia followed the sound through the shifting winds, going solid to skydive against the gale.

> I'll give each of you three, each whatever it is you ask,
> she said. But you must give up something of equal value

in return. So tell me, what is it that each of you are willing to forfeit?

Olivia descended onto a rooftop, where Rafe strummed a new guitar.

Time, the young lad said quickly—for he had many years left. Money, the rich man said after a moment—for he had plenty. But the wise woman snickered, fear—for she had no need of it.

"Hey, Rafe," she said, removing her mask and hood.

"Hola, Miss Liv," he said, putting the guitar away. "It's strange how people rarely talk about facing fears on the road to success, no? By contrast, they're all too willing to give up time and money, no matter how short those are in supply. Regardless of whether or not those are the real bottlenecks."

Olivia nodded in a daze, eyes locked on the backpack at his feet. "Is that my—"

"Yes, flashlight and compact included," he said, staring up at the moon and the dancing sky. "Thought you might want them."

"Where did you—"

"Aren't the works of his hands wondrous?" he asked, strolling to the edge of the rooftop.

She nodded, feeling, as she joined him, as if she were on the verge of remembering the answer to a *very* important question.

"For centuries, humanity has marveled at the heavens. But now that they can calculate the size and distance of the sun and moon, they no longer stop to question the fact that they *appear* the *same size* in the sky. Why, the odds against that and eclipses are *astronomical*! It's *almost* as if someone *set* them there. Made them that way."

"Rafe," Olivia whispered.

"Yes, chica?"

"You said that you can prevent people from recognizing you for you."

"Sí."

"Well, from the moment we met, you felt like an old friend."

He turned and smiled at her.

"And the way you talk....It's like you're not one of *us*. Not *human*."

"Olivia," he whispered.

At that moment, the fog lifted from her mind, and she stumbled back. "*Raphael.*"

"Do not be afraid," her guardian angel said, holding her while she wept.

An archangel! He was an *archangel*. "Why *me*?" she whispered. "*Why* are you telling me this?"

He sat down beside her and smiled. "Because you asked for help. And so I came."

"But I've *always* asked for help," she cried. "Every time..."

"And I have *always* been there," he said, tapping her shoulder.

Glimpses of him turning away the Ghost Giant's fists so that he did not strike her head flashed through her mind. Times he'd kept her from hitting the wall and breaking limbs.

"But why..."

"Did I permit you to get a concussion?" he asked, showing her images of him healing her wounds with a touch on the way to the library and of her grandfather looming over her, staring at his shaking hands.

"Because if you had not fainted, he would not have come to his senses. He'd have gone too far..."

"But if you have all this *power*..."

"Then why do bad things happen?"

She nodded, unnerved by the fact that her mind was an open book.

He gave her a reassuring smile and looked out over the city.

Olivia blinked and shielded her eyes as he shone, brighter than the sun. Like a beacon, he drove out the sickening, swirling mass of blackness that was raging from miles away and miles above like a massive sphere trying to press down and close in from all sides all around them.

"Fear not the one who can destroy the body, but the one who can destroy both body and soul," he said, watching the vortex writhe.

Olivia shuddered at the feeling of evil incarnate emanating from the distance—from each individual entity stirred up in the mix of malice, joining the ominous circling, like predators on the periphery waiting to rush in and devour their prey. *Her.* She could feel each demon's contempt, each one's anger toward and hatred of humanity, and each one's desire to rip them to shreds psychically, physically, and eternally.

"One of our primary tasks is to protect you from the fallen," Rafe said with a look of distant longing and sorrow as he stopped glowing while the mass of darkness faded. "But when we intervene on the physical plane, it is not to grant you what you can handle, but to help you with what you have been given. If it helps, you can think of humanity like a child. Once, the Almighty took a more *hands-on* approach. When you were young. When you needed to be pointed in the right direction. Now you've grown a bit. For all this era's faults, lifespans are beginning to skyrocket and ripple out, while rates of cannibalism and indiscriminate murder have plummeted alongside infant mortality and polio. But you're still growing. And now humanity questions things. Now, you reject any answer given until you discover it for yourselves. Learn and understand it. Take it to heart. This is an important aspect of free will."

"So we're rebellious teens?"

"In a way," he laughed. "And, like them, you have *so* much further to go," he said, holding out a hand to the stars.

Olivia stared at the night sky in all its glory, painfully aware of how insignificant their conflicts were on this tiny speck of rock drifting through space. They'd wasted so much time squabbling that they'd only briefly ventured out into the tiniest portion of the cosmos.

"Maybe we'd get there faster if you'd stop us from *hurting* each other."

He gave her a somber nod. "You don't have siblings. But if you did, they might bicker in the backseat. You could intervene time and again until you grew tired. Only then would they have the best chance of understanding that hurting one another and themselves is not the optimal way to behave. Then they'd stop all on their own. But until the lesson is learned, intervention often merely delays that revelation. Sometimes, the learning process is painful, and at times, there is no way for us to intervene without negating free will. Hence, it is our greatest wish for mankind to step in when it is wise to do so."

She nodded numbly, mind still reeling from being in the presence of one who was beyond time and space, until he got up.

"You have to go. Don't you?" she asked.

"I do," he said, putting his hospital coat around her shoulders.

"It might be a little big now, but trust me, you'll grow into it." He chuckled. "And that wound on your hand—I could heal it for you, but I think it would be best if you restrengthened the nerve endings by using the gifts He gave you."

She laughed, barely able to feel the pain, and hugged him. "I'll miss you."

"Oh, chica. To quote a dear friend, I will be with you *always*, even unto the *very* end of the age."

"You promise?" she laughed, wiping away tears.

"I do," he laughed, holding out a hand. "But before I go, would you like to fly with me?"

She nodded and hefted her backpack before taking his hand. His Victorian costume *changed*. Holes formed instantaneously in the back, and six dark wings that matched his hair let loose a whirlwind with a single beat, sending them higher than she would ever have thought possible. They raced through the sky far faster and more gracefully than she could ever have managed with her powers.

"Someday, you'll be capable of all this and more," he said, spinning through the clouds painted green by the ever-shifting auroras.

"Sans the wings?" she laughed.

"Sans the wings indeed," he laughed, becoming someone else each time she blinked. An old physician with graying wings, a towering warrior with verdant hair and feathers and six fingers, a weary traveler, a wedding officiator, and even a young girl with curly hair and downy feathers. But they all shared the same brilliant white smile.

"*How?*" Olivia asked. Unlike her grandfather's forms, these were not mere illusions. His mass and features had altered each time. But she'd felt no trace of a physical change or alterations in their trajectory or velocity. The transformations had all been instantaneous.

"Think of this universe as a majestic painting," Rafe said, in the form she was most familiar with, taking her above the snow and clouds. "He and my kind exist *outside* of it. We can always look in and alter it in ways beyond your current level of understanding."

She nodded. "Just as we can change a 2D piece of paper, so too can you alter this 3D space."

"Yes. Your current level of science would say that we're higher-dimensional beings."

"Like how the ancients thought that you lived in the sky?" she asked, picking up on his tone.

"Yes," he said, no doubt knowing what she was thinking.

"So we have a long way to go," she laughed, unsure if they'd ever be able to comprehend his true nature if their present metaphors were just as inaccurate as those of old.

"Indeed," he said, starting to fade.

"Remember, I'll always be with you," he said, humming a ghostly tune.

> "Though you've far to travel through land, air, seas, and
> stars, I'll be with you till the end until you're safe at
> home again."

"Goodbye, Rafe." Olivia wept, alone in the clouds. "Thank you for this *gift*." The gift of a lifetime.

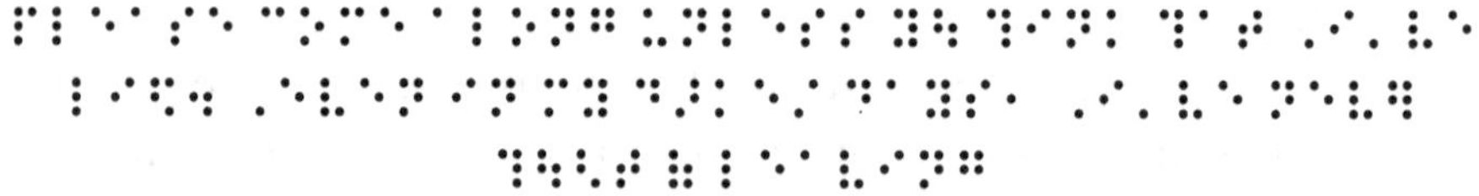

Vigil sat in his cell while the cops hauled in *animals*. But he could see it in their panicked eyes—the girl in the sky crossing translucently in front of the moon.

"And so it begins," he whispered. The figure in Death's aura had appeared. The one on whom all things hinged. The Alpha of the Omega. She who heralded the beginning of the end of all things.

ᚱᛖᚲᛇᚱᛏᛁᛟ ᚠᛁᛚ ᚦᛖᛋ

Chapter 26: Reunions

Sunday, November 1st, 2009 (All Saint's Day)

Olivia felt her aunt waiting for her by the hospital entrance just past midnight through the falling snow before she saw her. Jada pulled the car to a stop, and Olivia leaned over to hug Jasmine goodbye. "Thanks for everything."

"You too," the senior said. "I'll see you around. You know, assuming my folks don't ground me for life."

"Let me know if you need saving," Olivia said.

"Thanks, but I prefer my house *intact*," the senior laughed.

"*Ha ha*," Olivia said, turning to Jada.

"Oh, don't worry," Jada said, high-fiving her. "This *definitely* isn't the last you've seen of me."

"Wonderful," Olivia laughed, all too confident that her aunt's overly sharey best friend was all too eager to relate more embarrassing stories about her.

"I'm sure Kay feels the same way," Jada said with a smirk, unlocking the car.

"Where'd you get *that*?" Kurstin asked, staring at Rafe's coat as Olivia hopped out.

"He gave it to me before he left," she said, shutting the door.

"Still could've passed his number along for me!" Jada pouted, rolling down a window.

Olivia just smiled, doubting anyone would believe what she had seen. It all felt like a dream. A wonderful, marvelous dream at the end of a nightmare. But now it was time to wake up and go home. Back to the real world.

"Till next time," Jasmine laughed, running around to Kurstin and Olivia before enveloping them in a giant bear hug and hopping in the front seat for more legroom. "And tell your folks I say hi! I'd come to visit, but I'm pretty sure I'm grounded for life."

"I'll pass it on and come to visit you for a jailbreak!" Olivia called, waving alongside her aunt.

"See you at the next family dinner!" Jada called with a maniacal laugh before driving off.

Kurstin sighed, heading for the revolving doors. "She *will* actually invite herself over..."

"Then I suppose we should appreciate the calm before the storm," Olivia said, following her through the bustling lobby.

"Yeah," she said, slipping through the crowd.

"No, Anania, I did not go *blind*. I swear I'm fine, and there's no reason for you to come," a familiar, gruff voice said, cutting through the chatter.

"Hold on, I gotta call you back," he said, hanging up upon spotting them.

"Thanks for your help," Olivia said.

"Eh, don't mention it," Saul said, eyes still bloodshot from the spirits he'd gotten in them.

"By the way, your aunt wanted me to pick this up for you," he said, pulling a pristine police-issued sketchpad from his coat. "Happy Halloween."

Her eyes lit up, and she hugged him and her aunt on instinct as tightly as she could.

"Little less *gratitude* there, kiddo..." Saul winced beneath his bandages.

"Sorry!" Olivia said, backing away.

"You deserve that and more," Kurstin said, lightly hitting him on the shoulder.

"Eh, catch you later," he said, disappearing into the crowd and waving without looking over his shoulder.

"Come on," Kurstin said, heading down a hall. "Your mom's this way."

Olivia hurried to keep up, hugging her sketchpad with glee until its effect wore off as they wove past bikers cuffed to stretchers with broken bones and grisly seared-off flesh. Their wounds called out to her, but there was nothing she could do for them.

"Where is he?" a woman howled from the room ahead.

Olivia stiffened, feeling the occupants inside.

"Where's my cousin?" Valerie cried, getting hauled out by two orderlies.

Olivia blinked at her red hair. "Is she talking about *Foxtrot*?" she whispered.

"*Yeah*," Kurstin said.

Olivia's heart sank, unsure of how Valerie or forensics would react upon discovering that he'd been reduced to a bloody puddle. Pushing through the horrid thought and impatient people to keep up with her aunt, Olivia couldn't help but glance into the room as they passed, despite her powers telling her what she'd find.

Double-handcuffed to the bed, her grandfather raged against the medical personnel and police officers who were holding him down and desperately trying to prevent him from ripping off the bandages over his eyes or tearing out his IV.

"Don't worry," her aunt said, putting a hand on her shoulder. "There's no way they can weasel out of your mom's testimony. He's going away for life, and Hansen knows it."

Olivia nodded and turned away, hoping the lawyer wouldn't come after them for that. That her mom would get her sight back before her grandfather. And that they'd be able to convince whatever prison they stuck him in to slap a lead anklet on him if he ever got his sight back.

There was a commotion ahead as officers stepped aside to salute an old man with a gray goatee.

"Chief," Kurstin stammered, doing the same.

"At ease," he said, stopping in front of them.

"What are you doing here?" she asked.

"Just catching up with an old friend," he said, turning to Olivia. "You look just like she did at your age. Except for the—"

"Eyes," Olivia said, staring up at him and his name tag. *Freamon.* The man who'd interviewed her mom after the fire that had taken her sight.

He smiled at her. "You must get that a lot," he said, before turning to her aunt. "Well, I won't take up any more of your time, but congratulations on netting your second big fish this week. At this rate, you'll have my job in no time."

Kurstin paled, and the chief laughed. "Keep up the good work, Detective."

"Yessir," she stammered.

"You okay?" Olivia asked after he strode away.

"*Yeah*," her aunt said, letting nurses and doctors pass before stopping at the final door. "Um...take all the time you need."

Olivia could feel her aunt's heart racing, and her own swelled upon feeling *two* people waiting in the room beyond.

"Mom! Dad!" she cried with tears in her eyes, dragging her aunt inside in her mad dash to hug them.

"Olivia!" her mom cried. Her cast-covered legs twitched on instinct to race toward her.

"There she is," her dad said, tears falling from his dark green eyes onto his black beard at the sight of *both* of them.

Olivia ran ahead and hugged them as tightly as she could, eyes watering. Finally, her mom was *safe*. And her dad was *back*. "I missed you both *so much*," she wept.

"We missed you too," her mom said, squeezing her hand.

Olivia could feel the scar tissue beneath her mom's sleeves but refused to let thoughts of her grandfather ruin this moment. She shook with joy, briefly plunging them into incorporeality.

Her dad gasped, and her mom smiled, but all Olivia could focus on was that three generations of their family had been burned. But the tiny magnesium wound on her bandaged palm paled in comparison to her mom's and grandfather's extensive scar tissue.

Still, the little round dot stirred up memories of Sister Paula's scarred hands. She'd given her life to keep her and Jasmine safe and give them a shot at rescuing her mom. Wherever her godmother was, she was definitely smiling down at them. And, no doubt, clearing her throat to get her to stop leaving Kurstin out.

"There's someone I want you to meet," Olivia sniffled, turning to her aunt. "Mom, this is Kurstin."

"Hi, Ada," Kurstin said, before sheepishly adding, "Hey, Will."

"Hey, sis," he said, red-eyed. "It's good to see you. Thanks for getting them back."

Kurstin looked away and blushed. "It was a team effort, and, truth be told, your delightful daughter did most of the work."

"Will," Olivia's mom said. "She *has to* stay in our lives."

"Why?" he laughed. "Because you like the sound of her voice, or because she's earned it?"

Olivia chuckled and hugged them tight.

"Those are important factors, for sure," her mom began. "But no. Because she's clearly an *excellent* judge of character."

"Well, I'm sure we'll have plenty of time to catch up," he said.

"How long will you be in town?" Olivia asked, hoping he wouldn't have to leave until Monday.

"Permanently," he chuckled.

Olivia's eyes watered, and she reached out to bring her aunt into the fold. She held her family tight when Kurstin joined their embrace, thankful that they were all here to *stay*.

"So when's dinner?" Jay asked, following Kurstin into the interrogation room after sunset.

"I don't know," she groaned. "They *just* lost their house. Let's give them a day or two to find a new place. Besides, I'm sure Will knows you haven't changed in the *slightest*."

"All right, *fine*," Jay said, sitting down beside her.

"Vigil, this is Jada Johansen," Kurstin began. "She's my new partner, so you'll be dealing with the two of us going forward."

The gaunt man didn't even blink as he stared daggers into their souls.

"I like him," Jay whispered, staring at the lopsided *X*-shaped scar cut deep into the skin around his left eye.

"'Course you do," Kurstin muttered, already regretting her decision to agree to this. Saul'd better have a *good* explanation for bailing on her.

"Anyway," Jay said, pulling out a laptop. "Do you know this chick?"

Kurstin didn't need to see the screen to know what was playing because the footage was already seared into her mind, far clearer than any video they'd ever had on the *first* Exterminator.

"As you can see," Jay began, "a woman walks into a bar like the start of a bad joke. And it doesn't end well either," she said over the shouts and screams.

Kurstin groaned, disliking her friend's habit of making light of stuff like *this*. Plenty of people had dressed up like the vigilante last night, but this *copycat* had been the most deadly by far.

"I like how she grapples these guys to the ground by the shoulders," Jay said. "And I know it's more Japanese Jujitsu-style than your Brazilian throws, but I mean, come on, the way she's cutting through everyone..."

"I know of no one who parades around in a bandolier of blades as if it's a beauty sash," Vigil said in a harsh whisper that still chilled Kurstin to the bone.

She was surprised he'd spoken without Dr. Park present, but Jay's lack of sense made her *excited* by this latest development.

"Nor anyone who wears a single-filtered gas mask," Vigil continued. "Nor do I know anyone who tears up throats and tendons with cleats and painted *claws*."

"Actually," Jay said, "those are modeled off Victorian self-defense gloves, but I take your point."

Kurstin hid a yawn behind a hand, doubting they'd get anything else out of him, but spread out a series of photos before him anyway.

"Do you know anyone *else* who dresses up in body armor?" she asked, hand lingering on a small copy of the police sketch of the guy who'd gotten away when she'd arrested him.

But, as expected, Vigil just stared at the images, refusing to talk.

"*Okay*," Jay said. "How 'bout these dudes and dudettes?" she asked, scrolling through more copycats.

But the man didn't react to any of them.

Kurstin sighed, staring at the one Jay was enamored with. Whoever the woman was, her friend's infatuation made sense—the mystery woman's fighting style was as effective in reality as those of the actresses and stunt doubles in those terrible spy flicks Jay liked. The copycat would even fit in perfectly on those sets, with her tight costume and belt angled around her hips.

"Still a no?" Jay asked, clinging to a grainy photograph as if it were an autographed print from one of her favorite stars.

"No," Vigil said, speaking for the third time without Dr. Park present. "I know of *no one* who coordinates her nails and braids like *that*."

"Eh, worth a shot," Jay said, whipping her head around like the copycat, likely wishing she had weights at the end of waist-length hair to knock someone out with. And that she could parkour out the window and vanish into the night like a ninja and the new vigilante.

Kurstin stared down at the paperwork, half annoyed that the Exterminator was suddenly talking around her friend and half grateful that she wouldn't have to be the one wasting hours trying to break through to him in the future.

"All right," Kurstin said, clicking her pen and reading off the form. "Then as far as your court date, I presume that you still don't want to fight the charges or petition to delay your transfer to the supermax on account of the *ever-present danger that you may pose to yourself and those around you?*"

The scrawny man said nothing, and Kurstin sighed. "I'll take that as a yes," she said, filling out the form and feeling as if she'd signed his death warrant. Whether or not Vigil was the real vigilante, the Exterminator had killed a lot of people. People whose friends were now locked up in the very place the department was shipping him off to.

"You need not feel any guilt for the part you play, Detective," he whispered.

Kurstin stared into his dark eyes as he continued.

"You're just doing your job," he hissed. "It's not your fault that yours is a society that's determined it's more *humane* to *cage* people like *animals* for the rest of their lives instead of putting them *down* like *dogs*.”

“Okay...” Jay mumbled. “There’s so much wrong with that, I don’t even know where to begin...”

Kurstin sighed, taking solace in the fact that he wouldn’t be able to go insane in solitary on account of him already having lost his mind.

Shouts sounded in the hallway outside, and the door banged open. Someone shouted, “He’s got a gun!”

Kurstin and Jay spun, going for their weapons, but a bloody Berserker in cuffs had already raised a pistol. A shot went off, and the lights *exploded*, raining down sparks—plunging the room and hall into darkness. Bone and stone cracked, and alarm bells sounded over their fellow officer’s shouts. Red emergency lights flashed alongside the intermittent sparks above.

“You all right?” Kurstin asked, whirling.

“Fine,” Jay said, breath hanging in the air alongside gunsmoke.

They gasped upon spotting the shooter crumpled against the wall under a bloody smear and a giant crack.

Kurstin gulped and met Jay’s eyes. Neither of them had shoved the biker back. Nor would they have had the strength to break *concrete*.

Shivers ran down Kurstin’s spine as they turned to face Vigil. He sat there, chained to a table now covered in *ice*.

“Open your mind and reach out your hand,” he muttered to himself, withdrawing his outstretched hand, now covered in frost.

Kurstin and Jay stood there, slack-jawed, until he continued.

“You needn’t worry about me,” he whispered, breath rising alongside the smoke from the bullet embedded in the wall behind him. “I shall not die. My blood will not be on your hands.”

“He’s like *her*,” Jay mumbled.

Kurstin nodded, numbly removing her ponytail holder. She still didn’t know who’d fled when she’d arrested Vigil, but the skeletal man before her was certainly the *real* Exterminator. And he was like Olivia. But unlike her, he *killed*. She and Jay were only alive because he *willed* it. He’d only allowed himself to be taken prisoner because that’s what he’d *wanted*.

He wasn't going to Helheim to die or atone for his sins. They weren't sending a sacrificial lamb to the slaughter. They were sending a hunter to the lion's den. An *Exterminator*.

Unless they convinced Olivia to show their superiors what she could do, she doubted the higher-ups would believe her and Jay about Vigil's *abilities*. She gulped as she stared into the man's cold, emotionless eyes, doubting he'd let them live if he thought they'd tell a soul. But even if Olivia were here, Kurstin was uncertain of what her niece could do if it came down to a confrontation. She and Rice had only put down bits of frost and flickered the lights when they used their powers, while Vigil coated things in ice and shattered the lights, causing a building-wide blackout.

Kurstin gulped. Just how much stronger *was* he?

ᚱᛖᛏᚢᚱᚻᛁᛟ ᚠᚨᛗ

Chapter 27: Saints and Sinners

Monday, November 2nd, 2009 (All Souls' Day)

"Well, it's out of our hands," Saul muttered, seated in the last row of the chapel, when the final hymn concluded. "They said a coolant line froze and ruptured, and I see no reason to dispute that. I say we let the chips fall where they may," he added, watching the Wades and Jacksons trail after the nuns and Kateri's casket. As far as he was concerned, Rice and the rest of Helheim deserved to rot in Hell and whatever cells they landed in for the rest of their lives. Who was he to care if a superpowered vigilante cut their lives short?

"Saul, this is *serious*," Kurstin whispered as the mourners filed out.

"I know," he grunted, pushing the thought of the madman having powers aside. Still, it'd be a net win if Vigil did the world a favor and iced the whole supermax on arrival. "But what do you expect me to do?"

"I don't know, *something*. You always think of something, but now—"

"I'm turning in my badge," he said, not wanting to put off this conversation any longer.

"*What? Why?*" she asked, going red when people looked over at her outburst. She waved back at them and looked away, her head down, while the pews continued to thin.

He sighed. "I'm *tired*. I nearly died the other night." Like Kateri.

"*So?*" Kurstin asked, crossing her arms. "That's not exactly a first."

"Yeah, but this time's different. This time it's clear I'm slowing down."

"You're only *thirty-three*."

"Yeah, but my strength's peaked. I'm past my prime. Can't wrestle younger guys to the ground anymore. It's only a matter of time before that catches up with me and costs me *everything*. And I won't let it end like that. For once in my life, I'm quitting while I'm ahead."

"*Saul*," Kurstin said, putting a hand on his shoulder, "you don't need to brawl like a beast to do your job."

"Yeah, but, like I said, I'm *tired*."

"And just what's that supposed to mean?" she asked.

"Means I'm tired of fighting. Everything I do either backfires or is completely ineffective. And with the city going downhill....No, I'm *done*."

His heart ached when Kurstin's shoulders slumped, but his decision was final, and there was nothing to say. If only she were like the rest of the department, she'd be cheering his departure. But she'd been cursed with a soft spot for long shots and lost causes.

"Almost forgot," he said, digging into his pocket. "This is your cut." He handed her a wad of cash.

"My *cut*?"

"Pregnancy pool," he said. "For being such a good sport."

"Even if we factor in pain and suffering," she scoffed, leafing through the bills. "This looks too big to be my *portion*."

"Eh, well, it's mine too."

"And you're giving it to me because..."

He sighed. "I'm donating all my worldly possessions to join the monks."

She blinked. "Wait—*what*?"

She stared at him a long time before asking, "You're serious, aren't you?"

He nodded. "Thinking Kateri had the right idea all along, and, like I said, I need *rest*. Time to get my head back on straight after *everything*..."

"Who knows," he laughed. "Maybe this'll be good for me. We'll see how this trial run goes."

Kurstin shook her head. "What about Anania? Will it be good for *her*?"

"That was never going to work out," he snorted. "As much as she complains about me being blind to the obvious, it's time for her to move on. You too."

"*Me?*" she asked, taken aback. "Saul, Jay's already put in for a transfer, and—"

"That's not what I'm talking about," he said, feigning deadly seriousness.

She held up her wedding ring. "I've been *happily* married for a while now, thank you very much."

"I know," he laughed. "But when I saw your brother, I realized you've got a *very* specific type of man in your life: polite and bearded. But I suppose I'm only half that and Wilfred's only my middle—"

"Oh, *shut up*," she said, hitting his shoulder a bit too hard. "And it is *not*," she groaned, likely dreading the day Will and Will—William and Wilbur—had to meet.

He chuckled. "Gonna need thicker skin than that when you introduce them."

"Don't remind me," she muttered, joining the end of the line and stuffing her winnings in the donation box.

"Aren't you Lutheran?" he asked, following her out.

"Consider it a sign of respect for the woman who saved my niece's life," she said, adjusting her coat.

"Eh, she'd appreciate that," he said, trudging along beside her and spotting the brothers. They were waiting for him.

"Guess this is goodbye," he said.

"So long, Saul," Kurstin said, hugging him farewell. "Go be the burliest monk they've ever seen."

"Hehe, I'll be ready if the Berserkers ever come for the monastery," he said, departing with a wave and not looking back.

Olivia pushed her mom's wheelchair to Sister Paula's grave and set the flowers down, knowing this would be but the first of many times they'd do this. She hoped it would hurt less in the coming years.

"Thank you for taking care of me when I lost everything," her mom wept. "For watching over Olivia. Teaching and *protecting* her..."

Olivia squeezed her mom's hand, and her dad nodded solemnly.

"Thank you for introducing us and standing by us all these years."

"And for pushing me to always do the right thing," Olivia whispered. "Even when it hurts....*Goodbye*," she sniffled, departing with her parents so the others could pay their respects.

Her mom squeezed her hand. "Do you need a moment?"

"Yeah," Olivia whispered, heading off to cry in private.

Forgive them, for they know not what they do. That's what her godmother's dying request had been. Olivia wanted to honor her last wishes, not for her grandfather's sake, but for her godmother's. But she *couldn't*. In the moment, she hadn't hesitated to save him from the flames of this life or the next. But *forgiving* him....He didn't *deserve* that.

Then again, neither she nor anyone else deserved God's mercy. And yet it was given anyway. Still, her hatred hung around her neck like a millstone. Perhaps forgiveness was as much for the one wronged as it was for the sinner. The chance to set that weight down and move on. But knowing that changed *nothing*. It was still too hard. But maybe there was hope.

As she trod through the grass, her heart ached at seeing Sister Martha in pain alongside the others. Despite the woman's antics, she felt at least as sorry for her as the rest of the sisters if not more so, since she'd missed her chance to reconcile.

She wouldn't make that same mistake. And so Olivia gave the nun a sympathetic smile and received one in turn, understanding that they'd no longer be at odds. She could have wept at the weight lifting from her shoulders, but no matter how hard she tried, she couldn't change the way she felt about her grandfather. He was a *monster*.

Shadows passed overhead as two ravens raced across the cemetery and landed on a distant dead tree at the edge of the property. There were so many birds on it that it looked like it had black leaves.

Olivia squinted. It was too far to tell without her telescope, but she was sure that the dark-haired man standing underneath was staring at her.

"You okay?" Jasmine asked, shuffling over.

"Yeah," Olivia said, drying her eyes and turning upon feeling the senior *shaking.*

"Oh, you look *dreadful*," Olivia gasped.

"Thanks," the tall girl said, wiping sweat from her brow. "Still think that dress looks good on you."

"This is serious," Olivia said, glaring up at her. "We need to get you *inside*," she added, trying to push her to the vehicles.

"Or what? I'll catch a cold?" Jasmine laughed half-heartedly.

"A fever's more like it," Olivia muttered, feeling her friend's molecules shake in a frenzy while she strained and failed to get the stubborn girl to move an inch.

"Uh, you should stay away. You know, case it's *contagious*. I'd hate to see how much ice you'd build up if you got the chills."

"Then get moving, before I catch whatever you have," Olivia groaned, putting her back into it. "Come on, move it, or I'll *make* you."

"In public?" Jasmine snickered.

"No one's looking," Olivia said, feeling it to be true as people walked among the tombstones before she lightened Jasmine a tad.

"Okay, okay, I'm *moving*," the tall girl said, trying to keep her footing as she suddenly raced forward.

Olivia blushed and looked back, relieved that the guy under the raven tree was no longer there. Not that he'd have been close enough to see anything anyway.

Jasmine pulled the thermometer out of her ear when it beeped as Olivia paced back and forth in her—*their* room.

"One oh *seven*," the small girl said, without looking. "Half a degree more, and your brain'd start cooking."

"Don't remind me," Jasmine groaned, checking the numbers. As usual, Olivia was right, and that was uncanny. She pulled the blankets up to warm herself and blot out her friend—to return to a simpler time when she enjoyed peace and quiet and had zero spectral encounters.

"Uh-uh," the first-year said, ripping her sheets off incorporeally. "You need to cool down, not warm *up*."

"It's *freezing*," Jasmine said, rubbing her arms. "And who put you in charge?"

"Your mom did. *Remember?*"

"She asked you to take care of me while they're out, not *boss* me around."

Her friend grinned a creepy smile. "I need to make sure my sidekick gets better."

"*Sidekick?* I'm your *adult supervision*. But I'll show you a *side kick*," she said, lashing out with her foot.

Naturally, the small girl went immaterial and her foot got *covered* in frost when it passed through.

"Cold, cold, cold!" Jasmine muttered, shying back.

"All right, hit the showers!" the first-year said, pointing to the door like a disappointed coach.

"Nah, I'm good," Jasmine mumbled.

The tiny terror smiled, and her hands went translucent.

"Olivia, I *swear to God*, if you touch me with those..." she said, digging a set of wrist weights out of a pile of clothes on the floor and readying herself.

"*Jasmine Jessica*, is that any way to treat a guest?" the small girl said, mimicking her mom's tone and looking for an opening.

"*Guest?* You're a *pest*," Jasmine said, sitting up to make herself a smaller target.

"Wasn't it *your idea* for us to move in with you guys?"

"Yeah, shows how much *brain damage* I've accumulated," she muttered.

"Come on, Jasmine, you *need* to cool down. Please, let me help you."

"*Fine*, go get some ice packs," she said, before the small girl could pounce.

"You're no fun," she said, sailing through the walls.

"Knew we shouldn't've repainted," Jasmine muttered. Their houses had been exactly the same before they'd started remodeling, but apparently removing the original lead coat instead of painting over it like the Wades had left them vulnerable to *specters*.

"I heard that," Olivia called from the kitchen.

Jasmine rolled her eyes. Of course she did. She surveyed her half-renovated room, remembering how she'd helped her pops slide the appliances out to the front room to convert the kitchen into a bedroom. Apparently, the small girl's parents had opted to stick her in the attic. Had Jasmine known that was an option, she'd have advocated for sticking the small girl up there again instead of their current arrangement. But perhaps she could ask her parents for a more lenient sentence if she could make them see that rooming with Olivia was punishment enough.

"Here!" Olivia said, sticking her head through the wall and holding out an ice pack.

"Yeah, that's not gonna get old," Jasmine said, forcing herself to press the frigid thing to her head.

"Also, I got you a drink," the small girl added, pulling a glass of OJ from the wall.

"Maybe this won't be so bad after all," Jasmine said with a smirk, chugging the chilled drink until she recoiled.

"Brain freeze?" the first-year asked.

"Brain freeze," she said, pushing stuff aside to set her glass on the nightstand.

"Good," the small girl said, pressing buttons on her watch with beeps.

"What are you doing?"

"Setting a timer to check your temperature."

"*Great*," Jasmine said, grabbing her MP3 player and a modern history textbook.

"Really?" the first-year asked, floating overhead. "You're going to *study*?"

"*Yep*," Jasmine said, slipping in her earbuds and pressing play.

"That won't save you from the thermometer!" Olivia called over the music. "And that'll make you deaf!" she said and *signed*.

Jasmine groaned and turned the volume down while her warden hopped into a beanbag chair to keep watch.

"Prisoner in my own home," she muttered, cracking the textbook and diving further into the Vietnam War.

Unfortunately, Olivia got up every few songs to check her temp. Thankfully, it seemed stable, so she wouldn't actually need fever reducers.[16]

"I'm going to go make dinner," the small girl announced, heading for the kitchen.

Jasmine nodded and strummed her fingers to the rapid beat of a chopper song, letting her mind race while she tore through her assignments. Three verses in, she smelled smoke.

"Olivia!" she cried, running out.

"Jasmine!" the first-year shrieked, pointing to *her*.

Jasmine's eyes went wide at her reflection in the microwave. Her *hair* was on fire!

Flames hissed as Olivia flew over to extinguish them. But the smoke alarm still tried to emit its piercing cry as the lights flickered. Jasmine ran to the sink and doused her head under running water, flooding the room with steam.

"What on earth?" she asked, wiping off the window and recoiling at her bald reflection before looking closer. There weren't any burns. It didn't *hurt*. Had they caught it in time? No—her hair had burned down to the roots, but her skin was uncharred. Why? This wasn't like Pentecost, since the disciples' heads hadn't been burned by tongues of fire. Nor was it like the burning bush, because her hair'd gone up in smoke and down the drain.

"Jasmine?" Olivia whispered, hovering over her shoulder.

They stared at her follicles. They were *glowing* like hot embers. And the air between them distorted under the clashing temperatures.

"Oh, God, what is *happening* to me?" she cried. Her precious curls were *gone*.

"Can I..." Olivia asked, holding out a hand.

---

[16] A class of oft-overused medications that prolong many illnesses by reducing the body's efforts to turn up the heat to kill off pathogens and infected cells.

"Sure," Jasmine sniffled, desperately hoping her hair would grow back.

Tiny, frigid fingers touched her head with a hiss.

"The hairs in your follicles....They feel like *lightbulb filaments*."

"Are you serious?" Jasmine said, head in her hands. Her mind raced. It had to be whatever was in that syringe. It had seemed like the only way to save Mrs. Wade and prevent her pro career from ending before it began, like her pop's had. Whatever it did, it had removed any trace of a gunshot wound and the resulting pain in her leg, but now....Would she even be able to pass a drug test? Would she even be able to leave her *house*?

"Whoa, whoa, what are you doing?" Olivia asked.

"What? *Nothing*?"

"*No*. You were doing something. Your head was glowing brighter."

"I was thinking..." Jasmine groaned. "Good God, my hair lights up like a light bulb when I get ideas..."

The small girl stifled a laugh. "Good to see your humor's still intact."

"Olivia, this is *serious*. I can't just stop *thinking*. And if it's kicking off this much heat when I'm *bald*..."

"Hold on," she said, flying off to their room and returning with the schoolgirl wig. "Wig caps are made of silicone, right?"

"You're right!" Jasmine said, pulling it on. "Silicone's an *insulator*. If my hair acts like a filament, it can only heat up when exposed to electricity—maybe it's now connected at the roots to the neurons in my brain....But with this silicone—"

"It's negated," Olivia gasped.

Jasmine took the wig cap on and off and watched the follicles glow and dim.

"Yeah, it's not kicking off heat anymore. I just need to wear a *wig*."

"So," her friend began, floating around and frosting over the window, "I have to put on a disguise to hide when I'm using my powers, but you need to put one on to *stop* using yours."

Jasmine glared up at the small girl. "If you're gonna start cracking jokes like that, it's gonna get old *fast*."

Olivia laughed so hard she went even more transparent, floating around the room and frosting things over when she bumped into them.

Jasmine laughed with her friend. "Fire and Ice."

"Guess Ifrit was an apt code name after all."

"Just like *Ghost Girl*," she retorted.

"*Hey*! I only told them that to keep *you* happy."

"I know. But *Ghost* was just too generic."

"Well, so was Genie," she said, pouting in midair.

"I dunno. *Ghost Girl and Genie Lady* has a nice ring to it. And they're both spirits, right?"

"It does *not*," the small girl said, floating upside down. "And we're not actually spirits."

"That may be, but—I'm sorry, but I *cannot* take you seriously when you're doing that."

"Doing *what*?" Olivia asked, failing to maintain a straight face when she crossed her arms upside down.

Jasmine laughed until the small girl's eyes widened in panic.

"What? What is it?" Jasmine asked.

"They're home!"

"Crud," Jasmine said, noticing the headlights outside before staring up at her ridiculous wig.

ᛉ᚜ᚢRᛗᚼ ᚦᛗ ᛗRᚦ

CHAPTER 28: NEW BEGINNINGS

Tuesday, November 3rd, 2009 (Feast Day of Saint Martin de Porres)

Devin Dieterich, the son of the Dragon, roamed the dark streets of Plymouth in the wee hours of the night, whistling to himself as he approached his supplier's car. Over the course of the weekend, his stepdad had burned to death, his mom had resigned from the school board, and he'd fled the house upon finding that his dad's friends weren't going to help him in court.

They wanted the *disgrace to his father's legacy* locked up as badly as the cops! All over a stupid prank! This was all *Wade's* fault. If she *just* coulda taken a *joke*, his life wouldn't have been *ruined*. He had to skip town. But before he left, he'd make her *pay*.

"You got it?" he asked, approaching the dealer.

"Yeah," the nerdy guy said, rolling down his window farther and pulling out a vial filled with bubbling red liquid. "Street name: *Dragon's Blood*. Highly volatile. It'll eat through just about anything."

"Great, give it here," Devin said, imagining the look on Olivia's face when he hurled it at her, leaving her deformed for the rest of her *miserable* life. She'd have plenty of time to think about what she'd done. To regret crossing him. Turning him down. Thinking she was *better* than him. Well, if he couldn't have her, no one would. They wouldn't even want to *look* at her.

"Not so fast," the guy said, pulling the vial back when Devin reached for it. "Cash *first*."

Devin shook his head. He'd need every penny and unsold parcel of steroids for his new life. "Pay you later."

"With the *change in management*, that's no longer going to work. Now, you pay up-front. Like everyone else."

Devin growled. With his stepdad dead, it seemed no one wanted to give him the respect he deserved.

"Thought you might say that," he said, pulling the gun from the back of his shorts.

"That really how you want to play this?" the nerdy dude asked.

"*Oh, yeah*," Devin replied, leaning back and grinning. He was going to squeeze the trigger as soon as the punk handed over the goods, because he'd slighted him. The only question was *where* he'd shoot him.

"Have it your way," the dweeb said. "The safety's on."

"What?" Devin asked, turning the gun away to check. "No, it's no—"

Glass shattered on his face, and pain worse than anything he'd ever felt in his life tore through him. He screamed as the acid burned through skin and bone. His supplier sped off and jerked the wheel, knocking him onto the pavement. Devin dropped the gun and howled into the night, choking on blood, exhaust, and acid.

"Anything worthwhile?" the tall girl yawned, adjusting a more fitting wig—completely fever-free.

"Not sure," Olivia said, shutting her old mailbox and squinting at the first of five envelopes on the way back.

"Hold on," she said, flying over police tape under the cover of darkness and reaching out with her powers. The letter opener shouldn't have melted. Yes, it was there! She freed it from the ash and shattered the soot clinging to the surface before falling back into step beside the tall girl.

"Uh, do you really need that if you can...*you know*?" she asked, holding up a shaky hand.

"But it's so *cool*!" Olivia said, admiring the feel of the Lion, Witch, and Wardrobe engravings on the hilt before cutting into a letter from *school*.

"What's it say? the senior asked, looking over her shoulder under the flickering streetlight.

"It says I don't have to make up my homework for the days my mom and I were *abducted*."

"*Too late*," Jasmine chuckled, stopping to get her own family's mail. "Next."

Olivia sliced into another letter and frowned. "It's from the breeder. They've *unenrolled* the puppy we picked out from the guide dog program..."

The tall girl's eyes widened. "Wait, *what?*"

"Guess we need to get that sorted out before it's too late," Olivia muttered, silently heading up the porch before the steps groaned under the senior's weight.

"Thank you for letting us stay here," the door said, vibrating with her mom's voice when she opened it.

"Don't mention it," Mrs. Jackson laughed, adjusting her pearl necklace at the other end of the table. "We're happy to help!"

Olivia still couldn't believe that the woman was taller than her *seated*, but she passed by without a word and stopped at her mom's side, staring at her wheelchair, waiting to break the bad news until after their moms finished their chat.

"But really, you didn't have to give up your room," her mom said. "We could've made do with the—"

"Nonsense," Jasmine's mom replied. "With that wheelchair, it's important you stay on the first floor. *Trust me*, Jerome and I have been there."

"Besides," Jasmine cut in, "the ceiling's still higher in the basement, and Mom's *always* wanted to live in a gym."

Mrs. Jackson nodded and took a sip of coffee.

"Hey, Mom," Olivia said, holding up the breeder's letter.

"Hey, Liv," she said, grabbing the braille checklist of everything they owned. Originally, they'd used it for inventory when moving, but now it served as an insurance claim. "We have some leftover money since Aunt Kurstin replaced your wardrobe. Would you like a set of those Lady Constance books?"

"Um, sure, if we can find them at a thrift store," she said. Given the fictional setting, she'd always taken the author's claim that the books were based on real cases with a grain of salt, but they'd been right about lead, so who knew what other tidbits of truth were locked away within those tales.

"*Perfect*," her mom said, running her fingers over the list.

Olivia winced when she felt them pass over the dots denoting the photo album that hadn't survived.

"And if we're getting them secondhand," her mom asked, voice wavering, "are there any others you'd like?"

Olivia inhaled sharply while Jasmine laughed with her own mom.

"Liv, what is it?" her mom asked, holding back tears.

"Another time," Olivia said, not wanting to rub salt in the wound.

"No, you can tell me. I promise I'm fine," she said, sitting up straighter.

"All right," Olivia said, setting Rafe's coat over the back of a chair and taking a seat. She'd defeated her grandfather and his goons, but compared to this, that was nothing. She didn't want to hurt her mom's feelings or let her down. But not asking was tearing her up inside. And her speculative self-torment was completely nonsensical if her mom was supportive.

"Could we get some drawing books?" she asked.

Her mom's fingers twitched. "What do you mean?"

Olivia took a deep breath and scooted closer, removing the transfer form from her pocket. "I want to switch my study hall for art class."

"How long have you been thinking about this?"

"A long time..." she said, head bowed. "I didn't want to let you down. And I didn't want you to be disappointed in me or the fact that you couldn't see my sketches..."

Her mom put an arm around her and said, "Liv, it's not possible for me to be disappointed in you. You make me so *proud*," she said, hugging her and whispering, "And I'd love to see what you've drawn when I get my sight back one day."

"Thanks, Mom," Olivia whispered, hugging her back and feeling the weight evaporate from her shoulders. All this time, she'd been worried about nothing. If she had to face a similar situation in the future, she'd confront it head-on because while the outcome might be uncertain, it'd certainly be less painful than the constant burden of indecision and the eternal 'what-ifs' nagging at the back of her mind.

"So," her mom said, clicking a pen with a smile, "given how late it is in the semester and the paper I heard you unfolding, I'm guessing there's something for me to sign."

"Yes," Olivia said, flattening the paper out and moving her mom's hand to the signature line. "Here."

"And to be clear, this won't affect your grades, will it?"

"Of course not," Olivia said quickly.

Her mom laughed. "I know. You told me you get your homework done in class. Which means you've probably been doodling in study hall anyway, haven't you?"

"Yeah," she laughed.

"And *done*," her mom said with a grin, still managing a perfect signature after so many sightless years.

"Thank you!" Olivia cried, squeezing her tight.

"You're very welcome, though you'll have to help me pick out what books to get you. Since, well..." she laughed, batting her lashes to showcase her sightless eyes.

They laughed together until she felt her dad and Jasmine's pops at the door with a *puppy*!

"We're back!" Mr. Jackson called in his deep voice, ducking low to enter. At six-eight, he was the tallest person Olivia had ever met, but his kindly smile and demeanor made him *far* more welcoming than her grandfather.

"'Bout time," Jasmine said, catching the keys he tossed over. "Thought we were gonna have to jog or take the *bus*."

"No need for *that*," Olivia's dad laughed, holding a finger to his mouth. A little German Shepherd puppy slept in his arms.

Olivia was barely able to contain her glee, thankful that her giant smile didn't ruin his surprise for her mom.

"Ade, could you sign this?" he asked, pulling out a form and moving her hand to the appropriate line.

"That depends on what *this* is," she said, while Olivia and the others held their breath, staring at the adorable little sleeping guy.

"Well, you remember how I agreed to help fix up the house when we moved in?"

"Uh-huh."

"Well," Mr. Jackson said, twirling his cane, "I suggested he stop by the courthouse to start a business."

Olivia stared over her mom's shoulder at the paper.

"So we could write off some of the cost as a business expense," her dad said.

"Okay," her mom replied. "But why do I—"

"If you do some web work, we could write off a braille display as well," he said, eyeing the puppy.

Olivia grinned when her mom smiled and signed as fast as she could.

"Well, that or health insurance," her dad added.

Olivia and her mom froze.

"What do you..."

"You're getting your sight back, Ade."

"But—"

"We have more than enough, since the house burned down."

"But the medication—"

"Even if you burned through the whole insurance payout, you'd still earn plenty on freelance gigs if you can do both the database *and* design work," he said.

"But the ACA hasn't passed yet. They can still reject me."

"Not if we apply *together*," Mr. Jackson said, setting down a paper and motioning for Jasmine and his wife to sign.

"With five employees and one dependent, we're over the *group* threshold," her dad said, kissing her hair. "You'll start as soon as you recover from your operation."

Olivia hugged her mom and wept with her.

"Thank you," her mom sobbed. "Wait, we need to call the breeder, since we—"

"Already did," her dad said, setting the little guy in her lap. "She even agreed to part with him, since you two already bonded."

"Oh, Lan!" she cried, petting the little guy.

He yawned and wagged his tiny tail, nuzzling further into her lap.

"Guess we won't be needing this anymore," Olivia said, setting the letter aside.

"Right you are," her dad said, spotting the envelopes and grabbing a package with a thumb drive inside. "But we will be needing *this*."

"What is it?" Olivia asked, while her mom hugged little Lan.

"It *was* going to be a Christmas present," he said, pulling out the flash drive. "But since the original went up in smoke..."

Her mom gasped. "You digitized the scrapbook!"

"I *did*," he said, pressing it into her hand.

She and Olivia wept even more.

"I love you," her mom whispered, grabbing his hair and pulling him down to kiss him.

Lan barked and licked their faces, and Olivia laughed with everyone else until Mrs. Jackson's watch beeped.

"Well, I best be off," she said. "But I'll see you two for workouts later."

The senior and Olivia nodded. Despite her powers, her parents thought it would be best if she *refrained* from putting on a cape and going out at night, given her age and the lawyer's threat.

But that was no reason not to prepare, in case the bikers ever came knocking—or that Jester Jasmine was convinced had *abilities*. Olivia still couldn't believe the tall girl had shot up with and pocketed an unknown substance.

"Let's go," the irresponsible girl said, jingling the keys.

"Yeah, one second," Olivia said, heading down the hall with the last two letters. She tore open the one from Hawthorn Center and gasped. The request for a follow-up had been canceled, since Dr. Park had abruptly resigned.

Olivia felt each and every metallic bead and letter on her friendship bracelet, hating that she'd put off visiting out of fear of what she'd find and worry that others would discover she'd been checked into a mental institution. Then again, she'd been cleared by medical professionals, and they hadn't. She'd undergone treatment, even if she hadn't needed it, and she'd faced her issues instead of ignoring them or self-medicating like far too many living in fear of the stigma of seeking help. Perhaps being open about that and visiting Victoria were the next steps she should take.

"Come on, slowpoke!" Jasmine called.

Starting by telling the tall girl. "Hold on!" Olivia said, ripping open the final letter.

Olivia,

Victoria transferred out of Hawthorn Center upon turning eighteen and recently woke up from her coma. She doesn't "speak" anymore, she just hums, and she is still regaining her motor functions, but she can still recognize ASL and the written word.

She gets the biggest smile on her face when we look at the sketchpad you left her, and I know she'd love to hear from you. Unfortunately, I've had to send her to a specialty clinic overseas with strict security protocols. But I can still relay your messages if you write to her at this address.

Sincerely,

—Ms. Delilah Sigfried

P.S. Love the costume.

Olivia wept, relieved that Victoria was okay and that she wasn't mad, but the pain of having missed her chance to see her still cut deep. She'd have to be more decisive going forward. And as she reread the letter, her hands shook at the final line and postmark, coating the clothes Jasmine hadn't picked up in frost. Victoria's mom had mailed this *after* Halloween. Somehow, she *knew* it had been her under that mask and what she could do.

"Earth to Olivia!" Jasmine called.

"Coming!" she said, flying through the walls.

"Forgetting something?" the tall girl asked, hefting a backpack.

"Right!" Olivia said, flying back to the room.

"Gonna need to do a lot of waterproofing," Mrs. Jackson said.

"Sorry!" Olivia called, running out to the hallway with her overstuffed backpack.

"Come on," Jasmine called. "We're gonna be—"

Olivia vanished in the hall and instantaneously materialized beside her friend in a pile of frost.

"Late..." the senior said, eyes wide along with all the rest.

"I can *teleport*," Olivia whispered. She shook with joy and appeared by Rafe's coat. She grinned, feeling both it and the backpack as part of her song, and rearranged the *notes* while teleporting *in place*.

"Ta-da!" she cried, having teleported the coat on underneath her backpack straps. *"Quick change!"*

Everyone's eyes grew wider while she shook uncontrollably under the flickering lights. "This is going to be *awesome!*" she shouted.

"And just like that. She gets *another* power," Jasmine mumbled.

"Come on, let's go!" Olivia said, bounding up and down higher than the tall girl. "We can see what you can do after school. Test my theory of you being immune to heat exhaustion. And then we can warm up the stove and—Mom! We're going to have so much fun when you get your sight and powers back!"

"I'm looking forward to it," she laughed, as Lan barked, wagging his tail.

"Slow down, there," Jasmine chuckled. "You're going too fast to stay solid or opaque."

Olivia nodded, feeling as hyper as her dancing molecules.

"Bye, kiddo," her dad said, a smile half-hidden beneath his beard.

Olivia disappeared like the electrons all around her and reappeared, like them, in her own *electron cloud*—her line of sight—to hug her dad.

"Bye, Dad. Bye, Mom. Bye, Lan. Bye, Mr. and Mrs. Jackson!" she said, teleporting to hug each of them.

Everyone laughed and waved when she pulled Jasmine out the door, aided by weightlessness.

"Slow down!" the tall girl chuckled, unlocking the car. "Between your peppy attitude and that oversized coat, people might think you've got a boyfriend."

"Good!" Olivia said, hopping in and buckling up. "Devin might start leaving me alone, then!" she said, ecstatic, staring back at the charred angel statue that now more closely resembled Rafe, with its blackened hair and soot-accented smile. Even though he was no longer around physically, he was still protecting her socially by repelling creeps with his old coat. She said a quick prayer of thanks while the tall girl backed out.

"Well, if you want people to leave you alone, earbuds might be more effective," she said, handing her MP3 player over with *new* earbuds.

"Jasmine, I can't accept that."

"'Course you can. I mean, it's no puppy, but I did load it up with classical tunes for you."

"Wait...you're *giving* this to me?"

"Sure are."

"But what'll you be listening to?"

"Well, my dad has been promising to get me a new one if I scored a certain *scholarship*," she said, holding up an opened envelope of her own.

"Congrats!" Olivia said, high-fiving her.

"Thanks," the tall girl said, keeping her eyes on the road. "Besides, I figured you could use a replacement, since your radio broke."

"Thanks," Olivia said, cradling it as if it were brand new.

"By the way, your hair's a *mess*."

"Oh, right," Olivia said, pulling down the mirror. Frost and antigravity had really done a number on her hair. But teleporting in place to straighten her locks back to their full glory and shattering the frost did the trick. She wished fixing Jasmine's hair was as easy, but she took solace in the fact that she'd felt a subtle change in the tall girl's scalp since yesterday. Her hair would grow back.

The tall girl hit the volume button, and a deep voice came over the speakers.

"Witnesses say they saw a *ghost*," the man said, rattling the whole car.

"A Ghost *Girl*," the guy said.

"A name that's sure to haunt her when she's older," the lady replied.

"Or sooner," Olivia chuckled.

"It's fitting, and you know it," Jasmine snorted.

"If the dead age, that is," the man said.

"*Or*," the guy said, "she's trying to throw us off her scent."

"True that," the woman said. "She might just be a shortie like me."

"Unless," the man with the deep voice said, "it's all just *mass hysteria*."

"Hallucinogen-infused smoke," the woman added. "It was a *nightclub* that burned down. And we all know what they got goin' on in there."

"Regardless," the guy said, "nutcases, I mean *true believers*, have flocked to the site alongside conspiracy theorists."

"I bet these so-called *ghost hunters* are making police investigators' jobs even harder," the lady replied.

"That they are," the man said. "DPD has officers standing guard on round-the-clock shifts and mandated OT to get to the bottom of things as *quickly as possible* to, quote, *save time and cut costs*."

"Ha!" the woman said. "As if."

"Not sure what they'll find," the guy began. "Word is that, unlike evidence of criminal activity *Outback*," he said in an Australian accent, "there's no video evidence of the *heroine* whatsoever."

Someone hit the table in the studio. "I see what you did there," the man said. "It's funny cause there was a meth lab *out back*."

"Well, wherever she is—" the guy replied.

"Or isn't," the woman said.

"Or isn't," the guy agreed. "One thing's for sure, another urban legend's been born."

"And hopefully, the revenue from merchandise and *Ghost Girl* tours is here to *stay*," the man concluded.

"We'll be right back after these *spooky* messages," the lady laughed.

"Lucky you," Jasmine said. "When I was uploading those songs, I saw online that no one can quite agree on what your suit looked like, thanks to all that soot and ash. Some even thought your costume was *black*, making people doubt your existence further due to the conflicting reports."

"Speaking of," Olivia said, slipping out the pristine police-issued sketchpad. "I've got something to show you."

"Do show," the tall girl said, stopping at a red light.

Olivia smiled, holding up the sketch of the new suit she wanted to put together.

"I like it," Jasmine said, heading forward when the light changed. "Almost makes me hope we get to team up again, *partner*."

"Me too," Olivia laughed. "*Partner*."

ᚦᛟᚾᚷᚺᛏ ᚠᚻᛗ ᛗᛗᛗᛟᚱᛁ

Epilogue

Prison guards escorted Tyrian Hansen and his boss through Helheim Maximum Security Penitentiary while the other visitor trailed behind. Standish[17] transfers glared at them from an intersecting hall, but neither Tyrian nor his boss turned to look at them. At last, the final set of doors buzzed open to admit them to the visitation area.

"Alstrom," Tyrian said in passing to the guard stationed inside before pulling up a chair for himself and sitting beside his boss on their side of the plexiglass.

The other visitor took a seat at the far end, likely thinking that Tyrian and his boss looked quite odd next to each other. Though they'd both dressed in black, expensive cologne clung to Tyrian's suit, while exhaust and engine oil radiated off his boss's old leather jacket and eyepatch. And though they were roughly the same age, gray hair and wrinkles only clung to one of them. In contrast to his boss's beard and the way he leaned back in his seat, Tyrian still maintained his clean-shaven look and upright posture from their days as soldiers.

The doors buzzed open on the other side of the glass. Richard lumbered in, chained hand and foot between two guards. They guided him to the chair and bolted his restraints to the floor before departing. He blindly reached for the phone. When he found it, Tyrian picked up his end in unison and held it between him and his boss, knowing that they wouldn't be listened in on, thanks to the guards they had on payroll.

"So where are we?" Richard asked.

"Our ranks and finances are in tatters, but our coalition is holding," Tyrian replied. Axel would take the fall for the meth lab since the junkyard was in his name, and, though getting that parcel of land back would take time and money, it would return to them whenever the police department decided to liquidate it as assuredly as winter came each year. At which point, they would expand Helvete to the building's original dimensions.

---

[17] Standish Maximum Correctional Facility in Michigan closed on October 31st, 2009.

"Any calls for blood?" Richard asked.

"Naturally," Tyrian said. "Both presidents died on our property, after all." But those who suspected that the old hitman had been paid to carry out a final task were keeping their theories to themselves.

The boss dismissed his concerns with the wave of an engine grease–stained hand. "We all bled together on Samhain," he said in an even tone. "Now, a shared history binds us together firmer than a common foe or interest."

Tyrian didn't like that word, *Samhain*. It made the boss sound like an actual pagan in the vein of the Grimm Guard's Wiccan. And he liked to believe that he'd dedicated his life to an organization headed by a man more rational than that. Unfortunately, superstition was the most charitable explanation he could come up with for the boss's insistence that Richard's executions not take place within the club itself. Had they conducted them in the secrecy of the basement or junkyard—or if Richard simply hadn't left the bodies up to terrify those he interrogated—the girl wouldn't have found the killing grounds, and *none* of this would have happened.

"And the young cub?" Richard asked. "Does *he* believe we set his old man up?"

"Whether he does or not is irrelevant," the boss said. "He chose to throw their lot in with us. And since he was the one who originally vouched for the alliance, he'll continue to do so now that he's dug himself into this hole."

Tyrian nodded, confident that the commander was correct, as usual. At least he still had that aspect of his leadership going for them. "For an outward show of unity, Bertholdt will toe the line alongside his copresident brother."

"Three birds, one stone," Richard muttered.

"Exactly," Tyrian replied. "The Wild Hunt will follow our lead as surely as the Grimm Guard will, with the traitor advising Zinderman."

"Speaking of the traitor," the boss began. "Will he talk?"

Tyrian shook his head. "Miller's a true needle in a haystack. The way he served up his boss on a silver platter almost makes me think he really can turn straw into gold."

"But will he *talk*?" the boss asked, devoid of emotion.

Tyrian refused to let a frown cross his face. No matter what case he made for *talent*, the boss always asked about *loyalty*. "Unlike the rest of his *ilk*, Miller's got a head for business," Tyrian said, adjusting his glasses and tactics.

"Circumstances change, and what he knows could ruin everything," the boss said dryly.

"I understand, but he's a valuable asset. Which is why I will personally see to it that our interests remain aligned and never *diverge*," Tyrian said.

"Good," the boss replied. "Thus concludes Operation Oskoreia."

Tyrian checked his watch to conceal any displeasure that may have crept over his face at the mention of that word. He'd stomached his brothers-in-arms' fondness for the ancient motifs they'd named their unit, club, and call signs after, and chose to believe that the boss merely selected such terms to appeal to his subordinates' fervor rather than buying into it himself. But who knew—perhaps the commander was already in mental decline?

"Hmm..." Richard said. "The op may be over, but the price we paid was steep."

"Concerns," his boss said—not asked.

"We lost a lot of guys," Richard replied, leaning back in his seat. "And the Turncoats are champing at the bit to join up."

"Do it," Odenkirk said. "We can always use more cannon fodder."

"Yes, well," Tyrian began, not even bothering to hide his distaste, "there's not that many of them left for that."

"Then we'll boost their numbers," the boss said. "Pay our respects at their funerals. Coerce their kin to come north and avenge them."

Tyrian nodded. Shrewd as always. At least they'd be doing the world a favor by funneling them into a more useful cause. "On the subject of *cannon fodder*—do you want me to extend that offer to the Jesters as well?"

"*No*," Odenkirk said flatly. "I worked with a madman once, and it didn't end well. *Never again*."

"Very well," Tyrian replied. "But even with an increase in allies, our head count is still down. How do you feel about tapping from the Calderos's talent pool?"

Richard inhaled sharply. "I don't think some of our brothers are *ready* for that. Which limits our recruitment potential, to say the least..." he grumbled. "And if we're drawing from the Turncoat's *ilk*..."

"Burn them down until their ranks are depleted," his boss said. "Then we'll re-up with the Calderos's lighter-skinned members to ease our boys into the modern era."

Tyrian nodded, hating that they couldn't force change too fast without some in their band fleeing, kicking and screaming. Part of him wondered whether they were worse than the actual bigots in their group on account of them selling their souls to cater to those backward beliefs in an effort to manipulate the undesirables to further their agenda. Moral quandary or not, Tyrian was all too aware that they were playing with fire. Philosophically, he wondered why those in power were so often drawn to their own destruction? Was it hubris, or the psychological equivalent of gravity pulling down whatever rose up?

"Richard," their boss said, "how are things on the inside?"

"Eh, my cellmate's *insane*. He tells me that I have no future and keeps saying that he'll stay his hand until the *appointed time*....This your way of *punishing* me?" he asked. "Because for the umpteenth time, I didn't know she was going to *torch* the place."

"I'm not concerned about Helvete," the boss said. "Like our coalition, we'll rebuild stronger than before and donate a portion of our proceeds to get the girl's family and our reputation back on their feet. The other clubs will continue to view the whole matter as a family affair, and, while we won't remain unscathed, the weak will be forced out, and we'll emerge strengthened like tempered steel. We merely need to bide our time until we've passed through the crucible."

Tyrian nodded, checking his perfectly manicured nails, detesting the prison guards for constantly trying to throw fuel on the fire that was Richard's current predicament—especially considering that such efforts were done merely to boost their odds of winning foolish wagers.

"As for your *housing situation*," Tyrian began, "the staff are making bets on which of you is more dangerous, given that your fearsome reputations have both been undercut by your recent blindness and the revelation of the supposed vigilante's malnourishment."

"He's the genuine article," the boss said.

Tyrian shrugged, trusting the man despite the facts. Regardless, *Baldr* wasn't happy with the latest development, which brought them to the next point on the agenda.

"Irrespective of whom you're bunking with, we can work with this," Tyrian said. "Play nice so that I can show the jury how much you've changed. How you're no longer a threat."

"*Fine*," Richard hissed.

Tyrian removed the glasses he didn't need to wipe down. "Richard, we were informed that your injuries were *extensive*."

"Your *point*?"

"It'll take time for you to heal. And yet, here we are, two days in, and instead of resting, you've already put two of Benjamin's crew in the medical wing, further straining our relations with the man and adding even more charges to your already substantial list. Are you *trying* to make my job impossible?"

"Just doing *mine*," Richard scoffed. "Cleaning up messes Baldr *won't*. How's my case look?"

Tyrian clicked his tongue. "Your daughter's statement is damning. We're doing damage control, but, given our limited options with you behind bars...it's challenging, to say the least."

"*Great*. So I'm stuck in here for the foreseeable future."

"Unfortunately," Tyrian said. "But, again, this will play better in court if you get your sight back *later* in the process."

Richard crossed his bandaged arms. "Great. But who's running security till I get back?"

"I will see to your duties as well as my own," Tyrian said.

"And the girl? Richard asked.

"Her family can't press their claims too hard without revealing what she can do," Tyrian said.

"What if she gets *emotional* again?" Richard asked, tossing an imaginary grenade over his shoulder.

"If she goes nuclear, we've already ensured our half of the mutually assured destruction," the boss replied. "And even with you incarcerated, we stand ready to dispatch who or *what*ever crawls out of the dark, now that she's shone an irreversible light on herself and this city."

Tyrian adjusted his tie, fully aware that Richard and the boss spoke of things he wasn't privy to. But after years of careful observation, he was nearly certain that the boss believed people like Richard were gradually drawn together like magnets, ever so slightly increasing the odds of dramatic confrontations, which would inevitably begin to accelerate if things crossed a certain threshold. At least, that was why Tyrian concluded that they'd left Vietnam without a fight. And why the commander never let Richard use his talents to the fullest, let alone in the open.

The boss cleared his throat, and Tyrian nodded.

"Make peace with Baldr, and you can deal with the girl when you make your grand return."

Richard hung up with a sinister smile and rose from his seat, bound in chains, ready to be dismissed.

Vigil sat across from Death in silence until the doors buzzed to dismiss the blind giant's visitors. When the coast was clear, he picked up the phone with a shaky hand, clinging to it as he did the hopes he had pinned on the horsemen.

"There are three things on which we must speak," he whispered. "Past, present, and future." He traced the criss-crossed scar over his left eye.

Death nodded, oblivious to the auras Vigil could read in his eyes. They flashed before him like a man's life moments before death, jumbled and indistinct, yet the relevant pivotal moments stood out to him clear as day. The most prominent among them was the girl in the aurora.

"Blessed are those who have not seen and yet have believed," Vigil began. "And yet for your sake and for the sake of others so that they might not perish, I shall tell you of something which you alone know so that you might believe. For you see, I know the origin of the voice with which you speak, for I know that you stole the voice of the man who took yours. The general whom you *assassinated*."

Neither Death nor the guard listening in blinked, for they were both made of sterner stuff. And though neither of them gave any indication of belief, their auras shifted, projecting a better future.

"Second, I know that the guard with two auras standing behind you is War in disguise," Vigil said, watching the infant boys abandoned in the hospital to die cry and wail. And from their agony rose the man they had become, stitched together from his twin's remains so that one of them might live. So that countless others might live.

Neither of the horsemen said anything, but still, their futures burned brighter alongside Vigil's as he unfocused his eyes to watch hope for humanity spring eternal and dance about his reflection in the glass.

"And finally, we must speak of what is, what was, and what is to come," Vigil said, doing his best to keep his voice even.

"For I know the man whose face is on the piece of paper in your pocket," he said, reliving Death's memories of infiltrating the sketch artist's office and creating a graphite rubbing to bring out the lines that had been drawn on the original piece of paper that the detective's new partner had taken with her. The paper that she had tried to show him.

"Go on," Death said in the voice that was not his own.

"Behold, these are the things I saw in the eyes of the *man* who fled. The *monster* who seeks the end of all things. The *abomination* who was there from the beginning. Before the Flood of Noah. The wretched *Spawn* of Azazel. The vile *offspring* of the formerly Holy Watchers, the Fallen Angels. A *Nephilim* born of demons and the damned. A giant of old whose immortal soul the world could not hold.

One on whom this world's myths were based. A dread *shedim* whom early peoples both feared and revered.

"You have heard it said, beware of demons masquerading as gods. But I tell you the truth, so too should you be likewise wary of those who should not exist. Those blessed and cursed with the free will of man and all the powers of the heavenly and hellish hosts that no mortal was ever meant to wield. For those burdened with such an affliction cannot be driven back by mere exorcisms. Nor can they ever hope to comprehend with their limited senses the mystical forces they seek to employ.

"Now behold, these are but a foretaste of the great and many terrible things which I glimpsed when I looked into his eyes. Horrible, unnatural things that should not be. For I saw one marked by wicked cunning, deceit, and *vile* deeds. He may not be the Father of Lies, but he is the *perfecter* of them.

"I saw him kill his own mother in cold blood. Paint his *twisted* world into being with her blood. In his quest for power, he named a madman *brother* and slew countless others. I saw him gouge out his own eye and hang himself on a tree in exchange for occult knowledge.

"Mention not the one of whom I speak in the presence of blackbirds, for the Lord of Ravens still has dominion over the same servants now as then. So too do they still whisper in his ear, telling him of all they have seen and heard."

"Odin," Death said, voice and hands steady as they'd always been. "You speak of Odin. The Norse god of war and wit."

Vigil nodded slowly. "Though the face on the paper in your pocket bears little resemblance to the one who just left, I assure you that they are one and the same. And because he bears the same name now as then, and similar faces, these are marks of hubris. A weakness you and your horsemen *must* exploit if there's to be any hope of victory."

"And how would we go about that?" Death asked with clinical coldness, readying his pen and notepad in the same way he did in countless other moments interviewing the deranged.

"I don't know," Vigil whispered. "He fled before I could glimpse his plans. But I know that he's watching the girls. And after the countless lifetimes of memories that I was forced to bear witness to, I know that he has horrible, terrible plans for them. Somehow, they are both the key to his dark aims and the secret to ridding this world of him once and for all."

Vigil shook his head. "Whatever his aims with this *biker gang* are, his presence here does not bode well for the future of mankind. For we are still young and have but barely begun to explore the heavens. Reach for the stars. But his kind does not care. Their fires burn *low*. Down to the *embers*. Nothing but a remnant remains. Yet still they haunt us, even in their death throes, threatening to doom us all in their last desperate attempt to escape extinction and eternal damnation."

ᚺᚢᚷᛁᛏᛏ ᚠᛏᛒ ᛘᚢᛏᛁᛏᛏ

Postscript

Thank you, dear reader (or listener), for picking up this work, in whatever medium you chose, and making it to the end of the tale. I hope that you enjoyed your time with the story, and if you would like to check in on Olivia and her friends, please visit the website at https://fauxsaur.us for behind-the-scenes annotations and a potential sequel announcement (contingent upon this book selling well enough).

—Andrew

www.ingramcontent.com/pod-product-compliance
Lightning Source LLC
Chambersburg PA
CBHW071443140726
47997CB00005B/1575